Aus...
Playboys

*These sexy playboys are guaranteed to
make the best husbands!*

*Praise for three bestselling authors –
Helen Bianchin, Margaret Way
and Marion Lennox*

About A CONVENIENT BRIDEGROOM:
'Helen Bianchin turns up the heat…in this fast-paced, intensely sensual tale.'
—*Romantic Times*

About Margaret Way:
'Margaret Way creates a richly drawn love story with an intriguing premise and captivating scenes.'
—*Romantic Times*

About Marion Lennox:
'Marion Lennox pens a truly magnificent fairy tale. The romance is pure magic and the characters are vibrant and alive.'
—*Romantic Times*

Australian Playboys

A CONVENIENT BRIDEGROOM
by
Helen Bianchin

MAIL-ORDER MARRIAGE
by
Margaret Way

DR McIVER'S BABY
by
Marion Lennox

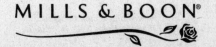

MILLS & BOON®

*MILLS & BOON and MILLS & BOON with the Rose Device
are registered trademarks of the publisher.
Harlequin Mills & Boon Limited,
Eton House, 18-24 Paradise Road, Richmond, Surrey, TW9 1SR*

AUSTRALIAN PLAYBOYS
© by Harlequin Enterprises II B.V., 2003

*A Convenient Bridegroom, Mail-Order Marriage and Dr McIver's Baby
were first published in Great Britain by Harlequin Mills & Boon Limited
in separate, single volumes.*

A Convenient Bridegroom © Helen Bianchin 1999
Mail-Order Marriage © Margaret Way Pty., Ltd. 1999
Dr McIver's Baby © Marion Lennox 1998

ISBN 0 263 83591 X

05-0603

*Printed and bound in Spain
by Litografia Rosés S.A., Barcelona*

Helen Bianchin was born in New Zealand and travelled to Australia before marrying her Italian-born husband. After three years they moved, returned to New Zealand with their daughter, had two sons then resettled in Australia. Encouraged by friends to recount anecdotes of her years as a tobacco sharefarmer's wife living in an Italian community, Helen began setting words on paper and her first novel was published in 1975. An animal lover, she says her terrier and Persian cat regard her study as much theirs as hers.

A CONVENIENT BRIDEGROOM

by

Helen Bianchin

CHAPTER ONE

'NIGHT, *cara*. You will be staying over, won't you?'

Subtle, very subtle, Aysha conceded. It never ceased to amaze that her mother could state a command in the form of a suggestion, and phrase it as a question. As if Aysha had a choice.

For as long as she could remember, her life had been stage-managed. The most exclusive of private schools, extra-curricular private tuition. Holidays abroad, winter resorts. Ballet, riding school, languages...she spoke fluent Italian and French.

Aysha Benini was a product of her parents' upbringing. Fashioned, styled and presented as a visual attestation to family wealth and status.

Something which must be upheld at any cost.

Even her chosen career as an interior decorator added to the overall image.

'Darling?'

Aysha crossed the room and brushed her lips to her mother's cheek. 'Probably.'

Teresa Benini allowed one eyebrow to form an elegant arch. 'Your father and I won't expect you home.'

Case closed. Aysha checked her evening purse, selected her car key, and turned towards the door. 'See you later.'

'Have a good time.'

What did Teresa Benini consider a *good time*? An exquisitely served meal eaten in a trendy restaurant with Carlo Santangelo, followed by a long night of loving in Carlo's bed?

Aysha slid in behind the wheel of her black Porsche Carrera, fired the engine, then eased the car down the driveway, cleared the electronic gates, and traversed the quiet tree-lined street towards the main arterial road leading from suburban Vaucluse into the city.

A shaft of sunlight caught the diamond-studded gold band with its magnificent solitaire on the third finger of her left hand. Brilliantly designed, horrendously expensive, it was a befitting symbol representing the intended union of Giuseppe Benini's daughter to Luigi Santangelo's son.

Benini-Santangelo, Aysha mused as she joined the flow of city-bound traffic.

Two immigrants from two neighbouring properties in a northern Italian town had travelled in their late teens to Sydney, where they'd worked two jobs every day of the week, saved every cent, and set up a cement business in their mid-twenties.

Forty years on, Benini-Santangelo was a major name in Sydney's building industry, with a huge plant and a fleet of concrete tankers.

Each man had married a suitable wife, sadly produced only one child apiece; they lived in fine homes, drove expensive cars, and had given their children the best education that money could buy.

Both families had interacted closely on a social and personal level for as long as Aysha could remember. The bond between them was strong, more than friends. Almost family.

The New South Head Road wound down towards Rose Bay, and Aysha took a moment to admire the view.

At six-thirty on a fine late summer's evening the ocean resembled a sapphire jewel, merging with a sky clear of cloud or pollution. Prime real estate overlooked numerous coves and bays where various sailing craft lay anchored. Tall city buildings rose in differing architectural design, structured towers of glass and steel, providing a splendid backdrop to the Opera House and the wide span of the Harbour Bridge.

Traffic became more dense as she drew close to the city, and there were the inevitable delays at computer-controlled intersections.

Consequently it was almost seven when she drew into the curved entrance of the hotel and consigned her car to valet parking.

She could, *should* have allowed Carlo to collect her, or at least driven to his apartment. It would have been more practical, sensible.

Except tonight she didn't feel *sensible*.

Aysha nodded to the concierge as she entered the lobby, and she hadn't taken more than three steps towards the bank of sofas and single chairs when a familiar male frame rose to full height and moved forward to greet her.

Carlo Santangelo.

Just the sight of him was enough to send her heart racing to a quickened beat. Her breath caught in her throat, and she forced herself to monitor the rise and fall of her chest.

In his late thirties, he stood three inches over six feet and possessed the broad shoulders and hard-muscled body of a man who coveted physical fitness. Sculpted raw-boned facial features highlighted planes and angles, accenting a powerful jaw, strong chin, and a sensuously moulded mouth. Well-cut thick dark brown hair was stylishly groomed, and his eyes were incredibly dark, almost black.

Aysha had no recollection of witnessing his temper. Yet there could be no doubt he possessed one, for his eyes could darken to obsidian, the mouth thin, and his voice assume the chill of an ice floe.

'Aysha.' He leant down and brushed his mouth against her own, lingered, then he lifted his head and caught both of her hands in his.

Dear God, he was something. The clean male smell of him teased her nostrils, combining with his subtle aftershave.

Her stomach executed a series of somersaults, and her pulse hammered heavily enough to be almost audible. Did she affect him the way he affected her?

Doubtful, she conceded, aware of precisely where she fitted in the scheme of things. Bianca had been his first love, the beautiful young girl he'd married ten years ago, only to lose her in a fatal car accident mere weeks after the honeymoon. Aysha had cried silent tears at the wedding, and wept openly at Bianca's funeral.

Afterwards he'd flung himself into work, earning

a reputation in the business arena as a superb strategist, able to negotiate with enviable skill.

He had dated many women, and selectively taken what they offered without thought of replacing the beautiful young girl who had all too briefly shared his name.

Until last year, when he'd focused his attention on Aysha, strengthening the affectionate bond between them into something much more personal, more intimate.

His proposal of marriage had overwhelmed her, for Carlo had been the object of her affection for as long as she could remember, and she could pinpoint the moment when teenage hero-worship had changed and deepened into love.

A one-sided love, for she was under no illusion. The marriage would strengthen the Benini-Santangelo conglomerate and forge it into another generation.

'Hungry?'

At the sound of Carlo's drawled query Aysha offered a winsome smile, and her eyes assumed a teasing sparkle. 'Starving.'

'Then let's go eat, shall we?' Carlo placed an arm round her waist and led her towards a bank of elevators.

The top of her head came level with his shoulder, and her slender frame held a fragility that was in direct contrast to strength of mind and body.

She could, he reflected musingly as he depressed the call button, have turned into a terrible brat. Yet for all the pampering, by an indulgent but fiercely

protective mother, Aysha was without guile. Nor did
she have an inflated sense of her own importance.
Instead, she was a warm, intelligent, witty and very
attractive young woman whose smile transformed her
features into something quite beautiful.

The restaurant was situated on a high floor offering
magnificent views of the city and harbour. Expensive, exclusive, and a personal favourite, for the chef
was a true artiste with an expertise and flair that had
earned him fame and fortune in several European
countries.

The lift doors slid open, and she preceded Carlo
into the cubicle, then stood in silence as they were
transported with electronic speed.

'That bad, hmm?'

Aysha cast him a quick glance, saw the musing
cynicism apparent, and didn't know whether to be
amused or resigned that he'd divined her silence and
successfully attributed it to a ghastly day.

Was she that transparent? Somehow she didn't
think so. At least not with most people. However,
Carlo was an entity all on his own, and she'd accepted a long time ago that there was very little she
could manage to keep hidden from him.

'Where would you like me to begin?' She wrinkled her nose at him, then she lifted a hand and proceeded to tick off each finger in turn. 'An irate client,
an even more irate floor manager, imported fabric
caught up in a wharf strike, or the dress fitting from
hell?' She rolled her eyes. 'Choose.'

The elevator slid to a halt, and she walked at his
side to the restaurant foyer.

'Signor Santangelo, Signorina Benini. Welcome.' The maître d' greeted them with a fulsome smile, and accorded them the deference of valued patrons. He didn't even suggest a table, merely led them to the one they preferred, adjacent the floor-to-ceiling window.

There was, Aysha conceded, a certain advantage in being socially well placed. It afforded impeccable service.

The wine steward appeared the instant they were seated, and Aysha deferred to Carlo's choice of white wine.

'Iced water, please,' she added, then watched as Carlo leaned back in his chair to regard her with interest.

'How is Teresa?'

'Now there's a leading question, if ever there was one,' Aysha declared lightly. 'Perhaps you could be more specific?'

'She's driving you insane.' His faint drawling tones caused the edges of her mouth to tilt upwards in a semblance of wry humour.

'You're good. Very good,' she acknowledged with cynical approval.

One eyebrow rose, and there was gleaming amusement evident. 'Shall I try for excellent and guess the current crisis?' he ventured. 'Or are you going to tell me?'

'The wedding dress.' Visualising the scene earlier in the day brought a return of tension as she vividly recalled Teresa's calculated insistence and the seamstress's restrained politeness. Dammit, it should be so easy. They'd agreed on the style, the material. The fit was perfect. Yet Teresa hadn't been able to leave it alone.

'Problems?' He had no doubt there would be many, most of which would be of Teresa's making.

'The dressmaker is not appreciative of Mother's interference with the design.' Aysha experienced momentary remorse, for the gown was truly beautiful, a vision of silk, satin and lace.

'I see.'

'No,' she corrected. 'You don't.' She paused as the wine steward delivered the wine, and went through the tasting ritual with Carlo, before retreating.

'What don't I see, *cara*?' Carlo queried lightly. 'That Teresa, like most Italian *mammas*, wants the perfect wedding for her daughter. The perfect venue, caterers, food, wine, *bomboniera*, the cake, limousines. And the dress must be outstanding.'

'You've forgotten the flowers,' Aysha reminded him mildly. 'The florist is at the end of his tether. The caterer is ready to quit because he says *his* tiramisu is an art form and he will not, *not*, you understand, use my grandmother's recipe from the Old Country.'

Carlo's mouth formed a humorous twist. 'Teresa is a superb cook,' he complimented blandly.

Teresa was superb at everything; that was the trouble. Consequently, she expected others to be equally superb. The *trouble* as such, was that while Teresa Benini enjoyed the prestige of employing the *best* money could buy, she felt bound to check every little detail to ensure it came up to her impossibly high standard.

Retaining household staff had always been a problem for as long as Aysha could remember. They came and left with disturbing rapidity due to her mother's refusal to delegate even the most minor of chores.

The waiter arrived with the menu, and because he was new, and very young, they listened in silence as he explained the intricacies of each dish, gave his considered recommendations, then very solicitously noted their order before retreating with due deference to relay it to the kitchen.

Aysha lifted her glass and took a sip of chilled water, then regarded the man seated opposite over the rim of the stemmed goblet.

'How seriously would you consider an elopement?'

Carlo swirled the wine in his goblet, then lifted it to his lips and savoured the delicate full-bodied flavour.

'Is there any particular reason why you'd want to incur Teresa's wrath by wrecking the social event of the year?'

'It would never do,' she agreed solemnly. 'Although I'm almost inclined to plug for sanity and suffer the wrath.'

One eyebrow slanted, and his dark eyes assumed a quizzical gleam.

The waiter delivered their starters; minestrone and a superb linguini with seafood sauce.

'Two weeks, *cara*,' Carlo reminded her.

It was a lifetime. One she wasn't sure she'd survive intact.

She should have moved out of home into an apartment of her own. Would have, if Teresa hadn't dismissed the idea as ridiculous when she had a wing in the house all to herself, complete with gym, sauna and entertainment lounge. She had her own car, her own garage, and technically she could come and go as she pleased.

Aysha picked up her fork, deftly wound on a portion of pasta and savoured it. Ambrosia. The sauce was *perfecto*.

'Good?'

She wound on another portion and held it to his lips. 'Try some.' She hadn't intended it to be an intimate gesture, and her eyes flared slightly as he placed his fingers over hers, guided the fork, and then held her gaze as he slid the pasta into his mouth.

Her stomach jolted, then settled, and she was willing to swear she could hear her own heartbeat thudding in her ears.

He didn't even have to try, and she became caught up with the alchemy that was his alone.

A warm smile curved his lips as he dipped a spoon into his minestrone and lifted it invitingly towards her own. 'Want to try mine?'

She took a small mouthful, then shook her head when he offered her another. Did he realise just how difficult it was for her to retain a measure of sangfroid at moments like these?

'We have a rehearsal at the church tomorrow evening,' Carlo reminded her, and saw her eyes darken.

Aysha replaced her fork, her appetite temporarily diminished. 'Six-thirty,' she concurred evenly. 'After which the wedding party dine together.'

Both sets of parents, the bride and groom to-be, the bridesmaids and their attendants, the flower girls and page boys and *their* parents.

Followed the next day by a bridal shower. Hardly a casual affair, with just very close friends, a few nibblies and champagne. The guest list numbered fifty, it was being catered, and Teresa had arranged entertainment.

To add to her stress levels, she'd stubbornly refused to begin six weeks' leave of absence from work until a fortnight before the wedding.

On the positive side, it kept her busy, her mind occupied, and minimised the growing tension with her mother. The negative was hours early morning and evening spent at the breathtaking harbourside mansion Carlo had built, overseeing installation of carpets, drapes, selecting furniture, co-ordinating colours. And doing battle with Teresa when their tastes didn't match and Teresa overstretched her advisory capacity. Something which happened fairly frequently.

'Penny for them.'

Aysha glanced across the table and caught Carlo's teasing smile.

'I was thinking about the house.' That much was true. 'It's all coming together very well.'

'You're happy with it?'

'How could I not be?' she countered simply, visualising the modern architectural design with its five sound-proofed self-contained wings converging onto a central courtyard. The interior was designed for light and space, with a suspended art gallery, a small theatre and games room. A sunken area featured spa and sauna, and a jet pool.

It was a showcase, a place to entertain guests and business associates. Aysha planned to make it a home.

The wine waiter appeared and refilled each goblet, followed closely by the young waiter, who removed their plates prior to serving the main course.

Carlo ate with the enjoyment of a man who consumed nourishment wisely but well, his use of cutlery decisive.

He was the consummate male, sophisticated, dynamic, and possessed of a primitive sensuality that drew women to him like a magnet. Men envied his ruthlessness and charm, and knew the combination to be lethal.

Aysha recognised each and every one of his qualities, and wondered if she was woman enough to hold him.

'Would you care to order dessert, Miss Benini?'

The young waiter's desire to please was almost embarrassing, and she offered him a gentle smile. 'No, thanks, I'll settle for coffee.'

'You've made a conquest,' Carlo drawled as the waiter retreated from their table.

Her eyes danced with latent mischief. 'Ah, you say the nicest things.'

'Should I appear jealous, do you think?'

She wanted to say, *only if you are*. And since that was unlikely, it became easy to play the game.

'Well, he *is* young, and good-looking.' She pretended to consider. 'Probably a university student working nights to pay for his education. Which would indicate he has potential.' She held Carlo's dark gleaming gaze and offered him a brilliant smile. 'Do you think he'd give up the room he probably rents, sell his wheels…a Vespa scooter at a guess…and be a kept toy-boy?'

His soft laughter sent shivers over the surface of her skin, raising fine body hairs as all her nerve-endings went haywire.

'I think I should take you home.'

'I came in my own car, remember?' she reminded him, and saw his eyes darken, the gleam intensify.

'A bid for independence, or an indication you're not going to share my bed tonight?'

She summoned a winsome smile, and her eyes shone with wicked humour. 'Teresa is of the opinion catering to your physical needs should definitely be my priority.'

'And Teresa knows best?' His voice was silky-smooth, and she wasn't deceived for a second.

'My mother believes in covering all the bases,' Aysha relayed lightly.

His gaze didn't shift, and she was almost willing to swear he could read her mind. 'As you do?'

Her expression sobered. 'I don't have a hidden agenda.' Did he know she was in love with him? Had loved him for as long as she could remember? She hoped not, for it would afford him an unfair advantage.

'Finish your coffee,' Carlo bade gently. 'Then we'll leave.' He lifted a hand in silent summons, and the waiter appeared with the bill.

Aysha watched as Carlo signed the slip and added a generous tip, then he leaned back in his chair and surveyed her thoughtfully.

She was tense, but covered it well. His eyes narrowed faintly. 'Do we have anything planned next weekend?'

'Mother has something scheduled for every day until the wedding,' she declared with unaccustomed cynicism.

'Have Teresa reorganise her diary.'

Aysha looked at him with interest. 'And if she won't?'

'Tell her I've surprised you with airline tickets and accommodation for a weekend on the Gold Coast.'

'Have you?'

His smile held humour. 'I'll make the call the minute we reach my apartment.'

Her eyes shone, and she broke into light laughter. 'My knight in shining armour.'

Carlo's voice was low, husky, and held amusement. 'Escape,' he accorded. 'Albeit brief.' He stood to his feet and reached out a hand to take hold of hers. His gleaming gaze seared right through to her heart. 'You can thank me later.'

Together they made their way through the room to the front desk.

The maître d' was courteously solicitous. 'I'll arrange with the concierge to have your cars brought to the front entrance.'

Both vehicles were waiting when they reached the lobby. Carlo saw her seated behind the wheel of her Porsche, then he crossed to his Mercedes to fire the engine within seconds and ease into the line of traffic.

Aysha followed, sticking close behind him as he traversed the inner city streets heading east towards Rose Bay and his penthouse apartment.

When they reached it she drove down into the underground car park, took the space adjoining his private bay, then walked at his side towards the bank of lifts in companionable silence.

They didn't *need* a house, she determined minutes later as she stepped into the plush apartment lobby.

The drapes weren't drawn, and the view out over the harbour was magnificent. Fairy lights, she mused as she crossed the lounge to the floor-to-ceiling glass stretching across one entire wall.

City buildings, street lights, brightly coloured neon vying with tall concrete spires and an indigo sky.

Aysha heard him pick up the phone, followed by the sound of his voice as he arranged flights and accommodation for the following weekend.

'We could have easily lived here,' she murmured as he came to stand behind her.

'So we could.' He put his arms around her waist and pulled her back against him.

She felt his chin rest on the top of her head, sensed the warmth of his breath as it teased her hair, and was unable to prevent the slight shiver as his lips sought the vulnerable hollow beneath the lobe of one ear.

She almost closed her eyes and pretended it was real. That *love* not lust, and *need* not want, was Carlo's motivation.

A silent groan rose and died in her throat as his mouth travelled to the edge of her neck and nuzzled, his tongue, his lips erotic instruments as he tantalised the rapidly beating pulse.

His hands moved, one to her breast as he sought a sensitive peak, while the other splayed low over her stomach.

She wanted to urge him to quicken the pace, to dispense with her clothes while she feverishly tore every barrier from his body until there was nothing between them.

She wanted to be lifted high in his arms and sink down onto him, then clutch hold of him as he took her for the ride of her life.

Everything about him was too controlled. Even in bed he never lost that control completely, as she did.

There were times when she wanted to cry out that while she could accept Bianca as an important part of his past, *she* was his future. Except she never said the words. Perhaps because she was afraid of his response.

Now she turned in his arms and reached for him, her mouth seeking his as she gave herself up completely to the heat of passion.

He caught her urgency and effortlessly swept her into his arms and carried her into the bedroom.

Aysha's fingers worked on his shirt buttons, unfastened the buckle on his belt, then pulled his shirt free.

His nipples were hard, and she savoured each one in turn, then used her teeth to tease, aware that Carlo had deftly removed most of her clothes.

She heard his intake of breath seconds ahead of the soft thud as he discarded one shoe and the other, then dispensed with his trousers.

'Wait.' His voice was low and slightly husky, and she ran her hands over his ribcage, searched the hard plane of his stomach and reached for him.

'So you want to play, hmm?'

CHAPTER TWO

CARLO caught hold of her arms and let his hands slide up to cup her shoulders as he buried his mouth in the vulnerable hollow at the edge of her neck.

Her subtle perfume teased his senses, and he nuzzled the sensitive skin, tasted it, nipped ever so gently with his teeth, and felt the slight spasm of her body's reaction to his touch.

She was a generous lover. Passionate, with a sense of adventure and fun he found endearing.

He trailed his lips down the slope of her breast and suckled one tender peak, savoured, then moved to render a similar supplication to its twin.

Did he know what he did to her? Aysha felt a stab of pain at the thought that his lovemaking might be contrived. A practised set of moves that pushed all the right buttons.

Once, just once she wanted to feel the tremors of need shake his body…for her, only her. To know that she could make him so crazy with desire that he had no restraint.

Was it asking too much to want *love*? She wore his ring. Soon *she* would bear his name. It should be enough.

She wanted to mean so much more to him than just a satisfactory bed partner, a charming hostess.

Take what he's prepared to give, and be grateful,

a tiny voice prompted. *A cup half-full is better than one that is empty.*

Her hands linked at his nape and she drew his head down to hers, exulting in the feel of his mouth as he shaped her own.

She let her tongue slide against his, then conducted a slow, sweeping circle before initiating a probing dance that was almost as evocative as the sexual act itself.

His hand shaped her nape and held fast her head, while the other slipped low over one hip, cupped her bottom and drew her close in against him.

She wanted him *now*, hard and fast, without any preliminaries. To be able to feel the power, the strength, without caution or care. As if he couldn't bear to wait a second longer to effect possession.

The familiar slide of his fingers, the gentle probing exploration as he sought the warm moistness of her feminine core brought a gasping sigh from her lips.

Followed by a despairing groan as he began an evocative stimulation. It wasn't fair that he should have such intimate knowledge and be aware precisely how to wield it to drive a woman wild.

His mouth hardened, and his jaw took control of hers, moving it in rhythm with his own.

She clutched hold of his shoulders and held on as his fingers probed deeper, and just as she thought she could bear it no longer he shifted position.

A cry rose and died in her throat as he slid into her in one long, thrusting movement.

Dear God, that felt good. So good. She murmured

her pleasure, then gave a startled gasp as he tumbled her down onto the bed and withdrew.

His mouth left hers, and began a seeking trail down her throat, tasting the vulnerable hollows at the base of her neck, the soft, quivering flesh of each breast, the indentation of her navel.

She knew his intention, and felt the flame lick along every nerve-end, consuming every sensitised nerve-cell until she was close to conflagration.

Her head tossed from one side to the other as sensation took hold of her whole body. Part of her wanted to tell him to stop before it became unbearable, but the husky admonition sounded so low in her throat as to be indistinguishable.

He was skilled, so very highly skilled in giving a woman pleasure. The slight graze of his teeth, the erotic laving of his tongue. He knew just where to touch to urge her towards the edge. And how to hold her there, until she begged for release.

Aysha thought she cried out, and she bit down hard as Carlo feathered light kisses over her quivering stomach, then paused to suckle at her breast,

His mouth closed on hers, and she arched up against him as he entered her in one surging movement, stretching delicate tissues to their utmost capacity.

He began to move, slowly at first, then with increasing depth and strength as she became consumed with the feel of him.

His skin, her own, was warm and slick with sweat, and the blood ran through her veins like quicksilver.

It was more than a physical joining, for she gifted

him her heart, her soul, everything. She was *his*. Only his. At that moment she would have died for him, so complete was her involvement.

Frightening, shattering, she reflected a long time later as she lay curled into the warmth of his body. For it almost destroyed her concept of who and what she had become beneath his tutelage.

The steady rise and fall of his chest was reassuring, the beat of his heart strong. The lazy stroke of his fingers along her spine indicated he wasn't asleep yet, and the slight pressure against the indentations of each vertebrae was soothing. She could feel his lips brush lightly over her hair as she drifted into a peaceful sleep.

It was the soft, hazy aftermath of great lovemaking. A time for whispered avowals of love, Aysha thought as she woke, the affirmation of commitment.

Aysha wanted to utter the words, and hear them in return. Yet she knew she would die a silent death if he didn't respond in kind. She pressed a light butterfly kiss to the muscled ridge of his chest and traced a gentle circle with the tip of her tongue.

He tasted of musk, edged with a faint tang that was wholly male. She nipped the hard flesh with her teeth and bestowed a love-bite, then she soothed it gently before moving close to a sensitive male nipple.

She trailed her fingers over one hip, lingered near his groin, and felt his stomach muscles tense.

'That could prove dangerous,' Carlo warned as she began to caress him with gentle intimacy.

The soft slide of one finger, as fleeting as the tip of a butterfly's wing, in a careful tactile exploration. Incredible how the male organ could engorge and enlarge in size. Almost frightening, its degree of power as instrument to a woman's pleasure.

Aysha had the desire to tantalise him to the brink of madness, and unleash everything that was wild and untamed, until there were no boundaries. Just two people as one, attuned and in perfect accord on every level. Spiritual, mental and physical.

A gasp escaped her throat as he clasped both hands on her waist and swept her to sit astride him.

Excitement spiralled through her body as he arched his hips and sent her tumbling down against his chest.

One hand slid to her nape as he angled her head to his, then his mouth was on hers, all heat and passion as he took possession.

The kiss seared her heart, branding her in a way that made her *his*…totally. Mind, body, and soul. She had no thought for anything but the man and the storm raging within.

It made anything she'd shared before seem less. Dear Lord, she'd ached for his passion. But this…this was raw, primitive. Mesmeric. Ravaging.

She met and matched his movements, driven by a hunger so intense she had no recollection of time or place.

Aysha wasn't even aware when he reversed positions, and it was the gentling of his touch, the gradual loss of intensity that intruded on her conscious mind and brought with it a slow return to sanity.

There was a sense of exquisite wonderment, a sensation of wanting desperately to hold onto the moment in case it might fracture and fragment.

She didn't feel the soft warmth of tears as they slid slowly down her cheeks. Nor was she aware of the sexual heat emanating from her skin, or the slight trembling of her body as Carlo used his hands, his lips to bring her down.

He absorbed the dampness on one cheek, then pressed his lips against one closed eyelid, before moving to effect a similar supplication on the other. His hands shifted as he gently rolled onto his back, carrying her with him so she lay cradled against the length of his body.

Slight tremors shook her slim form, and he brought her mouth to his in a soft, evocative joining. His fingers trailed the shape of her, gently exploring the slim supple curves, the slender waist, the soft curve of her buttocks.

It was Carlo who broke contact long minutes later, and she trailed a hand down the edge of his cheek.

'I get first take on the shower. You make the coffee,' she whispered.

His slow smile caused havoc with her pulse-rate. 'We share the shower, then I'll organise coffee while you cook breakfast.'

'Chauvinist,' Aysha commented with musing tolerance.

His lips caressed her breast, and desire arrowed through her body, hot, needy, and wildly wanton. 'We can always miss breakfast and focus on the shower.'

His arousal was a potent force, and her eyes danced with mischief as she contemplated the option. 'As much as the offer attracts me, I need *food* to charge my energy levels.' She placed the tip of a finger over his lips, then gave a mild yelp as he nipped it with his teeth. 'That calls for revenge.'

Carlo's hands spanned her waist and he shifted her to one side, then he leaned over her. 'Try it.'

She rose to the challenge at once, although the balance of power soon became uneven, and then it hardly seemed to matter any more who won or lost.

Afterwards she had the quickest shower on record, then she dressed, swept her hair into a twist at her nape, added blusher, eye colour and mascara.

She looked, Carlo noted with respect, as if she'd spent thirty minutes on her grooming instead of the five it had taken her.

'Sit down and eat,' he commanded as he slid an omelette onto a plate. 'Coffee's ready.'

'You're a gem among men,' Aysha complimented as she sipped the coffee. Pure nectar on the palate, and the omelette was perfection.

'From chauvinist to gem in the passage of twenty minutes,' he drawled with unruffled ease, and she spared him a wicked grin in between mouthfuls.

'Don't get a swelled head.'

She watched as he poured himself some coffee then joined her at the table. The dark navy towelling robe accented his breadth of shoulder, and dark curling hair showed at the vee of the lapels. Her eyes slid down to the belt tied at his waist, and lingered.

'You don't have time to find out,' he mocked lazily, and she offered a stunning smile.

'It's my last day at work.' She rose to her feet and gulped the last mouthful of coffee. 'But as of tomorrow…'

'Promises,' Carlo taunted, and she reached up to brush her lips to his cheek, except he moved his head and they touched his mouth instead.

'Got to rush,' she said with genuine regret. 'See you tonight.'

Her job was important to her, and she loved the concept of using colour and design to make a house a home. The right furnishings, furniture, fittings, so that it all added up to a beautiful whole that was both eye-catching and comfortable. She'd earned a reputation for going that extra mile for a client, exploring every avenue in the search to get it right.

However, there were days when phone calls didn't produce the results she wanted, and today was one of them. Added to which she had to run a final check over all the orders that were due to come in while she was away. An awesome task, just on its own.

Then there was lunch with some of her fellow staff, and the presentation of a wedding gift…an exquisite crystal platter. The afternoon seemed to fly on wings, and it was after six when she rode the lift to Carlo's penthouse.

'Ten minutes,' she promised him as she entered the lounge, and she stepped out of heeled pumps *en route* to the shower.

Aysha was ready in nine, and he snagged her arm as she raced towards the door.

'Slow down,' he directed, and she threw him an urgent glance.

'We're late. We should have left already.' She tugged her hand and made no impression. 'They'll be waiting for us.'

He pulled her close, and lowered his head down to hers. 'So they'll wait a little longer.'

His mouth touched hers with such incredible gentleness her insides began to melt, and she gave a faint despairing groan as her lips parted beneath the pressure of his.

Minutes later he lifted his head and surveyed the languid expression softening those beautiful smoky grey eyes. Better, he noted silently. Some of the tension had ebbed away, and she looked slightly more relaxed.

'OK, let's go.'

'That was deliberate,' Aysha said a trifle ruefully as they rode the lift down to the underground car park, and caught his musing smile.

'Guilty.'

He'd slowed her galloping pace down to a relaxed trot, and she offered a smile in silent thanks as they left the lift and crossed to the Mercedes.

'How was your day?' she queried as she slid into the passenger seat and fastened her belt.

'Assembling quotes, checking computer print-outs, checking a building site. Numerous phone calls.'

'All hands-on stuff, huh?'

The large car sprang into instant life the moment he turned the key, and he spared her a wry smile as they gained street level.

'That about encapsulates it.'

The church was a beautiful old stone building set back from the road among well-tended lawns and gardens. Symmetrically planted trees and their spreading branches added to the portrayed seclusion.

There was an air of peace and grace apparent, meshing with the mystique of blessed holy ground.

Aysha drew a deep breath as she saw the several cars lining the curved driveway. Everyone was here.

Attending someone else's wedding, watching the ceremony on film or television, was a bit different from participating in one's own, albeit this was merely a rehearsal of the real thing.

'I want to carry the basket,' Emily, the youngest flower girl, insisted, and tried to wrest it from Samantha's grasp.

'I don't want to hold a pillow. It looks sissy,' Jonathon, the eldest page boy declared.

Oh, my. If he thought carrying a small satin lace-edged pillow demeaned his boyhood, then just wait until he had to get dressed in a miniature suit, satin waistcoat, buttoned shirt and bow-tie.

'Sissy,' the youngest page boy endorsed.

'You have to,' Emily insisted importantly.

'Don't.'

'Do so.'

Aysha didn't know whether to laugh or cry. 'What if Samantha carries the basket of rose petals, and Emily carries the pillow?'

It was almost possible to see the ensuing mental tussle as each little girl weighed the importance of each task.

'I want the pillow,' Samantha decided. Rings held more value than rose-petals to be strewn over the carpeted aisle.

'You can have the basket.' Emily, too, had done her own calculations.

Teresa rolled her eyes, the girls' respective mothers attempted to pacify, and when that failed they tried bribery.

The four bridesmaids looked tense, for they'd each been assigned a child to care for during the formal ceremony.

'OK.' Aysha lifted both hands in a gesture of expressive defeat. 'This is how it's going to be. Two baskets, so Emily and Samantha get to carry one each.' She cast both boys a stern look. 'Two pillows.'

'Two?' Teresa queried incredulously, and Aysha inclined her head.

'Two.'

The little girls beamed, and both boys bent their heads in sulky disagreement.

Maybe it would have been wiser not to give the children a rehearsal at all, and simply tell them what to do on the day and hope they'd concentrate so hard there wouldn't be the opportunity for error.

Celestial assistance was obviously going to be needed, Aysha mused as she listened to the priest's instructions.

An hour later they were all seated at a long table in a restaurant nominated as children-friendly. The food was good, the wine did much to relax fraught nerves, and Aysha enjoyed the informality of it all as she leaned back against Carlo's supporting arm.

'Tired?'

She lifted her face to his, and her eyes sparkled with latent intimacy. 'It's been a long day.'

He leaned in close and brushed his lips to her temple. 'You can sleep in in the morning.'

'Generous of you. But I need to be home early to help Teresa with preparations for the bridal shower. Remember?'

It was almost eleven when everyone began to make a move, and a further half-hour before Aysha and Carlo were able to leave, for the bridesmaids lingered and Teresa had last-minute instructions to impart.

The witching hour of midnight struck as she preceded Carlo into the penthouse, and she slipped off her shoes, took the clip from her hair and shook it loose, then she padded through to the kitchen.

'Coffee?'

Aysha sensed rather than heard him move behind her, and she murmured her approval as his hands kneaded tense shoulder muscles.

'Good?'

Oh, yes. So good, she was prepared to beg him to continue. 'Please. Don't stop.' It was bliss, almost heaven, and she closed her eyes as his fingers worked a magic all on their own.

'Any ideas for tomorrow night?'

She heard the lazy quality in his voice and smiled. 'You mean we have a free evening?'

'I can book dinner.'

'Don't,' she said at once. 'I'll pick up something.'

'I could do this much better if you lay down on the bed.'

Her senses were heightened, and her pulse began to quicken. 'That might prove dangerous.'

'Eventually,' Carlo agreed lazily. 'But there are advantages to a full body massage.'

Aysha's blood pressure moved up a notch. 'Are you seducing me?'

His soft laughter sounded deep and husky close to her ear. 'Am I succeeding?'

'I'll let you know,' she promised with wicked intent. 'In about an hour from now.'

'An hour?'

'The quality of the massage will govern your reward,' Aysha informed him solemnly, and he laughed as he swept her into his arms and carried her through to the bedroom.

To lay prone on towels as Carlo slowly smoothed aromatic oil over every inch of her body was sensual torture of the sweetest kind.

Whatever had made her think she'd last an hour? After thirty minutes the pleasure was so intense, it was all she could do not to roll onto her back and beg him to take her.

'I think,' she said between gritted teeth, 'that's enough.'

His fingertips smoothed up her thighs and lingered a hair's breadth away from the apex, then shaped each buttock before settling at her waist.

'You said an hour,' Carlo reminded her, and gently rolled her onto her back.

Aysha looked at him from beneath long-fringed

lashes. 'I'll make you pay,' she promised as liquid heat spilled through her veins.

He leaned down and took her mouth in a brief hard kiss. 'I'm counting on it.'

The sweet sorcery of his touch nearly sent her mad, and afterwards it was she who drove him to the brink, aware of those dark eyes watching her with an almost predatory alertness that gradually shifted and changed as she tried to break his control.

Desire, raw and primitive, tore through her body, and she felt bare, exposed, as her own fragile control shredded into a thousand pieces.

Aysha had no recollection of the tears that slowly spilled down each cheek until Carlo cupped her face and erased them with a single movement of his thumb.

His lips brushed hers, gently, back and forth, then angled in sensual possession.

Afterwards he simply held her until her breathing slowed and steadied into a regular beat, then he gently eased her to lie beside him and held her close through the night.

She barely stirred when he rose at eight, and he showered in a spare bathroom, then dressed and made breakfast.

The aroma of freshly brewed coffee stirred Aysha's senses, and she fought through the final mists of sleep into wakefulness.

'The tousled look suits you,' Carlo teased as he placed the tray down onto the bedside pedestal. Her cheeks were softly flushed, her eyes slumberous, the dilated pupils making them seem too large for her face.

'Hi.' She made an attempt to pull the sheet a little higher, and incurred his husky laughter.

'Your modesty is adorable, *cara*.'

'Breakfast in bed,' she murmured appreciatively. 'You've excelled yourself.'

He lowered his head and bestowed an open-mouthed kiss to the edge of her throat, teased the tender skin with his teeth, then trailed a path to the gentle swell of her breast.

'I aim to please.'

Oh, yes, he did that. She retained a very vivid memory of just how well he'd managed to please her. Not that it had been entirely one-sided... She'd managed to take him further towards the edge than before. One of these days...*nights*, she amended, she planned to tip him over and watch him free-fall.

'Naturally, your mind is more on food than me at this point, hmm?'

Go much lower, and I won't get to the food. 'Of course,' she offered demurely. 'I'm going to need stamina to make it through the day.'

'The bridal shower,' he mused. His eyes met hers, and she regarded him solemnly.

'Teresa wants the occasion to be memorable.'

Carlo sank down onto the bed. 'There's orange juice, and caffeine to kick-start the day.'

Together with toast, croissants, fruit preserve, cheese, wafer-thin slices of salami and prosciutto. A veritable feast.

Aysha slid up in the bed, paying careful attention

to keep the sheet tucked beneath her arms, and took the glass of juice from Carlo's extended hand. Next came the coffee, then a croissant with preserve, followed by a piece of toast folded in half over a layer of cheese and prosciutto.

'More coffee?'

She hesitated, checked the time, then shook her head. 'I said I'd be home around nine.'

Carlo stood to his feet and collected the tray. 'I'll take this downstairs.'

Ten minutes later she had showered, dressed and was ready to face the day. Light blue jeans sheathed her slim legs, hugged her hips, and she wore a fitted top that accentuated the delicate curve of her breasts.

She skirted the servery, reached up and planted a light kiss against the edge of his jaw. 'Thanks for breakfast.'

He caught her close and slanted his mouth over hers with a possession that wreaked havoc with her equilibrium. Then he eased the pressure and brushed his lips over the swollen contours of her own, lingered at one corner, then gently released her.

'I consider myself thanked.'

Her eyes felt too large, and she quickly blinked in an effort to clear her vision. That had been... 'cataclysmic' was a word that came immediately to mind. And passionate, definitely passionate.

Maybe she was beginning to scratch the surface of his control after all.

That thought stayed with her as she took the lift down to the underground car park, and during the few kilometres to her parents' home.

CHAPTER THREE

AYSHA'S four bridesmaids were the first to arrive, followed by Gianna and a few of Teresa's friends. Two aunts, three cousins, and a number of close friends.

There were beautifully wrapped gifts, much laughter, a little wine, some champagne, and the exchange of numerous anecdotes. Entertainment was provided by a gifted magician whose expertise in pulling at least a hundred scarves from his hat and jacket pockets had to be seen to be believed.

Coffee was served at three-thirty, and at four Teresa was summoned to the front door to accept the arrival of an unexpected guest.

The speed with which Lianna, Aysha' chief bridesmaid, joined Teresa aroused suspicion, and there was much laughter as a good-looking young man entered the lounge.

'You didn't—' Aysha began, and one look at Lianna, Arianne, Suzanne and Tessa was sufficient to determine that her four bridesmaids were as guilty as sin.

A portable tape-recorder was set on a coffee table, and when the music began he went into a series of choreographed movements as he began to strip.

It was a tastefully orchestrated act, as such acts went. The young man certainly had the frame, the body, the muscles to execute the traditional bump-and-grind routine.

'You refused to let us give you a ladies' night out, so we had to do something,' Lianna confided with an impish grin as everyone began to leave.

'Fiend,' Aysha chastised with affectionate remonstrance. 'Wait until it's your turn.'

'What'll you do to top it, Aysha? Hire a group of male strippers?'

'Don't put thoughts into my head,' she threatened direly.

The caterers tidied and cleaned up, then left fifteen minutes later, and Aysha crossed to the table where a selection of gifts were on display.

From the intensely practical to the highly decorative, they were all beautiful and reflected the giver's personality. A smile curved her lips. Lianna's gift of a male stripper had been the wackiest.

'You had no idea of Lianna's surprise?' Teresa queried as she crossed to her side.

'None,' Aysha answered truthfully, and curved an arm around her mother's waist. 'Thanks, Mamma, for a lovely afternoon.'

'My pleasure.'

Aysha grinned unashamedly. 'Even the stripper?' she teased, and glimpsed the faint pink colour in her mother's cheeks.

'No comment.'

She began to laugh. 'All right, let's change the subject. What shall we do with these gifts?'

They set them on a table in one of the rooms Teresa had organised for displaying the wedding

presents, and when that was done Aysha went upstairs and changed into tailored trousers and matching silk top.

It was after six when she entered Carlo's penthouse apartment, and she crossed directly into the
kitchen to deposit the carry-sack containing a selection of Chinese takeaways she'd collected *en route*
from home.

'Let me guess. Chinese, Thai, Malaysian?' Carlo
drawled as he entered the kitchen, and she directed
him a winsome smile.

'Chinese. And I picked up some videos.'

'You have plans to spend a quiet night?'

She opened cupboards and extracted two plates,
then collected cutlery. 'I think I've had enough excitement for the day.' And through last night.

'Care to elaborate on the afternoon?'

Her eyes sparkled with hidden devilry. 'Lianna ordered a male stripper.' She decided to tease him a
little. 'He was young, *built*, and gorgeous.' She wrinkled her nose at him. 'Ask Gianna; she was there.'

'Indeed?' His eyes speared hers. 'Perhaps I need
to hear more about this gorgeous hunk.'

Carlo had her heart, her soul. It never ceased to
hurt that she didn't have his.

'Well…' She deliberated. 'There was the body to
die for.' She ticked off each attribute with teasing
relish. 'Longish hair, tied in this cute little ponytail,
and when he let it free…wow, so sexy. No apparent
body hair.' Her eyes sparkled with devilish humour.
'Waxing must be a pain…literally. And he had the
cutest butt.'

Carlo's eyes narrowed fractionally, and she gave him an irrepressible grin. 'He stripped down to a thong bikini brief.'

'I imagine Teresa and Gianna were relieved.'

She tried hard not to laugh, and failed as a chuckle emerged. 'They appeared to enjoy the show.'

His lips twitched. 'An unexpected show, unless I'm mistaken.'

'Totally,' she agreed, and viewed the various cartons she'd deposited on the servery. 'Let's be *really* decadent,' she suggested lightly. 'And watch a video while we eat.'

The first was a thriller, the acting sufficiently superb to bring an audience to the edge of their seats, and the second was a comedy about a wedding where everything that could go wrong, did. It was funny, slapstick, and over the top, but in amongst the frivolity was a degree of reality Aysha could identify with.

In between videos she'd tidied cartons and rinsed plates, made coffee, and now she carried the cups through to the kitchen.

She felt pleasantly tired as she ascended the stairs to the main bedroom, and after a quick shower she slid between the sheets to curl comfortably in the circle of Carlo's arms with her head pillowed against his chest.

Within minutes she fell asleep, and she was unaware of the light touch as Carlo's lips brushed the top of her head, or the feather-light trail of his fingers as they smoothed a path over the surface of her skin.

They woke late, lingered over breakfast, then took

Giuseppe's cabin cruiser for a day trip up the Hawkesbury River. They returned as the sun set in a glorious flare of fading colour and the cityscape sprang to life with a myriad of pin-prick lights.

Magic, Aysha reflected, as the wonder of nature and manmade technology overwhelmed her.

Tomorrow the shopping would begin in earnest as Teresa initiated the first of her many lists of Things to Do.

'Mamma, is this really necessary?'

As shopping went, it had been a profitable day with regard to acquisitions. Teresa, it appeared, was bent on spending money... *Serious* money.

'You're the only child I have,' Teresa said simply. 'Don't deny me the pleasure of giving my daughter the best wedding I can provide.'

Aysha tucked her hand through her mother's arm and hugged it close. 'Don't rain on my parade, huh?'

'Exactly.'

'OK. The dress, if you insist. But...' She paused, and cast Teresa a stern look. 'That's it,' she admonished.

'For today.'

They joined the exodus of traffic battling to exit choked city streets, and made it to Vaucluse at five-thirty, leaving very little time to shower, change and be ready to leave the house at six thirty.

'You go on ahead,' Teresa suggested. 'I'll put these in the room next to yours. We can sort through them tomorrow.'

Aysha raced upstairs to her bedroom, then discarded her clothes and made for the shower. Minutes later she wound a towel round her slim curves, removed the excess moisture from her hair and wielded the hairdrier to good effect.

Basic make-up followed, then she crossed to the walk-in robe, cast a quick discerning eye over the carefully co-ordinated contents, and extracted a figure-hugging gown in black.

The hemline rested at mid-thigh, the overall length extended slightly by a wide border of scalloped lace. The design was sleeveless, backless, and cunningly styled to show a modest amount of cleavage. Thin shoulder straps ensured the gown stayed in place.

Sheer black pantyhose? Or should she settle for bare legs and almost non-existent thong bikini briefs? And very high stiletto-heeled pumps?

Minimum jewellery, she decided, and she'd sweep her hair into a casual knot atop her head.

Half an hour later she descended the stairs to the lower floor and entered the lounge. Teresa and Giuseppe were grouped together sharing a light aperitif.

Her father turned towards her, his expression a comedic mix of parental pride and male appreciation. Any hint of paternal remonstrance was absent, doubtless on the grounds that his beloved daughter was safely spoken for, on the verge of marriage, and therefore he had absolutely nothing to worry about.

Teresa, however, was something else. One glance was all it took for those dark eyes to narrow fractionally and the lips to thin. *Appearance* was everything, and tonight Aysha did not fit her mother's required image.

'Don't you think that's a little…?' Teresa paused delicately. 'Bold, darling?'

'Perhaps,' Aysha conceded, and directed her father a teasing glance. 'Papà?'

Giuseppe was well versed in the ways of mother and daughter, and sought a diplomatic response. 'I'm sure Carlo will be most appreciative.' He gestured towards a crystal decanter. 'Can I fix you a spritzer?'

She hadn't eaten much throughout the day, just nibbled on fresh fruit, sipped several glasses of water, and taken three cups of long black coffee. Alcohol would go straight to her head. 'I stopped by the kitchen when I arrived home and fixed some juice,' she declined gently. 'I'm fine.'

'Unless I'm mistaken, that's Carlo now.'

The light crunch of car tires, the faint clunk of a door closing, followed by the distant sound of melodic door chimes heralded his arrival, and within seconds their live-in housekeeper ushered him into the lounge.

Aysha crossed the room and caught hold of his hand, then offered her cheek for his kiss. It was a natural gesture, one that was expected, and only she heard the light teasing murmur close to her ear. 'Stunning.'

His arm curved round the back of her waist and he drew her with him as he moved to accept Teresa's greeting.

'A drink, Carlo?'

'I'll wait until dinner.'

It would be easy to lean in against him, and for a moment she almost did. Except there was no one to impress, and the evening lay ahead.

Giuseppe swallowed the remainder of his wine, and placed his glass down onto the tray. 'In that case, perhaps we should be on our way. Teresa?'

At that moment the phone rang, and Teresa frowned in disapproval. 'I hope that's not going to make us late.'

Not unless the call heralded something of dire consequence; there wasn't a chance. Aysha bit back on the mockery, and sensed her mother's words even before they were uttered.

'You and Carlo go on ahead. We won't be far behind you.'

Sliding into the passenger seat of the car was achieved with greater decorum than she expected, and she was in the process of fastening her seatbelt when Carlo moved behind the wheel.

A deft flick of his wrist and the engine purred to life. Almost a minute later they had traversed the curved driveway and were heading towards the city.

'Am I correct in assuming the dress is a desire to shock?'

Aysha heard the drawling voice, sensed the underlying cynicism tinged with humour, and turned to look at him. 'Does it succeed?'

She was supremely conscious of the amount of bare thigh showing, and she fought against the temptation to take hold of the hemline and attempt to tug it down.

He turned slightly towards her, and in that second

she was acutely aware of the darkness of his eyes, the faint curve of his mouth, the gleam of white teeth.

'Teresa didn't approve.'

'You know her so well,' she indicated wryly. 'Papà seemed to think you'd be appreciative.'

'Oh, I am,' Carlo declared. 'As I'm sure every other man in the room will be.'

She directed him a stunning smile. 'You say the nicest things.'

'Careful you don't overdo it, *cara*.'

'I'm aiming for brilliance.'

For one brief second her eyes held the faintest shadow, then it was gone. He lifted a hand and brushed light fingers down her cheek.

'A few hours, four at the most. Then we can leave.'

Yes, she thought sadly. And tomorrow it will start all over again. The shopping, fittings, social obligations. Each day it seemed to get worse. Fulfilling her mother's expectations, having her own opinions waved aside, the increasing tension. If only Teresa wasn't bent on turning everything into such a *production*.

Suburban Point Piper was a neighbouring suburb and took only minutes to reach.

Carlo turned between ornate wrought-iron gates and parked behind a stylish Jaguar. Four, no, five cars lined the curved driveway, and Aysha experienced a moment's hesitation as she moved towards the few steps leading to the main entrance.

There had been countless precedents of an evening

such as this, Aysha reflected as she accepted a light wine and exchanged pleasantries with fellow guests.

Beautiful home, gracious host and hostess. The requisite mingling over drinks for thirty minutes before dinner. Any number between ten to twenty guests, a splendid table. An exquisite floral centrepiece. The guests carefully selected to complement each other.

'Carlo, *darling*.'

Aysha heard the greeting, recognised the sultry feminine purr, and turned slowly to face one of several women who had worked hard to win Carlo's affection.

Now that the wedding was imminent, most had retired gracefully from the hunt. With the exception of Nina di Salvo.

The tall, svelte fashion consultant was a *femme fatale*, wealthy, widowed, and selectively seeking a husband of equal wealth and social standing.

Nina was admired, even adored, by men. For her style, beauty and wit. Women recognised the predatory element existent, and reacted accordingly.

'Aysha,' Nina acknowledged. 'You look…' The pause was deliberate. 'A little tired. All the preparations getting to you, darling?'

Aysha summoned a winsome smile and honed the proverbial dart. 'Carlo doesn't permit me enough sleep.'

Nina's eyes narrowed fractionally, then she leaned towards Carlo, brushed her lips against his cheek, and lingered a fraction too long. 'How are you, *caro*?'

'Nina.' Carlo was too skilful a strategist to give anything away, and too much the gentleman to do other than observe the social niceties.

He handled Nina's overt affection with practised ease and minimum body contact. Although Nina more than made up for his reticence, Aysha noted, wondering just how he regarded the glamorous brunette's attention.

She saw his smile, heard his laughter, and felt the tender care of his touch. Yet how much was a façade?

'Do get me a drink, *caro*,' Nina commanded lightly. 'You know what I like.'

Oh, my, Aysha determined as Carlo excused himself and made his way to the bar. This could turn into one hell of an evening.

'I hope you don't expect fidelity, darling,' Nina warned quietly. 'Carlo has...' she paused fractionally '...certain needs not every woman would be happy to fulfil.'

Cut straight to the chase, a tiny voice prompted. 'Really, Nina? I'll broach that with him.'

'What will you broach, and with whom?'

Speak of the devil... Aysha turned towards him as he handed Nina a slim flute of champagne.

Quite deliberately she tilted her chin and gazed into his dark gleaming eyes with amused serenity. She'd had plenty of *smile* practice, and she proffered one of pseudo-sincerity. 'Nina expressed her concern regarding my ability to fulfil your needs.'

Carlo's expression didn't change, and Aysha

dimly registered that as a poker player he would be almost without equal.

'Really?'

It seemed difficult to comprehend a single word could hold such a wealth of meaning. Or the quiet tone convey such a degree of cold anger.

The tension was evident, although Carlo hadn't moved so much as a muscle. Anyone viewing the scene would assume the three of them were engaged in pleasant conversation.

'Perhaps Nina and I should get together and compare notes,' Aysha declared with wicked humour.

Nina lifted the flute to her lips and took a delicate sip. 'What for, darling? My notes are bound to be far more extensive than yours.'

Wasn't that the truth? She caught a glimpse of aqua silk and saw Teresa and Giuseppe enter the room, and wasn't sure whether to be relieved or disappointed at their appearance.

Her mother would assess Nina's presence in an instant, and seek to break up their happy little threesome.

Aysha began a silent countdown… Three minutes to greet their hosts, another three to acknowledge a few friends.

'There you are, darling.'

Right on cue. Aysha turned towards her mother and proffered an affectionate smile. 'Mamma. You weren't held up too long, after all.' She indicated the tall brunette. 'You remember Nina?'

Teresa eyes sharpened, although her features bore

a charming smile. 'Of course. How nice to see you again.'

A lie, if ever there was one. Polite society, Aysha mused. Good manners hid a multitude of sins. If she were to obey her base instincts, she'd tell Nina precisely where to go and how to complete the journey.

There was an inherent need to show her claws, but this wasn't the time or place.

'Shall we go in to dinner?'

A respite, Aysha determined with a sense of relief. Unless their hostess had chosen unwisely and placed Nina in close proximity.

The dining room was large, the focal point being the perfectly set table positioned beneath a sparkling crystal chandelier of exquisite design.

The scene resembled a photograph lifted out of the social pages of a glossy magazine. It seemed almost a sacrilege for guests to spoil the splendid placement precision.

Although there were, she noted, a waiter and waitress present to serve allotted food portions at prearranged intervals. Likewise the imported wine would flow, but not at a rate that was considered too free.

Respectability, decorum, an adherence to exemplary good manners, with carefully orchestrated conversational topics guaranteed to stimulate the guests' interest.

Aysha caught Nina's gleam of silent mockery, and had an insane desire to disrupt it. A little, just a little.

Nothing overt, she decided as she selected a spoon

and dipped it into the part-filled bowl of mushroom soup.

The antipasto offered a superb selection, and the serving of linguini with its delicate cream and mushroom sauce couldn't be faulted.

'Could you have the waiter pour me some wine, darling?' Aysha cast Carlo a stunning smile. She rarely drank alcohol, and he knew it. However, she figured she had sufficient food in her stomach to filter the effect if she sipped it slowly.

Her request resulted in a slanted eyebrow, and she offered him the sweetest smile. 'Please.'

If he hesitated, or attempted to censure her in any way, she'd kill him.

A glance was all it took for the waiter to fill her glass, and seconds later she lifted the crystal flute to her lips and savoured the superb Chablis.

Giuseppe smiled, and lifted his own glass in a silent salute.

A few glasses of fine wine, good food, pleasant company. It took little to please her father. He was a man of simple tastes. He had worked hard all his life, achieved more than most men; he owned a beautiful home, had chosen a good woman as his wife, and together they had raised a wonderful daughter who was soon to be married to the son of his best friend and business partner. His life was good. Very good.

Dear Papà, Aysha thought fondly as the wine began to have a mellowing effect. He was everything a father should be, and more. A man who had managed to blend the best of the Old Country with the best of the new. The result was a miscible blend of wisdom and warmth tempered with pride and passion.

The main course was served...tender breast of chicken in a delicate basil sauce with an assortment of vegetables.

Her elbow touched Carlo's arm, and she lowered her hand to her lap as she unconsciously toyed with her napkin. His thigh was close to her own. Very close.

Slowly, very slowly, she moved her leg until it rested against his. It would be so easy to glide her foot over his. With extreme care, she cautioned silently. Stiletto heels as fine as hers should almost be registered as a dangerous weapon. The idea was to arouse his attention, not cause him an injury.

Gently she positioned the toe of her shoe against his ankle, then inched it slowly back and forth without moving her heel, thereby making it impossible for anyone to detect what she was doing.

This could be fun, she determined as she let her fingers slide towards his thigh. A butterfly touch, fleeting.

Should she be more daring? Perhaps run the tip of her manicured fingernail down the outer seam of the trousered leg so close to her own? Maybe even...

Ah, that brought a reaction. Slight, but evident, nonetheless. And the slight but warning squeeze of his fingers as they caught hold of her own.

Aysha met his gaze fearlessly as he turned towards her, and she glimpsed the musing indolence apparent beneath the gleaming warmth of those dark brown depths.

Without missing a beat, he lifted her hand to his lips and kissed each finger in turn, watching the way her eyes dilated in startled surprise. Then he returned her hand to rest on his thigh, tracing a slow pattern over the fine bones, aware of her slight tremor as he deliberately forestalled her effort to pull free.

It was fortunate they were between courses. Aysha looked at the remaining wine in her glass, and opted for chilled water. Wisdom decreed the need for a clear head. Each brush of his fingers sent flame licking through her veins, and she clenched her hand, then dug her nails into hard thigh muscle in silent entreaty.

She experienced momentary relief when Carlo released her hand, only to suppress a faint gasp as she felt his fingers close over her thigh.

CHAPTER FOUR

AYSHA reached for her glass and took a sip of iced water, and cast the table's occupants a quick, encompassing glance.

Her eyes rested briefly on Nina, witnessed her hard, calculating glance before it was quickly masked, and felt a shiver glide down the length of her spine.

Malevolence, no matter how fleeting, was disconcerting. Envy and jealousy in others were unenviable traits, and something she'd learned to deal with from a young age. It had accelerated with her engagement to Carlo. Doubtless it would continue long after the marriage.

She wanted love…desperately. But she'd settle for fidelity. Even the thought that he might look seriously at another woman made it feel as if a hand took hold of her heart and squeezed until it bled.

'What do you think, Aysha?'

Oh, hell. It wasn't wise to allow distraction to interfere with the thread of social conversation. Especially not when you were a guest of honour.

She looked at Carlo with a silent plea for help, and met his humorous gaze.

'Luisa doesn't agree I should keep our honeymoon destination a surprise.'

A second was all it took to summon a warm smile.

'I need to pack warm clothes.' Her eyes gleamed and a soft laugh escaped her lips. 'That's all I know.'

'Europe. The snowfields?' The older woman's eyes twinkled. 'Maybe North America. Canada?'

'I really have no idea,' Aysha declared.

Dessert comprised individual caramelised baskets filled with segments of fresh fruit served with brandied cream.

'Sinful,' Aysha declared quietly as she savoured a delectable mouthful.

'I shouldn't, but I will,' Luisa uttered ruefully. 'Tomorrow I'll compensate with fresh juice for breakfast and double my gym workout.'

Teresa, she noted, carefully removed the cream, speared a few segments of fruit, and left the candied basket. As mother of the bride, she couldn't afford to add even a fraction of a kilo to her svelte figure.

It was half an hour before the hostess requested they move into the lounge for coffee.

Aysha declined the very strong espresso brew and opted for a much milder blend with milk. The men took it short and sweet, added *grappa*, and converged together to exchange opinions on anything from *bocce* to the state of the government.

Argue, Aysha amended fondly, all too aware that familiar company, good food, fine wine all combined to loosen the male Italian tongue and encourage reminiscence.

She loved to listen to the cadence of their voices as they lapsed into the language of their birth. It was expressive, accompanied by the philosophical shrug of masculine shoulders, the hand movements to emphasise a given point.

'Giuseppe is in his element.'

Aysha mentally prepared herself as she turned to face Nina. One glance was all it took to determine Nina's manner was the antithesis of friendly.

'Is there any reason why he shouldn't be?'

'The wedding is a major coup.' The smile didn't reach her eyes. 'Congratulations, darling. I should have known you'd pull it off.'

Aysha inclined her head. 'Thank you, Nina. I'll take that as a compliment.'

There was no one close enough to overhear the quiet exchange. Which was a pity. It merely offered Nina the opportunity to aim another poisoned dart.

'How does it feel to be second-best? And know your inherited share in the family firm is the sole reason for the marriage?'

'Considering Carlo is due to inherit his share in the family firm, perhaps you should ask him the same question.'

Successfully fielded. Nina didn't like it. Her eyes narrowed, and the smile moved up a notch in artificial brilliance.

'You're the one who has to compete with Bianca's ghost,' Nina offered silkily, and Aysha waited for the punchline. 'All cats are alike in the dark, darling. Didn't you know?'

Oh, my. This was getting dirty. 'Really?' Her cheeks hurt from keeping a smile pinned in place. 'Perhaps you should try it with the lights on, some time.'

As scores went, it hardly rated a mention. And the victory was short-lived, for it was doubtful Nina would allow anyone to gain an upper hand for long.

'Aysha.' Luisa appeared at her side. 'Teresa has just been telling me about the flowers for the church. Orchids make a lovely display, and the colour combination will be exquisite.'

She was a guest of honour, the focus her wedding day. It was easy to slip into animated mode and discuss details. Only the wedding dress and the cake were taboo.

Except talking and answering questions merely reinforced how much there still was to do, and how essential the liaison with the wedding organiser Teresa had chosen to co-ordinate everything.

The invitation responses were all in, the seating arrangements were in their final planning stage. According to Teresa, any one of the two little flower girls and two page boys could fall victim to a malicious virus, or contract mumps, measles or chicken pox. Alternately, one or all could become paralysed with fright on the day and freeze half-way down the aisle.

At ages three and four, anything was possible.

'My flower girl scattered rose petals down the aisle perfectly at rehearsal, only to take three steps forward on the day, tip the entire contents of the basket on the carpet, and run crying to her mother,' recalled one of the guests.

Aysha remembered the incident, and another wedding where the page boy had carried the satin ring-cushion with such pride and care, then refused to give it up at the appropriate moment. A tussle had ensued, followed by tears and a tantrum.

It had been amusing at the time, and she really didn't care if one of the children made a mistake, or missed their cue. It was a wedding, not a movie which relied on talented actors to perform a part.

Her mother, she knew, didn't hold the same view.

Aysha glanced towards Carlo, and felt the familiar pull of her senses. Dark, well-groomed hair, a strong shaped head. Broad shoulders accentuated by perfect tailoring.

A slight inclination of his head brought his profile into focus. The wide, sculpted bone structure, the strong jaw. Well-defined cheekbones, and the glimpse of his mouth.

Fascinated, she watched each movement, her eyes clinging to the shape of him, aware just how he felt without the constriction of clothes. She was familiar with his body's musculature, the feel and scent of his skin.

At this precise moment she would have given anything to cross to his side and have his arm curve round her waist. She could lean in against him, and savour the anticipation of what would happen when they were alone.

He was fond of her, she knew. There were occasions when he completely disconcerted her by appearing to read her mind. But that special empathy between two lovers wasn't there. No matter how desperately she wanted it to be.

Did he know she could tell the moment he entered a room? She didn't have to see him, or hear his voice. A developed sixth sense alerted her of his presence, and her body reacted as if he'd reached out and touched her.

All the fine hairs moved on the surface of her skin, and the back of her neck tingled in recognition.

Damnable, she cursed silently.

It was after eleven when the first of the guests took their leave, and almost midnight when Teresa and Giuseppe indicated an intention to depart.

Aysha thanked their hosts, smiled until her face hurt, and quivered slightly when Carlo caught hold of her hand as they followed her parents down the steps to their respective cars.

'Goodnight, darling.' Teresa leaned forward and brushed her daughter's cheek.

Aysha stood as Carlo unlocked the car, then she slid into the passenger seat, secured her belt, and leaned back against the headrest as Carlo fired the engine.

'Tired?'

She was conscious of his discerning glance seconds before he set the car in motion.

'A little.' She closed her eyes, and let the vehicle's movement and the quietness of the night seep into her bones.

'Do you want me to take you home?'

A silent sigh escaped her lips, and she effected a rueful smile. 'Now there's a question. Which home are you talking about? Yours, mine or ours?'

'The choice is yours.'

Was it? The new house was completely furnished, and awaiting only the final finishing touches. Her own bedroom beckoned, but that was fraught with implication Teresa would query in the morning.

Besides, she coveted the touch of his hands, the feel of his body, his mouth devastating her own.

Then she could pretend that good lovemaking was a substitute for *love*. That no one was meant to have it all, and in Carlo, their future together, she had more than her share.

'The penthouse.'

Carlo didn't comment, and she wondered if it would have made any difference if she'd said *home*.

An ache started up in the pit of her stomach, and intensified until it became a tangible pain as he slowed the car, de-activated the security system guarding entrance to the luxury apartment building, then eased down into the underground car park and brought the vehicle to a halt in his allotted space.

They rode the lift to the top floor in silence, and inside the apartment Aysha went willingly into his arms, his bed, an eager supplicant to anything he chose to bestow.

It was just after nine when Aysha eased the Porsche into an empty space in an inner city car park building, and within minutes she stepped off the escalator and emerged onto the pavement.

It was a beautiful day, the sky a clear azure with hardly a cloud in sight, and the sun's warmth bathed all beneath it with a balmy summer brilliance. Her needs were few, the purchases confined to four boutiques, three of which were within three blocks of each other.

Two hours, tops, she calculated, then she'd meet her bridesmaids for lunch. At two she had a hair appointment, followed by a manicure, and tonight she was attending an invitation-only preview of the first in a series of foreign films scheduled to appear over the next month.

Each evening there was something filling their social engagement diary. Although last night when Carlo had suggested dining out she'd insisted they eat in...and somehow the decision hadn't got made one way or the other. She retained a vivid recollection of *why*, and a secret smile curved her lips as she slid her sunglasses into place.

Selecting clothes was something she enjoyed, and she possessed a natural flair for colour, fashion and design.

Aysha had three hours before she was due to join her bridesmaids for lunch, and she intended to utilise that time to its fullest potential.

It was nice to be able to take time, instead of having to rush in a limited lunch-hour. Selective shopping was fun, and she gradually added to a growing collection of glossy carry-bags.

Bags she should really dispense with before meeting the girls...which meant a walk back to the car park to deposit her purchases in the boot of her car.

Lianna, Arianne, Suzanne and Tessa were already seated when Aysha joined them. Two brunettes, a redhead, and a blonde. They'd attended school together, suffered through piano and ballet lessons, and, although their characters were quite different from each other, they shared an empathy that had firmed over the years as an unbreakable bond.

'You're late, but we forgive you,' Lianna began before Aysha was able to say a word. 'Of course, we do understand.' She offered one of her irrepressible smiles. 'You have serious shopping on the agenda.' She leaned forward. 'And your penance is to relay every little detail.'

'Let me order a drink first,' Aysha protested, and gave her order to a hovering waiter. 'Mineral water, slice of lemon, plenty of ice.'

'What did you buy to change into after the wedding?' Arianne quizzed, and Lianna pulled a face.

'Sweetheart, she won't *need* anything to wear after the wedding except skin.'

'Sure. But she should have something sheer and sexy to start off with,' Suzanne interceded.

'Honest, girls, can you see Carlo helping Aysha out of the wedding gown and into a nightgown? Come on, let's get real here!'

'Are you done?' Aysha queried, trying to repress a threatening laugh.

'Not yet,' Lianna declared blithely. 'You need to suffer a little pain for all the trouble we're going to for you.' She began counting them off on each finger. 'Dress fittings, shoe shopping, church rehearsals, child chaperoning, in church and out of it, organising the bridal shower, not to mention make-up sessions and hair stylists practising on our hair.' Her eyes sparkled with devilish laughter. 'For all of which our only reward is to kiss the groom.'

'Who said you get to do that?' Aysha queried with

mock seriousness. 'Married men don't kiss other women.'

'No kiss, we decorate the wedding car,' Lianna threatened.

'Are you ladies ready to order?'

'Yes,' they agreed in unison, and proceeded to completely confuse the poor young man who'd been assigned to their table.

'You're incorrigible,' Aysha chastised as soon as he'd disappeared towards the kitchen, and Lianna gave a conciliatory shrug.

'This is a *feel-good* moment, darling. The last of the great single-women luncheons. Saturday week you join the ranks of married ladies, while we, poor darlings, languish on the sideline searching for the perfect man. Of which, believe me, there are very few.' She paused to draw breath. 'If they look good, they sound terrible, or have disgusting habits, or verge towards violence, or, worst of all, have no money.'

Suzanne shook her head. 'Cynical, way too cynical.'

They ordered another round of drinks, then their food arrived.

'So, tell us, darling,' Lianna cajoled. 'Is Carlo as gorgeous in bed as he is out of it?'

'That's a bit below the belt,' Arianne protested, and Lianna grinned.

'Got it in one. Hey, if Aysha ditches him, I'm next in line.' She cast Aysha a wicked wink. 'Aren't you glad I'm your best friend?'

'Yes,' she responded simply. Loyalty and integrity

mattered, and Lianna possessed both, even if she was an irrepressible motor-mouth. The fun, the generous smile hid a childhood marred by tragedy.

'You haven't told us what you bought this morning.'

'You didn't give me a chance.'

'I'm giving it to you now,' Lianna insisted magnanimously, and Aysha laughed.

She needed the levity, and it was good, so good to relax and unwind among friends.

'What social event is scheduled for tonight? Dinner with family, the theatre, ballet, party? Or do you just get to stay home and go to bed with Carlo?'

'You have the cheek of old Nick,' Aysha declared, and caught Lianna's wicked smile.

'You didn't answer the question.'

'There's a foreign film festival on at the Arts Centre.'

'Ah, eclectic entertainment,' Arianne sighed wistfully. 'What are you going to wear?'

'Something utterly gorgeous,' Lianna declared, her eyes narrowing speculatively. 'Long black evening trousers or skirt, matching top, shoestring straps, and that exquisite beaded evening jacket you picked up in Hong Kong. Minimum jewellery.'

'OK.'

'*OK?* I'm in fashion, darling. What I've just described is considerably higher on the scale of gorgeous than just *OK*.'

'All right, I'll wear it,' Aysha conceded peaceably.

They skipped dessert, ordered coffee, and Aysha barely made her hair appointment on time.

'No dinner for me, Mamma. I'll just pick up some fruit. I had a late lunch,' she relayed via the mobile phone prior to driving home. With the way traffic was moving, it would be six before she reached Vaucluse. Which would leave her just under an hour to shower, dress, tend to her hair and make-up, and be at Carlo's apartment by seven-fifteen.

'*Bella,*' he complimented warmly as she used her key barely minutes after the appointed time.

Aysha could have said the same, for he looked devastatingly attractive attired in a dark evening suit, snowy white cotton shirt, and black bow tie. Arresting, she added, aware of her body's reaction to his appreciative appraisal. Heat flooded her veins, activating all her nerve-ends, as she felt the magnetic pull of the senses. It would be so easy just to hold out her arms and walk into his, then lift her face for his kiss. She wanted to, badly.

'Would you like a drink before we leave?'

Alcohol on a near-empty stomach wasn't a good idea, and she shook her head. 'No. Thanks.'

'How was lunch with the girls?'

A smile lifted the edges of her mouth, and her eyes gleamed with remembered pleasure. 'Great. Really great.'

Carlo caught hold of her hand and lifted it to his lips. 'I imagine Lianna was at her irrepressible best?'

'It was nice just to sit, relax and laugh a little.' Her smile widened, and her eyes searched his. 'Lianna is looking forward to kissing the groom.'

Carlo pulled back the cuff of his jacket and checked his watch. 'Perhaps we should be on our way. Traffic will be heavy, and parking probably a problem.'

It was a gala evening, and a few of the city's social scions numbered among the guests. The female contingent wore a small fortune in jewels and French designer gowns vied with those by their Italian equivalent.

Aysha mingled with fellow guests, nibbled from a proffered tray of hors d'oeuvres, and sipped orange juice with an added dash of champagne.

'Sorry I'm a little late. Parking was chaotic.'

Aysha recognised the light feminine voice and turned to greet its owner. 'Hello, Nina.'

The brunette let her gaze trail down to the tips of Aysha's shoes, then slowly back again in a deliberately provocative assessment. 'Aysha, how—pretty, you look. Although black is a little stark, darling, on one as fair as you.'

She turned towards Carlo, and her smile alone could have lit up the entire auditorium. '*Caro*, I really need a drink. Do you think you could organise one for me?'

Very good, Aysha silently applauded. Wait for the second Carlo is out of earshot, and…any minute now—

'I doubt you'll satisfy him for long.'

Aysha met that piercing gaze and held it. She even managed a faint smile. 'I'll give it my best shot.'

'There are distinct advantages in having the wedding ring, I guess.'

'I get to sleep with him?'

Nina's eyes glittered. 'I'd rather be his mistress

than his wife, darling. That way I get most of the pleasure, all of the perks, while you do the time.'

The temptation to throw the contents of her glass in Nina's face was almost irresistible.

'Champagne?' Carlo drawled, handing Nina a slim flute.

The electronic tone summoning the audience to take their seats came as a welcome intrusion, and she made her way into the theatre at Carlo's side, all too aware of Nina's presence as the usherette pointed them in the direction of their seats.

Now why wasn't she surprised when Nina's seat allocation adjoined theirs? Hardly coincidence, and Aysha gritted her teeth when Nina very cleverly ensured Carlo took the centre seat. Grr.

The lights dimmed, and her fingers stiffened as Carlo covered her hand with his own. Worse was the soothing movement of his thumb against the inside of her wrist.

So he sensed her tension. Good. He'd sense a lot more before the evening was over!

The theatre lights went out, technicolor images filled the screen, and the previews of forthcoming movies showed in relatively quick sequence. The main feature was set in Paris, the French dubbed into English, and it was a dark movie, *noir*, with subjective nuances, no comedy whatsoever. Aysha found it depressing, despite the script, directorship and acting having won several awards.

The final scene climaxed with particular violence, and when the credits faded and the lights came on she saw Nina withdraw a hand from Carlo's forearm.

Aysha threw her an icy glare, glimpsed the glittering satisfaction evident, and wanted to scream.

She turned towards the aisle and moved with the flow of exiting patrons, aware, as if she was a disembodied spectator, that Nina took full advantage of the crowd situation to press as close to Carlo as decently possible.

They reached the auditorium foyer, and Aysha had to stand with a polite smile pinned to her face as the patrons were served coffee, offered cheese and biscuits or minuscule pieces of cake.

'Why don't we go on to a nightclub?' Nina suggested. 'It's not late.'

And watch you attempt to dance and play kissy-face with Carlo? Aysha demanded silently. Not if I have anything to do with it!

'Don't let us stop you,' Carlo declined smoothly as he curved an arm along the back of Aysha's waist. Tense, definitely tense. He wanted to bend his head and place a placating kiss to the curve of her neck, then look deep into those smoky grey eyes and silently assure her she had nothing whatsoever to worry about.

A slight smile curved his lips. Nina saw it, and misinterpreted its source.

'The music is incredible.' She tucked her hand through his arm, and cajoled with the guile of a temptress. 'You'll enjoy it.'

'No,' he declined in a silky voice as he carefully disengaged her hand. 'I won't.'

Nina recognised defeat when she saw it, and she

lifted her shoulders with an elegant shrug. 'If you must miss out…'

His raised eyebrow signalled her departure, and she swept him a deep sultry glance. 'Another time, maybe.'

Aysha drew a deep breath, then released it slowly. Of all the nerve! She lifted her cup and took a sip of ruinously strong coffee. It would probably keep her awake half the night, but right at this precise moment she didn't give a damn.

'Carlo, *come stai*?'

A business acquaintance, whose presence she welcomed with considerable enthusiasm. The man looked mildly stunned as she enquired about his wife, his children, their schooling and their achievements.

'You overwhelmed him,' Carlo declared with deceptive indolence, and she fixed him with a brilliant smile.

'His arrival was timely,' she assured him sweetly. 'I was about to hit you.'

'In public?'

She drew in a deep breath, and studied his features for several long seconds. 'This is not a time for levity.'

'Nina bothers you?'

Aysha forced herself to hold his gaze. 'She never misses an opportunity to be wherever we happen to go.'

His eyes narrowed fractionally. 'You think I don't know that?'

'Were you ever lovers?' she demanded, and a faint

chill feathered across the surface of her skin as she waited for his response.

'No.'

The words tripped out before she could stop them. 'You're quite sure about that?'

Carlo was silent for several seconds, then he ventured silkily, 'I've never been indiscriminate with the few women who've shared my bed. Believe me, Nina didn't number among them.' He took her cup and placed it together with his own on a nearby table. 'Shall we leave?'

He was angry, but then so was she, and she swept him a glittering look from beneath mascaraed lashes. 'Let's do that.'

Their passage to the car wasn't swift as they paused momentarily to chat to fellow patrons whom they knew or were acquainted with.

'Your silence is ominous,' Carlo remarked with droll humour as he eased the Mercedes into the flow of traffic.

'I'm going with the saying…*if you can't find anything nice to say, it's better to say nothing at all.*'

'I see.'

No, you don't. You couldn't possibly know how terrified I am of not being able to hold your interest. Petrified that one day you'll find someone else, and I'll be left a broken shell of my former self.

The drive from the city to Rose Bay was achieved in a relatively short space of time, and Carlo cleared security at his apartment underground car park, then manoeuvred the car into his allotted space.

Aysha released the door-clasp, slid to her feet,

closed the door, and moved the few steps to her car.

'What are you doing?'

'I would have thought that was obvious. I'm going home.'

'Your keys are in the apartment,' Carlo said mildly.

Dammit, so they were. 'In that case, I'll go get them.'

She turned and stalked towards the bank of lifts, stabbed the call button, and barely contained her impatience as she waited for it to arrive.

'Don't you think you're overreacting?'

There was something in his voice she failed to recognise, although some deep, inner sixth sense did and sent out a red alert. 'Not really.'

The doors slid open and she stepped into the cubicle, jabbed the top panel button, and stood in icy silence as they were transported to the uppermost floor.

Carlo unlocked the apartment door, and she swept in ahead of him, located the keys where she'd put them on a table in the foyer, and collected them.

'Your parents aren't expecting you back tonight.'

It didn't help that he was right. 'So I'll ring them.'

He noted the proud tilt of her chin, the firm set of her mouth. 'Stay.'

Her eyes flared. 'I'd prefer to go home.' Nina's vitriolic words had provided too vivid an image to easily dispel.

'I'll drive you.'

The inflexibility evident in his voice sent chills

scudding down the length of her spine. 'The hell you will.'

His features hardened, and a muscle tensed at the side of his jaw. 'Try to walk out of this apartment, and see how far you get.'

Aysha allowed her gaze to travel the length of his body, and back again. He had the height, the sheer strength to overcome any evasive tactics she might employ.

'Brute force, Carlo? Isn't that a little drastic?'

'Not when your well-being and safety are at stake.'

Her chin tilted in a gesture of defiance. 'Somehow that doesn't quite add up, does it?' She held up her hand as he began to speak. 'Don't.' Her eyes held a brilliant sheen that was a mixture of anger, pride, and pain. 'At least let there be honesty between us.'

'I have never been dishonest with you.'

She felt sick inside, a dreadful gnawing emptiness that ripped away any illusions she might have had that affection and caring on his part were enough.

Without a further word she turned and walked towards the front door, released the locking mechanism, then took the few steps necessary to reach the bank of lifts.

Please, *please* let there be one waiting, she silently begged as she depressed the call button.

The following twenty seconds were among the longest in her life, and she gave an audible sigh of relief when the heavy stainless steel doors slid open.

Aysha stepped inside and turned to jab the appropriate floor panel, only to gasp with outraged indignation as Carlo stepped into the cubicle.

'Get out.'

Dark eyes lanced hers, mercilessly hard and resolute. 'I can drive you, or follow behind in my car.' The ruthlessness intensified. 'Choose.'

The lift doors slid closed, and the cubicle moved swiftly down towards the car park.

'Go to hell.'

His smile held little humour. 'That wasn't an option.'

'Unfortunately.'

The flippant response served to tighten his expression into a grim mask, and his anger was a palpable entity.

'Believe you wouldn't want me to take you there.' His drawl held a silky threat that sent shivers scudding down the length of her spine.

The doors whispered open, and without a word she preceded him into the huge concrete cavern. Her car was parked next to his, and she widened the distance between them, conscious of her heels clicking against the concrete floor.

Carlo crossed to the Mercedes, unlocked the passenger door, and held it open. 'Get in.'

Damned if she'd obey his dictum. 'I'll need my car in the morning.'

His expression remained unchanged. 'I'll collect you.'

Aysha felt like stamping her foot. 'Or I can have Teresa drop me, or take a cab, or any one of a few other options.' Her eyes were fiery with rebellion. 'Don't patronise me, dammit!'

It had been a long night, fraught with moments of sheer anger, disillusionment, and introspective rationalisation. None of which had done much to ease the heartache or the sense of betrayal. Each of which she'd examined in detail, only to silently castigate herself for having too high an expectation of a union based solely in reality.

Worse, for allowing Nina's deviousness to undermine her own ambivalent emotions. Nina's success focused on Aysha's insecurity, and it irked unbearably.

Carlo watched the fleeting emotions chase across her expressive features and divined each and every one of them.

'Get in the car, *cara*.'

His gentle tone was almost her undoing, and she fought against the sudden prick of tears. Damn him. She wanted to maintain her anger. Lash out, verbally and physically, until the rage was spent.

Conversely, she needed his touch, the soothing quality of those strong hands softly brushing her skin, the feel of his mouth on hers as the sensual magic wove its own spell.

She wanted to re-enter the lift and have it transport them back to his apartment. Most of all, she wanted to lose herself in his loving, then fall asleep in his arms with the steady beat of his heart beneath her cheek.

Yet pride prevented her from taking that essential

step, just as it locked the voice in her throat. She felt raw, and emotionally at odds.

Did most brides suffer this awful ambivalence? *Get real*, a tiny voice reminded her. You don't represent *most* brides, and while you have the groom's affection, it's doubtful he'll ever gift you his unconditional love.

With a gesture indicating silent acquiescence she slid into the passenger seat, reached for the safety belt as Carlo closed the door, and fastened it as he crossed in front of the vehicle. Seconds later he fired the engine and cruised up the ramp leading to street level.

'Call your parents.'

Aysha reached into her purse and extracted the small mobile phone, and keyed in the appropriate digits.

Giuseppe answered on the third ring. 'Aysha? Something is wrong?'

'No, Papà. I'll be home in about fifteen minutes. Can you fix security?'

Thank heavens it wasn't Teresa who'd answered, for her mother would have fired off a string of questions to rival the Spanish Inquisition.

Aysha ignored Carlo's brief encompassing glance as the car whispered along the suburban street, and she closed her eyes against the image of her mother slipping on a robe in preparation for a maternal chat the instant Aysha entered the house.

A silent laugh rose and died in her throat. At this precise moment she didn't know which scenario she preferred... The emotive discussion she'd just had with Carlo, or the one she was about to have with Teresa.

Aysha had no sooner stepped inside the door than her mother launched into a series of questions, and it was easier to fabricate than spell out her own insecurities.

She justified her transgression by qualifying Teresa had enough on her plate, and nothing could be achieved by the confidence.

'Are you sure there is nothing bothering you?' Teresa persisted.

'No, Mamma.' Inspiration was the mother of invention, and she used it shamelessly. 'I forgot to take the samples I need to match up the shoes tomorrow, so I thought I'd come home.'

'You didn't quarrel with Carlo?'

Quarrel wasn't exactly the word she would have chosen to describe their altercation. 'Why would I do that?' Aysha countered.

'I'll make coffee.'

All she wanted to do was go to bed. 'Don't bother making it for me.'

'You're going upstairs now?'

'Goodnight, Mamma,' she bade gently. 'I'll see you in the morning.'

'Gianna and I will meet you for lunch tomorrow.' She mentioned a restaurant. 'I'll book a table for one o'clock.'

She leaned forward and brushed lips to her mother's cheek. 'That sounds nice.'

Without a further word she turned and made for the stairs, and in her room she slowly removed her clothes, cleansed her face of make-up, then slid in between the sheets.

CHAPTER FIVE

'I'LL be there in half an hour,' Carlo declared as Aysha took his call early next morning. 'Don't argue,' he added before she had a chance to say a word.

Conscious that Teresa sat within hearing distance as they shared breakfast she found it difficult to give anything other than a warm and friendly response.

'Thanks,' she managed brightly. 'I'll be ready.' She replaced the receiver, then drained the rest of her coffee. 'That was Carlo,' she relayed. 'I'll go change.'

'Will you come back here, or go straight into the city?'

'The city. I need to choose crockery and cutlery for the house.' Pots and pans, roasting dishes. Each day she tried to accumulate some of the necessities required in setting up house. 'I may as well make an early start.'

In her room, she quickly shed shorts and top and selected a smart straight skirt in ivory linen, added a silk print shirt and matching jacket, slid her feet into slim-heeled pumps, tended to her hair and make-up, and was downstairs waiting when Carlo's Mercedes slid to a halt outside the front door.

Aysha drew a calming breath, then she walked out to the car and slipped into the passenger seat. 'There was no need for you to collect me,' she assured him, conscious of the look of him, the faint aroma of his cologne.

'There was every need,' he drawled silkily as he sent the car forward.

'I don't want to fight with you,' she said ingenuously, and he spared her a swift glance.

'Then don't.'

A disbelieving laugh escaped her throat. 'Suddenly it doesn't seem that easy.'

'Nina is a woman who thrives on intrigue and innuendo.' Carlo's voice was hard, his expression an inscrutable mask.

Oh, yes, Aysha silently agreed. And she's so very good at it. 'She wants *you*.'

'I'm already spoken for, remember?'

'Ah, now there's the thing. Nina abides by the credo of *all being fair in love and war*.'

'And this is shaping up as war?'

You'd better believe it! 'You're the prize, *darling*,' she mocked, and incurred his dark glance.

'Yours.'

'You have no idea how gratifying it is to hear you say that.'

'Cynicism doesn't suit you.' Carlo slanted her a slight smile, and she raised one eyebrow in mocking acquiescence.

'Shall we change the subject?'

He negotiated an intersection, then turned into Rose Bay.

'I've booked a table for dinner tonight. I'll collect you at six.'

They'd had tickets for tonight's première performance by the Russian *corps de ballet* for a month. How could she not have remembered?

The remainder of the short drive was achieved in silence, and Carlo deposited her beside her car, then left as she slid in behind the wheel of the Porsche.

City traffic was horrific at this hour of the morning, and it was after nine when Aysha emerged onto the inner city street.

First stop was a major department store two blocks distant, and she'd walked less than half a block when her mobile phone rang.

She automatically retrieved the unit from her bag and heard Teresa's voice, pitched high in distress.

'Aysha? I've just had a call from the bridal boutique. Your headpiece has arrived from Paris, but it's the wrong one!'

She closed her eyes, then opened them again. It had taken a day of deliberation before making the final choice... How long ago? A month? Now the order had been mixed up. Great. 'OK, Mamma. Let's not panic.'

Her mother's voice escalated. 'It was perfect, just perfect. There wasn't another to compare with it.'

'I'll go sort it out.' A phone call from the boutique to the manufacturer in Paris, and the use of a courier service should see a successful result.

Aysha should have known it couldn't be that simple.

'I've already done that,' the boutique owner relayed. 'No joy, unfortunately. They don't have another in stock. The design is intricate, the seed pearls needed are held up heaven knows where, and the gist of it is, we need to choose something else.'

'OK, let's do it.' It took an hour to select, ascertain the order could be filled and couriered within the week.

'That's definite,' the vendeuse promised.

Now why didn't that reassure her? Possibly because she'd heard the same words before.

An hour later she had to concede there were diverse gremlins at work, for the white embroidered stockings ordered hadn't arrived. The lace suspender belt had, but it didn't match the garter belt, as it was supposed to do.

Teresa would consider it a catastrophe. Aysha merely drew in a deep breath, ascertained the order might be correctly filled in time, decided *might* wasn't good enough, and opted to select something else with a guaranteed delivery.

It was after midday when she collected the last carry-bag and added it to the collection she held in each hand. Shoes? Did she have time if she was to meet Teresa and Gianna at Double Bay for lunch at one? She could always phone and say she'd be ten or fifteen minutes late.

With that thought in mind she entered the Queen Victoria building and made her way towards the shoe shop.

It was a beautiful old building, historically preserved, and undoubtedly heritage-listed. Aysha loved the ambience, the blend of old and modern, and she admired a shop display as she rode the escalator to the first floor.

She'd only walked a few steps when an exquisite bracelet showcased in a jeweller's window caught her eye, and she paused to admire it. The gold links were of an unusual design, and each link held a half-carat diamond.

'I'm sure you'll only have to purr prettily in Carlo's ear, and he'll buy it for you.'

Aysha recognised the voice and turned slowly to face the young woman at her side. 'Nina,' she acknowledged with a polite smile, and watched as Nina's expression became positively feline.

She took in the numerous carry-bags and their various emblazoned logos. 'Been shopping?'

Aysha effected a faint shrug. 'A few things I needed to collect.'

'I was going to ring and invite you to share a coffee with me. Can you manage a few minutes now?'

The last thing she wanted was a tête-à-tête with Nina…with or without the coffee. 'I really don't have time. I'm meeting Teresa and Gianna for lunch.'

'In that case…' She slid open her attaché case, extracted a large square envelope and slipped it into one of Aysha's carry-bags. 'Have fun with these. I'm sure you'll find them enlightening.' Closing the case, she proffered a distinctly feline smile. '*Ciao*. See you tomorrow night at the sculpture exhibition.'

Given the social circle in which they both moved, their attendance at the same functions was inevitable. Aysha entertained the fleeting desire to give the evening exhibition a miss, then dismissed the idea. Bruno would never forgive their absence.

Aysha caught the time on one of the clocks featured in the jeweller's window, and hurriedly made for the bank of escalators.

Five minutes later she joined the flow of traffic and negotiated a series of one-way streets before hitting the main arterial one that would join with another leading to Double Bay.

Teresa and Gianna were already seated at a table when she entered the restaurant, and she greeted them both warmly, then sank into a chair.

'Shall we order?'

'You were able to sort everything out with the bridal boutique?'

It was easier to agree. Afterwards she could go into detail, but right now, here, she didn't want Teresa to launch into a long diatribe. 'Yes.'

'*Bene.*' Her mother paused sufficiently long for the waiter to take their order. 'You managed to collect everything?'

'Except shoes, and I'm sure I'll find something I like in one of the shops here.' Double Bay held a number of exclusive shops and boutiques. 'I'll have a look when we've finished lunch.'

It was almost two when they emerged onto the pavement, and Aysha left both women to complete their shopping while she tended to the last few items on her list.

A rueful smile played at the edges of her mouth. In a little over a weeek all the planning, the shopping, the organising…it would all be over. Life could begin to return to normal. She'd be Aysha Santangelo, mistress of her own home, with a husband's needs to care for.

Just thinking about those needs was enough to send warmth coursing through her veins, and put wickedly sensuous thoughts in her head.

During the next two hours she added to the number of carry-bags filling the boot of her car. The envelope Nina had slid into one of them drew her attention, and she pulled it free, examined it, then, curious as to its contents, she undid the flap.

Not papers, she discovered. Photographs. Several of them. She looked at the first, and saw a man and a woman embracing in the foyer of a hotel.

Not any man. Carlo. And the woman was Nina.

Aysha's insides twisted and began to churn as she put it aside and looked at the next one, depicting the exterior and name of a Melbourne hotel, the one where Carlo had stayed three weeks ago when he'd been there for a few days on business. Supposedly business, for the following shot showed Carlo and Nina entering a lift together.

Aysha's fingers shook as she kept flipping the photographs over, one by one. Nina and Carlo pausing outside a numbered door. About to embrace. Kissing.

The evidence was clear enough. Carlo was having an affair…with Nina.

Her legs suddenly felt boneless, and her limbs began to shake. How dared he abuse her trust, her love…everything she'd entrusted in him?

If he thought she'd condone a mistress, he had another think coming!

Anger rose like newly ignited flame, and she thrust

the photographs back into the envelope, closed the boot, then slid in behind the wheel of her car.

There were many ways to hurt someone, but betrayal was right up there. She wanted to march into his office and instigate a confrontation. *Now*.

Except she knew she'd yell, and say things it would be preferable for no one else to overhear.

Wait, an inner voice cautioned as she negotiated peak hour traffic travelling the main east suburban road leading towards Vaucluse.

The car in front braked suddenly, and only a split-second reaction saved her from running into the back of it.

All her fine anger erupted in a stream of language that was both graphic and unladylike. Horns blared in rapid succession, car doors slammed, and there were voices raised in conflict.

Traffic banked up behind her, and it was ten minutes before she could ease her car forward and slowly clear an intersection clogged with police car, ambulance, tow-truck.

Consequently it was after five when she parked the car out front of her parents' home, and she'd no sooner entered the house than Teresa called her into the kitchen.

'I'll be there in a few minutes,' Aysha responded. 'After I've taken everything up to my room.'

A momentary stay of execution, she reflected as she made her way up the curved staircase. The carrybags could be unpacked later. The photographs were private, very private, and she tucked them beneath her pillow.

She took a few minutes to freshen up, then she retraced her steps to the foyer. The kitchen was redolent with the smell of herbs and garlic, and a small saucepan held simmering contents on the ceramic hotplate.

Teresa stood, spoon in hand, as she added a little wine, a little water, before turning to face her daughter.

'You didn't tell me what happened at the bridal boutique.'

Aysha relayed the details, then waited for her mother's anticipated reaction. She wasn't disappointed.

'Why weren't they couriered out? Why weren't we told before this there might be a problem? I'll never use that boutique again!'

'You won't have to,' Aysha said drily. 'Believe me, I've no intention of doing a repeat performance in this lifetime.'

'We should have used someone else.'

'As most of the bridal boutiques get all their supplies from the same source, I doubt it would have made a difference.'

'You don't know that,' Teresa responded sharply. 'I should have dealt with it myself. Can't they get anything right? Now we learn the wedding lingerie doesn't match.'

'I'm sure Carlo won't even notice.'

Teresa gave her a look which spoke volumes. 'It doesn't matter whether he notices or not. You'll know. *I'll* know. And so will everyone else when you lift your dress and he removes the garter.' The vol-

ume of her voice increased. 'We spent hours selecting each individual item. Now nothing matches.'

'Mother.' *Mother* was bad. Its use forewarned of
frazzled nerves, and a temper stretched close to
breaking point. 'Calm down.' One look at Teresa's
face was sufficient to tell a verbal explosion was imminent, and she took a deep breath and released it
slowly. 'I'm just as disappointed as you are, but we
have to be practical.' Assertiveness probably wasn't
a good option at this precise moment. 'I've already
chosen something I'm happy with and they've guaranteed delivery within days.'

'I'll check it out in the morning.'

'There's no need to do that.'

'Of course there is, Aysha.' Teresa was adamant.
'We've put a great deal of business their way.'

If she stayed another minute, she'd spit the dummy
and they'd have a full-scale row. 'I haven't got time
to discuss it now. I have to shower and change, and
meet Carlo in less than an hour.'

It was a cop-out, albeit a diplomatic one, she decided as she quickly ascended the stairs. Differences
of opinion were one thing. All-out war was another.
Teresa was *Teresa*, and she was unlikely to change.

Damn Nina and her Mission. She was a bitch of
the first order. Desperate, and dangerous.

The worst kind, Aysha determined viciously as she
stripped off her clothes and stepped beneath the cascade of water.

Five minutes later she emerged, wound a towel
around her slender curves and crossed into the bed-

room bent on selecting something mind-blowing to wear.

Dressed to kill. What a marvellous analogy, she decided. One look at her mirrored reflection revealed a slender young woman in a black beaded gown that was strapless, backless, with a hemline that fell to her ankles. A long chiffon scarf lay sprawled across the bed and she draped it round her neck so both ends trailed down her back.

Make-up was, she determined, a little overstated. Somehow it seemed appropriate. Warriors painted themselves before they went into battle, didn't they? And there would be a battle fought before the night was over. She could personally guarantee it.

Teresa was setting the table in the dining room. 'Mamma, I'm on my way.'

Was it something in her voice that caused her mother to cast her a sharp glance? When it came to maternal instincts, Teresa's were second to none. 'Have a good time.'

That was entirely debatable. Dinner *à deux* followed by an evening at the ballet had definitely lost its appeal. 'Thanks.'

Fifteen minutes later she garaged her car in the underground car park, then rode the lift to Carlo's apartment. The envelope containing the photographs was in her hand, and the portrayed images on celluloid almost scorched her fingers.

He opened the door within seconds, and she saw his pupils widen in gleaming male appreciation. A shaft of intense satisfaction flared, and she took in the immaculate cut of his dark suit, the startling white cotton shirt, the splendid tie.

The perfectly groomed, wildly attractive fiancé. Loving, too, she added a trifle viciously as he drew her close and nuzzled the sensitive curve of her neck.

The right touch, the expert moves. It was almost too much to expect him to be faithful as well. His love, she knew, would never be hers to have. But fidelity… That was something she intended to insist on.

'What's wrong?'

Add *intuitive*, Aysha accorded. At least some of his senses were on track. She moved back a step, away from the traitorous temptation of his arms. It would be far too easy to lean in against him and offer her mouth for his kiss. But then she'd kiss him back, and that wouldn't do at all.

'What makes you think that?' she queried with deliberate calm, and saw his eyes narrow.

'We've never played guessing games, and we're not going to start now.'

Games, subterfuge, deception. They were one and the same thing. 'Really?'

His expression sharpened, accentuating the broad facial bone structure with its strong angles and planes. 'Spit it out, Aysha. I'm listening.'

Aysha rang the tip of one fingernail along the edge of the envelope. Eyes like crystallised smoke burned with a fiery heat as she thrust the envelope at him. 'You've got it wrong. You talk. I get to listen.'

He caught the envelope, and a puzzled frown creased his forehead. 'What the hell is this about?'

'*Hell* is a pretty good description. Open the damned thing. I think you'll get the picture.' She certainly had!

His fingers freed the flap and she watched him carefully as he extracted the sheaf of photos and examined them one by one.

His expression barely altered, and she had to hand it to him... He had tremendous control. Somehow his icy discipline had more effect than anger.

'Illuminating, wouldn't you agree?'

His gaze speared hers, dark, dangerous and as hard as granite. 'Very.'

Her eyes held his fearlessly. 'I think I deserve an explanation.'

'I stayed in that hotel, and, yes, Nina was there. But without any prior knowledge or invitation on my part.'

How could she believe him when Nina continued to drip poison at every turn?

'That's it?' She was so cool it was a wonder the blood didn't freeze in her veins.

'As far as I'm concerned.'

'I guess Nina just happened to be standing outside your room?' She swept his features mercilessly. 'I don't buy it.'

'It happens to be the truth.' His voice was inflexible, and Aysha's eyes were fearless as she met his.

'I'm fully aware our impending marriage has its base in mutual convenience,' she stated with restrained anger. 'But I insist on your fidelity.'

Carlo's eyes narrowed and became chillingly

calm. There was a leashed stillness apparent she knew she'd be wise to heed.

Except she was past wisdom, beyond any form of rationale. Did he have any conception of what she'd felt like when she'd sighted those photos? It was as if the tip of a sword pierced her heart, poised there, then thrust in to the hilt.

'My fidelity isn't in question.'

'Isn't it?'

'Would you care to rephrase that?'

'Why?' Aysha countered baldly. 'What part didn't you understand?'

'I heard the words. It's the motive I find difficult to comprehend.'

With admirable detachment she raked his large frame from head to toe, and back again. 'It's simple. In this marriage, there's only room for two of us.' She was so angry, she felt she might self-destruct. 'There's no way I'll turn a blind eye to you having a mistress on the side.'

'Why would I want a mistress?' Carlo queried with icy calm.

Her eyes flashed, a brilliant translucent grey that had the clarity and purity of a rare pearl. 'To complement my presence in the marital bed?'

His gaze didn't waver, and she fought against being trapped by the depth, the intensity. It was almost hypnotic, and she had the most uncanny sensation he was intent on dispensing with the layers that guarded her soul, like a surgeon using a scalpel with delicate precision.

'Nina has done a hatchet job, hasn't she?' Carlo

offered in a voice that sounded like silk being razed by tempered steel. 'Sufficiently damaging, that any assurance I give you to the contrary will be viewed with scepticism?' He reached out a hand and caught hold of her chin between thumb and forefinger. 'What we share together,' he prompted. 'What would you call that?'

She was breaking up inside, slowly shattering into a thousand pieces. *Special*, a tiny voice taunted. So special, the mere thought of him sharing his body with someone else caused her physical pain.

'Good sex?' Carlo persisted dangerously.

Her stance altered slightly, and her eyes assumed a new depth and intensity. 'Presumably not good enough,' she declared bravely.

It was possible to see the anger build, and she watched with detached fascination as the fingers of each hand clenched into fists, watched the muscles bunch at the edge of his jaw, the slight flaring of nostrils, and the darkening of his eyes.

He uttered a husky oath, and she said with deliberate facetiousness, 'Flattery isn't appropriate.'

Something moved in the depths of his eyes. An emotion she didn't care to define.

'Nina,' Carlo vented emotively, 'has a lot to answer for.'

Didn't she just! 'On that, at least, we agree.'

'Let's get this quite clear,' he said with dangerous quietness. 'You have my vow of fidelity, just as I have yours. Understood?'

She wanted to lash out, then pick up something

and smash it. The satisfaction would be immensely gratifying.

'Aysha?' he prompted with deadly quietness, and she forced herself to respond.

'Even given that Nina is a first-class bitch, I find it a bit too much of a coincidence for you both to be in Melbourne at the same time, staying in the same hotel, the same floor.' Aysha drew in a deep breath. 'Photographic proof bears considerable weight, don't you think?'

He could have shaken her within an inch of her life. For having so little faith in him. So little trust.

'Did it not occur to you to consider it strange that a photographer just happened to be in the hotel lobby at the time Nina and I entered it…coincidentally together? Or that her suite and mine were very conveniently sited opposite each other?' It hadn't taken much pressure to discover Nina had bribed the booking receptionist to reshuffle bookings. 'Perhaps a little too convenient the same photographer was perfectly positioned to take a shot Nina had very carefully orchestrated?'

'You were kissing her!'

'Correction,' he drawled with deliberate cynicism. 'She was kissing me.'

Nina's words rose to the forefront of Aysha's mind. Vicious, damaging, and incredibly pervasive. 'Really? There didn't seem a marked degree of distinction to me.'

He extended his hands as if to catch hold of her shoulders, only to let them fall to his sides. 'A few seconds either way of that perfectly timed shot, and the truth would have been clearly evident.'

'According to Nina,' Aysha relayed bitterly, 'you represent the ultimate prize in the *most suitable husband* quest. Rich, handsome, and, as reputation has it...*a lover to die for.*' Her smile was a mere facsimile. 'Her words, not mine.'

Something fleeting darkened his eyes. A quality that was infinitely ruthless.

'An empty compliment, considering it's completely false.'

The celluloid print of that kiss rose up to haunt her. 'A willing, voluptuous female well-versed in every sexual trick in the book.' Her eyes swept his features, then focused on the unwavering depth of those dark eyes. 'You mean to say you refused what was so blatantly offered?' It took considerable effort to keep her voice steady. 'How noble.'

Carlo reached forward and caught hold of her chin, increasing the pressure as she attempted to twist out of his grasp.

'Why would I participate in a quick sexual coupling with a woman who means nothing to me?'

He was almost hurting her, and her eyes widened as he slid a hand to her nape and held it fast.

'A moment's aberration when your libido took precedence?' she sallied, hating the way his cologne teased her nostrils and began playing havoc with her equilibrium.

Oh, God, she didn't know anything any more. There were conflicting emotions warring inside her head, some of which hardly made any sense.

'Aysha?'

Her eyes searched his, wide, angry, and incredibly hurt. 'How would you feel if the situation were reversed?'

A muscle bunched at the side of his jaw, and something hot and terrifyingly ruthless darkened his eyes.

'I'd kill him.'

His voice was deadly quiet, yet it held the quality of tempered steel, and she felt as if a hand took hold of her throat and squeezed until it choked off her breath.

Her chest tightened and her heart seemed to beat loud, the sound a heavy, distant thud that seemed to reverberate inside her ears.

'A little extreme, surely?' Aysha managed after several long seconds.

'You think so?'

'That sort of action would get you long service, perhaps even life, in gaol.'

'Not for the sort of death I have in mind.' His features assumed a pitiless mask.

He had the power, the influence, to financially ruin an adversary. And he would do it without the slightest qualm.

A light shivery sensation feathered over the surface of her skin. She needed time out from all the madness that surrounded her. Somewhere she could gain solitude in which to think. A place where she had an element of choice.

'I'm going to move into the house for a few days.'

The words emerged almost of their own accord, and she saw his eyes narrow fractionally.

'It's the house, or a hotel,' Aysha insisted, meaning every word.

He wanted to shake her. Paramount was the desire to wring Nina's neck. Anger, frustration, irritation…each rose to the fore, and he banked them all down in an effort to conciliate.

'If that's what it takes.'

'Thank you.'

She was so icily polite, so remote. Pain twisted his gut, and he swore beneath his breath.

'We're due at the ballet in an hour.'

'Go alone, or don't go at all, Carlo. I really don't care.'

Aysha walked into the bedroom and caught up a few essentials from drawers, the wardrobe, aware that Carlo stood watching her every move from the doorway.

For one tragic second she felt adrift, homeless. Which was ridiculous. The thought made her angry, and she closed the holdall, then slung the strap over one shoulder.

'Aysha.'

She'd taken only a token assortment of clothing. That fact should have been reassuring, yet he'd never felt less assured in his life.

Clear grey eyes met his, unwavering in their clarity. 'Right now, there isn't a word you can say that will make a difference.'

She walked to the doorway, stepped past him, and made her way through the apartment to the front door. She half expected him to stop her, but he didn't.

The lift arrived swiftly, and she rode it down to the car park, unlocked her car, then drove it up onto the road.

Carlo leaned his back against the wall and stared sightlessly out of the wide plate-glass window. After a few tense minutes, he picked up the receiver, keyed in a series of digits, then waited for it to connect.

The private detective was one of the best, and with modern technology he should have the answer Carlo needed within days.

He made three more calls, offered an obscene amount of money to ensure that his requests... *orders*, he amended with grim cynicism, were met within a specified time-frame.

Now, he had to wait. And continue to endure Aysha's farcical pretence for a few days. Then there would be no more room for confusion.

He moved away from the wall, prowled the lounge, then in a restless movement he lifted a hand and raked fingers through his hair.

Yet strength wasn't the answer. Only proof, irrefutable proof.

In business, it was essential to cover all the bases, and provide back-up. He saw no reason why it wouldn't work in his personal life.

CHAPTER SIX

AYSHA was hardly aware of the night, the flash of headlights from nearby vehicles, as she traversed the streets and negotiated the Harbour Bridge. She handled the car with the movements of an automaton, and it was something of a minor miracle she reached suburban Clontarf.

Celestial guidance, she decided wryly as she activated the wrought-iron gates guarding entrance to the architectural masterpiece Carlo had built.

Remote-controlled lights sprang on as she reached the garage doors, and she checked the alarm system before entering the house.

It was so quiet, so still, and she crossed into the lounge to switch on the television, then cast a glance around the perfectly furnished room.

Beautiful home, luxuriously appointed, every detail perfect, she reflected; except for the relationship of the man and woman who were to due to inhabit it.

A weary sigh escaped her lips. Was she being foolish seeking a temporary escape? What, after all, was it going to achieve?

Damn. Damn Nina and the seeds she'd deliberately planted.

A slight shiver shook her slender frame, and she resolutely made her way to the linen closet. It was late, she was tired, and all she had to do was fetch fresh linen, make up the bed, and slip between the sheets.

She looked at the array of linen in their neat piles, and her fingers hovered, then shifted to a nearby stack.

Not the main bedroom. The bed was too large, and she couldn't face the thought of sleeping in it alone.

A guest bedroom? Heaven knew there were enough of them! She determinedly made her way towards the first of four, and within minutes she'd completed the task.

In a bid to court sleep she opted for a leisurely warm shower. Towelled dry, she caught up a cotton nightshirt and slid into bed to lie staring into the darkness as her mind swayed every which way but loose.

Carlo. Was he in bed, unable to sleep? Or had he opted to attend the ballet, after all?

What if Nina was also there? The wretched woman would be in her element when she discovered Carlo alone. Oh, for heaven's sake! Be sensible.

Except she didn't *feel* sensible. And sleep was never more distant.

Perhaps she did fall into a fitful doze, although it seemed as if she'd been awake all night when dawn filtered through the drapes and gradually lightened the room.

She lifted her left wrist and checked the time. A few minutes past six. There was no reason for her to rise this early, but she couldn't just lie in bed.

Aysha thrust aside the covers and padded barefoot

to the kitchen. The refrigerator held a half-empty bottle of fruit juice, a partly eaten sandwich, and an apple.

Not exactly required sustenance to jump-start the day, she decided wryly. So, she'd go shopping, stop off at a café for breakfast, then come back, change, and prepare to meet Teresa at ten. Meantime she'd try out the pool.

It was almost seven when she emerged, and she blotted off the excess moisture, then wrapped the towel sarong-wise and re-entered the house.

Within minutes the phone rang, and she reached for it automatically.

'You slept well?'

Aysha drew in a deep breath at the sound of that familiar voice. 'Did you expect me not to?'

There was a faint pause. 'Don't push it too far, *cara*,' Carlo drawled in husky warning.

'I'm trembling,' she evinced sweetly.

'So you should be.' His voice tightened, and acquired a depth that sent goosebumps scudding over the surface of her skin.

'Intimidation isn't on my list.'

'Nor is false accusation on mine.'

With just the slightest lack of care, this could easily digress into something they both might regret.

With considerable effort she banked down the anger, and aimed for politeness. 'Is there a purpose to your call, other than to enquire if I got any sleep?' She thought she managed quite well. 'I have a host of things to do.'

'*Grazie.*'

She winced at the intended sarcasm. *'Prego,'* she concluded graciously, and disconnected the phone.

On reflection, it wasn't the best of days, but nor was it the worst. Teresa was in fine form, and so consumed with her list of Things to Do, Aysha doubted her own preoccupation was even noticed. Which was just as well, for she couldn't have borne the string of inevitable questions her mother would deem it necessary to ask.

'You're looking a little peaky, darling. You're not coming down with something, are you?'

'A headache, Mamma.' It wasn't too far from the truth.

Teresa frowned with concern. 'Take some tablets, and get some rest.'

As if *rest* was the panacea for everything! 'Carlo and I are attending the sculpture exhibition at the Gallery tonight.'

'It's just as well Carlo is whisking you away to the Coast for the weekend. The break will do you good.'

Somehow Aysha doubted it.

The Gallery held a diverse mix of invited guests, some of whom attended solely to be seen and hopefully make the social pages. Others came to admire, with a view to adding to their collection.

Carlo and Aysha fell into a separate category. A close friend was one of the exhibiting artists and they wanted to add their support.

'Ciao, bella,' a male voice greeted, and Aysha

turned to face the extraordinarily handsome young man who'd sent his personal invitation.

'Bruno!' She flung her arms wide and gave him an enthusiastic hug. 'How are you?'

'The better for seeing you.' He lowered his head and bestowed a kiss to each cheek in turn. 'Damn Carlo for snaring you first.' He withdrew gently and looked deeply into those smoky grey eyes, then he turned towards Carlo and lifted one eyebrow in silent query. 'Carlo, *amici. Come stai?*'

Something passed between both men. Aysha glimpsed it, and sought to avert any swing in the territorial parameters by tucking one hand through Carlo's arm.

'Come show us your exhibits.'

For the next half-hour they wandered the large room, pausing to examine and comment, or converse with a few of the fellow guests.

Aysha moved towards a neighbouring exhibit as Carlo was temporarily waylaid by a business acquaintance.

'Your lips curve wide with a generous smile, yet your eyes are sad,' said Bruno. 'Why?'

'The wedding is a week tomorrow.' She gave a graceful shrug. 'Teresa and I have been shopping together every day, and nearly every night Carlo and I have been out.'

'Sad, *cara*,' Bruno reiterated. 'I didn't say tired. If Carlo isn't taking care of you, he will answer to me.'

She summoned a wicked smile and her eyes sparkled with hidden laughter. 'Swords at dawn? Or should that be pistols?'

'I would take pleasure in breaking his nose.'

She turned to check on the subject of their discussion, and stiffened. Bruno, acutely perceptive, shifted his head and followed her gaze. 'Ah, the infamous Nina.'

The statuesque brunette looked stunning in red, the soft material hugging every curve like a well-fitting glove.

Bruno leant down and said close to Aysha's ear, 'Shall we go break it up?'

'Let's do that.' The smile she proffered didn't reach her eyes, and her heart hammered a little in her chest as she drew close.

Nina's tapered red-lacquered nails rested on Carlo's forearm, and Aysha watched those nails conduct a gentle caressing movement back and forth over a small area of his tailored jacket.

Nina's make-up was superb, her mouth a perfect glossy red bow.

'Want me to charm her?' Bruno murmured, and Aysha responded equally quietly.

'Thanks, but I can fight my own battles.'

'Take care, *cara*. You're dealing with a dangerous cat.' He paused as they reached Carlo's side. 'Your most precious possession,' Bruno said lightly, and inclined his head with deliberate mockery, 'Nina.' Then he smiled, and moved through the crowd.

Wise man, Aysha accorded silently, wishing she could do the same.

'Darling, do get me a drink. You know what I like.'

Aysha began a mental countdown the moment Carlo left to find a waitress.

'I imagine you've checked the photographs?' Nina raised one eyebrow and raked Aysha's slender frame. 'Caused a little grief, did they?'

'Wasn't that your purpose?' Aysha was cold, despite the warmth of the summer evening.

'How clever of you,' Nina approved. 'Have you decided to condone his transgressions? I do hope so.' Her smile was seductively sultry. 'I would hate to have to give him up.'

Her heart felt as if it was encased in ice. 'You've missed your vocation,' she said steadily.

'What makes you say that, darling?'

She needed the might of a sword, but a verbal punch-line was better than nothing. 'You should have been an actress.' A smile cost her almost every resource she had, but she managed one beautifully, then she turned and threaded her way towards one of Bruno's sculptures.

'Who won?'

Bruno could always be counted on, and she cast him a wry smile. 'You noticed.'

'Ah, but I was looking out for you.' He curved an arm around the back of her waist. 'Now, tell me what you think about this piece.'

She examined it carefully. 'Interesting,' she conceded. 'If I say it resembles my idea of an African fertility god, would it offend you?'

'Not at all, because that's exactly what it is.'

'You're just saying that to make me feel good.'

He placed a hand over his heart. 'I swear.'

She began to laugh, and he smiled down at her. 'Why not me, *cara*?' he queried softly, and hugged her close. 'I'd treat you like the finest porcelain.'

'I know,' she said gently, and with a degree of very real regret.

'You love him, don't you?'

'Is it that obvious?'

'Only to me,' he assured her quietly. 'I just hope Carlo knows how fortunate he is to have you.'

'He does.'

Aysha heard that deep musing drawl, glimpsed the latent darkness in his eyes, and gently extricated herself from Bruno's grasp. 'I was admiring Bruno's sculpture.'

Carlo cast her a glittering look that set her nerves on edge. How dared he look at her like that when he'd been playing *up close and personal* with Nina?

'Don't play games, *cara*,' Carlo warned as soon as Bruno was out of earshot.

'Practise what you preach, *darling*,' she said sweetly. 'And *please* get me a drink. It'll give Nina another opportunity to waylay you.'

He bit off a husky oath. 'We can leave peaceably, or not,' he said with deceptive quietness. 'Your choice.' He meant every word.

'Bruno will be disappointed.'

'He'll get over it.'

'I could make a scene,' Aysha threatened, and his expression hardened.

'It wouldn't make any difference.'

It would, however, give Nina the utmost pleasure

to witness their dissension. 'I guess we get to say goodnight,' she capitulated with minimum grace.

Ten minutes later she was seated in the Mercedes as it purred across the Harbour Bridge towards suburban Clontarf.

She didn't utter a word during the drive, and she reached for the door-clasp the instant Carlo drew the car to a halt. It would be fruitless to tell him not to follow her indoors, so she didn't even try.

'Bruno is a friend. A good friend,' she qualified, enraged at his high-handedness. 'Which is more than I can say for Nina.'

'Neither Bruno nor Nina are an issue.'

Her chin tilted as she glared up at him. 'Then what the hell is the issue?'

'We are,' he vouchsafed succinctly.

'Well, now,' Aysha declared. 'There's the thing. Nina is quite happy for you to marry me, just as long as she gets to remain your mistress.'

His eyes filled with chilling intensity. 'Nina has one hell of an imagination.'

She'd had enough. 'Go home, Carlo.' Her eyes blazed with fury. 'If you don't, I'll be tempted to do something I might regret.'

She wasn't prepared for the restrained savagery evident as his mouth fastened on hers, forcing it open and controlling it as his tongue pillaged the inner sweetness. It was a deliberate ravishment of her senses. Claim-staking, punishing. She lost all sensation of time as one hand slid through her hair to hold fast her head, while the other curved low down her back.

Then the pressure eased, and the punishing quality changed to passion, gradually dissipating to a sensuous gentleness that curled round her inner core and tugged at her emotions, seducing until she was weak-willed and malleable.

From somewhere deep inside she dredged sufficient strength to tear her mouth free, and her body trembled as he traced the edge of his thumb across the swollen contours of her lips.

'Nina is nothing to me, do you understand? She never has been. Never will be.'

She didn't say a word. She just looked at him, glimpsed the faint edge of regret, and was incapable of moving.

He pulled her close and buried her head in the curve of his shoulder, then he pressed his lips to her hair.

Aysha could feel the power in that large body, the strength, and she felt strangely ambivalent. 'I don't want you to stay.'

'Because you'll only hate me in the morning?'

She drew a shaky breath. 'I'll hate myself even more.'

All he had to do was kiss her, and she'd change her mind. Part of her wanted him so much it was an impossible ache. Yet if she succumbed she'd be lost, and that wouldn't achieve a thing.

He held her for what seemed an age, then he turned her face to his and brushed his lips across her own, lingered at one corner and angled his mouth into hers in a kiss that was so incredibly evocative it dispensed with almost all her doubts.

Almost, but not quite. He sensed the faint barrier, and gently put her at arm's length.

'I'll pick you up at seven, OK?'

It was easy to simply nod her head, and she watched as he turned and walked to the door. Seconds later she heard his car's engine start, and she checked the lock, then activated security before crossing to her room.

Sleep seemed a distant entity, and she switched on the television in the hope of discovering something which would occupy her interest. Except channel-hopping provided nothing she wanted to watch, and she retired to her bedroom, then lay staring at the ceiling for what seemed hours before finally slipping into a restless slumber in which vivid dreams assumed nightmarish proportion as Nina took the role of vamp.

CHAPTER SEVEN

AYSHA woke early, padded barefoot to the kitchen, poured herself some fresh orange juice, then headed outdoors to swim several laps of the pool.

After fifteen minutes or so she emerged, towelled off the excess moisture, then retreated indoors to change and make breakfast.

The ambivalence of the previous evening had disappeared, and in the clear light of day it seemed advantageous for she and Carlo to spend the weekend apart.

With that thought in mind she crossed to the phone and punched in his number. The answering machine picked up, and she replaced the receiver down onto the handset.

He was probably in the shower, or, she determined with a glance at her watch, he could easily have left. She keyed in the digits that connected with his mobile, and got voicemail.

Damn. It would have been less confrontational to cancel via the phone than deal with him in person.

It was almost seven when Carlo walked into the kitchen, and his eyes narrowed at the sight of her in cut-off denims and skimpy top.

'You're not ready.'

'No.' Her response was matter-of-fact. 'I think we both need the weekend apart.'

His expression was implacable. 'I disagree. Go change and get your holdall. We don't have much time.'

'Give me one reason why I should go?' she demanded, tilting her chin at him in a way that drove him crazy, for he wanted to kiss her until all that fine anger melted into something he could deal with.

'I can give you several. But right now you're wasting valuable time.'

Without a word he strode through the lounge and ascended the stairs. She followed after him, watching as he entered the bedroom, opened a cupboard, extracted a leather holdall and tossed it down onto the bed, then he riffled through her clothes, selected, discarded, then opened drawers and took a handful of delicate underwear and dumped it in the holdall.

'What in hell do you think you're doing?'

A pair of heeled pumps followed sandals.

'I would have thought it was obvious.'

He moved into the *en suite* bathroom, collected toiletries and make-up, and swept them into a cosmetic case. He lifted his head long enough to spare her a searching look.

'You might want to change.'

Her eyes flashed fire. 'I might not,' she retaliated swiftly.

He shrugged his shoulders, pressed everything into the holdall, then closed the zip fastener.

'OK, let's go.'

'Don't you *listen*?' His implacability brought her to a state of rage. 'I am not going anywhere.'

Carlo was dangerously calm. Too calm. 'We've already done this scene.'

Aysha was too angry to apply any caution. 'Well, *hell*. Let's do it again.'

'No.' He slung the holdall straps over one shoulder, then he curved an arm round her waist and hoisted her over one shoulder with an ease that brought forth a gasp of outrage.

'You fiend! What do you think you're doing?'

'Abducting you.'

'In the name of God… *Why?*'

Carlo strode out of the room and began descending the short flight of stairs. 'Because we're flying to the Coast, as planned.'

She struggled, and made no impression. In sheer frustration she pummelled both hands against his back. 'Put me down!'

He didn't alter stride as he negotiated the stairs, and she aimed for his ribs, his kidneys, anywhere that might cause him pain. All to no avail, for he didn't so much as grunt when each punch connected.

'If you don't put me down this *instant*, I'll have you arrested for attempted kidnapping, assault, and anything else I can think of!'

Carlo reached the impressive foyer, took three more steps, then lowered her to stand in front of him.

'No, you won't.'

He was bigger, broader, taller than her, yet she refused to be intimidated. 'Want to bet?'

'Cool it, *cara*.'

'I am not your darling.'

His mouth curved with amusement, and she poked him several times in the chest.

'Don't you *dare* laugh!'

He curled his hands over her shoulders and held her still. 'What would you have me do? Kiss you? Haul you across one knee and spank your deliciously soft *derrière*?'

'Soft?' She worked out, and while her butt might be curved, it was tight.

'If you keep opposing me, I'll be driven to effect one or the other.'

'Lay a hand on me, and I'll—'

He was much too swift, and any further words she might have uttered were lost as his mouth closed over hers in a deep, punishing kiss which took hold of her anger and turned it into passion.

Aysha wasn't conscious when it changed, only that it did, and the fists she lashed him with gradually uncurled and crept up to his nape to cling as emotion wrought havoc and fragmented all her senses.

Carlo slowly eased the heat, and his mouth softened as he gently caressed the swollen contours of her lips, then pressed light butterfly kisses along the tender curve to one corner and back again.

When he lifted his head she could only look at him with drenched eyes, and he traced a forefinger down the slope of her nose.

'Now that I have your full attention… A weekend at the Coast will remove us from all the madness. No pressures, no demands, no social engagements.'

And no chance of accidentally bumping into Nina.

'Last call, Aysha,' Carlo indicated with a touch of mockery. 'Stay, or go. Which is it to be?'

It wasn't the time for deliberation. 'Go,' she said decisively, and heard his husky laughter.

They made the flight with ten minutes to spare, and touched down at Coolangatta Airport just over an hour later. It was almost ten when they checked into the hotel, and within minutes of entering into their suite Aysha crossed to the floor-to-ceiling glass window fronting the Broadwater, and released the sliding door.

She could hear the muted sound of traffic, voices drifting up from the pool area. Adjacent was an enclosed man-made beach with a secluded cave and waterfall.

In the distance she could see the architecturally designed roof resembling a collection of sails atop an exclusive shopping centre fronting a marina and connected by a walkway bridge to an exclusive ocean-front hotel.

A few minutes later she sensed rather than heard him move to stand behind her.

'Peaceful.'

It was, and she said so. 'Yes.'

His arms curved round her waist and he pulled her close. 'What do you want to do with the day?'

There was a desperate need to get out of the hotel suite, and lose herself among the crowds. 'A theme park?' She said the first one that came into her head. 'Dreamworld.'

He hid a wry smile. 'I'll organise it.'

'Just like that?'

'We can hire a car and drive into the mountains, take any one of several cruises.' His shoulders shifted as he effected a lazy shrug. 'You get to choose.'

'For today?'

'All weekend,' he said solemnly.

'Give me too much power, and it might go to my head,' Aysha teased, suddenly feeling more in control.

'I doubt it.'

He knew her too well. 'After dinner we go to the Casino, then tomorrow we do Movieworld.' Crowds, lots of people. Which left only the hours between midnight or later and dawn spent in this beautiful suite, with its very large, prominently positioned bed.

Dreamworld was fun. They played tourist and took a bus there, went on several rides, ate hot dogs and chips as they wandered among the crowd. Aysha laughed at the white tigers' antics, viewed the Tower of Terror and voiced an emphatic *no* to Carlo's suggestion they take the ride.

It was almost six when the bus deposited them outside the hotel.

'I'll have first take on the shower,' Aysha indicated as they rode the lift to their designated floor.

'We could share.'

'I don't think that's a good idea,' she said evenly. Just remembering how many showers they'd shared and their inevitable outcome set all her fine body hairs on edge.

The lift slid to a stop and she turned in the direction of their suite.

Inside, she collected fresh underwear and entered

the large bathroom. The water was warm and she adjusted the dial, undressed, then stepped into the tiled stall.

Seconds later the door slid open and her eyes widened as Carlo joined her.

'What do you think you're doing?'

'Sharing a shower isn't necessarily an invitation to have sex,' he said calmly, and took the soap from her nerveless fingers.

He was too close, but there was no further room to move.

'Want me to shampoo your hair?'

'I can do it,' she managed in a muffled voice, and she missed his slight smile as he uncapped the courtesy bottle and slowly worked the gel into her hair.

His fingers began a gentle massage, and she closed her eyes, taking care to stifle a despairing groan as he rinsed off the foam.

Not content, he palmed the soap and proceeded to smooth it over her back, her buttocks, thighs, before tending to her breasts, then her stomach.

'Don't,' Aysha begged as he travelled lower, and she shook her head in mute denial when he placed the soap in her hand, then guided it over his chest.

Her fingers scraped the curling hair there, and she felt the tautness of his stomach, then consciously held her breath as he'd traversed lower.

His arousal was a potent force, and she began to shake with the need for his possession. It would be so easy to let the soap slip from her hand and reach for him. To lift her face to his, and invite his mouth down to hers.

Then he turned and his voice emerged as a silky drawl. 'Do my back, *cara*.'

She thrust the soap onto its stand, and slid open the door. 'Do it yourself.'

Aysha escaped, only because he let her, she was sure, and she caught up a towel, clutched hold of her underwear, and moved into the bedroom.

It was galling to discover her hands were trembling, and she quickly towelled herself dry, then wound the towel turban-wise round her head.

By the time Carlo emerged she was dressed, and she re-entered the bathroom to utilise the hairdrier, then tend to her make-up.

White silk evening trousers, a gold-patterned white top, minimum jewellery, and white strapped heeled pumps made for a matching outfit.

Black trousers and a white chambray shirt emphasised his dark hair and tanned skin. He'd shaved, and his cologne teased her nostrils, creating a havoc all its own with her senses.

'Ready?'

They caught a taxi to the Casino, enjoyed a leisurely meal, then entered the gambling area.

Aysha's luck ran fickle, while Carlo's held, but she refused to use his accumulated winnings, choosing instead to watch him at the blackjack table. Each selection was calculated, his expression impossible to read. Much like the man himself, she acknowledged silently.

It was after one when they returned to the hotel. Aysha felt pleasantly tired, and in their suite she slipped out of her clothes, cleansed her face of make-up, then slid into bed to lie quietly with her eyes closed, pretending sleep.

Moments later she felt the mattress depress as Carlo joined her, and she measured her breathing into a slow, steady rise and fall. Grateful, she told herself, that Carlo's breathing gradually acquired a similar pattern.

Why was it that when you didn't want something, you felt cheated when you didn't receive it? Aysha queried silently. The size of the bed precluded any chance of accidentally touching, and she didn't feel inclined to instigate the contrived kind...

'Come on, sleepyhead, rise and shine.'

Aysha heard the voice and opened her eyes to brilliant sunshine and the aroma of freshly brewed coffee. It was *morning* already?

'Breakfast,' Carlo announced. 'You have three quarters of an hour to eat, shower and dress before we need to take the bus to Movieworld.'

What had happened to the night? You slept right through it, a tiny voice taunted. Wasn't that what you wanted?

They boarded the bus with a few minutes to spare, and there were thrills and spills and fun and laughter as the actors went through their paces. The various stuntmen and women earned Aysha's respect and admiration as more than once a scene made her catch her breath in awe of the sensitive degree of timing and expertise involved.

They caught the early evening-flight out of Coolangatta Airport, and arrived in Sydney after nine. Carlo collected the car, then headed towards the city.

For one brief moment Aysha was tempted to choose the apartment, except Carlo pre-empted any decision by driving to Clontarf.

She told herself fiercely that she wasn't disappointed as he checked the house and re-set the alarm.

His kiss was brief, a soft butterfly caress that left her aching for more. Then he turned and retraced his steps to the car.

Half an hour later Carlo crossed to the phone and punched in a series of digits, within minutes of entering his apartment.

Samuel Sloane, a legal eagle of some note, picked up on the seventh ring, and almost winced at the grim tone of the man who'd chosen to call him at such an hour on a Sunday evening at home. He listened, counselled and advised, and wasn't in the least surprised when he was ignored.

'I don't give a damn for the what-if's and maybes protecting my investments, my interests. I'm not consulting you for advice. I'm instructing you what to do. Draw up that document. I'll be in your office just before five tomorrow. Now, do we understand each other?'

The impulse to slam the receiver down onto the handset was uppermost, and Carlo barely avoided the temptation to do so.

Aysha spent the morning organising the final soft furnishing items she'd ordered several weeks previously. A message alerting her of their arrival had been on her answering machine when she'd checked it on her return from the Coast.

At midday she stood back and surveyed the results, and was well pleased with the effect. It was perfect, and just as she'd envisaged the overall look.

It was amazing how a few cushions, draped pelmets in matching fabric really set the final touch to a room.

All it needed, she decided with a critical eye, was a superbly fashioned terracotta urn in one corner to complete the image she wanted. Maybe she'd have time to locate the urn before she was due to meet Teresa at one.

Aysha made it with minutes to spare, and together they spent the next few hours with the dressmaker, checked a few minor details with the wedding organiser, then took time to relax over coffee.

'You haven't forgotten we're dining with Gianna and Luigi tonight?'

Aysha uttered a silent scream in sheer frustration. She didn't want to play the part of soon-to-be-married adoring fiancée. Nor did she want to dine beneath the watchful eyes of their respective parents.

When she arrived at the house she checked the answering machine and discovered a message from Carlo indicating he'd collect her at six. An identical message was recorded on her mobile phone.

Her fingers hovered over the telephone handset as she contemplated returning his call and cancelling out, only to retreat in the knowledge that she had no choice but to see the evening through.

A shower did little to ease the tension, and she

deliberately chose black silk evening trousers and matching halter-necked top, added stiletto pumps, twisted her hair into a simple knot atop her head, and kept make-up to a minimum.

She was ready when security alerted her that the front gate had been activated, and she opened the front door seconds ahead of Carlo's arrival.

He was a superb male animal, she conceded as she caught her first glimpse of him. Tall, broad frame, honed musculature, and he exuded a primitive alchemy that was positively lethal.

Expensively tailored black trousers, dark blue shirt left unbuttoned at the neck, and a black jacket lent a sophistication she could only admire. 'Shall we leave?' Aysha asked coolly, and saw those dark eyes narrow.

'Not yet.'

Her stomach executed a slow somersault, and she tensed involuntarily. 'We don't want to be late.'

He was standing too close, and she suppressed the need to take a backward step. She didn't need him close. It just made it more difficult to maintain a mental distance. And she needed to, badly.

He brushed his fingers across one cheek and pressed a thumb to the corner of her mouth. 'You're pale.'

She almost swayed towards him, drawn as if by a magnetic force. Dammit, how could she love him, yet hate him at the same time? It was almost as if her body was detached from the dictates of her brain.

'A headache,' she responded evenly, and his expression became intensely watchful.

'I'll ring and cancel.'

It was easier to handle him when he was angry. At least then she could rage in return. Now, she merely felt helpless, and it irked her that he knew.

'That isn't an option, and you know it,' she refuted, and lifted a hand in expressive negation.

'You've taken something for it?'

'Yes.'

'Povera piccola,' he declared gently as he lowered his head and brushed his lips against her temple.

Sensation curled inside her stomach as his mouth trailed down to the edge of her mouth, and she turned her head slightly, her lips parting in denial, only to have his mouth close over hers.

He caught her head between both hands, and his tongue explored the inner tissues at will, savouring the sweetness with such erotic sensuousness that all rational thought temporarily fled.

His touch was sheer magic, exotic, intoxicating, and left her wanting more. Much more.

It's just a kiss, she assured herself mentally, and knew she was wrong. This was seductive claim-staking at its most dangerous.

Aysha pushed against his shoulders and tore her mouth from his, her eyes wide and luminous as they caught the darkness reflected in his. Her mouth tingled, and her lips felt slightly swollen.

'Let's go.' Was that her voice? It sounded husky, and her mouth shook slightly as she moved away from him and caught up her evening bag.

In the car she leaned her head back against the

cushioned rest, and stared sightlessly out of the window.

Summer daylight saving meant warm sunshine at six in the evening, and peak-hour traffic crossing the Harbour Bridge had diminished, ensuring a relatively smooth drive to suburban Vaucluse.

Aysha didn't offer anything by way of conversation, and she was somewhat relieved when Carlo brought the Mercedes to a halt behind Teresa and Giuseppe's car in the driveway of his parents' home.

'Showtime.'

'Don't overdo it, *cara*,' he warned quizzically, and she offered him a particularly direct look.

Did he know just how much she hurt deep inside? Somehow she doubted it. 'Don't patronise me.'

She saw one eyebrow lift. 'Not guilty,' Carlo responded, then added drily, 'on any count.'

Now there was a *double entendre* if ever there was one. 'You underestimate yourself.'

His eyes hardened fractionally. 'Take care, Aysha.'

She reached for the door-clasp. 'If we stay here much longer, our parents will think we're arguing.'

'And we're not?'

'Now you're being facetious.' She opened the door and stood to her feet, then summoned a warm smile as he crossed to her side.

Gianna Santangelo's affectionate greeting did much to soothe Aysha's unsettled nerves. This was *family*, although she was under no illusions, and knew that both mothers were attuned to the slightest nuance that might give hint to any dissension.

Dinner was an informal meal, although Gianna had gone to considerable trouble, preparing *gnocchi* in a delicious sauce, followed by chicken pieces roasted in wine with rosemary herbs and accompanied by a variety of vegetables.

Gianna was a superb cook, with many speciality dishes in her culinary repertoire. Even Teresa had the grace to offer a genuine compliment.

'*Buona*, Gianna. You have a flair for *gnocchi* that is unsurpassed by anyone I know.'

'*Grazie*. I shall give Aysha the recipe.'

Ah, now there was the thing. Teresa's recipe versus that of Gianna. Tricky, Aysha concluded. Very tricky. She'd have to vary the sauce accordingly whenever either or both sets of parents came to dinner. Or perhaps not serve it at all? Maybe she could initiate a whole new range of Italian cuisine? Or select a provincial dish that differed from Trevisian specialities?

'I won't have time for much preparation except at the weekends.' She knew it was a foolish statement the moment the words left her mouth, as both Teresa and Gianna's heads rose in unison, although it was her mother who voiced the query.

'Why ever not, *cara*?'

Aysha took a sip of wine, then replaced her glass down onto the table. 'Because I'll be at work, Mamma.'

'But you have finished work.'

'I'm taking a six-week break, then I'll be going back.'

'Part-time, of course.'

'Full-time.'

Teresa stated the obvious. 'There is no need for you to work at all. What happens when you fall pregnant?'

'I don't plan on having children for a few years.'

Teresa turned towards Carlo. 'You agree with this?'

It could have been a major scandal they were discussing, not a personal decision belonging to two people.

'It's Aysha's choice.' He turned to look at her, his smile infinitely warm and sensual as he took hold of her hand and brushed his lips to each finger in turn. His eyes gleamed with sensual promise. 'We both want a large family.'

Bastard, she fumed silently. He'd really set the cat among the pigeons now. Teresa wouldn't be able to leave it alone, and she'd receive endless lectures about caring for a husband's needs, maintaining an immaculate house, an excellent table.

Aysha leaned forward, and traced the vertical crease slashing Carlo's cheek. His eyes flared, but she ignored the warning gleam. 'Cute, plump little dark-haired boys,' she teased as her own eyes danced with silent laughter. 'I've seen your baby pictures, remember?'

'Don't forget I babysat you and changed your nappies, *cara*.'

Her first memory of Carlo was herself as a four-year-old being carried round on his shoulders, laughing and squealing as she gripped hold of his hair for dear life. She'd loved him then with the innocence of a child.

Adoration, admiration, respect had undergone a subtle change in those early teenage years, as raging female hormones had labelled intense desire as sexual attraction, infatuation, lust.

He'd been her best friend, confidant, big brother, all rolled into one. Then he'd become another girl's husband, and it had broken her heart.

Now she was going to marry him, have his children, and to all intents and purposes live the fairy tale dream of happy-ever-after.

Except she didn't have his heart. That belonged to Bianca, who lay buried beneath an elaborate bed of marble high on a hill outside the country town in which she'd been born.

Aysha had wanted to hate her, but she couldn't, for Bianca had been one of those rare human beings who was so genuinely kind, so *nice*, she was impossible to dislike.

Carlo caught each fleeting expression and correctly divined every one of them. His mouth softened as he leant forward and brushed his lips to her temple.

She blinked rapidly, and forced herself to smile. 'Hands-on practice, huh? You do know you're going to have to help with the diapering?'

'I wouldn't miss it for the world.'

Aysha almost believed him.

'I'll serve the *cannoli*,' Gianna declared. 'And afterwards we have coffee.'

'You women have the *cannoli*,' Luigi dismissed with the wave of one hand. 'Giuseppe, come with me. We'll have a brandy. With the coffee, we'll have *grappa*.' He turned towards his son. 'Carlo?'

Women had their work to do, and it was work which didn't involve men. Old traditions died hard, and the further they lived away from the Old Country, Aysha recognised ruefully, the longer it took those traditions to die.

Carlo rose to his feet and followed the two older men from the room.

Aysha braced herself for the moment Teresa would pounce. Gianna, she knew, would be more circumspect.

'You cannot be serious about returning to work after the honeymoon.'

Ten seconds. She knew, because she'd counted them off. 'I enjoy working, Mamma. I'm very good at what I do.'

'Indeed,' Gianna complimented her. 'You've done a wonderful job with the house.'

'*Ecco*,' Teresa agreed, and Aysha tried to control a silent sigh.

Her mother invariably lapsed into Italian whenever she became passionate about something. Aysha sank back in her chair and prepared for a lengthy harangue.

She wasn't disappointed. The use of Italian became more frequent, as if needed to emphasise a point. And even Gianna's gentle intervention did little to stem the flow.

'If you had to work, I could understand,' Teresa concluded. 'But you don't. There are hundreds, thousands,' she corrected, 'without work, and taking money from the government.'

Aysha gave a mental groan. Politics. They were in for the long haul. She cast a pleading glance at Carlo's mother, and received a philosophical shrug in response.

'I'll make coffee,' Gianna declared, and Aysha stood to her feet with alacrity.

'I'll help with the dishes.'

It was only a momentary diversion, for the debate merely shifted location from the dining room to the kitchen.

Aysha's head began to throb.

'Zia Natalina has finished crocheting all the baskets needed for the *bomboniera*,' Gianna interceded in a bid to change the subject. 'Tomorrow she'll count out all the sugared almonds and tie them into tulle circles. Her daughter Giovanna will bring them to the house early on the day of the wedding.'

'*Grazie*, Gianna. I want to place them on the tables myself.'

'Giovanna and I can do it, if it will help. You will have so much more to do.'

Teresa inclined her head. 'Carlo has the wedding rings? Annalisa has sewn the ring pillow, but the rings need to be tied onto it.' A frown furrowed her brow. 'I must phone and see if she has the ribbon ready.' She gathered cups and saucers together onto the tray while Gianna set some almond biscuits onto a plate.

'The men won't touch them, but if I don't put a plate down with something Luigi will complain.' She lifted a hand and let it fall to her side. 'Yet when I produce it, he'll say they don't want biscuits with coffee.' Her humour was wry. 'Men. Who can understand them?' She cast a practised eye over the tray. 'We have everything. Let's join them, shall we?'

All three men were grouped together in front of the television engrossed in a televised, soccer match.

Luigi was intent on berating the goal keeper for presumably missing the ball, Aysha determined, and her father appeared equally irate.

'Turn off the set,' Gianna instructed Luigi as she placed the tray down onto a coffee table. 'We have guests.'

'Nonsense,' he grumbled. 'They're family, not guests.'

'It is impossible to talk with you yelling at the players.' She cast him a stern glance. 'Besides, you are taping it. When you replay you can yell all you like. Now we sit down and have coffee.'

'La moglie.' He raised his eyes heavenward.

'Dio madonna. A man is not boss in his own house any more?'

It was a familiar by-play, and one Aysha had heard many times over the years. Her father played a similar verbal game whenever Gianna and Luigi visited.

Her eyes sought Carlo's, and she glimpsed the faint humorous gleam evident as they waited silently for Gianna to take up the figurative ball.

'Of course you are the boss. You need me to tell you this?'

Luigi cast the tray an accusing glance. 'You

brought biscuits? What for? We don't need biscuits with coffee. It spoils the taste of the *grappa*.'

'Teresa and Aysha don't have *grappa*,' she admonished. 'You don't think maybe we might like biscuits?'

'After *cannoli* you eat biscuits? You won't sleep with indigestion.'

'I won't sleep anyway. After *grappa* you snore.'

'I don't snore.'

'How do you know? Do you listen to yourself?'

Luigi spread his hands in an expansive gesture. 'Ah, *Mamma*, give it up, huh? We are with friends. You cooked a good dinner. Now it is time to relax.' He held out a beckoning hand to Aysha. 'Come here, *ma tesora*.'

She crossed to his side and rested against the arm he curved round her waist.

'When are you going to invite us to dinner at the new house?'

'After they get back from the honeymoon,' Gianna declared firmly. 'Not before. It will bring bad luck.'

Luigi didn't take any notice. 'Soon there will be *bambini*. Maybe already there is one started, huh, and you didn't tell us?'

'You talk too much,' his wife chastised. 'Didn't you hear Aysha say she intends to wait a couple of years? Aysha, don't listen to him.'

'Ah, grandchildren. You have a boy first, to kick the soccer ball. Then a girl. The brother can look after his sister.'

'Two boys,' Giuseppe insisted, joining the conversation. 'Then they can play together.'

'Girls,' Aysha declared solemnly. 'They're smarter, and besides they get to help me in the house.'

'A boy and a girl.'

'If you two *vecchios* have finished planning our children,' Carlo intruded mildly as he extricated Aysha from his father's clasp. 'I'm going to take Aysha home.'

'*Vecchios*? You call us old men?' Giuseppe demanded, a split second ahead of Luigi's query,

'What are you doing going home? It's early.'

'Why do you think they're going home?' Gianna disputed. 'They're young. They want to make love.'

'Perhaps we should fool them and stay,' Aysha suggested in an audible aside, and Carlo shook his head.

'It wouldn't make any difference.'

'But I haven't had my coffee.'

'You don't need the caffeine.'

'Making decisions for me?'

'Looking out for you,' Carlo corrected gently. 'A few hours ago you had a headache. Unless I'm wrong, you're still nursing one.'

So he deserved full marks for observation. Without a further word she turned towards Luigi and pressed a soft kiss to his cheek, then she followed suit with her father before crossing to Teresa and Gianna.

Saying goodbye stretched out to ten minutes, then they made it to the car, and seconds later Carlo eased the Mercedes through the gates and out onto the road.

CHAPTER EIGHT

'YOU threw me to the lions.'

'Wrong century, *cara*,' he informed her wryly. 'And the so-called lions are pussy cats at heart.'

'Teresa doesn't always sheath her claws.' It was an observation, not a condemnation. 'There are occasions when being the only chick in the nest is a tremendous burden.'

'Only if you allow it to be.'

The headache seemed to intensify, and she closed her eyes. 'Intent on playing amateur psychologist, Carlo?'

'Friend.'

Ah, now there's a descriptive allocation, Aysha reflected. *Friend*. It had a affectionate feel to it, but affection was a poor substitute for love. The all-encompassing kind that prompted men to kill and die for it.

She lapsed into silence as the car headed down towards Double Bay.

'How's the headache?'

It had become a persistent ache behind one eye that held the promise of flaring into a migraine unless she took painkillers very soon. 'There,' she informed succinctly, and closed her eyes against the glare of oncoming headlights.

Carlo didn't offer another word during the drive

to Clontarf, for which she was grateful, and she reached for the door-clasp as soon as the car drew to a halt outside the main entrance to the house.

Aysha turned to thank him, only to have the words die in her throat at his bleak expression.

'Don't even think about uttering a word,' he warned.

'Don't tell me,' she dismissed wearily. 'You're intent on playing nurse.'

His silence was an eloquent testament of his intention, and she slid from the car and mounted the few steps to the front door.

Within minutes he'd located painkillers and was handing them to her together with a tumbler of water.

'Take them.'

She swallowed both tablets, then spared him a dark glance. 'Yessir.'

'Don't be sassy,' he said gently.

Damn him. She didn't need for him to be considerate. Macho she could handle. His gentleness simply undid her completely.

Aysha knew she should object as he took hold of her hand and led her to one of the cushioned sofas, then pulled her down onto his lap, but it felt so *good* her murmur of protest never found voice.

Just close your eyes and enjoy, a tiny imp prompted.

It would take ten minutes for the tablets to begin to work, and when they did she'd get to her feet, thank him, see him out of the door, then lock up and go to bed.

In a gesture of temporary capitulation she tucked

her head into the curve of his neck and rested her cheek against his chest. His arms tightened fractionally, and she listened to the steady beat of his heart.

She'd lain against him like this many times before. As a young child, friend, then as a lover.

Memories ran like a Technicolor film through her head. A fall and scraped knees as a first-grade kid in school. When she'd excelled at ballet, achieved first place at a piano recital. But nothing compared with the intimacy they'd shared for the past three months. That was truly magical. So mesmeric it had no equal.

She felt the drift of his lips against her hair, and her breathing deepened to a steady rise and fall.

When Aysha woke daylight was filtering into the room.

The main bedroom. And she was lying on one side of the queen-size bed; the bedcovers were thrown back on the other. She conducted a quick investigation, and discovered all that separated her from complete nudity was a pair of lacy briefs.

Memory was instant, and she blinked slowly, aware that the last remnants of her headache had disappeared.

The bedroom door opened and Carlo's tall frame filled the aperture. 'You're awake.' His eyes met hers, their expression inscrutable. 'Headache gone?'

'You stayed.' Was that her voice? It sounded breathless and vaguely unsteady.

He looked as if he'd just come from the shower. His hair was tousled and damp, and a towel was hitched at his waist.

'You were reluctant to let me go.'

Oh, God. Her eyes flew to the pillow next to her own, then swept to meet his steady gaze. Her lips parted, then closed again. Had they…? No, of course they hadn't. She'd remember…wouldn't she?

'Carlo—'

Her voice died in her throat as he discarded the towel and pulled on briefs, then thrust on a pair of trousers and slid home the zip.

Each movement was highlighted by smooth rippling muscle and sinew, and she watched wordlessly as he shrugged his arms into a cotton shirt and fastened the buttons.

He looked up and caught her watching him. His mouth curved into a smile, and his eyes were warm, much too warm for someone she'd chosen to be at odds with.

'Mind if I use a comb?'

Her lips parted, but no sound came out, and with a defenceless gesture she indicated the *en suite* bathroom. 'Go ahead.'

She followed his passage as he crossed the room, and she conducted a frantic visual search for something to cover herself with so she could make it to the walk-in wardrobe.

Carlo emerged into the bedroom as she was about to toss aside the bedcovers, and she hastily pulled them up again.

'I'll make coffee,' he indicated. 'And start breakfast. Ten minutes?'

'Yes. Thanks,' she added, and wondered at her faint edge of disappointment as he closed the door behind him.

What had she expected? That he'd cross to the bed and attempt to kiss her? *Seduce* her?

Yet there was a part of her that wanted him to…badly.

With a hollow groan she tossed aside the covers and made for the shower.

Ten minutes later she entered the kitchen to the aroma of freshly brewed coffee. Carlo was in the process of sliding eggs onto a plate, and there were slices of toasted bread freshly popped and ready for buttering.

'Mmm,' she murmured appreciatively. 'You're good at this.'

'Getting breakfast?'

Dressed, she could cope with him. 'Among other things,' she conceded, and crossed to the coffee-maker.

Black, strong, with two sugars. There was nothing better to kick-start the day. 'Shall I pour yours?'

'Please.' He took both plates and placed them on the servery. 'Now, come and eat.'

Aysha took a seat on one of four bar stools and looked at the food on her plate. 'You've given me too much.'

'Eat,' bade Carlo firmly.

'You're as bad as Teresa.'

He reached out a hand and captured her chin. 'No,' he refuted, turning her head towards him. 'I'm not.'

His kiss was sensuously soft and incredibly sensual, and she experienced real regret when he gently put her at arm's length.

'I have to leave. Don't forget we're attending the

Zachariahs' party tonight. I'll call through the day and let you know a time.'

With only days until the wedding, the pressure was beginning to build. Teresa seemed to discover a host of last-minute things that needed organising, and by the end of the day she began to feel as if the weekend at the Coast had been a figment of her imagination.

The need to feel supremely confident was essential, and Aysha chose a long, slim-fitting black gown with a sheer lace overlay. The scooped neckline and ribbon shoulder straps displayed her lightly tanned skin to advantage, and she added minimum jewellery: a slender gold chain, a single gold bangle on one wrist, and delicate drop earrings. Stiletto-heeled evening pumps completed the outfit, and she spared her reflection a cursory glance.

Black was a classic colour, the style seasonally fashionable. She looked OK. And if anyone noticed the faint circles beneath her eyes, she had every excuse for their existence. A bride-to-be was expected to look slightly frazzled with the surfeit of social obligations prior to the wedding.

Carlo's recorded message on the answering machine had specified he'd collect her at seven-thirty. The party they were to attend was at Palm Beach, almost an hour's drive from Vaucluse, depending on traffic.

She would have given anything not to go. The thought of mixing and mingling with numerous social friends and acquaintances didn't appeal any more than having to put on an act for their benefit.

Security beeped as Carlo used the remote module

to release the gates, and Aysha's stomach executed a series of somersaults as she collected her evening purse and made her way down to the lower floor.

She opened the front door as he alighted from the car, and she crossed quickly down the few steps and slid into the passenger seat.

His scrutiny was swift as he slid in behind the wheel, encompassing, and she wondered if he was able to define just how much effort it cost her to appear cool and serene.

Inside, her nerves were stretched taut, and she felt like a marionette whose body movements were governed by a disembodied manipulator.

She met his dark gaze with clear distant grey eyes. No small acting feat, when her body warmed of its own accord, heating at the sight of him and his close proximity.

His elusive cologne invaded her senses, stimulating them into active life, and every nerve-end, every fibre seemed to throb with need.

The *wanting* didn't get any better. If anything, each passing hour made it worse. Especially the long, empty nights when she hungered for his touch.

'How are you?'

Three words spoken in a commonplace greeting, yet they had the power to twist Aysha's stomach into a painful knot.

'Fine.' She didn't aim to tell him anything different.

Carlo eased the car forward, past the gates, then he accelerated along the suburban street with controlled ease.

She directed her attention beyond the windscreen and didn't see the muscle bunch at the edge of his jaw.

Would Nina be an invited guest? Dear Lord, she hoped not. Yet it was a possibility. A probability, she amended, aware that with each passing day the wedding drew closer. Which meant Nina would become more desperate to seize the slightest opportunity.

Aysha cursed beneath her breath at the thought of playing a part beneath Nina's watchful gaze. Worse, having to clash polite verbal swords with a woman whose vindictiveness was aimed to maim.

The harbour, with its various coves and inlets provided a scenic beauty unsurpassed anywhere in Australia, and she focused on the numerous small craft anchored at various moorings, cliff-top mansions dotted in between foliage.

Peak hour traffic had subsided, although it took the best part of an hour to reach their destination. A seemingly endless collection of long minutes when polite, meaningless conversation lapsed into silence.

'I guess our presence tonight is essential?'

Carlo cast her a direct look. 'If you're concerned Nina might be there…don't be. She won't have the opportunity to misbehave.'

'Do you really think you'll be able to stop her?' Aysha queried cynically.

He met her gaze for one full second, then returned his attention to the road. 'Watch me.'

'Oh, I intend to.' It could prove to be an interesting evening.

They reached the exclusive Palm Beach suburb at

the appointed time, and Aysha viewed the number of cars lining the driveway with interest. At a guess there were at least thirty guests.

Fifty, she re-calculated as their host drew them through the house and out onto the covered terrace.

It was strictly smile-time, and she was so well versed in playing the part that it was almost second nature to circulate among the guests and exchange small-talk.

A drink in one hand, she took a sip of excellent champagne and assured the hostess that almost every wedding detail was indeed organised, Claude, the wedding organiser, was indeed a gem, and, yes, she was desperately looking forward to the day.

Details she repeated many times during the next hour. She was still holding on to her first glass of champagne, and she took a hot savoury from a proffered platter, then reached for another.

'You missed dinner?'

Aysha spared Carlo a slow, sweet smile. 'How did you guess?'

His mouth curved, and his dark eyes held a musing gleam. 'You should have told me.'

'Why?'

The need to touch her was paramount, and he brushed fingertips down her cheek. 'We could have stopped somewhere for a meal.'

Her eyes flared, then dilated to resemble deep grey pools. 'Please don't.'

'Am I intruding on a little tiff?'

Aysha heard the words, recognised the feminine voice, and summoned a credible smile.

'Nina.'

Nina avidly examined Aysha's features, then fastened on the object of her obsession. She pressed exquisitely lacquered nails against the sleeve of Carlo's jacket. 'Trouble in paradise, *caro*?'

'What makes you think there might be?' His voice was pleasant, but there was no mistaking the icy hardness in his eyes as he removed Nina's hand from his arm.

Her pout was contrived to portray a sultry sexiness. 'Body language, darling.'

'Really?' The smile that curved his lips was a mere facsimile. 'In that case I would suggest your expertise is sadly lacking.'

Oh, my, Aysha applauded silently. If she could detach herself emotionally, the verbal parrying was shaping into an interesting bout.

'You know that isn't true.'

'Only by reputation. Not by personal experience.'

His voice was silk-encased steel, tempered to a dangerous edge. Only a fool would fail to recognise the folly of besting him.

'Darling, *really*. Your memory is so short?'

'We've frequented the same functions, sat at the same table. That's all.'

Nina spared Aysha a cursory glance. 'If you say so.' She gave a soft laugh and shook her head in telltale disbelief. 'The question is…will Aysha believe you?'

Aysha glimpsed the vindictive smile, registered the malevolence apparent in Nina's sweeping glance, before she turned back towards Carlo.

'*Ciao*, darlings. Have a happy life.'

Aysha watched Nina's sylph-like frame execute a deliberately evocative sway as she walked across the terrace.

'I think I need some fresh air.' And another glass of champagne. It might help dull the edges, and diminish the ugliness she'd just been witness to.

Strong fingers closed over her wrist. 'I'll come with you.'

'I'd rather go alone.'

'And add to Nina's satisfaction?'

Bright lights lit the garden paths, and there were guests mingling around the pool area. Music filtered through a speaker system, and there was the sound of muted laughter.

'Believe me, Nina's satisfaction is the last thing I want to think about.'

His grip on her hand tightened fractionally. 'I've never had occasion to lie to you, *cara*.' His eyes speared hers, fixing them mercilessly.

'There's always a first time for everything.'

Carlo was silent for several long seconds. 'I refuse to allow Nina's malicious machinations to destroy our relationship.'

The deadly softness of his voice should have warned her, but she was beyond analysing any nuances.

'Relationship?' Aysha challenged. 'Let's not delude ourselves our proposed union is anything other than a mutually beneficial business partnership.' She was on a roll, the words tripping easily, fatalistically, from her tongue. 'Cemented by holy matrimony in a bid to preserve a highly successful business empire for the next generation.' Her smile was far too bright, her voice so brittle she scarcely recognised it as her own.

Carlo's appraisal was swift, and she was totally unprepared as he lifted her slender frame over one shoulder.

An outraged gasp left her throat. 'What in *hell* do you think you're doing?'

'Taking you home.'

'Put me down.'

His silence was uncompromising, and she beat a fist against his ribcage in sheer frustration. With little effect, for he didn't release her until they reached the car.

'You *fiend*!' Aysha vented, uncaring of his ruthless expression as he unlocked the passenger door.

'Get in the car,' Carlo said hardily.

Her eyes sparked furiously alive. 'Don't you *dare* give me orders.'

He bit off a husky oath and pulled her in against him, then his head lowered and his mouth took punishing possession of her own.

Aysha struggled fruitlessly for several seconds, then whimpered as he held fast her head. His tongue was an invasive force, and she hated her traitorous body for the way it began to respond.

The hands which beat against each shoulder stilled and crept to link together at his nape. Her mouth softened, and she leaned in to him, uncaring that only seconds before anger had been her sole emotion.

She sensed the slight shudder that ran through his

large body, felt the hardening of his desire, and experienced the magnetising pulse of hunger in response.

Aysha felt as if she was drowning, and she temporarily lost any sense of time or where they were until Carlo gradually loosened his hold.

His lips trailed to the sensitive hollow at the edge of her neck and caressed it gently, then he lifted his head and bestowed a light, lingering kiss to her softly swollen mouth.

Sensation spiralled through her body, aching, poignant, making her aware of every nerve-centre, each pleasure spot.

Aysha didn't feel capable of doing anything but subsiding into the car, and she stared sightlessly out of the window as Carlo crossed to the driver's side and slid in behind the wheel.

She didn't offer a word for much of the time it took to reach Clontarf, for what could she say that wouldn't seem superfluous? The few occasions Carlo broached a query, her answer was monosyllabic.

Nina's image rose like a spectre in her mind, just as her voice echoed as the words replayed again and again.

CHAPTER NINE

THE Mercedes pulled off the main street and eased into a parking space. Carlo switched off the engine and undid his seatbelt.

Aysha looked at him askance. 'Why have you stopped?'

He reached sideways and unclasped her seatbelt. 'You didn't eat dinner, remember?'

The thought of food made her feel ill. 'I don't feel hungry.'

'Then we'll just have coffee.'

She looked at him in exasperation, and met the firm resolve apparent in his stance, the angle of his jaw.

'Do I get to have any say in this? Or will you employ strong-arm tactics?'

'You've dropped an essential kilo or two, you're pale, and you have dark circles beneath your eyes.'

'And I thought I was doing just fine,' Aysha declared silkily.

'It's here, or we raid the kitchen fridge at home.'

That meant him entering the house, making himself at home in the kitchen, and afterwards... She didn't want to contemplate *afterwards*. Having him stay was akin to condoning...

Oh, *damn*, she cursed wretchedly, and reached for the door-clasp.

The restaurant was well-patronised, and they were led to a centre table at the back of the room. Aysha heard the music, muted Mediterranean melancholy plucked from a boujouki, and the sound tugged something deep inside.

Carlo ordered coffee, and she declined. Greek coffee was ruinously strong.

'Tea. Very weak,' she added, and rolled her eyes when Carlo ordered moussaka from the menu. 'I don't want anything to eat.'

Moussaka was one of her favoured dishes, and when it arrived she spared it a lingering glance, let the aroma tease her nostrils. And she didn't argue when Carlo forked a portion and proffered a tempting sample.

It was delicious, and she picked up a spare fork and helped herself. Precisely as he'd anticipated she would do, she conceded wryly.

There was hot crusty bread, and she accepted a small glass of light red wine which she sipped throughout the meal.

'Better?'

It wasn't difficult to smile, and she could almost feel the relaxing effect of the wine releasing the knots of tension that curled tightly around her nerve-ends. 'Yes.'

'More tea?'

Aysha shook her head.

'Do you want to stay for a while, or shall we leave?'

She looked at him carefully, and was unable to define anything from his expression. There was a waiting, watchful quality apparent, a depth to his eyes that was impossible to interpret.

She spared a glance to the dance floor, and the few couples sharing it. Part of her wanted the contact, the closeness of his embrace. Yet there was another part that was truly torn.

Nina's accusations were too fresh in her mind, the image too vivid for it not to cloud her perspective.

Everything was wedding-related. And right now, the last thing she wanted to think about, let alone discuss, was the wedding.

'I adore the music. It's so poignant.'

Was she aware just how wistful she sounded? Or the degree of fragility she projected? Carlo wanted to smite a fist onto the table, or preferably close his hands around Nina's neck.

More than anything, he wanted to take Aysha to bed and make love with her until every last shred of doubt was removed. Yet he doubted she'd give him the opportunity. At least, not tonight.

Now, he had to be content to play the waiting game. Tomorrow, he assured himself grimly, he'd have everything he needed. And damned if he was going to wait another day.

He leaned across the table and caught hold of her hand, then lifted it to his lips.

It was an evocative gesture, and sent spirals of sensation radiating through her body. Her eyes dilated, and her lips shook slightly as he kissed each finger in turn.

'Dance with me.'

The shaking seemed to intensify, and she couldn't

believe it was evident. Dear God, dared she walk willingly into his arms?

And afterwards? What then? Let him lead her into the house, and into bed? That wouldn't resolve anything. Worse, the lack of a resolution would only condone her acquiescence to the status quo.

'Is dancing with me such a problem?' Carlo queried gently, and watched her eyes dilate to their fullest extent.

'It's what happens when I do.'

His eyes acquired a faint gleam, and the edges of his mouth tilted. 'Believe it's mutual.'

Aysha held his gaze without any difficulty at all. An hour ago she'd been furious with him. And Nina. *Especially* Nina.

'Pheromones,' she accorded sagely, and he uttered a soft laugh as he stood and drew her gently to her feet.

'The recognition by one animal of a chemical substance secreted by another,' Aysha informed him.

'You think so?'

She could feel her whole body begin to soften, from the inside out. A melting sensation that intensified as he brushed his lips against her temple.

'Yes.'

Would it always be like this? A smile, the touch of his mouth soothing the surface of her skin? *Is it enough*? a tiny voice taunted. Affection and sexual satisfaction, without love.

Many women settled for less. Much less.

He led her onto the dance floor and into his arms, and she didn't think about anything except the moment and the haunting, witching quality of the music as it stirred her senses and quickened the pace of her pulse.

Aysha wanted to close her eyes and think of nothing but the man and the moment.

For the space of a few minutes it was almost magic, then the music ceased as the band took a break, and she preceded Carlo back to the table.

'Another drink?'

'No, thanks,' she refused.

He picked up the account slip, summoned the waitress, paid, then led the way out to the car.

It didn't take long to reach Clontarf, and within minutes Carlo activated the gates, then drew the Mercedes to a halt outside the main entrance.

Aysha reached for the door-clasp as he released his seatbelt and opened the car door.

'There's no need—'

He shot her a glance that lost much of its intensity under cover of night. 'Don't argue,' he directed, and slid out from the car.

Indoors she turned to face him, and felt the sexual tension apparent. There was a slumberous quality in the depths of his eyes that curled all her nerve-ends, and she looked at him, assessing the leashed sensuality and matching it with her own.

'All you have to do is ask me to stay,' Carlo said quietly, and she looked at him with incredibly sad eyes.

It would be so easy. Just hold out her hand and follow wherever he chose to lead.

For a moment she almost wavered. To deny him

was to deny herself. Yet there were words she needed to say, and she wasn't sure she could make them sound right.

'I know.'

He lifted a hand and brushed his knuckles gently across her cheekbone. 'Go to bed, *cara*. Tomorrow is another day.'

Then he released her hand and turned towards the door.

Seconds later she heard the refined purr of the engine, and saw the bright red tail-lights disappear into the night.

He'd gone, when she'd expected him to employ unfair persuasion to share her bed. There was an ache deep inside she refused to acknowledge as disappointment.

If he'd pressed to stay, she'd have told him to leave. So why did she feel cheated?

Oh, for heaven's sake, this was ridiculous!

With a mental shake she locked the door and activated security, then she set the alarm and climbed the stairs to her room.

'Mamma,' Aysha protested. 'I don't *need* any more lingerie.'

'Nonsense, darling,' Teresa declared firmly. 'Nonna Benini sent money with specific instructions for you to buy lingerie.'

Aysha spared a glance at the exquisite bras, briefs and slips displayed in the exclusive lingerie boutique. Pure silk, French lace, and each costing enough money to feed an average family for a week.

After a sleepless night spent tossing and turning in her lonely bed, which had seen her wake with a headache, the last thing she needed was a confrontational argument with her mother.

'Then I guess we shouldn't disappoint her.'

Each garment had to be tried on for fit and size, and it was an hour before Aysha walked out of the boutique with bras and briefs in ivory, peach and black. Ditto slips, cobweb-fine pantyhose, and, the *pièce de resistance*, a matching nightgown and negligee.

'Superfluous,' she'd assured her mother when Teresa had insisted on the nightgown, and had stifled a sigh at her insistent glance.

Now, she tucked a hand beneath Teresa's arm and led her in the direction of the nearest café. 'Let's take five, Mamma, and share a cappuccino.'

'And we'll revise our list.'

Aysha thought if she heard the word *list* again, she'd scream. 'I can't think of a single thing.'

'Perfume. Something really special,' Teresa enthused. 'To wear on the day.'

'I already have—'

'I know. And it suits you so well.'

They entered the café, ordered, then chose a table near the window.

'But you should wear something subtly different, that you'll always associate with the most wonderful day of your life.'

'Mamma,' she protested, and was stalled in any further attempt as Teresa caught hold of her hands.

'A mother dreams of her child's wedding day from

the moment she gives birth. Especially a daughter. I want yours to be perfect, as perfect as it can be in every way.' Her eyes shimmered, and Aysha witnessed her conscious effort to control her emotions. 'With Carlo you'll have a wonderful life, enjoying the love you share together.'

A one-sided love, Aysha corrected silently. Many a successful marriage had been built on less. Was she foolish to wish for more? To want to be secure in the knowledge that Carlo had eyes only for her? That *she* was the only one he wanted, and no one else would do?

Chasing rainbows could be dangerous. If you did catch hold of one, there was no guarantee of finding the elusive pot of gold.

'Your father and I had a small wedding by choice,' Teresa continued. 'Our parents offered us money to use however we chose, and it was more important to use it towards the business.'

Aysha squeezed her mother's hand. 'I know, Mamma. I appreciate everything you've done for me.' Their love for each other wasn't in question, although she'd give almost anything to be able to break through the parent-child barrier and have Teresa be her friend, her equal.

However, Teresa was steeped in a different tradition, and the best she could hope for was that one day the balance of scales would become more even.

It was after eleven when they emerged into the arcade. Inevitably, Teresa's list had been updated to include perfume and a complete range of cosmetics and toiletries.

Aysha simply went with the flow, picked at a chicken salad when they paused for lunch, took two painkillers for her headache, and tried to evince interest in Teresa's summary of the wedding gifts which were beginning to arrive at her parents' home.

At three her mobile phone rang, and when she answered she heard Carlo's deep drawl at the other end of the line.

'Good day?'

Her heart moved up a beat. 'We're just about done.'

'I'll be at the house around seven.'

She was conscious of Teresa's interest, and she contrived to inject her tone with necessary warmth. 'Shall I cook something?'

'No, we'll eat out.'

'OK. *Ciao*.' She cut the connection and replaced the unit into her bag.

'Carlo,' Teresa deduced correctly, and Aysha inclined her head. 'He's a good man. You're very fortunate.'

There was only one answer she could give. 'I know.'

It was almost five when they parted, slipped into separate cars, and entered the busy stream of traffic, making it easy for Aysha to hang back at an intersection, then diverge onto a different road artery.

If Teresa discovered her daughter and prospective son-in-law were temporarily occupying separate residences, it would only arouse an entire host of questions Aysha had no inclination to answer.

The house was quiet, and she made her way upstairs, deposited a collection of brightly-coloured carry-bags in the bedroom, then discarded her clothes, donned a bikini and retraced her steps to the lower floor.

The pool looked inviting, and she angled her arms and dived into its cool depths, emerging to the surface to stroke several lengths before turning onto her back and lazily drifting.

Long minutes later she executed sufficient backstrokes to bring her to the pool's edge, then she levered herself onto the ledge and caught up a towel. Standing to her feet, she blotted excess moisture from her body, then she crossed to a nearby lounger and sank back against its cushioned depth.

The view out over the harbour was sheer magic, for at this hour the sea was a dark blue, deepening almost to indigo as it merged in the distance with the ocean.

There were three huge tankers drawing close to the main harbour entrance, and in the immediate periphery of her vision hundreds of small craft lay anchored at moorings.

It was a peaceful scene, and she closed her eyes against the strength of the sun's warmth. It had a soporific effect, and she could feel herself drifting into a light doze.

It was there that Carlo found her more than an hour later, after several minutes of increasing anxiety when he'd failed to locate her anywhere indoors.

His relief at seeing her lying supine on the lounger was palpable, although he could have shaken her for putting him through a few minutes of hell.

He slid open the door quietly, and stood watching her sleep. She looked so relaxed it was almost a shame to have to wake her, and he waited a while, not willing to disturb the moment.

A soft smile curved his mouth. He wanted to cross to her side and gently tease her into wakefulness. Lightly trail his fingers over the length of her body, brush his lips to her cheek, then find her mouth with his own. See her eyelids flutter then lift in wakefulness, and watch the warmth flood her eyes as she reached for him.

Except as things stood, the moment her lashes swept open her eyes were unlikely to reflect the emotion he wanted.

CHAPTER TEN

'AYSHA.'

She was dreaming, and she fought her way through the mists of sleep at the sound of her name.

The scene merged into reality. The location was right, so was the man who stood within touching distance.

It was the circumstances that were wrong.

She moved fluidly into a sitting position. 'Is it that late?' She swung her legs onto the ground and rose to her feet.

He looked impressive dressed in tailored trousers, pale blue cotton shirt, tie and jacket. She kept her eyes fixed on the knot of his tie. 'I'll go shower and change.'

He let her go, then followed her into the house. He crossed to the kitchen, extracted a cool drink from the refrigerator and popped the can, then he prowled around the large entertainment area, too restless to stand or sit in one place for long.

There were added touches he hadn't noticed before. Extra cushions on the chairs and sofas, prints hanging on the walls. The lines were clean and muted, but the room had a comfortable feeling; it was a place where it would be possible to relax.

Carlo checked his watch, and saw that only five minutes had passed. It would take her at least another thirty to wash and dry her hair, dress and apply make-up.

Forty-five, he accorded when she re-entered the room.

The slip dress in soft shell-pink with a chiffon overlay and a wide lace border on the hemline heightened her lightly tanned skin, emphasised her dark blonde hair, and clever use of mascara and shadow deepened the smoky grey of her eyes.

She'd twisted her hair into a knot atop her head, and teased free a tendril that curled down to the edge of her jaw.

Aysha found it easy to return his gaze with a level one of her own. Not so easy was the ability to slow the sudden hammering of her heart as she drew close.

'Shall we leave?' Her voice was even, composed, and at total variance to the rapid beat of her pulse.

'Before we do, there's something I want you to read.' Carlo reached for the flat manila envelope resting on the nearby table and handed it to her.

The warm and wonderful girl of a week ago no longer existed. Except in an acted portrayal in the presence of others.

Alone, the spontaneity was missing from her laughter, and her eyes were solemn in their regard. Absent too was the generous warmth in her smile.

The scene he'd initiated with Nina earlier in the day had been damaging, but he didn't give a damn. The woman's eagerness to accept his invitation to lunch had sickened him, and he hadn't wasted any time informing her exactly what he planned to do should she ever cause Aysha a moment's concern.

He'd gone to extraordinary lengths in an attempt to remove Aysha's doubts. Now he needed to tell her, *show* her.

'Read it, Aysha.'

'Can't it wait until later?'

He thrust a hand into a trouser pocket, and felt the tension twist inside his gut. 'No.'

There was a compelling quality evident in those dark eyes, and she glimpsed the tense muscle at the edge of his jaw.

She was familiar with every one of his features. The broad cheekbones, the crease that slashed each cheek, the wide-spaced large eyes that could melt her bones from just a glance. His mouth with its sensually moulded lips was to die for, and the firm jawline hinted at more than just strength of character.

'Please. Just read it.'

Aysha turned the envelope over, and her fingers sought the flap, dealt with it, then slid out the contents.

The first was a single page, sworn and signed with a name she didn't recognise. Identification of the witness required no qualification, for Samuel Sloane's prominence among the city's legal fraternity was legend.

Her eyes skimmed the print, then steadied into a slower pace as she took in the sworn affidavit testifying Nina di Salvo had engaged the photographic services of William Baker with specific instructions to capture Carlo Santangelo and herself in compromising positions, previously discussed and outlined, for the agreed sum of five hundred dollars per negative.

Aysha mentally added up the photographic prints Nina had shown her, and had her own suspicions confirmed. Carlo had been the target; Nina the arrow.

Her eyes swept up to meet his. 'I didn't think she'd go to these lengths.'

Carlo's eyes hardened as he thought of Nina's vitriolic behaviour. 'It's doubtful she'll bother either of us again.' He'd personally seen to it.

'Damage control,' Aysha declared, and saw his eyes darken with latent anger.

'Yes.'

It was remarkable how a single word could have more impact than a dozen or so. 'I see.'

She was beginning to. But there was still a way to go. 'Read the second document.'

Aysha carefully slipped the affidavit to one side. There were several pages, each one scripted in legalese phrased to confuse rather than clarify. However, there was no doubt of Carlo's instruction.

Any assets in whatever form, inherited from either parents' estates, were to remain solely in her name for her sole use. At such future time, Carlo Santangelo would assume financial responsibility for Benini-Santangelo.

There was only one question. 'Why?'

'Because I love you.'

Aysha heard the words, and her whole body froze. The stillness in the room seemed to magnify until it became a tangible entity.

Somehow she managed to dredge up her voice,

only to have it emerge as a sibilant whisper. 'If this is a trick, you can turn around and walk out of here.'

Her eyes became stricken with an emotion she couldn't hide, and his expression softened to something she would willingly give her life for.

He caught both her hands together with one hand, then lifted the other to capture her nape.

'I love you. *Love*,' he emphasised emotively. 'The heart and soul that is *you*.' He moved his thumb against the edge of her jaw, then slowly swept it up to encompass her cheekbone. His eyes deepened, and his voice lowered to an impassioned murmur. 'I thought the love Bianca and I shared was irreplaceable. But I was wrong.' He lowered his forehead down to rest against hers. 'There was you. Always you. Affection, from the moment you were born. Respect, as you grew from child to woman. Admiration, for carving out your own future.'

His hands moved to her shoulders, then curved down her back to pull her close in against him.

It would be all too easy to lean in and lift her mouth to meet his. As she had in the past. This time she wanted sanity unclouded by emotion or passion.

Aysha lifted her hands to his chest and tried to put some distance between them. Without success. 'I can't think when you hold me.'

Those dark eyes above her own were so deeply expressive, she thought she might drown in them.

'Is it so important that you think?' he queried gently, and she swallowed compulsively.

'Yes.' She was conscious of every breath she took, every beat of her heart.

Carlo let his hands drop, and his features took on a quizzical warmth.

What she wanted, she hardly dared hope for, and she looked at him in silence as the seconds ticked by.

His smile completely disarmed her, and warmth seeped into her veins, heating and gathering force until it ran through her body.

'You want it all, don't you?'

Her mouth trembled as she fought to control her emotions. She was shaking, inwardly. Very soon, she'd become a trembling mass. 'Yes.'

Carlo pushed both hands into his trouser pockets, and she was mesmerised by his mouth, the way it curved and showed the gleam of white teeth, the sensuous quirk she longed to touch.

'I knew marriage between us could work. We come from the same background, we move in the same social circles, and share many interests. We had the foundation of friendship and affection to build on.'

The vertical crease slashed each cheek as he smiled, and his eyes… She felt as if she could drown in their depths.

'In the beginning I was satisfied that it was enough. I didn't expect to have those emotions develop into something more, much more.'

She had to ask. 'And now?'

'I need to be part of your life, to have you need me as much as I need you. As my wife, my friend, the other half of my soul.' He released his hands and reached out to cup her face. 'To love you, as you deserve to be loved. With all my heart. For the rest of my life.'

Aysha felt the ache of tears, and blinked rapidly to dispel them. At that precise moment she was incapable of uttering a word.

Did she realise how transparent she was? Intimacy was a powerful weapon, persuasive, invasive, and one he could use with very little effort. It would be so easy to lower his head, pull her close and let her *feel* what she did to him. His hands soothing her body, the possession of his mouth on hers...

He did none of those things.

'Yes.'

He heard the single affirmative, and every muscle, every nerve relaxed. Nothing else mattered, except their love and the life they would share together. 'No qualifications?'

She shook her head. 'None.'

'So sure,' Carlo said huskily. He reached for her, enfolding her into the strength of his body as his mouth settled over hers. Gently at first, savouring, tasting, then with a passionate fervour as she lifted her arms and linked her hands together at his nape.

Aysha felt his body tremble as she absorbed the force of his kiss and met and matched the mating dance of his tongue as it explored and ravaged sensitive tissue.

His hands shaped and soothed as they sought each pleasure spot, stroking with infinite care as the fire ignited deep within and burst into flame.

It seemed an age before he lifted his head, and she

could only stand there, supported by the strength of his arms.

'Do you trust me?'

She heard the depth in his voice, sensed his seriousness, and raised her eyes to meet his. There was no question. 'Yes,' she said simply.

'Then let's go.'

'OK.'

'Such docility,' Carlo teased gently as he brushed his lips against one temple.

Aysha placed a hand either side of his head and tilted it down as she angled her mouth into his in a kiss that was all heat and passion.

His heart thudded into a quickened beat, and she felt a thrill of exhilaration at the sense of power, the feeling of control.

Carlo broke the contact with emotive reluctance. 'The temptation to love you now, *here*, is difficult to resist.'

A mischievous smile curved her mouth. 'But you're going to.'

His hands slid to her shoulders and he gave her a gentle shake. 'Believe it's merely a raincheck, *cara*.' He released her and took hold of her hand.

'Are you going to tell me *where* we're going?'

'Someplace special.'

He led her outside, then turned to the side path leading to the rear of the grounds.

'Here?' Aysha queried in puzzlement, as they traversed the short set of steps leading down to the gazebo adjacent the pool area.

Lights sprang to life as if by magic, illuminating

the gazebo and casting a reflected glow over the newly planted garden, the beautiful free-form pool.

Her eyes widened as she saw a man and two women standing in front of a small rectangular pedestal draped with a pristine white lace-edged cloth. Two thick candles displayed a thin flicker and a vaporous plume, and there was the scent of roses, beautiful white tight-petalled buds on slender stems.

'Carlo?'

Even as she voiced the query she saw the answer in those dark eyes, eloquent with emotive passion. And love.

'This is for us,' he said gently, curving an arm across the back of her waist as he pulled her into the curve of his body. 'Saturday's production will fulfil our parents' and the guests' expectations.'

She was melting inside, the warmth seeping through her body like molten wax, and she didn't know whether to laugh or cry.

An hour ago she'd been curled up on a soft-cushioned sofa contemplating her shredded emotions.

'OK?' Carlo queried gently.

Her heart kicked in at a quickened beat, and she smiled. A slow, sweet smile that mirrored her inner radiance. 'Yes.'

Introductions complete, Aysha solemnly took her position at Carlo's side.

If the celebrant was surprised at the bride and groom's attire, she gave no indication of it. Her manner appeared genuine, and the words she spoke held a wealth of meaning during the short service.

Carlo slipped a diamond-encrusted ring onto her

finger, and Aysha slid a curved gold band onto his, listening in a haze of emotions as they were solemnly pronounced man and wife.

She lifted her mouth to meet his, and felt the warmth, the hint of restrained passion as he savoured the sweetness and took his fill.

Oh, my, this was about as close to heaven as it was possible to get, Aysha conceded as he reluctantly loosened his hold.

The heat was there, evident in the depth of his eyes, banked down beneath the surface. Desire, and promised ecstasy.

She cast him a witching smile, glimpsed the hunger and felt anticipation arrow through her body.

There was champagne chilling in an ice bucket, and Carlo loosened the cork, then filled each flute with slightly frothy sparkling liquid.

The bubbles tingled her tastebuds and teased the back of her throat as she sipped the excellent vintage.

Each minute seemed like an eternity as she conversed with the celebrant and two witnesses, and accepted the toast.

With both official and social duties completed, the celebrant graciously took her leave, together with the couple who had witnessed the marriage.

Aysha stood in the circle of Carlo's arms, and she leaned back against him, treasuring the closeness, the sheer joy attached to the moment.

Married. She could hardly believe it. There were so many questions she needed to ask. But not yet. There would be time later to work out the answers.

For now, she wanted to savour the moment.

Carlo's lips teased her sensitive nape, then nuzzled an earlobe. 'You're very quiet.'

'I feel as if we're alone in the universe,' she said dreamily. Her mouth curved upwards. 'Well, almost.' A faint laugh husked low in her throat. 'If you block out the cityscape, the tracery of street lights, the suburban houses.'

'I thought by now you'd have unleashed a barrage of questions,' he said with quizzical amusement.

She felt the slide of his hand as he reached beneath her top and sought her breast. The familiar kick of sensation speared from her feminine core, and she groaned emotively as his skilled fingers worked magic with the delicate peak.

She turned in his arms and reached for him, pulling his head down to hers as she sought his mouth with her own in a kiss that wreaked havoc with her tenuous control.

Aysha was almost shaking when he gently disengaged her, and her lips felt faintly swollen, her senses completely swamped with the feel, the taste of him.

'Let's get out of here,' Carlo directed huskily as he caught hold of her hand and led her towards his car.

'Where are we going?'

'I've booked us into a hotel suite for the night. Dinner at the restaurant. Champagne.'

'Why?' she queried simply. 'When everything we need is right here?'

'I want the night to be memorable.'

'It will be.' Without a doubt, she promised silently.

'You don't want the luxurious suite, a leisurely meal with champagne?' he teased.

'I want *you*. Only you,' Aysha vowed with heart-felt sincerity. 'Saturday we get to go through the formalities.' The elegant bridal gown, the limousines, the church service, the extravagant reception, she mused silently. Followed by the hotel bridal suite, and the flight out the next morning to their honeymoon destination.

A bewitching smile curved her generous mouth, and her eyes sparkled with latent humour. 'Tonight we can please ourselves.'

Carlo pressed a light kiss to the edge of her lips. 'Starting now?'

'Here?' she countered wickedly. 'And shock the neighbours?'

He swept an arm beneath her knees and carried her into the house. He traversed the stairs without changing stride, and in the main bedroom he lowered her down to stand in front of him.

Slowly, with infinite care, he released her zip. Warm fingers slid each strap over her shoulders, then shaped the soft slip down over her hips, her thighs, to her feet. Only her briefs and bra remained, and he dispensed with those.

She ached for his touch, his possession, and she closed her eyes, then opened them again as he lightly brushed his fingers across her sensitised skin.

He followed each movement with his lips, each single touch becoming a torture until she reached for him, her fingers urgent as they released shirt buttons and tugged the expensive cotton from his muscular frame.

His eyes dilated as she undid the buckle of his belt, and he caught his breath as she worked the zip fastening.

'Not quite in control, huh?' she offered with a faintly wicked smile, only to gasp as his mouth sought a vulnerable hollow at the edge of her neck.

He had the touch, the skill to evoke an instant response, and she trembled as his tongue wrought renewed havoc.

His hands closed over hers, completing the task, and she clutched hold of his waist as he dispensed with the remainder of his clothes.

The scent of his skin, the slight muskiness of *man* intermingled with the elusive tones of soap and cologne. Tantalising, erotic, infinitely tempting, and inviting her to savour and taste.

Aysha felt sensation burgeon until it encompassed every nerve-cell. The depth, the magnitude overwhelmed her. Two souls melding, seamlessly forging a bond that could never be broken.

She lifted her arms and wound them round his neck as he lowered her down onto the bed and followed her, protecting her from the full impact of his weight.

His mouth closed over hers, devastatingly sensual, in a kiss that drugged her mind, her senses, until she hardly recognised the guttural pleas as her own.

She was on fire, the flames of desire burning deep within until there was no reason, no sensation of anything other than the man and the havoc he was caus-

ing as he led her through pleasure to ecstasy and
beyond.

Now, she wanted him *now*. The feel of him inside
her, surging again and again, deeper and deeper, until
she absorbed all of him, and their rhythm became as
one, in tune and in perfect accord as they soared
together, clung momentarily to the sexual pinnacle,
then reached the ultimate state of nirvana.

Did she say the words? She had no idea whether
they found voice or not. There was only the journey,
the sensation of spiralling ecstasy, the scent of sexual
essence, and the damp sheen on his skin.

She was conscious of her own response, *his*, the
shudder raking that large body as he spilled his seed,
and she exulted in the moment.

The sex between them had always been good.
Better than good, she accorded dimly as she clung to
him. But this, this was more. Intoxicating, exquisite,
wild. And there was *love*. That essential quality that
transcended physical expertise or skill.

There was no contest, Aysha acknowledged with
lazy warmth a long time later as she lay curled
against a hard male body.

Neither had had the will to indulge in leisurely
lovemaking the first time round. It had been hard and
fast, each one of them *driven* by a primal urge so
intense it had been electrifying, wanton, and totally
impassioned.

Afterwards they had shared the Jacuzzi, then towelled dry, they'd returned to bed for a lingering aftermath of touching, tasting…a *loving* that had had
no equal in anything they'd previously shared.

'Are we going to tell our parents?'

Carlo brushed his chin against the top of her head. 'Let a slight change in wording to *reaffirmation* of vows do it for us on the day.'

CHAPTER ELEVEN

AYSHA woke to the sound of rain, and she took a moment to stretch her limbs, then she checked the bedside clock. A few minutes past seven.

Any time soon Teresa would knock on her door, and the day would begin.

If she was fortunate, she had an hour, maybe two, before Teresa began checking on everything from the expected delivery time of flowers…to the house, the church, the reception. Followed by a litany of re-minders that would initiate various supervisors to re-check arrangements with their minions. The wedding co-ordinator was doubtless on the verge of a nervous breakdown.

Aysha slid out from the bed and padded barefoot across the carpet to the draped window. A touch to the remote control module activated the mechanism that swept the drapes open, and she stifled a groan at the sight of heavy rain drenching the lawn.

Her mother, she knew, would consider it an omen, and probably not a propitious one.

Aysha selected shorts and a top, discarded her nightshirt, then quickly dressed. With a bit of celes-tial help she might make it downstairs to the dining room—

Her mobile phone rang, and she reached for it.

'Carlo?'

170

'Who else were you expecting?'

His deep voice did strange things to her senses, and the temptation to tease him a little was difficult to resist. 'Any one of my four bridesmaids, your mother, Nonna Benini, phoning from Treviso to wish me *buona fortuna*, Sister Maria Teresa…' she trailed off, and was unable to suppress a light laugh. 'Is there any particular reason you called?'

'Remind me to exact retribution, *cara*,' he mocked in husky promise.

The thought of precisely how he would achieve it curled round her central core, and set her heart beating at a quickened pace.

'You weren't there when I reached out in the night,' Carlo said gently. 'There was no scent of you on my sheets, no drift of perfume to lend assurance to my subconscious mind.' He paused for a few seconds. 'I missed you.'

She closed her eyes against the vivid picture his words evoked. She could feel her whole body begin to heat, her emotions separate and shred. 'Don't,' she pleaded with a slight groan. 'I have to get through the day.'

'Didn't sleep much, either, huh?' he queried wryly, and she wrinkled her nose.

'An hour or two, here and there,' Aysha admitted.

'Are you dressed?'

'Yes.' Her voice was almost prim, and he laughed.

'Pity. If I can't have you in the flesh, then the fantasy will have to suffice.'

'And you, of course, have had a workout, showered, shaved, and are about to eat breakfast?'

Carlo chuckled, a deep, throaty sound that sent shivers slithering down her spine. 'Actually, no. I'm lying in bed, conserving my energy.'

Just the thought of that long muscular body resting supine on the bed was enough to play havoc with her senses. Imagining how he might or might not be attired sent her pulse beating like a drum.

'I don't think we'd better do this.'

'Do *what*, precisely?'

'Phone sex.'

His voice held latent laughter. 'Is that what you think we're doing?'

'It doesn't compensate for the real thing.'

His soft laughter was almost her undoing. 'I doubt Teresa will be impressed if I appear at the door and sweep you into the bedroom before breakfast.'

A firm tattoo sounded against the panelled door. 'Aysha?'

The day was about to start in earnest. 'In a moment, Mamma.'

'Don't keep me waiting too long at the church, *cara*,' Carlo said gently as she crossed the room.

'To be five minutes late is obligatory,' she teased, twisting the knob and drawing back the door. '*Ciao.*'

Teresa stood framed in the doorway. '*Buon giorno*, darling.' Her eyes glanced at the mobile phone. 'You were talking to Carlo?' She didn't wait for an answer as she walked to the expanse of plate glass window with its splendid view of the harbour and northern suburbs. 'It's raining.'

'The service isn't scheduled until four,' Aysha attempted to soothe.

'Antonio has spent so much time and effort on the gardens these past few weeks. It will be such a shame if we can't assemble outside for photographs.'

'The wedding organiser has a contingency plan, Mamma.' Photographs in the conservatory, the massive entry foyer, the lounge.

'Yes, I know. But the garden would be perfect.'

Aysha sighed. The problem with a perfectionist was that rarely did *anything* meet their impossibly high expectations.

'Mamma,' she began gently. 'If it's going to rain, it will, and worrying won't make it different.' She crossed to the *en suite* bathroom. 'Give me a few minutes, then we'll go downstairs and share breakfast.'

It was the antithesis of a leisurely meal. The phone rang constantly, and at nine the first of the day's wedding gifts arrived by delivery van.

'Put them in here,' Teresa instructed, leading the way into a sitting room where a long table decorated with snowy white linen and draped tulle held a large collection of various sized wrapped and beribboned packages.

The doorchimes sounded. 'Aysha, get that, will you, darling? It'll probably be Natalina or Giovanna.'

The first in line of several friends who had offered their services to help.

'Aysha, you look so calm. How is that?'

Because Carlo loves me. And we're already married. The words didn't find voice, but they sang through her brain like the sweetest music she'd ever heard.

'Ask me again a few hours from now,' she said with a teasing smile.

Organisation was the key, although as the morning progressed the order changed to relative chaos and went downhill from there.

The florist delivered the bridal bouquets, exquisitely laid out in their boxes...except there was one missing. The men's buttonholes arrived with the bouquets, instead of being delivered to Gianna's home.

Soon after that problem was satisfactorily resolved Teresa received a phone call from one of the two women who'd offered to decorate the church pews...they couldn't get in, the church doors were locked, and no one appeared to be answering their summons.

Lunch was hardly an issue as time suddenly appeared to be of the essence, with the arrival of Lianna, Arianne, Suzanne and Tessa.

'*Très* chic, darling,' Lianna teased as she appraised Aysha from head to toe and back again. 'Bare feet, cut-off jeans and a skimpy top. The ultimate in avant-garde bridal wear. Just add the veil, and you'll cause a sensation,' she concluded with droll humour.

'Mamma would have a heart attack.'

'Not something to be countenanced,' Lianna agreed solemnly. 'Now,' she demanded breezily, 'we're all showered and ready to roll. Command, and we'll obey.'

Together they went over the *modus operandi*, which went a little haywire, as the hairdresser arrived early and the make-up artist was late.

There followed a lull of harmonious activity until

it became volubly clear Giuseppe was insistent on wearing navy socks instead of black, and an argument ensued, the pitch of frazzled voices rising when Teresa laddered new tights.

'Ah, your *mamma*...' Giuseppe sighed eloquently as he entered the dining room where the hairdresser was putting the finishing touches to Aysha's hair.

'I love you, Papà,' Aysha said softly, and saw his features dissolve into gentleness.

'*Grazie.*' His eyes moistened, and he blinked rapidly. 'The photographer, he will be here soon. Better you go upstairs and get into that dress, or we'll both have your Mamma to answer to, hmm.'

She gave him a quick hug, touched her fingers to his cheek, and smiled as he caught hold of them and bestowed a kiss to her palm. 'A father couldn't wish for a more beautiful daughter. Now go.'

When she reached her bedroom Teresa was fussing over the bridesmaids' gowns in a bid to ensure every detail was perfect.

Lianna rolled her eyes in silent commiseration, then exhibited the picture of genteel grace. 'When are the little terrors due to arrive?'

'My God,' Teresa cried with pious disregard as she swept to face Aysha. 'The rose petals. Did you see a plastic container of rose petals in the florist's box?'

Aysha shook her head, and Teresa turned and all but ran from the room.

'For heaven's sake, darling,' Lianna encouraged. 'Get into that fairy floss of a dress, we'll zip you up, stick on the headpiece and veil—' An anguished wail rent the air. 'Guess the rose petals were a no-show, huh?' she continued conversationally. 'I'll go offer my assistance before dear Teresa adds a nervous breakdown to the imminent heart attack.'

Ten minutes later she was back, and Aysha merely lifted one eyebrow in silent query.

'One container of rose petals found safe and sound at Gianna's home. As we need *two*, Giuseppe has been despatched to denude Antonio's precious rose bushes.'

'Whose idea was that?' Aysha shook her head in a silent gesture of mock despair. 'Don't tell me. Yours, right?'

Lianna executed a sweeping bow. 'Of course. What the hell else were we going to do?' She inclined her head, then gave a visible shudder. 'Here come the cavalry of infants.'

Aysha removed her wedding dress from its hanger, then with the girls' help she carefully stepped into it and eased it gently into place. The zip slid home, and she adjusted the scalloped lace at her wrist.

The fitted bodice with its overlay of lace was decorated with tiny seed pearls, and the scooped neckline displayed her shoulders to perfection. A full-length skirt flowed in a cluster of finely gathered pleats from her slender waist and fell in a cascade of lace. The veil was the finest tulle, edged with filigree lace and held in place by an exquisite head piece fashioned from seed pearls and tiny silk flowers.

'Wow,' Lianna, Arianne, Suzanne and Tessa accorded with reverence as she turned to face them, and Lianna, inevitably the first to speak, declared, 'You're a princess, sweetheart. A real princess.'

Lianna held out her hand, and, in the manner of a surgeon requesting instruments, she demanded, 'Shoes? Garter in place? Head piece and veil.' That took several minutes to fix. 'Something borrowed?' She tucked a white lace handkerchief into Aysha's hand. 'Something blue?' A cute bow tucked into the garter. 'Something old?'

Aysha touched the diamond pendant on its thin gold chain.

Teresa re-entered the room and came to an abrupt halt. 'The children are waiting downstairs with the photographer.' Her voice acquired a betraying huskiness. '*Dio Madonna*, I think I'm going to cry.'

'No, you're not. Think of the make-up,' Lianna cajoled. 'Then we'd have to do it óver, which would make us late.' She made a comical face. 'The mother of the bride gets to cry *after* the wedding.' She patted Teresa's shoulder with theatrical emphasis. 'Now's the time you launch yourself into your daughter's arms, assure her she's the most beautiful girl ever born, and any other mushy stuff you want to add. Then,' she declared with considerable feeling, 'we smile prettily while the photographer does his thing, and get the princess here to the church on time.'

Teresa's smile was shaky, definitely shaky, as she crossed to Aysha and placed a careful kiss on first one cheek, then the other. 'It's just beautiful.' She swallowed quickly. 'You're beautiful. Oh, dear—'

'Whoa,' Lianna cautioned. 'Time to go.'

The photographer took almost an hour, utilising indoor shots during a drizzling shower. Then miraculously the sun came out as they took their seats in

no fewer than three stretch limousines parked in line
on the driveway.

'Well, Papà, this is it,' Aysha said softly. 'We're
on our way.'

He reached out and patted her hand. 'You'll be
happy with Carlo.'

'I know.'

'Did I tell you how beautiful you look?'

Aysha's eyes twinkled with latent humour.
'Mamma chose well, didn't she?'

His answering smile held a degree of philosophical
acceptance. 'She has planned this day since you were
a little girl.'

The procession was slow and smooth as the cav-
alcade of limousines descended the New South Head
Road.

Stately, Aysha accorded silently as the first of the
cars slowed and turned into the church grounds.

There were several guests waiting outside, and
there was the flash of cameras as Giuseppe helped
her out from the rear seat.

Lianna and Arianne checked the hem of her gown,
smoothed the veil, then together they made their way
to the church entrance, where Suzanne and Tessa
were schooling the children into position.

The entire effect came together as a whole, and
Aysha took a moment to admire her bridal party.

Each of the bridesmaids wore burgundy silk off-
the-shoulder fitted gowns and carried bouquets of
ivory orchids. The flower girls wore ivory silk full-
length dresses with puffed sleeves and a wide waist-
band, tied at the back in a large bow, with white

shoes completing their attire, while the two page boys each wore a dark suit, white shirt with a paisley silk waistcoat and black bow-tie.

Teresa arrived, and Aysha watched as her mother distributed both satin ring cushions and supervised the little girls with their baskets of rose petals.

This was as much Teresa's day as it was hers, and she smiled as she took Giuseppe's arm. 'Ready, Papà?'

He was giving her into the care of another man, and it meant much to him, Aysha knew, that Carlo met with his full approval.

The organ changed tempo and began the 'Bridal March' as they entered the church, and Aysha saw Carlo standing at the front edge of the aisle, flanked by his best man and groomsmen.

Emily and Samantha strewed rose petals on the carpet in co-ordinated perfection. Neither Jonathon nor Gerard dropped the ring cushions.

As she walked towards Carlo he flouted convention and turned to face her. She saw the glimpse of fierce pride mingling with admiration, love meshing with adoration. Then he smiled. For her, only for her.

Everything else faded to the periphery of her vision, for she saw only him, and her smile matched his own as she moved forward and stood at his side.

Carlo reached for her hand and covered it with his own as the priest began the ceremony.

The substitution *reaffirmation* of their vows seemed to take on an electric significance as the guests assimilated the change of words.

Renewed pledges, the exchange of rings, and the

long, passionate kiss that undoubtedly would become a topic of conversation at many a dinner table for months to come.

There was music, not the usual hymn, but a poignant song whose lyrics brought a lump to many a guest's throat. A few feminine tears brought the use of fine cotton handkerchiefs when the groom leaned forward and gently kissed his bride for the second time.

Then Aysha took Carlo's arm and walked out of the church and into the sunshine to face a barrage of photographers.

It was Lianna who organised the children and cajoled them to behave with decorum during the photographic shoot. Aysha hid a smile at the thought they were probably so intimidated they didn't think to do anything but obey.

'She's going to drive some poor man mad,' Carlo declared with a musing smile, and Aysha laughed, a low, sparkling sound that was reflected in the depths of her eyes.

'And he'll adore every minute of it,' she predicted.

The shift to the reception venue was achieved on schedule, and Aysha turned to look at Carlo as their limousine travelled the short distance from the church.

'You were right,' she said quietly. 'I wouldn't have missed the church service for the world.'

His smile melted her bones, and her stomach executed a series of crazy somersaults as he took her hands to his lips and kissed each one in turn.

'I'll carry the image of you walking towards me down the aisle for the rest of my life.'

She traced a gentle finger down the vertical crease of his cheek and lingered at the edge of his mouth. 'Now we get to cut the cake and drink champagne.'

'And I get to dance with my wife.'

'Yes,' she teased mercilessly. 'After the speeches, the food, the photographs…'

'Then I get to take you home.'

Oh, my. She breathed unsteadily. How was she going to get through the next few hours?

With the greatest of ease, she reflected several hours later as they circled the guests and made their farewells.

Teresa deserved tremendous credit, for without doubt she had staged the production of her dreams and turned it into the wedding of the year. Press coverage, the media, the church, ceremony, catering, cake… Everything had gone according to plan, except for a few minor hiccups.

A very special day, and one Aysha would always treasure. But it was the evening she and Carlo had exchanged their wedding vows that would remain with her for the rest of her life.

Saying goodbye to her parents proved an emotional experience, for among their happiness and joy she could sense a degree of sadness at her transition from daughter to wife.

Tradition died hard, and Aysha hugged them tight and conveyed her appreciation not only for the day and the night, but for the care and devotion they'd accorded her from the day she was born.

There was confetti, rice, and much laughter as they escaped to the limousine. A short drive to an inner city hotel, and then the ascent by lift to the suite Carlo had booked for the night.

Aysha gave a startled gasp as he released the door then swept her into his arms and carried her inside.

'Now,' he began teasingly, as he pulled her close. 'I get to do this.'

This was a very long, intensely passionate kiss, and she just held on and clung as she met and matched his raw, primitive desire.

Then he gently released her and crossed to the table, where champagne rested on ice.

Aysha watched as Carlo loosened the cork on the bottle of champagne.

Froth spilled from the neck in a gentle spume, and she laughed softly as he picked up a flute to catch the foaming liquid.

'I've done that successfully at least a hundred times.' He partly filled another, then he handed her one, and touched the rim with his own. 'To us.'

Her mouth curved to form a generous smile, and her eyes... A man could drown in those luminous grey depths, at times mysterious, winsome, wicked. Today they sparkled with warmth, laughter and love. He wanted to reach out and pull her into his arms. Hold and absorb her until she was part of him, and never let go.

'Happiness, always,' said Aysha gently, and sipped the fine champagne.

He placed the bottle and the flute down onto the

coffee table, then he gently cradled her face between both hands.

'I love you.' His mouth closed over hers in a soft, open-mouthed kiss which reduced her to a quivering boneless mass.

'Have I told you how beautiful you looked today?' Carlo queried long minutes later.

After three times she'd stopped counting. 'Yes,' she teased, pressing a finger against the centre of his lower lip. Her eyes dilated as he took the tip into his mouth and began to caress it slowly with his tongue.

Heat suffused her veins, coursing through her body until she was on fire with need.

'There's just one thing.'

He buried his mouth in its palm. 'Anything.'

'Fool,' she accorded gently, and watched in fascination as his expression assumed a seriousness that was at variance with the day, the hour, the moment.

'Anything, *cara*,' he repeated solemnly. 'Any time, anywhere. All you have to do is ask.'

She closed her eyes, then slowly opened them. It frightened her to think she had so much power over this man. It was a quality she intended to treat with the utmost respect and care.

'I have something for you.'

'I don't need anything,' Carlo assured her. 'Except *you*.'

She kissed him briefly. 'I'm not going anywhere.' What she sought reposed within easy reach, and she took the few steps necessary to extract the white envelope, then she turned and placed it in his hand.

'*Cara*? What is this?'

A telephone call, specific instructions, a lecture on the necessity to protect her interests, and time out in a very hectic schedule to attach her signature in the presence of her legal advisor.

'Open and read it.'

Carlo's eyes sharpened as he extracted the neatly pinned papers, and as he unfolded and began to scan the affidavit it became apparent what she'd done.

He lowered the papers and regarded her carefully. 'Aysha—'

'I love you. I always have, for as long as I can remember.' She thought she might die from the intensity of it. 'I always will.'

It was a gift beyond price. 'I know.' Carlo's voice was incredibly gentle. Just as his love for her would endure. It was something he intended to reinforce every day for the rest of his life.

'Come here,' he bade softly, extending his arms, and she went into them gladly, wrapping her own round his waist as he enfolded her close.

The papers fluttered to the floor as his lips covered hers, and she gave herself up to the sensual magic that was theirs alone.

Heaven didn't get much better than this, Aysha mused dreamily as he swept an arm beneath her knees and strode towards the stairs.

'*Ti amo,*' she whispered. '*Ti amo.*'

Carlo paused and took possession of her mouth with his own in a kiss that held so much promise she almost wept. '*In eterno.*' Eternity, and beyond.

Margaret Way takes great pleasure in her work and works hard at her pleasure. She enjoys tearing off to the beach with her family at weekends, loves haunting galleries and auctions and is completely given over to French champagne 'for every possible joyous occasion'. She was born and educated in the river city of Brisbane, Australia, and now lives within sight and sound of beautiful Moreton Bay.

Look out for Margaret Way's brilliant new mini-series *Koomera Crossing*:

RUNAWAY WIFE – August
OUTBACK BRIDEGROOM – October
OUTBACK SURRENDER – December

All brought to you by Tender Romance™!

MAIL-ORDER MARRIAGE

by

Margaret Way

CHAPTER ONE

When he reached the top of Warinna Ridge he reined his bay mare a few short of the cliff face. This was a favourite aboriginal resting place when on walkabout and a magnetic spot for him, too; the best vantage point on the whole of Jabiru. From the high elevation he could look down on the herd scattered over the shimmering, wonderful, emerald-green valley. From umber to emerald. All it took was a drop of rain. Only this time they got a mighty deluge courtesy Cyclone Amy. Danger was a woman, didn't they say? Now the danger had passed.

The rich-coated Brahmans with their distinctive floppy ears, dewlaps and humps didn't have to walk anywhere to graze. The country all around them was in splendid condition now that the floodwaters had withdrawn. Paruna Creek and the Oolong Swamp, home to countless waterbirds, pelicans, swans, ducks, brolgas, magpie geese, the jabirus, the large tropical storks that gave the station its name, were running a bumper and the cattle grazed face-high in rippling pastures. Blue and green couch, para grass, spear grass, you name it. The richest green feed any herd could need to thrive and fatten.

Deep pools of water like miniature lagoons glittered in the metallic noonday sun, a heat haze rising off the surface creating an illusion of hot mineral springs. The pools were everywhere, natural cooling-off spots for the herd, numbers of them wallowing in the silver lakes.

Cherish the earth, he thought, some of the restlessness in his mind quietening as he looked out over a vista that ravished the eye. It was still very hot and humid but a light aromatic breeze scented so sweetly of sandalwood cooled his dark-tanned skin. Though he had a million and one other things to do, it was hard to tear himself away. He looked for a long time, drawing strength from the land. Jabiru filled him with such a sense of pride, of achievement. Not bad for a kid born on the wrong side of the blanket. Nevertheless he felt the taste of bitterness on his tongue. Maybe he would never get rid of it.

The distant hills, spurs of the Great Dividing Range that separated the hinterland from the lush coastal strip, glowed a deep pottery purple, the colour the Aboriginal artist Namitjira had used so wonderfully. An extraordinary brilliance lay over the land. It gave him infinite pleasure. A compensation for the loneliness and isolation. Sometimes at night on long rides under the stars he felt at absolute peace. That wasn't easy for a man like him. Not that Jabiru was a glamour property. It was a lean commercial operation geared for results.

Jabiru cattle were becoming sought after now. But, God, it had taken years and years of backbreaking toil. Now, when he was starting to realise the rewards, he had no one to share it with. Not a soul. There had only ever been him and his mother. Going from town to town. Never staying long enough anywhere to be accepted, until they had come up to tropical North Queensland, over a thousand miles from where they had started, where no one went hungry or cold.

Abundant tropical fruit dropped off the trees, superb beef was cheap, the rivers and the glorious blue sea teemed with fish, and the weather ranged from halcyon to plain torrid.

He'd been around twelve at the time. A difficult age for a boy. At least it had been for him, his mum's protector. His mother, always so very pretty but so soft and vulnerable, had found permanent work helping out in a pub. Marcy Graham, the publican's wife, had taken the two of them under her wing. A good sort was Marcy. The sort that prompted the accolade "heart of gold." They had even lived at the pub for a time until Marcy found them a bungalow they could afford on the outskirts of town. It had been lonely but beautiful on the edge of the mysterious, green rainforest. He even got used to the snakes, mostly harmless. His mum never did.

It had taken a long time to make friends at the local school. Something about him made the other kids keep their distance. He had a wicked temper for one thing, mainly because he wouldn't take the least little gibe about his mother or him. And there had been plenty in those early days. He was tall for his age and strong. It had only taken a couple of fights for the bully boys to get the message.

It wasn't until he was around fourteen and the efforts of the school principal had paid off he found himself with the reputation for being "clever." He didn't know how it happened. He had missed out on so much schooling moving around, yet when he decided to throw himself into it—after all it was he who had to look after his mum—he took off like a rocket. He had graduated from high school with the highest score of any student, giving him the pick of the universities when places were hotly contested. Hell, he could even have become a doctor, a scientist, or a lawyer, only there was no money for all that stuff.

"It's a shame!" Bill Carroll, his old headmaster, told his mother, bewildered to be so confronted. "Matthew could have a great future. He could be anything he sets his mind to."

Only he was a cattleman. And hell, he enjoyed it. He thrived on it. Even when he was living a life of near slavery he'd been happy. He hadn't been able to realise any dream of university but he'd brought the brain and the spirit of an achiever to bear on all his endeavours.

It was Marcy who found him a job as a jackeroo on Luna Downs. Filthy rich absentee owner, swine of a manager. Absolute swine: he had made all the young guys' lives hell, but he got square for all of them before he left.

Once he was old enough—he was plenty strong enough—he bought a very rough slice of scrub with what he thought of then as a hefty loan from the local bank. Somehow despite his youth he had convinced the bank manager he could turn the wilderness into a viable cattle empire. Finally he had sold it three years ago for a handsome profit, launching a full-scale assault on Jabiru.

Jabiru was owned by the Gordon family. In their heyday the Gordons had held significant pastoral holdings, but times had changed. Jabiru had been allowed to run down. Everyone in the business knew it would take a lot of hard work to get it up and running again. Then, everyone knew he wasn't afraid of hard work. It worked for him, too, old man Gordon had taken quite a shine to him.

Of course Gordon knew the story. Everyone did. There were no secrets in the Outback. He was the skeleton in the closet. Jock Macalister's son. Illegitimate son. Difficult to hide it when even he knew he was the image of him as a young man. Sir John Macalister, nowadays referred to as the grand old man of the cattle industry. Macalister had three beautiful daughters but he had never conceived a son in wedlock. Wasn't that sad? He didn't even have a grandson to inherit. The daughters had married, had children. All girls. Perhaps it was the Big Fella up there getting square with Jock's dishonourable past.

His mother had always sworn Macalister had never forced himself upon her. He could have, as he flew around his cattle empire enjoying the traditional *droit de seigneur.* His mother, then working as a sort of nanny on one of Macalister's properties, swore she had wanted him as much as he had wanted her. Only when their relationship was suspected, she found herself shown the road by ''The Missus,'' her immediate employer, who gave her enough money to move far away. Macalister was the Boss; a man with a reputation that needed upholding if necessary by his staff. He was already married to the Mondale heiress at the time. With two small children to think about. Matthew's mother had been young, pretty. In the final analysis—*forgettable.*

He would have been, too, except for his red setter hair, the jet-black brows and his unusually blue eyes. Struth! He even had the same chiselled cleft in his chin. It hadn't taken that North Queensland town a week to uncover their secret.

He was Jock Macalister's kid. Only the rich and powerful Macalisters would never accept that. He had never set eyes on his so-called "father" in his life, though he had seen him plenty of times in the newspapers or on television. He wouldn't actually like to confront the old man. Only Sir John's age would prevent him from being beaten up.

Matthew's own burden in life was grief. Too deep for words. His mother had been killed two years before. She and a few friends had been enjoying a night out on the town, a night which ended in tragedy. His mother and her current boyfriend, not a bad guy, had inexplicably taken a wrong turn. They knew the area well, but ended up in a swollen canal. The dangers of drinking. The car with them in it had been fished out the next day. The same day he had been flown in by the police helicopter to identify the bodies. My God!

"You need to understand your mother, Red," Marcy had tried to console him. "She always felt so alone."

Alone? Who, then, was he? A nobody? He had worked like a slave getting a better home for his mother. It had been far too rough to take her out into the bush. Not that she would have gone. His mother loved people. But he had always provided her with money. Always made the journey into town looking like a wild man with his too long hair and beard, to see how she was faring. She couldn't have been too lonely. There was always a man. A couple of them he had personally thrown out.

His mother had come from England to Australia with her parents as a little girl. All had gone well for some years until her parents split up. She had stayed with her mother who eventually remarried.

"I never got on with my stepfather," was all his mother ever said, but anyone could read between the lines. His mother, pretty as a picture, was simply a born victim. It made him feel quite violent towards his natural father whose life must hide a multitude of sins.

He went by his mother's surname, of course, Carlyle, and his first name came from the grandfather in England she remembered with such affection. Matthew. But no one had ever called him anything but Red. No one outside his mother who always called him Matty even when he topped six-two and his body had developed hard muscle power. Well perhaps there were one or two others. His old headmaster and a Miss Westwood who had taught him to love books. Books were a great relaxation for a man who led a very solitary life. Not that he was a monk. He found time for women. There always seemed to be plenty but he picked ones who knew the score. No laying traps for any vulnerable little girls. And he took good care he never made one of them pregnant. That would have been carrying on the sins of his father.

Matthew lifted his battered akubra and raked a hand through his thick too long hair—heck, it touched the collar of his denim shirt, then set it back low down over his eyes. The sun was throwing back searing silver reflections off the serpentine line of the creek and multiple pools. He had five men working for him now, two part Aboriginals. Wonderful bushmen, stockmen and trackers. He wouldn't swap them for the top jackeroos off any of the stations. And they were real characters, always ready for a laugh despite the endless backbreaking work. He had no troubles with the other men, either, all tough self-reliant, occasionally given to terrible binges in town when he had to take the four-wheel drive on the long journey and haul them back home.

What he needed now was a woman. The right woman. But how the hell was she to be found? He didn't have the time to start up any courting. His life was packed from predawn to dusk and then he was too damned tired to throw himself into the Jeep and drive a couple of hundred kilometres into town. And back. He was thirty-four now. He was well on the way to seeing results, so he kept thinking about starting a little dynasty of his own. From scratch. He had no past anyone wanted to acknowledge. His much-loved and despaired-over mother was dead. He wanted family, he wanted kids of his own. He wanted to make something of his life. Only there would never be a woman he'd force or a child he'd abandon.

Late that afternoon, icy-cold beer in hand, he sat on the veranda of the modest homestead he had built himself, breathing in the pure aromatic air and contemplating his future. Single-storey, the bungalow had its feet planted in the rich tropical earth, a wide veranda that ran the length of the house and a roof that came down like a great shady hat. To him who had never had a real home it seemed like a miracle. It was then as he rocked back and forth, a solution of sorts came to him.

Why not advertise for a wife? Frontier men had had to advertise in the old days. In a way Jabiru was still frontier country. If he kept to what he really *wanted* in a wife he might weed out the empty-headed adventuress or the woman who just wanted to find herself a home.

The idea kept his mind occupied while he prepared himself a solitary but far from don't-give-a-damn dinner. Beef, of course. He ate lots of it and even if the health freaks had cut it out of their diet, the last time he'd seen Doc Sweeney in town he'd been labelled a superbly fit individual. So, grilled eye fillet served up with all the freshly picked salad greens he could lay his hands on.

Aboriginal Charlie, who must have been a Chinese market gardener in another life, had quite a garden going. Different kinds of lettuce, lots of herbs, cucumbers, peppers, tomatoes, shallots—you name it. Waxy little potatoes that came up so clean from the red volcanic soil they only needed a brush off to shine. There were already thirty or more avocado trees on the property that fruited heavily to add the finishing touch.

He didn't allow himself to fall into the habit of eating junk food or those frozen meals plenty of guys on their own settled for. He sat down to a civilised table, a couple of checked tablecloths he got Marcy to buy for him, decent plates.

"Damn it, I'm a civilised man," he told himself. His mother, very dainty herself, had instilled manners in him. He would offend no woman with rough talk or crude ways. Breeding had triumphed, he thought ironically. One day when he could, he would find his mother's family in England. Look them up.

Right now, an enormous gulf separated him from his roots. His maternal grandparents were dead. He knew that much. Strange, his mother had never attempted to go home. Was it pride, or a kind of shame? When he thought about her, which was every day, his heart, or what passed for it, broke. He shook his head. I've got to get a life. And a life means a woman. *A wife.*

CHAPTER TWO

It SHOULD have been perfect holidaying up here in the blue and gold tropics, but something was missing. It's a long time since I felt good, Cassie realised. Not that it seemed to matter to anyone. Not to her estranged socialite mother who spent her whole life partying and really had never wanted her. She'd had a nanny almost from the moment she was born. A nanny she had come to love until, when she was seven, Rose left.

She had a clear mental picture of herself running into her mother's bedroom after school, her eyes filled with a tearful dread. "Where is she? What happened to her?"

"Don't be tiresome, Cassandra." Her mother, seated at the dressing table, had waved her away. "The usual reason. You're too old for a nanny."

"But why couldn't we say goodbye?" All these years later she could still feel the terrible pull in her throat.

"Why? Because I can well do without your hysterics," her mother had said firmly, turning back to the mirror that showed her elegant reflection in triplicate. "You're growing up now, Cassandra, and you have to move on to a new stage. You're going to boarding school. St. Catherine's, the very best. I expect you to get used to the idea. Daddy and I will be doing a lot of travelling this year. All connected to the business."

Which simply wasn't true. Daddy was a very rich businessman who felt vaguely ill-at-ease with a small

14

girl. Tall, strikingly handsome, seldom at home. But whenever he saw Cassie he patted her kindly on the head then vanished again.

It was a big thing for her, going to boarding school. She learned quickly and, in the end she actually enjoyed it. She made good friends and became very popular both with her peers and the staff. She was head girl in her last year. The top student. That had her parents drooling. With her little successes they moved closer, expressing their pleasure in her achievements. Even better, she had grown from a rather frail, pale child into a highly gratifying reflection of her father's side of the family. Aunt Marian especially, a perennial beauty. There was a general feeling she had turned out rather well.

"It does a child no good at all to smother them with affection," her mother once told her friend Julie's mother, in Cassie's hearing. "Look at Cassie. While Stuart and I were off adventuring, she grew up, became self-reliant."

Julie's mother had smiled back, but the smile never did reach her eyes. Cassie always got the feeling though her mother was always invited everywhere and appeared to have scores of friends, it was just *noise*. No one genuinely *cared* about her. How could they when she had nothing to give?

As soon as she possibly could, Cassie tracked down her darling Rose living quietly in a dreary flat. They had fallen into each other's arms reliving the old grief of separation. She had set Rose up nicely. They couldn't stop her. She was eighteen and had come into a good deal of money, a legacy from her maternal grandmother who had always spoken up for her and was outraged when she was shunted off to boarding school. Grandma had died too early. There had been long-running differences between her grandmother and mother. Mostly about her.

"She might look like me, but honestly I don't know where your mother came from," Grandma often remarked. "Some other planet. Very cold."

Grandma had left Cassie well off. Something that shocked her mother out of her mind. It was a dreadful sin she had been excluded from the will except for a very valuable jade collection she had long coveted.

At university Cassie had a mild eating disorder. Not anorexia or anything like it, but still a bit of a problem. God knows what that was all about, but anyway she got over it. Maybe she'd been trying to take control of her own life. Her own body. Though she did extremely well with her studies, so far as her parents were concerned that was filling in time. Her job was to get married and marry well. Her mother introduced her around relentlessly and found her just the right man. God, he was awful. It was around that time she found the guts to challenge her mother. On *everything*. Instead of shutting up and going away, she found a highly articulate tongue. Heck, hadn't she been a valued member of the University Debating Group?

"What are you trying to do to me, Cassandra?" her mother had cried, off balance with the shock. "You're tearing me to strips."

She had no choice but to leave home. It was never hers anyway. Her mother and herself were very different people. Her father was a benevolent fringe figure. She realised now, in her various relationships since, she had always been looking for a father figure. The men she had gone out with were mostly older, wiser, established in their professions, but alas, no spark, no flame to feed on.

I wish I could share with someone, Cassie thought. I wish I could run into strong comforting arms. I wish I could look at a man with love and respect. Wishful thinking more like it! A consequence of her pretty dreadful childhood. She prayed if she ever became a mother she would know how to show love.

The sun was getting too hot, Cassie noticed now.

She moved languidly off the recliner and stood up. Another dip in the aquamarine pool then she and Julie could start thinking about lunch. Maybe that wonderful little Italian place built on a ridge overlooking the sea. The seafood up here was out of this world, fresh from the Reef waters and straight onto the table. Second thought, pasta. She loved pasta. Who didn't? Hadn't the ancient Etruscans made pasta? The Chinese? Didn't they make *everything?* Marco Polo was supposed to have enjoyed delicious pasta in China. Pasta and noodles were essentially the same thing. Many a time she'd tossed either pasta or noodles with a simple tomato, basil and extra-virgin olive oil sauce.

She was the cook here. Julie, her friend from their very first day at St. Catherine's was almost totally undomesticated. Sometimes it came with the territory. Cassie herself had barely been inside a kitchen until she had moved out of her parents' house. Her parents had a housekeeper, an excellent cook who presided over her domain jealously. Her father had a full-time chauffeur, as well.

Julie's father, head of the stockbroking firm for which they both worked, was a lovely man. Her mother, who did a great deal of charity work along with the partying, was lovely, too. Lucky Julie! It was their tropical hideaway—really a fabulous retreat—she and Julie were staying at. They were supposed to have come up much earlier, but Cyclone Amy had put a halt to that. They had had to wait a full month before things settled down and the weather returned to glorious. Now they would dress in something easy and go into town.

"Why not try the pub?" Julie suggested when they were out on the sea road. "They have a nice little setup out the back. The food's supposed to be very good. Heck—" she swung her head to admire the splendid produce in one of the many roadside stalls fronting the local farms "—can you believe the tropical fruit? The size and the variety. I don't recognise half of it."

Cassie sat stiffly upright, her face paling. "Goodness, Julie. Watch out!" A station wagon was rapidly approaching them and Julie, in a hired BMW—she didn't know how to drive anything else—was holding the middle of the road like some hooligan playing chicken.

"Sorry." Julie corrected her positioning with a loud gulp that turned into contrite giggles.

"In the interests of survival, I think I'll drive," Cassie said firmly. Julie had developed the very risky habit of turning her head to look at things when she should have been focused on the road. It was more pronounced up here where the scenery was astonishingly beautiful and the sea road was bordered on one side by an almost continuous rampart of blossoming white bougainvillea like great foaming breakers, on the other, the crystal blue seascape. "People like you need a chauffeur."

"Yeah. Like your dad. Spoken to him lately?" Julie asked wryly, knowing full well the answer.

"I plug away but I think he's aware I've gone missing."

Julie shook her head. "You've had a terrible time, Cass."

"Only with my parents," Cassie quipped, but didn't smile. "Pull over, lady." She did her imitation of a traffic cop. "Like *now*." Life mightn't be all that brilliant but she didn't fancy going off one of the steep slopes.

They were both standing at the side of the road getting ready to change positions when a dusty four-wheel drive with a formidable bull bar pulled up alongside them.

"Everything okay?" The driver, a man, lowered his head to look out at them.

Cassie, overcome by an intensity of awareness, stood rooted, but Julie let out a quite audible, "Wow!"

"Excuse me?" One distinctively black eyebrow shot up, mockery laced with a certain amount of mischief.

Cassie predictably was the first to gather her wits. "We're fine, thank you," her breath expelled on a rush of air as she tried to overcome her confusion. "Just changing drivers."

"Well, take care then." Brilliant blue eyes sought and challenged her gaze. "Next time I wouldn't pull up quite so close to the edge. We've had a lot of rain. There could be slippage."

"Many thanks." Cassie gave a quick jerk of her head, wondering why she was behaving like she was.

"No problem." He lifted a hand to her, the intensity of his own gaze undimmed.

The engine of the four-wheel drive started up with a roar, another brief salute and he was off.

They were silent for quite a few moments, then Julie burst out in amazed ecstasy. "Did you see that, Cass? That had to be the best-looking guy I've ever seen in my life. Colouring to die for! Dark red hair, copper skin, jet-black eyebrows, the hottest blue eyes on the planet. Where has he been all my life?"

"Out bush." Cassie was surprised her voice sounded normal. "At a guess, I'd say he's a cattleman on one of his periodic forays into town. The long hair and the physique, the gear."

"Boy!" Julie gave a feline growl. "Talk about ten years searching for my hero. I've found him." She gave Cassie a little punch on the arm. "Sure he wasn't an apparition?"

"I'm hoping not," Cassie laughed, suddenly sounding exuberant.

"So let's get our skates on," Julie urged, running to the passenger side of the car. "It'll take us another twenty minutes to get into town."

They recognised the battered four-wheel drive parked outside the pub. "What did I tell you? The best people eat here!" Julie crowed in delight.

"No." Cassie was surprised by her own reluctance. Normally she might have seen it as a bit of fun. But that guy, stunning as he was, wasn't a man to be trifled with.

Julie stared at her friend in amazement. "If you say you weren't impressed, you're lying in your teeth."

"He's very handsome, I agree."

Julie shook her blond head. "Handsome doesn't say it. I thought I was going to swoon."

"All right, he's terrific," Cassie conceded, yanking the thin strap of her camisole top back onto her shoulder. "But kind of dangerous, didn't you think?"

"As in what?" Julie reluctantly considered it. Cassie was extremely smart. Even her dad said so and he was sparing with the praise. "I thought he was very gallant, stopping like that."

"Well, we're not exactly bad-looking are we," Cassie retorted. "I know he wasn't giving us any come-on, rather the reverse, but he looked pretty complicated, complex, not your ordinary kind of guy. I'd say he's done a lot of living and done it hard."

"Heck, you noticed a lot." Julie, as usual, was impressed. "All I latched onto was the beauty of those *eyes!*"

"I know." Cassie smiled. "I saw the lightning strike. Don't follow it up, Julie. I'm only speaking in your best interests. Guys like that need a sign around their neck—Beware."

"Cassie, don't worry. Trust me." Julie shook her friend's arm. "Everything will be sweet. I only want to see him again. See if he's as stunning as I thought. Probably he'll sound like a redneck as soon as he opens his mouth."

Marcy looked up as the two young women entered the pub. She knew who they were, or she knew the cute little blond one, always laughing, shoulders bobbing, staring around her with wide blue-eyed interest. She was the daughter of the rich couple, the Maitlands, the people who had built a luxury retreat out at Aurora Bay. Marcy, who liked to give people private nicknames, called her Blondy. The other one was Sable.

She'd seen her a couple of times around town. Hard to miss her. Where the little blonde was pretty, her friend totally eclipsed her. Mane of darkest brown into black hair like a luxurious fur pelt so thick it formed a swirling hood around her face. Light, luminous eyes like a river in the rain, polished skin. She was tall and very slender, but healthy-looking, vibrant. The two of them were dressed almost exactly the same. White cotton jeans so tight they looked like they'd been poured on, little-nothing tops that made the most of high young breasts and delicate shoulders. The heads were already turning, as well they might.

To have looked like that even for a day, Marcy thought. "Can I help you, girls?" she greeted them with her wide infectious smile.

"Yes, please." Sable approached. For all her classy look she wasn't uppity. Nice and friendly. "I'm Cassie Stirling. This is my friend, Julie Maitland. We're staying at Julie's parents' place on the point."

As though I don't know everything that goes on in the town, Marcy thought. "Yes, I know, luv." She nodded pleasantly. "Aurora Bay. Big terracotta place on the point."

"That's it!" Julie moved up to join her friend at the counter. "We thought we might do lunch." She had an appealing slightly breathless delivery, but there was a touch of patronising there absent in her friend.

"Glad to have you," Marcy said. 'You're not looking for anyone are you?" Blondy was all but standing on tiptoes looking around.

"You have to understand this is confidential." The girl bent to Marcy with a stage whisper. "We're hard on the track of a gorgeous-looking guy with hair like a dark flame and burning blue eyes. We had an idea he might have come in here.''

''Well, you had the idea.'' Cassie coloured, wishing Julie would shut up.

''That would be Red. Red Carlyle.'' Marcy told them matter-of-factly, picking up a cloth and wiping off the already spotless counter.

''You know him?'' Julie asked hopefully.

''Twenty years and more.''

''Not married, is he?'' Julie asked.

''Funny you should say that.'' Marcy gave them a rather sardonic smile. ''He's advertisin' for a wife.''

''Then that's definitely not the one,'' Sable said.

''There's only one Red.'' Marcy shook her head. ''Matter of fact, the ad is in the local paper.''

''You're having us on, aren't you?'' Julie pulled a little face.

Sable smiled, too, but in a special way, kind of tender, Marcy thought. For some reason Marcy associated smiles like that with people who carried an inner sorrow. Red had a smile like that. Dazzling, lighting up his whole face, but with something that tugged at the heartstrings. At least that's what Marcy had always thought.

''What's wrong with the women of this town?'' Sable was asking with a humorous tilt of her brows.

''A man like that on the loose!'' Blondy rolled her eyes.

''Works too hard, that's his problem,'' Marcy told them. ''How's he ever gonna find a wife when he spends all his time on Jabiru?''

''And may I ask what Jabiru is?'' Blondy spoke in a facetious fashion that didn't do her justice. ''Make sense to you, Cass?'' Looking amused, she turned her head.

''I'm sure it's a property of some kind. A cattle station probably.'' Cassie gave Julie a little quelling shake of the head.

''Right in one,'' Marcy announced cheerfully. ''Red runs Brahmans. Very hardy breed. They do very well right throughout the North where the British breeds can't survive.''

''How interesting,'' said Julie. ''And this—Jabiru, is it *big?*''

''Up here, girlie, we take vastness for granted,'' Marcy said bluntly. She was starting to tire a little of Blondy, something that wasn't lost on her friend.

''Would you have a table for two free?'' Cassie intervened. By now she really wanted to get out of the pub but she was loath to offend this nice, cheerful woman with the smile lines creasing her vibrant green eyes.

''Sure, luv.'' Marcy reached under the counter and retrieved the local paper folded over to the page that carried Red's astonishing advertisement. She was still trying to take it in. All Red had to do was turn up Saturday night when the pub was full and holler. Chances are he would get knocked down in the stampede. ''The one with the ring around it.'' She stabbed the paper for emphasis. ''You can read it while you're waiting for lunch.''

The courtyard expanded magically, wonderfully, a cool and shadowy place with masses of flowers in pots, great baskets of ferns suspended from the rafters, latticed walls dripping with a dusky rose bougainvillea, circular tables, green and white bordered cloths, garden chairs. There was a lot of laughter, a lot of talking, with everyone dressed very casually, tourists and locals. It was almost full. Every male to a man gave the girls long appreciative looks. One around their own age raised his hand indicating there was plenty of room at his table. But Marcy ignored him, showing them towards the rear with its green-gold bars of light for all the world like the sun pouring through stained-glass panels.

"This is enchanting," Cassie said, gazing around her with real pleasure.

"We think so, Luv." Marcy was pleased. She and Bill had put quite an effort into getting it right. She stopped at a table for two centred like the others with a bud vase holding a spray of the lovely Cooktown orchid, the State flower. "Anything to drink?"

Both girls chose mineral water with lime.

"You'll find the chef's suggestions posted on the board." Marcy waved a plump arm towards the blackboard. "I'm sure you'll find something you fancy. Coral trout. Red Emperor, straight from the trawler. Gulf prawns big as bananas. We could make up a lovely seafood platter for two if you like. The crab is superb."

"I know, heavenly!" Cassie's mouth started to water.

"Think it over. I'll be back in a few minutes to take your order." Marcy started to move off, then turned. "By the way, Red will be in shortly. He has some business down the road."

The Lord works in strange ways, Marcy thought. The girl, Cassie, with the eyes clear as diamonds and her obviously privileged background, was at a crossroads in her life. There was something missing. Someone. Marcy had a sure instinct about such things. Bill often told her she had the second sight inherited they both thought from her Scottish grandmother. Besides, there wasn't anything she wouldn't do for Red.

Less than ten minutes later as the girls exclaimed over the delicious seafood platter Marcy was setting before them, Red Carlyle appeared at the entrance to the courtyard, instantly creating his own force field. He was greeted on all sides with shouts and waves, lifting an all-encompassing hand in acknowledgment. His gaze ranged over the courtyard for a moment until he caught sight of Marcy's short plump figure. Immediately he began to stride towards her, moving with such grace and pent-up energy, Cassie felt a thrust of excitement in the pit of her stomach. He had such a blaze about him she felt like ducking her head. He was heading towards them, abundant dark red hair swept back, touching the collar of his blue denim shirt. No short back and sides for him. The remarkable eyes glowed turquoise, sweeping over the girls as Marcy moved her body to follow the girls' stare.

"Red!" She greeted him with motherly pleasure.

He smiled and Cassie found herself gripping the arms of her chair. This was the man who was *advertising* for a wife? Why, he was so handsome, so vibrant, it made her eyes smart to look at him. The dark blue gaze was on her now, a long measuring scrutiny, then on Julie, who had her pretty pink mouth open like a fish.

"Well, I see you made it safely into town." He softly shook his head as though he was surprised.

"You know these young ladies, Red?" Marcy executed a double take.

"We passed one another back on the road. Didn't get to names."

"I'm Julie Maitland," Julie piped up, giving her best Drew Barrymore smile. "This is my friend—"

"Cassandra Stirling." Cassie wanted to identify herself.

"*Cassandra?* As in, daughter of Priam King of Troy?" He looked at her with those amazing eyes, the same long steady assessment.

"You'd better believe it," Julie quipped. The original Cassandra had been condemned by Apollo to prophetise correctly but never be believed.

"A beautiful dangerous name for a beautiful, dangerous woman," Matthew responded, seeing a woman he could want badly but was hopelessly out of reach. Her eyes put him in mind of a silver river, the lining lashes as thick as inky-black ferns. Skin like magnolia silk, lovely long neck. Dire consequences were attached to wanting a woman like that and he wasn't a man to long for things beyond hope of fulfilment.

"Red Carlyle." He introduced himself. "I wasn't christened that. My ma called me Matthew after my grandad in England, but it took less than a week to be rechristened up here."

"Gorgeous hair, that's why!" Marcy grasped a handful, fixing him with an affectionate gaze. He towered over her by a good foot. "I was telling the girls, here, you've been advertising for a bride."

Perhaps he would be embarrassed! He wasn't. Unflappable. A touch speculative.

"Sure have. Saves a lot of time. Only *one* thing. The frivolous needn't apply. A serious offer demands a serious response."

Julie raised her eyebrows, plainly dumbfounded. "It's hard to believe any woman could resist you."

He glanced at her and shook his head. "We're talking about a full partner in my business. Cattle ranch, name of Jabiru. I'm talking about a woman who can share my vision. A woman who's strong in her own right. A woman who can give me children we'll both love and enjoy. I'm not talking about a chick who wants to move in and play house. I'm talking about much, much more.''

Julie coughed. ''So this brings me to my application.'' She was only half joking.

He laughed. Warm and deep. His voice far from being country hick was educated, very attractive, with curiously an English accent.

''Write it down,'' he invited. ''No need to send along the photograph. I know what you look like. Pretty as a picture. I know, too, you're joking. You're the daughter of a very successful man and you've been looked after all your life. *Pampered.*''

Julie sighed. ''That's exactly the way my folks raised me. What about Cassie? What do you see in her?'' Julie had already gained the impression of some undercurrent.

He turned his attention to Cassie of the billowing hair. ''Oh, someone who's had sadness in her life at some point. But a person who won't let herself be overwhelmed.''

''Say that's spot-on. Tell us more. Sit down,'' Julie invited. ''Talk to us.''

He shook his head as though he had already said too much. ''Love to. Some other time maybe. I'm on a pretty tight schedule.''

''You have to grab a bite to eat, Red,'' Marcy jumped in. ''I can easily move you all to a larger table.''

''Really, please join us,'' Cassie said with so much

feeling it shocked her. In all her life she had never met anybody to match his shattering impact. Though he was acting friendly, she was smart enough to realise this was a man with a dangerous edge. There was an inner core of aloofness in him, as well, almost an arrogance. Maybe it was just a fiery pride.

"All right, then." He came to a quick decision. "I'm pretty hungry for Marcy's roast lamb. And vegetables, Marcy. Lots of them. I haven't cooked for days."

"You mean, you do your own *cooking?*" Julie, whose pièce de résistance was an overcooked omelette, asked.

"I'm an expert," he answered with no sense of false modesty.

"He is, too." Marcy gave him a proud smile. "His mum started him off and I took over by handing over a few cookbooks. Red, here, lives like a feudal lord."

Pleased with the way things were going, Marcy busied herself setting up a larger table two places down. Matthew, obviously used to helping her, picked up the girls' seafood platter arranged beautifully on a colourful ceramic plate and carried it down. He even went back and picked up the bud vase seeing there wasn't one on the new table. Finally, he seated both girls with a stunningly elegant flourish, before he flung himself into a chair with lavish pent-up grace.

"So, what are you doing up here?" he asked. "Holidaying?"

"Julie's parents have a hideaway up here," Cassie explained, turning her head to face him.

"Hideaway? I bet it's big enough to get lost in," he mocked.

Both girls nodded their assent. "It's on the point at Aurora Beach."

"Hell, I love that place," he said. "I haven't been there in a long time." Although he appeared to be addressing Julie, his eyes kept regarding Cassie as though he sought to commit her features to memory. He even moved his chair to a better angle.

Cassie found it as disconcerting as it was thrilling. She felt overexcited: racing in top gear.

"Jabiru keeps you very busy?" She allowed herself to look into his bronze face and saw chiselled features, a beautiful sensuous mouth, good jaw, cleft chin.

He nodded his handsome, flamboyant head. "It's taken years of my life. Years of backbreaking work to develop it."

"But you treasure it?"

His eyes glittered turquoise. "My Promised Land. The place I feel truly at home."

"Then you're a lucky man."

"I figure I am." He stared at her. So why did he catch that little note of sadness? It didn't make sense. Both of them were undoubtedly young women who lived in a style he could only imagine.

"But to advertise?" Julie had been avidly following their dialogue. "I bet you could get any woman you want."

"I'm thinking you're too kind. Getting the right woman might take a miracle, but I'll keep trying. I live an exhausting life, but soon I hope I can slow down. I'm not getting any younger. Thirty-four. Time to get a life."

Julie laughed. "But surely you know all the local girls?"

"As in saying 'good day,'" he admitted. "I haven't

invited them all out to the ranch.'' The turquoise eyes glinted. "You'd be surprised that local rag goes far and wide.''

"So how are you going to *know?*'' Cassie asked quietly. She turned her head, pinned by the charge he sent out like an electric thrill. Maybe he even *saw* it, because of what he said.

"A thunderbolt from Heaven.'' His tone was sardonic. "What do the French call it, a *coup de foudre?*''

"Does it *really* happen?'' Cassie asked from the depths of her soul. She hadn't meant to. She wasn't used to being fascinated by a man. Generally it was the other way about. She the object of desire who turned away.

"I'm *sure* it does,'' he answered in a strange, harsh voice. "Just as I don't think acting on it would be wise. I'm looking for something less extravagant than a dangerous passion.''

"You have to see you're just the person for it?'' Julie shot him a playful glance.

"No, ma'am.'' Not only did he shake his head emphatically, he waved a dismissive hand. Elegant, long-fingered, darkly tanned, calloused on the fingertips and palms, Cassie noted.

There's a story here, Julie thought, convinced of it.

"Headlong passion can be very destructive. Wouldn't you agree?'' he continued. "I wonder just how many people have been swept into an ocean of grief. I know it happens.''

"So you're planning a marriage of convenience?'' Cassie asked, a flicker of something very like antagonism in her voice. What was the matter with her? She felt as tight as a spring.

"Hey, it must be convenient, that's for certain. Perhaps something in between. Many cultures have arranged marriages. Had them for many centuries and they seem to work out. Have true worth."

"So you're saying falling love isn't the answer?" Cassie was persisting and didn't know why. If only he'd stop looking at her like that.

"I'm saying many, many love matches end in divorce," he retorted, his enunciation clear. "I've seen plenty of relationships flounder. The woman is generally left to make a home for any children involved."

"Yes," Cassie agreed, then abruptly changed the subject. "So, you're English."

"I'm as Australian as you are." His beautiful eyes stared her down.

"I only meant you have an *English* accent." She had to strive to smile. Her mouth felt dry. "Where did you pick it up?"

"My mother was English," he explained briefly.

"Oh, I see." Cassie realised it wasn't a subject he was going to talk about.

"Actually you sound great," Julie soothed. She could have sworn Red and Cassie were attracted to each other. Attraction with a dash of hostility. No, not *hostility,* she decided, something rather complex.

Marcy returned at just the right moment with Red's roast lamb and a large side dish of vegetables. For a while conversation stopped as they enjoyed their meal. He ate ravenously for a while, Cassie noted. No bad table manners, indeed not, just a man who was totally concentrating on good food. A man who probably had only in recent days been able to grab a meal on the run.

"This is wonderful." He looked up and reached for

his glass of beer. "We've been out on a four-day muster. Didn't stop for long. Pushed too damned hard. The floods have held us up but the country's in fine form now the waters have abated."

"It's like another world!" Cassie gazed at the stupendous hanging baskets of ferns. "I've never seen anything like the vegetation up here. Or the colours! The extraordinary depth and brilliance of the sky, the rich red and emerald earth, the endless white beaches, the sparkling blue sea."

"The Tropics, ma'am," he drawled. "I expect you know many of the islands of the Great Barrier Reef?"

"We know Hayman well," Julie volunteered, daintily downing a creamy rock oyster.

"Of course." Momentarily his lids came down. Hayman was one of the great resorts of the world. A resort for the wealthy.

"Actually I cruised the Whitsunday's with friends," Cassie said, smiling in remembrance of one of the most beautiful and peaceful holidays of her life. "We visited many of the lesser known islands and cays, explored the wonders of the coral reef, the gardens and grottoes, swam in beautiful lagoons. A heavenly blue world of infinite distances."

"Yes, it's glorious," he agreed, spearing the last morsel of roast potato. "So close yet I haven't been able to get away in years."

"You mean you haven't been able to take a *holiday*," Julie asked.

"More important things to do," he laughed. "I'm not complaining. Jabiru's mine and I love it. On the other hand it's good to have the company of two beautiful women." The dazzling eyes flashed over them, brilliant but impenetrable. "Do you know anything about ranching, as the Americans say?"

"Some." Cassie nodded. "I was invited once to a race meeting on Monaro Downs. A huge affair. The place belongs to Sir Jock Macalister," she said casually. "Being a cattleman you're bound to know of him. Monaro Downs is the Macalisters' flagship in the Channel Country."

"I know where it is," he interrupted, startling her with the curtness of his tone.

Colour moved under her high cheekbones. She spoke quietly. "What's the matter? Have I upset you in some way?"

A muscle in the clean line of his jaw jumped erratically. He nearly said yes. Such was her magic. "Not at all. Anyone in the Outback would know of Macalister and his empire. So you were impressed?"

"I sure was," Cassie replied, regarding him with an odd half smile. "I've never seen anything like the homestead. The finest mansion you could imagine set down in a million wild acres. Nothing except for endless miles of plains and towering sand hills. I missed the miracle of the wildflowers. It was the middle of the drought. My parents were lucky enough to witness the spectacle. They said it was unbelievable."

"So you weren't along on the trip?"

"I was at boarding school at the time."

"Boarding school?" One black eyebrow shot up. "I figure your parents must be on the land, as well?"

"My father is a Sydney businessman," she told him quietly. She didn't dare mention his strong business connections with Macalister.

"Nobody heard about day school?" The sensual mouth quirked. "I'm sorry." He gave Cassie a smile that heated her blood. "I have to watch my tongue. You have brothers and sisters?"

"I'm the only one."

"Tell me about it." He shrugged. "I was the only one, as well. And you, Miss Julie?" he addressed her with a light-hearted mockery.

"The only daughter, which I'm happy with. Two big brothers. Cass has been my best friend since our first day at St. Catherine's. A posh school for young ladies."

"You mean you were bundled off, as well?" he asked in amazement.

"No, I was a day pupil. Cassie's parents travelled a lot," Julie informed him.

"And when was this? How old?"

"Not yet eight." Cassie reached over to take Julie's hand affectionately.

"Really." Carlyle shook his head. "It hardly seems possible any parent could part with you. Even *now* the unhappiness is in your eyes, Cassandra."

It was like being caught in a passionate embrace. "Surely not," Cassie managed.

He regarded her with the kind of intensity she was just barely getting used to. "You've got the kind of shimmering eyes a heart's beat away from tears."

She took a deep breath, feeling a very real panic. "I can see I'll have to protect my gaze from you."

"Too observant?" he asked with a mixture of sympathy and challenge.

"No one else has mentioned it." She thought she was losing a layer of skin.

"I'm sure they've noticed." His smile was twisted. "Luminescent, isn't that the word? I didn't get past high school—'' this with a touch of self derision ''—whereas you two got to go to university I'll bet.''

Julie nodded. ''I did what I was told. I struggled through. Cassie is the brain. We both work for my father. He's a stockbroker.'' She didn't add ''big-time'' but she got his full attention.

''That's interesting. I've made quite a bit for myself playing the market. It's amazing what you girls are doing these days. Showing us guys up. All you need is the chance.''

''So, no chauvinist?'' Cassie asked, feeling another great surge of attraction but struggling against it.

He tossed back the rest of his beer. ''No way. Women have resources to call on we guys don't. I know a woman took over the running of a big station when her husband was killed, as tough and intelligent as the best of 'em. Actually I have an intense admiration for a woman's strength. And an intense sympathy for the soft little vulnerable ones some man always treats badly.''

''You're going to make a wonderful husband,'' Julie sighed.

''I'm going to give it my best shot. A commitment is a commitment. Isn't that right?''

Neither young woman was about to argue. If the truth be known, they were spellbound.

A moment later Matthew shoved his chair back, coiled ready to spring into action. ''That was great!'' he said with satisfaction. ''Marcy knows exactly the way to a man's heart.'' He pushed his chair in, a smile deepening the curve of his mouth. ''It's been a great pleasure meeting you, Julie, Cassandra.'' His eyes moved from one to the other. ''But I've got to get cracking. I hope you enjoy the rest of your holiday. Before you go back to your world of luxury.''

"No chance of seeing Jabiru, I suppose?" the irrepressible Julie asked.

He was about to shake his head, but suddenly relented. A split second's impulse. "Why not, if you're really interested," he found himself saying, much against his better judgment. "I can't come for you, much as I'd like to. This is a bad time. But by next week the pace should slacken off. If you'd like to make the drive, you're very welcome. But I think that'll put you off," he mocked.

"So, what day next week?" Julie persisted, wanting to follow it up by helicopter if she had to. This guy was something else.

"Ring me," he said, his voice deep and sonorous. "Marcy will give you my number."

God, how dumb can a man get! he thought as he made his way out onto the street. Little Julie with her wiggle was having a bit of fun, he could see that. But what the hell! He was sick of the quiet life. The other one—Cassandra—though she listened to her friend with a mixture of amused affection and dismay, was sending different signals. She didn't look like she wanted to come. There was even a kind of anxiety in her. He had sensed it. Anyway, she was way out of his league. A woman from a world he could never get into. A woman, it now seemed, from Jock Macalister's world. That alone suffused him with a chill, helpless anger. Nothing could be gained from even seeing her again. He regretted, too, ever looking into her eyes. There was a woman he could badly want but never have.

grandchildren. But what about those poor girls? I worry about them up to the brim to help.''

Matthew sat back, thinking. ''Well, Ned, I know what happened. Hell on earth. But I've found this remote place, a refuge. Out here I'll never be harmed again. I know well enough how my family operates.''

CHAPTER THREE

''WHAT in the world is goin' on, Red?'' Ned Croft, his old mate from town, asked him. They were sitting on the veranda enjoying a cold beer and a quick lunch of the fresh bread rolls Ned had brought from the town's bakehouse, stuffed with his own ham, cheese and pickles.

Ned, all of seventy-five, but very fit and wiry with a long bayonet scar on his right arm from the Second World War, often made the trek, lured by his old bush life and the fact that he and Red had struck up quite a friendship, kept glancing down at the swag of mail he had assured Mavis at the post office he would deliver to Red.

''Bloody advertisin', mate. I can't accept that,'' Ned said, scratching his balding, freckled scalp. ''A big handsome fella like yourself could have any girl you wanted. Especially now you've become so successful. It's a great life out here and you've made the homestead real nice.''

''I need a wife, Ned,'' Matthew said, straightening up to pick up another roll. Was there anything better than freshly baked bread and butter?

''You did mention that. But *advertisin'*, mate? Seems utterly wrong for a bloke like you.''

''The way I see it, Ned, it will save me a load of time.''

''Goin' on that.'' Ned pointed downwards with a

38

gnarled thumb. "But what about love, boy? Haven't you given a bit of thought to that?"

Matthew's eyes blazed. "Hell, Ned, I know what love is. I loved my mother. But I've found this romantic love business is a bit of a trap. Sometimes it's over before it's begun. Then there's my background. The past. At least everyone around here knows all about the skeleton in my family closet."

Ned shook his head. Given to lengthy considerations, he didn't say anything for a while. "Don't talk skeletons to me, lad. You're as good a bloke as any girl could get. Better. I know you take this illegitimate bit real serious, but no one else does. You was the victim. The unlucky one. It's Macalister who's the bastard."

"And no argument from me." Matthew grinned. "But some people place a lot of store on family. I remember life with Mum. Moving from place to place. Never having anyone. No relatives. No support group. No damned identity. Even some of the kids at school gave me hell until I found a way to shut their mouths. I have to find an ordinary girl who knows the truth and won't shy away from it."

"Why, did you have someone *else* in mind?" Ned asked shrewdly, turning his bony silver head.

"No," Matthew lied.

"You don't sound sure," Ned replied. "I don't know about this ordinary bit, either. There's nuthin' ordinary about you, Red. Don't you understand that?"

"I'm a realist, Ned. I've come a long way, but now I want to put down roots. Marry a good woman who'll give me a family. I want to build a relationship that will hold us together."

"That's some ambition," Ned, long divorced, said. "That girl, Fiona, didn't you like her?"

Matthew laughed. "Ned, Fiona left town ages ago. She went to Brisbane to find herself a nice solicitor."

"Don't know what she's missin'. Are you gunna read all of these?" Ned leaned down to loosen the neck of the mailbag.

"Every last one."

"Gunna take a while," Ned snorted, rubbing his jaw. "Want me to help you?"

"Thanks, Ned, but I have to look after these myself," Matthew declined. "You know, respecting a girl's confidence."

"Course. Fine," Ned nodded in agreement. "Looks like pretty hard work to me all the same." He finished off the rest of his tea. Good tea, too. Red made a nice cuppa. "Reckon I can stay overnight?" He was hoping Red would say yes, and he did.

"You know you can, Ned." Matthew gathered the few plates together, put them on the tray. "Listen, we're doing a little muster at Yanco Gully. Want to ride along?"

"Count me in!" Ned said with enthusiasm, jumping to his feet. "This Jabiru is a great place. And haven't you made it work!"

Red mightn't want to know it but he had surely inherited Macalister's legendary drive. It was an absolute tragedy when a man rejected his own son, Ned thought. Moreover, *such* a son! And his *only* son. Macalister for all his millions and his empire must have plenty of bad moments.

"I'm serious about this," Julie called as Cassie walked out onto the magnificent upper deck with its breathtaking views of a glorious blue sea and the off-shore islands that adorned it like rings of jade. "That guy's fantastic."

Outside the wind off the water was whipping through Cassie's hair. She hesitated a moment then returned to the huge open-plan living room. "I've told you before, Julie, this is one dangerous-edged man. He won't take kindly to any little jokes. He strikes me as a man with a real temper. He could confront you about it."

"Well—" Julie was seated at a table trying to answer Red's advertisement. "You're not *listening*, sweetie. I'm dead serious. I need some excitement in my life and he's offering."

"You're talking absolute rubbish." Cassie took a chair at the circular table. "And what about Perry?"

"You've got no idea, have you? I said I want *excitement*. Perry's nice, but no one could call him macho. Red is real *man!*"

"And too powerful for you. I wouldn't want to be the woman who tried to make a fool of him. You'd be left with a very sorrowful tale to tell."

"He's not a guy to beat a woman up," Julie scoffed. "He seemed very different from that."

"Well, what do you actually know about him? Zilch."

"I know the best already. I can work my way to the worst. It could just work out." At this Cassie shot out of her seat and Julie fired off, "If you weren't such a control freak you'd admit he got to you, too. I thought that was real sexy the way he kept calling you Cassandra. I wonder what happened to his mother?"

"Something bad," Cassie snapped. "It wasn't a subject he was about to discuss. You did see that."

"Simmer down, Cass," Julie begged. "I'm not clever like you. I want to find myself a *man*. So far, Red's it."

The shrill voice of the vacuum cleaner cut through their conversation. Molly Gannon who with her husband Jim, acted as caretakers for the Maitlands' very expensive retreat appeared from the hallway. "Not going to bother you am I, girls? I can come back later."

"No, come in Molly," Julie beckoned. "You might be able to help us here." Julie turned in her chair. "You know everyone around here. What do you know about a guy called Red Carlyle. Owns a cattle station in the hinterland."

"Red?" Molly switched off the vacuum cleaner and straightened up, pressing a hand against her aching back. "'Course I know Red. Everyone knows Red. He's a big success story around here."

"Ah," Julie cried in satisfaction. "Pull up a chair, Molly."

"Can't we leave this?" Cassie was exasperated and more upset than she knew why.

"It's not Red's ad?" Molly settled herself in an armchair.

"You know about it?" Cassie asked.

Molly gave her rich, rumbling laugh. "We *all* know about it. If I didn't have Jim I'd be applying myself. Mavis at the post office reckons she's flat out handling his mail."

"So they're answering already?" Julie bit her lip.

Molly just looked at her. "You've *seen* Red, haven't you?"

"Yes we have," Cassie told her quietly.

"Talk to him?"

"Just a few words."

"That'd be enough, I reckon." Molly nodded her head. Up and down several times. "He's really somethin', isn't he? He came here with his mum when he was about twelve years old. Wild kid then and for a long time after. A real hot temper. Typical redhead. Used to zip into anyone who said anything about him or his mum. His mum especially. He was very protective."

"What could they possibly *say?*" Cassie asked, somehow fearful of what was coming.

"Aa-ah!" Molly retorted, shaking her head from side to side.

"Come on, Moll," Julie urged. "You can't leave us up in the air. If you want to know, I'm thinking of answering his ad."

"What?" Molly couldn't hide her shock. "You're not *serious* are you, dear?"

"Sure." Julie gave her a challenging look. "I'm real interested."

The odd, shocked expression was still on Molly's face. "Deary, deary, be *warned.*" She gave it such emphasis.

Cassie turned to Julie. "Isn't that what I told you?"

"He hasn't spent time in jail, has he?" Julie demanded, her eyes turning steely.

"No, no, nothing like that." Molly scratched her springy grey head, locking eyes with Cassie, who she thought was far the more sensible of the two. "I said that badly. Red is a fine young man. He's worked very hard to get where he has. We all admire him, but he's got a bit of a cloud over his name. If you know what I mean. Doesn't mean anything to us up here, but it would to *your* folks. Take my advice, girls. Enjoy yourselves and go home. Your life's not up here."

"Is that today's lecture?" Cassie smiled to take the edge off her words. What Molly had said had only made her defensive. On Red's behalf.

"I'm only trying to give you good advice," Molly maintained, now staring at the floor. "Your parents wouldn't thank me, Julie, if I didn't put you straight."

"Why don't you?" Cassie invited. "What's Red's dark secret?"

Molly thought for a moment then sighed. "No *secret* in these parts. He's the flamin' image of his father at the same age, that's why. The colouring. The red setter hair, the blue eyes, the black eyebrows. You've got no idea, have you?"

"Obviously not," Cassie said, and Julie made a snorting sound.

"He's Jock Macalister's son," Molly announced like he was royalty.

Julie sat up, chin up. "For crying out loud!"

"Wait a minute." Cassie frowned. "Sir Jock doesn't have a son. He has three married daughters and as far as I know their children are little girls."

"How come you know so much?" Molly gave her a puzzled stare.

"My parents are quite friendly with Sir Jock," Cassie confided. "They've visited Monaro Downs a number of times. I've been there years ago when I was a child. I don't remember Sir Jock having red hair. It was thick and tawny, as I recall. But I do remember his black eyebrows and brilliant blue eyes."

"He's Macalister's son, all right," Molly said in such a stern voice her double chin trembled. Her disapproval of Macalister was very evident. "Won't acknowledge him though."

Cassie felt heat spread all over her skin. "But that's appalling!"

"It is, too." Molly gave another vigorous sideways jerk of her head. "I can't begin to tell you how that boy suffered. And his mum. The prettiest little thing you ever laid eyes on. Rather like you in style, Julie. Petite, blond. She was English. Posh accent. We all wondered about her background. Red sounds like a Pom to this day."

"But how did they meet?" Cassie asked, clamping her own hands together. "Red's mother and Macalister?"

Molly blew out a long, whinnying breath. "Appears she was employed as a governess, nanny, some such thing, on one of his stations."

"So he took advantage of her?" Cassie said, seeing the tragedy.

"Sure. Don't they all?" Molly retorted caustically, though sadness spread over her kind, homely features. "Little thing was killed a few years back. The whole town turned out for the funeral. Seems like yesterday. It was rough on Red. He really loved his mother. Did everything he could to look after her."

"How was she killed?" Cassie felt a little sick. Julie sat slumped in her chair as though all the wind had been knocked out of her.

"Road accident," Molly said vaguely. "Red's carrying a lot of baggage."

"One can understand that," Cassie mused.

"He'll make a good husband and a good father, mind you," Molly said loyally. "But don't you two young ladies go thinkin' of answering any advertisements. That would rock your folks to the core."

*   *   *

By mutual consent both girls left the house and headed for the beach, walking barefoot in the fine-grained white sand that ran like hot silk.

"Let's move down to the water's edge," Cassie murmured. "Easier going. We'll walk up to Leopard Rock."

The water at the edge was crystal, a beautiful aquamarine that deepened into brilliant blue.

"Well, that sure put a lid on it," Julie groaned. "Poor old Red. It must be awful to be illegitimate."

"It's not the social stigma it once was," Cassie said steadily. "And rightly so. The innocent can't be victimised. They can't pay for something that happened before they were born. Anyway, plenty of couples are having children without getting around to marriage."

Julie nodded, flipping a blond curl out of her eyes. "But it's not *our* way, is it? Our folk's way."

"I guess not. I don't really believe it's any woman's preferred way. Women want security, permanence, the best possible life for their children. There are enough hurdles surely?"

"But what an extraordinary story." Julie bent to pick up a very pretty sea-shell. "Your parents so friendly with Macalister yet they've never heard the rumours?"

"They could have for all I know." Cassie shrugged. "It seems to be common knowledge."

"Yet the family, the Macalisters, ignore it. Ignore Red. He's got a big family with tons of money yet he's an outcast."

They stopped to watch a flock of disturbed seagulls take to the air.

"You haven't met *Lady Macalister*." Cassie shuddered, turning to Julie with a theatrical expression.

"Even my mother said she's a woman with a very cold heart."

Julie would have laughed at the irony if it weren't so sad. "Well, she'd know." She put an arm around Cassie's waist. "Why don't we go and look at this place? Jabiru. It can't do any harm. I'd really like to see it, wouldn't you?"

Of one accord they walked into a foaming little breaker. "Actually I *would* but it'd be against my better judgement. We might be getting drawn into something here, Julie. Something about Red Carlyle scares me."

"Afraid of his attraction?" Julie gave her friend a shrewd glance. "I'd say you're even more interested in Red than I am."

Cassie frowned. "That's the part that bothers me. I can just imagine telling my parents I was interested in Jock Macalister's illegitimate son."

"Can't wait for that one," Julie quipped. "They'd give you a very hard time. Your dad would probably zap you out of his will."

"I don't care about that." Cassie threw back her head, letting the sea breeze whip her hair into a silk pennant. "I've had a good education. I can make my own way. Besides, there's Grandma's money."

"That's right!" Julie brightened. "Tell you what, we'll have a swim on the way back then I'm going up to the house to leave a message for Red. He did invite us and we've got the time. We could take care of his mail for him. Help him pick out the right bride."

In the end Red organised everything himself. He enlisted the help of a friendly neighbour, Bob Lester, a well-established cattleman, to ferry the girls back after his business meeting in town. Red himself would drive them home. But it meant an overnight stay.

"What do you think, Marcy?" Cassie whispered across the counter. They often came into the pub now and each time they had a conversation with a willing Marcy.

"Safe as houses," Marcy maintained stoutly.

"What a pity. I thought he'd grab me," Julie giggled.

"Not Red, I swear. He'll treat you like the fine young ladies you are. Bob and Bonnie Lester are pillars of the community. You'll be safe with Bob. You'll need riding gear. Big shady hats. Red has organised with me to send a few supplies out. You'll take them along on your trip. Bob doesn't mind. I think you're going to have a very good time."

I'll pray for that, Cassie thought.

Bob Lester turned out to be a tall, hale cattleman with a thick shock of prematurely snow-white hair and a full white moustache, handlebars and all. He picked them up at the house and entertained them with lots of stories on their long journey into the hinterland.

Cassie had thought it might be endless but the time flew. The scenery was remarkable. Under a cloudless cobalt-blue sky the countryside waved a lush emerald-green to the horizon. The spurs of the Great Dividing Range stood in stark relief above the plains, their colour the most wonderful moody grape-blue into purple. Small white and lavender-blue wildflowers floated on this sea of hardy green grasses and scattered all over were pools of tranquil water, relics of the floodwaters Cyclone Amy had brought down.

"You can consider yourselves fortunate, girls," Bob Lester told them. "Red don't have many visitors.

He's been pretty darn content on his own. Leastways up until now. I'm blessed if I know if he's serious about this advertisin' for a bride. There's already bagsful of mail arriving from all over. He'd be well advised to be serious, I reckon.''

"So how's he going to handle it?" Julie, in the back, piped up.

"I don't rightly know," Bob admitted. "What I *can* tell you is the woman who lands Red is one mighty lucky woman. Even I never imagined he could work the wonders he has. Jabiru was terribly rundown and the old homestead was in such a state it had to be demolished. Red built the new place with his own hands. It's a credit to him but you'll be able to see for yourselves. Course he's a chi—''

"Chip off the old block?" Julie promoted.

Bob gave a wry grin. "Everyone knows around here. Macalister ignoring his own son. Makes yah wonder!"

"There's no room for doubt?" Cassie asked.

Bob gave her a brief telling look. "None, unless a man has a double."

It was a paradise of the wild.

Flocks of magpie geese flew overhead and a solitary jabiru stood in stately silence at the edge of a silvery pool. A big sign above the iron gate announced the entry to Jabiru Station. Another sign on the fence carried the warning: This Gate Must Be Shut At All Times.

Cassie jumped out to open the gate, waited until the Land Rover had passed through, then swung the gate back into position. The metallic sound caused an amazing number of brilliantly coloured parrots to rise out of the magnificent gum that stood to one side of the gate, screeching their arrival. Not that Red would have heard. They had to travel a good mile up an unsealed drive before the homestead came into sight. A long, low-slung building that seemed completely at home in its verdant surroundings.

"Say, this is nice," Julie breathed. "But very isolated. He must find it hard out here all by himself."

"Well, he's aiming to change that," Bob said. "Probably he's had no time to feel lonely. He's slaved to get this place back to what it was."

Red was on hand to greet them, all taut and terrific male grace, coming down to the vehicle and opening up the front and back doors. "Right on time!" He looked beyond Cassie for a moment to smile at Bob. "Thanks a lot, neighbour. You'll stay and have a cup of tea?"

"Love to." Bob grinned. "Lots of supplies in the back, Red. Cold stuff in the esky. Marcy sent it along."

"Good. I'll take care of it. You hop out and stretch your legs. Well, now, Julie, Cassandra, I'm very pleased you could come."

The blue eyes made Cassie feel hot and helpless, but Julie answered for both of them. "It's great to be here. Worth working hard for, Red?" She swept out her arms.

"What do *you* think?" Suddenly he turned his head and pinned Cassie's eyes.

For a moment she forgot to breathe. "A paradise of the wild," she managed at last, her voice faintly husky.

"I'll accept that." He smiled. "Come on, come on up. Bob—" he turned his head "—leave those things I'll get them."

"Just the esky, then," Bob answered, reaching into the vehicle for the cold stuffs. "I'll have a cup of tea, then I'll be off."

Inside the bungalow both girls were astonished at how attractive Red had made it. It was rustic, admittedly, the furnishings were old, inexpensive, but comfortable-looking with several sofas, one good leather armchair in a rich burgundy. The scatter rugs on the polished floor were colourful, as were the fat cushions on the sofas. There were prints that looked like they'd been selected carefully, hung around one large main room with a whole wall taken up with books, books, books. Heaps too many to count. There were even two big planters containing luxuriant golden canes and sprays of yellow orchids in a copper pot in the middle of the dark-timbered old dining table that had been polished to quite a shine.

"Come on, a decorator did this," Julie cajoled. "What's her name?"

"This was put together by a man." Cassie looked around. "It's comfortable and relaxed and it has a great feel of home."

"Glad you like it." Red sketched a bow. "While you look around I'll bring your things in. My guest-room is to the left. Two single beds. Clean sheets. I hope you'll be comfortable."

What have I let myself in for? he thought as he lopped down the front steps. The cute little Julie didn't bother him. She was pretty, never giving herself a moment to get bored, but Cassandra of the luminous eyes. He was far from immune to her. In fact for a moment there when they had arrived he had hardly dared to look at her. But still, he had. Stared at her oval face, her skin, her eyes, the luscious tender curves of her mouth, the way her gleaming hair went into deep soft waves over her shoulders.

It was one hell of a risk to have her here, he thought as he reached into the Land Rover for the luggage. Why hadn't he just let it go? Last night when he wasn't cleaning house in preparation for their visit, he had sat reading a score of letters from young women who had given serious consideration to spending their life with him. Some of the letters moved him. Those were from young women from unhappy homes, desperate to find security and a new life. Some of them he even knew. Couple of kooks. One he put down fast. Dirty talk, for God's sake. He realised he might expect it.

Now this beautiful porcelain creature who stood inside the rough house he had built had said it had a great feel of home. She wasn't just saying it, either. He could see the sincerity in her lovely features. The princess he could fall in love with. The princess he couldn't wait to be gone. Jock Macalister's bastard he might be, but he wasn't any fool.

CHAPTER FOUR

BECAUSE Julie couldn't ride, he drove them around the station until late afternoon, stopping to watch the glorious tropical sunset from Warinna Ridge. Fiery reds, glowing rose, brilliant streaks of indigo and gold that illuminated the whole world.

"We'd better not delay," he murmured at last, "dusk will set in fast and we have to get down the ridge." They had left the Jeep at the bottom, making the fairly easy climb on foot. It would be easier still going down. Red went ahead, holding any low-slung branches out of their way, moving with his special rhythm that had Cassie's eyes glued to his wide back.

That was when it happened.

As Julie padded past her just a little out of breath, the ground seemed to move under Cassie's feet. Pebbles and small rocks rolled down the slope. She gave a little shriek as she lost balance, skidding forward, a sharp rock slashing at her ankle as she seemed all set to take a fall. Except it didn't happen that way. Red whipped around in a lightning flash, grabbed her body and hauled her to him, holding her strongly as she fell crushed against him on legs as wobbly as a new born foal's.

"Lord!" she gulped on something that sounded like a sob, her heartbeat driven up into her mouth.

His body was so beautiful. Beautiful! The male scent of him so clean and warm and so erotic. She felt wildly aroused in an instant. Sinking in a well of sensation. And he knew it. He *knew* it. She was more alive than she had ever been. More afraid.

"Cassandra." He bent his head, his mouth touching her hair. "You okay?"

While Julie called out anxiously, "You're not hurt, are you, Cass?"

"I might have hurt my ankle." She spoke breathlessly, betrayingly, feeling the shame of it.

"Here, let's have a look," he said with measured gentleness. "Rest your hand on my shoulder."

She had to get herself under control, glimpsing something wonderful but afraid to follow.

"You've gashed it," he told her. To a man he would have added, "No big deal." But this was a princess with a fine delicate ankle. "Have you got a clean handkerchief on you?"

He gazed up into her face, finding her pale with sexual feelings briefly glimpsed before the veil fell.

"I have." Julie came to the rescue. "Say, that looks nasty, Cass."

"It won't be when I clean it up," Red retorted, fixing a makeshift bandage. "Bad luck. Want me to carry you?" he asked, powerfully aware of his desire to hold her.

Her beautiful hair bounced loose all around her flushed face. "No, I'll be fine." She denied what she longed for. "It just shook me a little."

Understatement of the year. Inside she was burning hot. Imagining herself alone with him in the night. What it would be like?

When they returned to the house, Red insisted on cleaning up the gash straight away.

She protested again, jittery, not knowing what to do

with her hands. She couldn't believe she could feel this way. So soon.

"I think I should. I'm your host. While I'm attending to it, maybe Julie would like to pick the makings for a salad while it's still light?"

"Will do," Julie answered obligingly. "Just so long as you don't ask me to cook the dinner."

"You mean to tell me you can't cook?" He turned on her with sparkling eyes.

"No." Julie grinned. "I guess that means I can't respond to your advertisement."

"Cooking is pretty important. Bottom line." He smiled.

"Where are we going to do this?" Cassie asked as Julie picked up a basket used for the purpose and moved out of the back door to the vegetable garden.

"This way, please." He gestured towards the bathroom which was surprisingly spacious. Built to accommodate a big man, she supposed. Here again, on a limited budget and doing most of it himself, it was bright, attractive with floods of light in the daytime and timber screening. Privacy for guests, she guessed, because there was no one around for miles. There was a long bench in the shower recess and Red told her to sit down there while he hunted up his first-aid kit which lay behind the mirrored wall cabinet.

"This is silly. I can do it." Cassie swept her hair out of her eyes, determined not to let her guard down completely.

"Why so nervous?" His tone was moving them into a new zone.

For a moment she had a dazed, mindless feeling, knowing herself to be transparent. "I think you know the answer."

He stared at her for a moment, a stare as intimate as a kiss. "And what's that?"

Cassie set her delicate jaw, not rejoicing in her vulnerability. "I know you got a lot of mail, Matthew, but don't let it go to your head."

His eyes flickered. "Why not, with a highly desirable woman like you? Anyway, some of these letters would break your heart."

"I suppose." Somehow she wasn't surprised by his sensitivity. "Most of us are looking for something. Someone."

"*You* wouldn't have to look far, would you?" he asked ironically, filling a basin of water and tipping in antiseptic. "I bet you have a string of guys standing in line."

"Well—" A shadow crossed her face. "No one I care about. It takes time to find the right person."

He wanted to touch her cheek, stroke it, run a finger across the lush pad of her mouth. Have that mouth open to him. "And sometimes that person enters your life when you least expect it. The element of chance that can make or break a life. Who said you could call me Matthew?" he asked belatedly on a soft growl.

"It just seemed natural. You don't like it?"

"Maybe too much," he said with a trace of self-derision. Very gently, he removed Julie's blood-stained handkerchief, set it aside, then began to bathe Cassie's ankle. "You have very delicate ankles. Pretty toes." He traced his finger this way and that, slow and steady. Along her instep, over her ankle, down her toes, which she thought gratefully were as nice in their way as her fingers.

"Stop that, Matthew." Her voice was silky soft. Shaky. She knew how much she was giving away.

He paid little attention. "I just thought a little massage." The compulsion to draw her into his arms was becoming unbearable.

"It's not clear to me but, but are you flirting?" Best to sound a little angry.

"Flirting!" He threw back his handsome head and laughed. "Oh, Cassandra, I've never flirted in my life. Never had the time."

"All the same, I think you're dangerous to me."

"You're not going to interfere with my plans, either," he said with a taut smile, picking up the tension.

"If you want to put the bandage on."

"Bandage? Maybe a little Band-Aid?" he lightly mocked, his eyes sliding over her.

"Sure. Make fun of me."

"I'm not like that, Cassie." He held her foot gently and dabbed it dry. "In fact I'm going to kiss it better."

She didn't move. She didn't make a sound. This was seduction itself. Her eyes closed as he bent his glowing ruby head and kissed the smooth skin of her ankle.

"You devil!" she said softly. "No."

"No, what?" He smiled back at her.

"Mocking me again?"

"You know exactly what I'm doing, Cassie." He clipped his words, but his sapphire gaze held her with intensity. "Maybe you'd better make allowances for—"

"A pretty complicated guy?" she suggested, strong emotion leaping from him to her.

"Is that how you see me?" He rose from his haunches and stood up, towering over her, causing her to eye him with trepidation.

"I'm sure of it."

"Why did you come out here?" he challenged very quietly.

She clasped the bench with her two hands, fixing her gaze on the white duckwood floor in the shower. "You invited us. We had nothing else to do. And we genuinely wanted to see the place. Which I must tell you I love."

"For a visit of two days?" he asked cynically.

"What do you want me to say, Matthew?"

His eyes held hidden currents. "Nothing. Heaps. What does it matter?" He looked down at her, his attitude as intense as hers. "How does that feel?"

"Fine." She transferred her gaze to her ankle. "You're very competent in everything you do."

"A top guy."

"You really expect something to come of this advertising?" she burst out spontaneously, revealing part of her turbulent feelings.

"I'm sure something will."

"What about love?" What did it have to do with her, anyway?

"Love can be poisonous, Cassandra. I know that." He looked through and beyond her.

She stood up abruptly, pushing the heavy fall of her hair behind her ear. "You can't let what happened to your mother affect your life."

Too late, she realised her mistake, but she was hopelessly off balance in his presence.

His eyes burned into her like a blue jet of flame. "So the lovely Lady Cassandra has been gossiping?" His expression turned into hard arrogance.

She held up her hands, almost in supplication. "Sorry, Matthew. Please don't call it gossiping. It came out."

"Sure." He shrugged a shoulder. "Who did you ask?"

She could feel the hot blood suffusing her face. "I'd prefer not to say, but someone who's on your side."

"Not Marcy, surely?"

"No, not Marcy. I'm such a fool. I can't believe I blustered that out. But you unnerve me." Just how much she didn't want to fathom.

"If it comes to that, you unnerve me," he said in a grating voice. "So you know the other bit, as well."

She backed away, leaning against the far wall. "Jock Macalister is stuck with his wrong, Matthew. You aren't. You've made a successful life for yourself. You don't have to account to anyone."

There was a voice in the hall. Julie's.

"Hey, you guys, what's happening?"

Red straightened but there was tension in his lean powerful body.

"Coming, Julie," he called in a perfectly calm voice. "I've been attending to Cassandra's ankle."

"Want to tell Red about how I hurt myself skiing?" Julie called. "Boy, that's some vegetable patch, Red. It was hard not to pick the lot."

"Take some home with you tomorrow," Red said, leading Cassie back into the main room. "I'm not the market gardener, by the way. One of my men, Charlie, part Aboriginal, part Chinese in another life, handles that."

"Well, it's a credit to him," Julie said, beaming at them over a basket laden with lettuce, fat red tomatoes, shiny green and red capsicums, shallots and a few lemons she had pulled off a tree. "Say, everything all right here?" Her bright smile faltered after a moment.

"Of course it is," Red assured her so smoothly she

was put at her ease. He held out his hand and took the basket. "The ankle is giving Cassandra a bit of gip."

"Well, sit down girl." Julie hurried over to her. "Take the weight off it. Read a book. Red's got a whole library. Meanwhile he's going to give me a lesson on preparing— What's on the menu, Red?"

"What about peppered steak, Jabiru eye fillet, melt in your mouth. Salad and some little new potatoes. Just dug up. Nice bottle of red. White, if you prefer. Cheese for later. One thing I haven't gotten around to cooking is a cake."

Julie went on in her vivacious fashion. "Then let Cassie show you. She makes a wicked chocolate cake."

Red's two cattle dogs, Dusty and Jason, had returned at sundown and he went out and greeted them affectionately introducing them to the girls but not letting them through the door. They stayed out on the veranda, growling gently in the dark when some movement or sound alerted them.

"They're superb working dogs. Watch dogs, as well," Red said.

In the end they stayed up late, their conversation covering a wide range of topics. Cassie folded herself into the corner of a sofa while Julie took the armchair opposite Red and laughed delightedly at all his stories. And he, like Bob Lester, had a fund of them. In turn she regaled him with funny episodes from hers and Cassie's shared life. Which he appeared to enjoy.

"Now that I've run out of stories," she announced over a nightcap, "what about if we help you to run through a few more of your letters? You'll have to hire a secretary anyway."

"I don't think so, Julie." Red rubbed his forehead,

starting to debate with himself. "Maybe I should. I never expected anything like this, I have to tell you. I won't have the time to get 'round to all of them.

"We'll help you," Julie repeated.

"But they're *personal*," he stressed.

"They won't know."

"That's not the point, is it?" He gave her a wicked smile.

"We'll take the task very seriously, Matthew," Cassie promised. "Assemble the ones with the most appeal."

"All right. All right." A little exasperated, he rose to his six plus, went to a cabinet, selected another twenty letters and slammed them down on the old cedar wood chest he was using for a coffee table. "We won't speak and we won't dare laugh. We'll just set aside what seems to come from the heart. Ah, yes, the photograph, too," he added with humour. "I'm not aiming to ruin my life. I set the limit at thirty."

"The old biological clock, eh?" Julie muttered, selecting one of the pile.

"I want children." Red snatched up one, making short work of opening it out.

And I wouldn't mind mothering them, flashed into Cassie's head.

She woke from a sound sleep for a few moments almost completely disoriented. The clouds of mosquito netting, the narrow bed, the strange room, the incredibly fresh and balmy air that wafted through the windows. Where was she? Then full consciousness set in. She had chosen to visit Matthew Carlyle on Jabiru.

It was early. Very early. The predawn sky was a translucent pearl grey. She slipped her feet out of bed and reached for her robe. Julie, the night owl, was still fast asleep, her two hands tucked sweetly under her chin. Cassie found herself smiling. Julie had slept like that since she'd been a little girl.

Cassie walked to the tall window looking out over the green valley. There was a radiance on the horizon, a radiance that would turn into an explosion of light as the sun burst over the top of the range. Such a beautiful place! It made her feel rejuvenated, more at peace with herself than she had been for a while.

The dawn wind was stroking rustling sighs out of the trees that surrounded the homestead. Gums and acacias, a magnificent poinciana that would be something to see when in flower, numerous bauhinias, the orchid trees and a pair of tulip trees covered with opulent coral-red flowers. From this angle she could see an old tank stand smothered in cerise bougainvillea that cascaded right to the ground. She was truly fascinated by Matthew's world. No wonder he loved it.

Matthew. Matthew Carlyle. Red Carlyle. She tried the names over silently on her tongue. What exactly did he mean to her? How had she reached this stage of involvement—no, "involvement" didn't say it—in such an impossibly short time? True, he was stunningly handsome, bore himself like a prince, was uncommonly well read, highly intelligent. Those attributes hadn't blinded her before. Her ex-boyfriend, Nick Raeburn, with whom she worked, was all of these things as had been a few men before him. What they lacked, or significantly what they lacked for her, was Matthew's brand of magnetism. It penetrated to her very depths. She had been drawn headlong toward him at first sight. Up close and personal he stirred her even more, a combination of the physical and spiritual. He had such *power*.

She was twenty-four. She was moving along in her career, well paid, successful, but something vital was lacking in her life. She thought of it as her dream. To be blessed with the right man. To create a good future together. To love and above all to *share*. Was she crazy to think she could put her needs down on paper? Show them to him. Offer to become his wife.

She wasn't that brave. He would throw back that dark gleaming red head and laugh. A hard ironic laugh. He saw her, she knew, as someone who came from a different world, she didn't dare mention her parents weren't merely acquaintances but friendly with the man who had fathered him only to spend a lifetime ignoring his very existence. Thanks to Jock Macalister, Matthew trusted no one on earth. He wouldn't trust her, either.

Cassie turned away from the window, opened the bedroom door very quietly and listened for sound. Nothing stirred. The dogs weren't on the veranda. She padded down the hallway to the bathroom, found it empty and shut the door. Her towel was there in its allotted place, her bath things. She would have a quick shower and maybe cook breakfast. The truth was Matthew could fend for himself. The steaks last night had been cooked to perfection, the salad, which he'd insisted on making though she'd offered, at its simple best, crisp and fresh tossed in a good olive oil and red wine vinegar.

She was touched by the way he lived. Admired it, too. A man alone, yet keeping everything spick-and-span. He'd allowed her to set the table using an attractive cloth and napkins, good quality dinnerware, stainless-steel cutlery. He was a civilised man with innate good breeding. She wondered what his English mother had been like. A road accident, Molly had said. Leaving a lot more unsaid.

She knew what Matthew's mother looked like. There were several photographs atop an old pine chest in the living room. Photographs of a very pretty blond woman with a bubble of soft curls and a lovely smile, looking unselfconsciously at the camera. Others with her arm around a little boy so handsome he would bring tears to any woman's eyes. Matthew as an older boy, already inches over his mother's head, then an arresting young man, holding his petite mother in front of him, two hands resting on her shoulders. It was evident they were very close.

Cassie was returning very quietly to the bedroom when suddenly a door snapped shut.

Matthew. And no way to avoid him. It brought her close to trembling. Matthew Carlyle, a random element in her life but so compelling it seemed like he was everything she had ever wanted in a man. Cassie stood arrested, the blood coming up into her face.

At that moment Matthew, moving across the living room towards the kitchen, caught sight of Cassie in the hallway.

For a minute he felt like someone had struck him high in the chest. It was a terrible shock to discover he wanted this woman, this near stranger, so very badly. How had this happened? He wanted to touch her, to feel her touch him. She was wearing a blue robe with some sort of lustre, her hair, that wonderful crowning glory, billowing around her shoulders, the outline of her body, sloping shoulders, the small high breasts, delicate hips, just barely concealed by the satiny fabric of her robe.

"Hi there!" he managed when inside he felt hot and heavy, his heart squeezed by emotion. She started to walk towards him as if at a silent call, looking at him with luminous eyes.

She might have been a sleepwalker or someone in a dream so directed was her progress. He found himself putting out a hand, spearing his fingers through the long thick mass of her hair. It came to him he would love to brush it. Have her sit there while he brushed through its deep waves, listening to the electric crackle, revelling in the sable flow over her shoulders.

She should have been startled but she wasn't. She just stood there mesmerised letting him take control.

"How beautiful you are," he said very quietly, lost in the pool of her eyes. "I didn't want you to come, Cassandra," he told her.

"Why?" She knew the answer, her own heart quaking.

"Not difficult to explain. I'm trying to sort out my life, not get in way over my head."

"Of course, I understand that." Still she watched him.

"So why are you looking at me with those river eyes?"

"I thought you *knew,*" she said at last.

He nodded. "Sometimes things happen that should never happen." Despite himself his hand moved to her flawless flower skin. His desire for her was growing to the point he knew he should move away, say something about getting breakfast. Anything but pander to his own unparalleled sexual need. Something about her struck such a painful chord. The memory of love. *Real* love. The great love he had had for his mother. The sense of desolation and loss he had endured. His feeling for this woman, Cassandra, was undreamt of. In pursuing it he could cause great unhappiness for them both.

He heard her draw in a little shaken breath and his eyes dropped to her mouth, dwelt on its smooth cushiony curves. Her lips were parted and he could see the pearly nacre of her teeth. Did he imagine it or did she sway towards him? Her long-lashed eyes were wide open, yet so dreamy, so rapt, she might have lost all orientation.

It seemed to work both ways. He found himself taking her oval face in one hand and then he bent his head, caught up her lips with his own, kissing her so deeply, hungrily, it even seemed he was trying to eat her.

The scent of her! The wonderful woman fragrance mixed with the freshness of a lemony soap, and the talcum powder reminding him of a baby.

Quite slowly she wound an arm around his neck like a tendril, knowing what that would do to him. No stopping him now. He pulled her into his arms with a low cry, gathering her tightly against him, ravished by the imprint of her beautiful body on his hard frame. What was happening had never happened to him in the past. He had taken women thankfully with gentleness, glad of their responding pleasure. Now his longing was so harsh he felt the arms that closed around her turn to iron. She was afraid and excited at the same time, he could tell. Her head draped back over his arm as she offered up her mouth, kissing him back, exchanging this almost unbearable rapture. It drove him to half lift her from the ground, desperate not just for kisses but to go all the way. Spread her out on his bed, that beautiful hair fanning around her head.

It was outrageous. He knew that. He barely knew her. She was, after all, a rich girl from the city. A guest in his home. He should be treating her with respect. He had begun to run his hand across her breast, aware of an arousal that matched his own. Now, before another towering wave of heat broke over him, he reeled back, releasing her so abruptly her knees started to buckle and she clutched at him like a child.

"I'm sorry." His breath came out like a bitter gasp. This was fantasy. A dream. Not his rough-and-ready world.

"Wait a moment, Matthew," she answered, very gently, very sweetly. "It was my fault as much as yours."

"So what do we do now? Pretend it didn't happen?"

She saw the high mettled set of his head, the blaze in his eyes. "I'm not the girl you'd pick to marry?"

"You're way out of my league, Cassandra," he said, a nerve beating in his temple.

"How can you possibly say that?" She really meant it. He was the kind of man with the vital force to make a mark in the world. The fact of his birth meant little to her beyond the deep well of sympathy she felt for his abandoned mother and a fatherless child.

"Would you introduce me to Daddy?" he asked in a very crisp, confronting way.

"I'd be happy to." None of the young men her parents had lined up could match Matthew.

"Doesn't it upset you, knowing my background?" He frowned, black brows drawn down.

"It upsets me only in the sense it upsets you," she answered simply. "You're your own man, Matthew. You're an achiever. You can take your place anywhere."

"Sure, I know that," he shrugged, "but it doesn't mean your parents mightn't hate me."

It was possible. Matthew Carlyle was very different. "Matthew, I want to tell you my parents have put me through hell. My father is a very successful, clever, overbearing man. My mother lives a highly social life. That's all she cares about."

"Be that as it may, they wouldn't want their daughter to throw herself away on a guy like me. I know without your telling me they've got someone lined up for you. Someone they're accustomed to. Someone with the same background as themselves. Hell, he's probably already chosen."

She couldn't deny it and it showed on her face.

"You'd have to be totally mad to settle for a small-time cattleman, a beautiful creature like you, to spend your life hidden away in the wilds." He laughed ironically. "Now, what about if you get dressed," he suggested, starting to put distance between them. "I'll make breakfast. Orange juice. Pawpaw. Bacon and eggs."

"You'll make someone a wonderful husband," Cassandra said, suddenly feeling humiliated. Put back on some pedestal. Shut away.

"Good of you to tell me," Matthew said with a suave bow. "All I will admit to is that was the best kiss I've ever had in my life. It's quite possible I'll remember it as an old man."

CHAPTER FIVE

"You're fascinated by him, aren't you?" Julie said, her pretty face betraying her anxiety.

"No," Cassie denied, adjusting her sunglasses.

"You can't fool me, girl. I've been your best friend for sixteen years." Julie shook her head.

"You sound worried, Julie." They were sitting out on the deck enjoying the earthly paradise that surrounded them.

"I am." Julie reached for the sun cream, rubbing some more on her tanned legs. "I'm not such a fool I can't tell you and Red are wildly attracted to one another. You haven't been the same since we arrived home, even I'm getting out of my depth. I know I started all this, but you must know your parents have their own hopes for you. It has to be someone they approve of, Cassie. Someone who will fit in."

"That's right. Aren't you relieved, then, Matthew wouldn't dream of considering me? He actually told me to my face."

Julie laughed nervously. "He *did?*"

"Meeting Matthew Carlyle was like having an abyss open up in front of me," Cassie said.

"Lord, Cassie." Julie sighed deeply. "Not that I can blame you. Red is just amazing. Bright, breezy, arrogant, fun. In truth, quite a guy. I could have fallen in love with him myself but it was perfectly plain he had no interest in me. It was you who caught his gaze that first day on the highway. I can't think why when

I'm far more beautiful.'' She laughed softly then sobered. "I'm sorry, Cassie. I could have spared you the heartache. You're usually so sensible." She shook her head again.

"You think it's a disaster to allow myself to fall in love with Matthew."

"Oh, boy. *Yes!* I know you've shown plenty of spirit but in a way you're still a mite afraid of your parents. Your father especially. Goodness knows he's a regular despot though he's been a little more human of late."

"Well, that's because he thinks finally I'm going to toe the line."

"In a sense my own parents aren't that different," Julie admitted. "They'll want a say in my marriage. That's the only way, according to Mum, I'll get the perfect match. I'm still a kid in the classroom to her."

"You poor thing! Anyway, it was quite an experience. I'm none the worse for it."

"You must excuse me if I don't believe that," Julie burst out. "Red's the one person I've ever seen get to you. It would have to be someone totally unsuitable."

"Ah, yes—" Now the about-face. "I've thought a lot about it," Cassie said. "I'm going to answer Matthew's advertisement."

Horror and a kind of admiration broke over Julie's pretty face. "But he'll think you're trying to make a fool of him. Heck, Cassie, didn't you warn me not to think of upsetting Red?"

"I'm dead serious."

This affected Julie so much she jumped up and went to the balustrade, looking out sightlessly over the glorious blue sea. Finally she turned with a sympathetic frown. "There *is* such a thing as love at first sight obviously."

"The poets say so." Cassie had a clear picture of Matthew's face. "I just didn't think it could happen to me."

"Usually I'm the mad, impulsive one," Julie moaned, "and you're so calm and controlled." She came back, dropped a kiss on the top of Cassie's head, then sat down. "This is like a romance novel. It can't be real. Do you realise your parents would blame *me?*"

"Well, I'll tell them you advised me against anything so crazy."

"A wise move for me." Julie sounded wry. "What is it you want, Cassie?" she asked. "Adventure, a rip-roaring life? Can't you have a good old time? Get Red out of your system."

"I want him," Cassie said very carefully.

"Then it's not just sex?" Julie looked hard at her.

Cassie drew off her sunglasses. "We didn't get into that, Julie."

"Oh, yeah, no time?"

"Surprise, surprise. Matthew goes a long way towards being a very chivalrous guy."

Julie shrugged. "I find myself agreeing. You can see his mother's story has affected him deeply."

"Sad but no bad thing," Cassie said with a slight hardening of her tone. "We've both met guys with a callous hand for all their so-called eligibility."

"You're absolutely right. But I should stop you," Julie said.

"Sorry, kiddo," Cassie answered staring up at the sky. "Too much time has passed. I've already written

the letter. In fact Matthew should have it by tomorrow.''

The morning had barely dawned before Julie took a
call from her mother telling her of the sudden death
of her great-aunt.

''You don't have to come with me,'' Julie said, seeing the torn expression on Cassie's face. ''Aunt Sarah
lived a good life. At some point in her eighties she
decided she didn't want to go on. All the family knew
it. I'll have to go to the funeral, show my respects, but
you can stay on. We still have to the end of the week.''

''But your parents will expect me to come home
with you,'' Cassie said.

''Not in the least. They're very happy to have you
enjoy this. Molly and Jim are here to look after you.''

''We both know the reason why I want to stay,
Julie.'' Cassie met her friend's eyes.

''It might come to nothing, Cassie,'' Julie warned.
''You said yourself Red is one complex man.''

''I know, but I have to hear what he has to say.''

''It could be painful,'' Julie stressed, ''and I won't
be here to offer comfort.''

''He could simply ignore me,'' Cassie said as
calmly as she could.

''I don't think that's possible.'' Julie's answer was
wry. ''Different backgrounds or not, you both seem to
identify. It's more than chemistry, I can see that. Just
as I can see it might involve a lot of trauma.''

Cassie sipped at her coffee meditatively. ''I think I
know, Julie, who I am and what I want. I've been
drifting unsatisfied, unfulfilled. We've talked about it
often enough. I want commitment. A mature relationship before I'm too much older. I want children. I want

to share all the pleasure and the pains of my life. I want a husband to love. I want to be able to tell him I love him. I could never say it to my mother and father. Maybe that's one of the reasons I'm drawn to Matthew. I know he wants commitment, too. Family. The stable relationship he never had in his childhood.''

''I know, and it's just beautiful,'' Julie all but wailed, ''but your parents will kill you when they find out.''

Two hours later Julie was on her flight to Sydney, pretty flustered by all that was happening, but vowing not to say anything at all about Cassie's reason for staying on. ''You'll ring me just as soon as you get Red's response.'' She gave Cassie instructions. ''I'm really desperate to know how this turns out. This is your *life,* Cassie. Your future. I thought you were the one who had wisdom.''

Cassie didn't protest. ''I have to pin my faith on my deepest intuitions, Julie.'' She kissed her friend on the cheek and walked her to the departure gate. ''There are no guarantees in life. I've only known Matthew a very short time but I feel in my bones he's a fine human being.''

The same fine human being arrived on Cassie's doorstep late afternoon, eyes flashing blue fire under a fine head of steam.

''What's this supposed to mean?'' he demanded of Cassie without preamble, waving her letter in the air.

''Are you going to come in?'' she invited.

''No, I'm not,'' he returned bluntly. ''How do I know Julie isn't in this with you? Two cruel little city cats having a bit of fun.''

''It's not like that at all, Matthew. No way. I promise. Anyway, Julie has gone home. I drove her to the airport this morning. A member of her family died suddenly.''

''That's awful.'' His anger dimmed briefly. ''I'm sorry. Death hits even the rich. In the meantime, you're staying on. What are you hoping for? An outback adventure. Some fantastic sex?''

She almost laughed then, sobering quickly, said, ''No!''

''Come on, Cassandra. I'm a realist. You're playing a game. Well, I'll tell you, lady, with the *wrong* man.''

There were heavy footsteps in the hall. The next moment Molly hove into sight, carrying a huge vase of tropical lilies she had picked that morning. ''Cassie, I thought I heard you talking to someone,'' she exclaimed. Then, when Cassie moved, ''Ah, Red, how nice to see you. What brings you to town?''

''Business, Molly.'' He managed to sound casual. ''How did Jim get on on his fishing trip with Deputy Dan?''

''Hear about that, did you?'' Molly smiled broadly. ''There's nobody knows more about what's goin' on than Red,'' she told Cassie, placing the spectacular floral arrangement on the circular table. ''Don't know how he does it so far out of town.''

''You'd be surprised, Molly, who drops by.''

''The girls certainly enjoyed themselves,'' Molly stood back to admire her handiwork. ''Had a lovely time. I suppose Cassie's told you Julie had to fly off home.''

''Well, yes, but I've just arrived.''

''Come in and have a cup of coffee, then,'' Molly invited. ''Expect you're staying overnight at the pub?''

He nodded. "I'll start back before dawn."

"So, are you comin' in or what?" Molly looked from one to the other, her broad smile fading as she picked up on the atmosphere.

This time Matthew shook his head. "No thanks, Molly. I have a problem to address."

Molly moved uncomfortably. "Oh, sure, right."

"Don't mean to be rude, Moll. I was hoping Cassandra, here, would come back into town with me. We have something to discuss."

"A date, is that it?" Molly asked cautiously.

"Not at all. A *discussion*," Matthew said impassively. "Coming, Cassandra?" He transferred his hard gaze to Cassie's face. Her beautifully sculpted cheekbones were tinged with colour, but her eyes were calm and level.

"If you wait just a moment I'll grab a shirt." Some sort of cover-up. She was wearing a sleeveless indigo top with matching drawstring trousers, but it felt right to put something over the top. For one thing, she wasn't wearing a bra. Matthew's gaze was like a lick of flame.

Molly was staring at them both with a hint of puzzlement. "Everything okay with you two?"

Red flashed her his beautiful smile. "I promise I'll bring Cassandra back safe and sound."

Inside Matthew's Jeep all was quiet but for the knocking of Cassie's heart. Matthew was silent driving on down the coast road, stopping at a point where the beach became accessible.

"Let's go for a walk," he said in a clipped voice, putting the vehicle into park and switching off the ignition.

"All right." She opened out her door and sprang onto the grassy verge.

Everywhere was radiant light, the cobalt-blue sea stretched to the horizon, floating coral cays and emerald islands surrounded by blazing white sand. The throbbing heat of midday had cooled off and the breeze swished through the tall coconut palms and the dense vegetation that gave life and colour to the cascading slopes. Armies of little wildflowers in scarlet, vermilion, deep blue, and gold embroidered the foliage while all about an array of bougainvillea blossomed prolifically.

It was ravishingly beautiful, tranquil, the golden sand shifting beneath Cassie's feet. The water near the edge was so crystal clear she could see all the pretty little shells lying on the seabed. She turned her head, seeing the long stretch of beach to the headland was deserted. There was no one around but the flocks of gulls that took to the air at her unexpected appearance.

Matthew, vigorously crunching his way across the sand, caught up with her and took hold of her arm. She was forced to stop.

"What do you expect to come of all this?"

Her breath caught in her throat at the severity of his expression. She remembered then the stories about his temper.

"Is it so incredible to believe I meant it?" She spoke, emotionally seduced by his gaze. "After all, you've had dozens of letters."

"Dear God." He turned his handsome head towards the sea where a shoal of small fish were leaping from the waves. "I want the truth, Cassandra," he gritted.

"I meant every word." She gave a choked little cry and tried to break away.

He held her hard. "Sorry. I'm not buying it. I suppose the two of you laughed yourselves sick at your boldness."

"Did you think my letter bold?" A stab of deepest anxiety pierced her. She had tried so hard to get it right.

"It would have been a beautiful letter. From a stranger. Not from *you*." He stood proudly, unsmilingly, cleft chin upthrust.

"That's it? Not from *me*." Her spirits lifted. *A beautiful letter*. "I'm like you, Matthew. I want a life. I want a husband, family. I'm longing to live my dream."

"So you said in your letter," he cut her off. "The brutal fact is, you'd hate every moment of living Outback. Even the town is only a very small community. There aren't any theatres, nightclubs, concert halls. No flash department stores and boutiques to go shopping. No luxury. Only peace and quiet and the land."

"You don't think I feel its tremendous attraction?" She looked at him, challenging him to deny it.

"I feel you and I have something utterly different going," he said with hard meaning.

Cassie bent her head in acknowledgment. "I only know I've never felt like this before."

His hands took her shoulders. "How do I know you're not some consummate actress? Why don't you level with me? What do you want, a quick affair before you vanish?"

She blushed. "Do you intend to talk to all the other women who wrote to you like this?"

He ignored her. "Hell, don't you realise you could have been taking a big risk?"

"I trust you, Matthew," she said, and she really did.

Something flashed in his eyes and he grasped the long fall of her hair with one hand.

"What sort of a future could *we* have?"

"A good one if we work at it. I'm not so very different from you. In my own way I was abandoned. That's not going to happen to my children."

He reflected on this with a daunting frown. "You're dreaming," he said at last. "Fantasising. All on the basis of one kiss." Even then there was residual passion in his voice.

"You felt what I felt," she returned simply. "You can't deny it."

"So? It's only because you're so beautiful." He spoke coolly. "A magnolia who shouldn't be uprooted. You don't know anything about loneliness or isolation. Doing it hard. This idea about living happily ever after isn't enough. It takes much more than sexual fascination to make a marriage. Or is it like I said, you're just plain bored?"

It seemed to her she might never convince him. "The first moment I saw you I sensed some part of what was going to happen," she offered.

"Are you going to call it Fate?" His voice was tight.

"Is that so strange?"

"Don't you dare cry," he said sharply, uncertainly.

"It's the salt air in my eyes." She blinked and her voice began to falter. "I promise you, Matthew, my letter was written in all sincerity. I know how you might think it was some kind of joke. I know I'm as much a mystery to you as you are to me, but I'm not like that. Cruelty, insensitivity, is something I've had turned on me most of my life. The more I see of you, the more I want to learn.''

"This is so damned crazy," he muttered in a low voice. "Dangerous. Aren't you scared?"

"Of course I am." She spoke nervously. In reality she was intoxicated, out of balance. It was wonderful just to be with him again. Even if he was angry. He was like some marvellous ray of attraction with his intensely male sexuality, his power and vigour, the eyes of a visionary. Who needed safety?

The sky above them began to fill with long billowing clouds to set the sun to rest. Broad golden beams of sunlight were pervaded by a pink mist. Sunset was approaching to silence them with its beauty.

"You know nothing about me, nothing at all." He raised a hand to his temple, a gesture of uncertainty, exasperation.

"Some things we take on faith without *knowing* it." Cassie was disturbed by her own headlong behaviour.

"You want to escape. You're not happy."

"I haven't been happy for a while now," she said after some moments, staring up at the splendour of the sky.

"I'm surprised to hear that. You're beautiful, rich. Ah, I get it, you've had an unhappy love affair." His tone was dry. "You're trying to forget."

"I don't give a damn about anyone." She faced him, catching at her skeining hair. "There is no one. Do you want a wife or not, Matthew?" she challenged.

"Stop it. Damn it, Cassandra," he said as though she was making him feel desperate and trapped. "You're not the right girl to come into my life. You don't understand what you're letting yourself in for."

"So, I'm rejected?" She felt a weight of terrible dismay.

"Listen, why don't we go into town?" His eyes creased against the setting sun. A glory of crimson rose-pink and gold. "Have something to eat."

She hated herself for agreeing. Tormented now by her vulnerability to the man. "All right," she replied almost curtly.

"I'm sorry, Cassandra, if I don't respond to the shots as you call them."

"I'll keep trying."

"Why would you? Why *should* you?"

"Because it's important," Cassie said with surprising conviction.

By mutual accord they sought something more private than Marcy's, choosing Francesco's, an excellent small restaurant run by a local family with strong Italian roots. Arriving early as they did, the place was almost empty, but as they took their time over a pre-dinner drink other customers began to arrive, some with children, their voices bright and cheerful as they greeted their host and different members of the family, all accomplished cooks, who took turns manning the restaurant. Cassie felt too intense to be hungry but delicious aromas kept wafting from the kitchen whenever the swinging doors opened and shut.

"The ravioli here is wonderful," Matthew mentioned, himself infected by her mood. His face uplit by the blossoming candlelight was all planes and angles. "A simple enough dish yet plenty get it wrong. Frank uses the finest, freshest ingredients. They speak for themselves. Come to think of it, I've never been here when the food wasn't good. We'll eat whenever you're ready, Cassandra. Maybe after that you'll be ready to talk.''

Cassie laughed wryly. Not a terribly good beginning, she thought, but from the first bite of a beautifully tender pillow of pasta with a delectable filling of eggplant and a marvellous sauce which turned out to be melted zucchini flowers, Cassie began to unwind. If only there was no...issue between them, this would be a joy.

Matthew ordered a bottle of red wine and for the space of the meal, which included the classic *vitello tonnato,* they simply savoured the food. Francesco came over to the table smiling broadly, complimenting Cassie on her beauty while they in turn complimented him on a memorable meal.

"How have I never seen you before?" Francesco asked Cassie with a wide grin which embraced Matthew.

"This is my first time." Cassie smiled. "I sincerely hope it won't be the last."

"Not the first time for Red." Francesco clapped hand on Matthew's shoulder. "But the first time I see such a light in his eyes!"

"Hell, Italians are such romantics," Matthew said in a throw-away voice after Francesco had moved on. "I can see what the candlelight is doing to your face, let alone my eyes."

"What is it doing?" Cassie looked at him, her wineglass cupped like a chalice between her two slender hands.

He didn't answer for a moment. "Your skin has turned to pale gold," he began. "Your eyes are no longer silver-grey, they've taken on the violet of your shirt. Your mouth is as tender as a child's but very much a woman's. You're powerfully beautiful, Cassandra. I don't know how to describe what you've got. On the one hand it's all sensuality and plenty of it, on the other, there's high intelligence, a flame of purity, goodness, sensitivity. It's enormously intriguing. Tell me about your childhood.'' He gave her a straight, interested look.

It touched her that he didn't just consider her a body. She sipped at her wine then put it down. ''Not uncommon, Matthew.'' When goodness knows it was. ''As I've told you, my father is a very successful businessman. Making money is his life. My mother, in her own way, is devoted to him. He provides her with just the sort of life she craves. They travel a great deal. My father never embarks on a business trip without my mother. Their marriage works for them. It's solid.''

''So, material success and high social position are at the heart of it?''

''Very much so,'' she said softly, like a sigh. ''A great many people feel that way.''

''You seem a little traumatised by it all.'' He reached across the table, unexpectedly putting a hand over her own, a gesture that made tears sting her eyes.

''I probably was when I was very young. I was a sort of formless little kid. I didn't quite know what my place was in the scheme of things. I wasn't the light of my parents' eyes. I couldn't fail to know that even if I didn't understand it. I had a nanny from birth until I was seven. I loved her and I continue to see her. Then when she left, I was sent off to boarding school. It was there I met Julie. We looked into one another's eyes and were friends. Just like that. Julie's a lot of fun.''

"Yet on the face of it, you don't seem to have a lot in common?" He said it as he saw it, from his own observation.

"Actually we share a great deal of affection and loyalty. Opposites attract." She gave him a slight mocking smile. "Maybe being opposites is essential to balance. You have a dark side to *you*, Matthew."

He nodded his red head. "So I have. We've both lived our little dramas. You seem to have found out about mine." This with a tinge of bitterness.

"It wasn't simple curiosity." She held his gaze. "I wanted to see into your heart and your mind and your soul."

The muscle along his taut jawline worked. "How in earth did it happen?" He ran his fingertips across his wide brow.

"You mean, our attraction? It's not just me, is it, Matthew?"

His handsome face was so still it looked carved. She didn't move, either, waiting on his reply.

"On the basis of one kiss? A couple of days together? Showing you all Jabiru has to offer?"

"It's possible." In the soft warmth she felt a little chill. "I believe there is a connection between events no matter how seemingly random. I don't remember you being so hard on the writers of your other letters."

Still he said, "With a couple of exceptions, they weren't trying to make an ass of me."

Her quick flush answered him. "You know I'm not."

The hardness inside of him softened at her expression. "All right, I accept that, but I have this troubled feeling about it, Cassandra." He looked at her levelly with his piercing eyes.

"You know what it is?" She felt the two of them were locked in a bubble. "You're scared of loving someone, Matthew, and you're trying to protect yourself. You want a woman who'll accommodate all your needs but won't get under your skin. Really falling in love hurts."

A harsh protest rose in his throat. "Not only that, it can muck up a life." He turned his head, looking for a waiter. "Let's have a coffee."

"I don't mind." She lifted the heavy fall of her hair at the back of her neck. The restaurant was entirely filled now, people around them exclaiming at the food, the children tucking into thick crusty bread, mopping up the remains of spaghetti.

"And you'd have to give up your very comfortable life in Sydney, your very good job, the prospects of promotion Julie was talking about, to settle down on an Outback cattle station?" Matthew said eventually. He stopped talking as the waiter arrived with their short black espresso coffees, then left.

"I don't know all that's coming, Matthew," she conceded. "How could I? I thought I wanted a career. It seemed to be important to be a success as my father expected. And I am. I'm well regarded in the firm. But I wouldn't give my life to a career. I told you what I want. Love. Family. Husband, wife, children. The full traditional bit. I've given a lot of thought to this. I've enjoyed the adrenaline rush of my job, the rock beat of big business, getting all the calculations right, but it's not the full picture. The *right* picture. I could love you if you let me. I could love your way of life. I want to share your vision. I admire you so for all you've achieved."

"Have you ever been in love?" he suddenly shot at her. "Tell me *now* before you have time to think."

"No." She paused.

"Is that the truth?"

She looked up at his handsome face and found it taut and hawkish. "Once I thought I was."

"Thank you," he said dryly, his handsome mouth twisting.

"The feeling didn't last."

"So where is he now?" The brilliant eyes stared into her face.

"Actually, I work with him," Cassie admitted, wondering if she should have told a white lie.

"So in a way it *is* flight?" A little cloud of hostility had set in, breaking up the fragile rapport.

She shook her head and said in a neutral tone, which was actually a quiet challenge, "I've no more argument to present, Matthew. I can see your unease. We've only had this short time together, I know, but either you accept me or push me out of your life forever. I have to go home Friday." Either way I've been burnt badly.

"You started this, Cassandra." The words burst from Matthew with the force of pent-up passion. "Now we both have to live with it. I'm damned well not going to give you an instant answer. I know what it's like running around with a ring through the nose. I'm a cattleman remember?"

Francesco came to see them off, exclaiming again at Cassie's beauty, bowing over her hand, giving Matthew another thump on the shoulder, making it look like happy, earthy congratulations. Matthew thought it was time to get out before Frank started teasing him unmercifully. He and Adelina, Frank's wife, were always encouraging him to get married.

"Get someone to wait on *you*," Frank often said, and laughed. "No good, a man being on his own."

He could run off with a beautiful princess. Be totally enraptured until the princess decided she'd had enough of the back blocks and left him sick of heart and forsaken. Both of them lapsed into a silence while he drove back to the luxury hideaway on the headland.

"I haven't asked you what Julie thinks of all this," Matthew said finally into the fraught silence.

She didn't turn her face to him. "She's concerned."

"Well, hell, she isn't a fool, exactly."

Her own anger surfaced. "Let it alone, Matthew. I hear you loud and clear."

"Meanwhile we lust after each other." That when the beginnings of love were flowing into him and with it a lot of unexpected stress.

It must have hurt her because she dropped her head, giving a little smothered cry to which he responded powerfully.

He braked and scanned the road he knew so well. A minute later he turned the Jeep off the road, pulling into a scenic vista bordered by white timber rails. The sea was shining all around them, the sky fantastic, glittering with stars, the air smelling so sweetly of the sea and the thousands of little wildflowers that rioted across the vegetation and down the sandy slopes.

"Ah, Cassie." Beyond composure, finding himself with her in the melting dark, he moved to clasp her face between his hands, feeling the trembling that broke over her as he lowered his head.

She had no standard by which to measure his enormous fascination. It was enchantment, emotion running so deep she could feel the heat of it on their skin. There was a buzzing in her ears, in her veins. She wanted him with all her body. Very nearly so with all her heart. But she knew he was a lot tougher than she could ever be. She knew he was a man who could make hard decisions. Who would do anything to arrange his life.

His hands moved to her shoulders and stopped there. The bones so delicate, so elegant, he felt steam was actually coming off him, his desire for her was so powerful, burning him up. She wasn't wearing a bra. How could he not notice? That pretty little top all that was between her and her bare skin. The filmy shirt that changed the colour of her eyes fell back like a shawl so all evening he could see the tender, shadowed cleavage, imagining the rose-pink of the nipples that peaked so erotically against the indigo-blue fabric.

The beauty of the night, the scents and the burning diamond-white of the stars were increasing his feelings of wildness, of going out of control.

It shouldn't be. He had worked hard at being his own master. He wasn't going to let go of it for a woman. She was right. It scared him. This feeling of being spellbound like she had stolen his soul.

Her eyes were closed. He knew there were tears behind her eyelids. He kissed them, staring down into her beautiful, luminous face. Was this the woman to take to the rough bush? She deserved the finest mansion. A man who had no stain on his background, not Jock Macalister's bastard son. He thought he had risen above it. Now, with this woman, it was a source of exquisite pain.

"I want you," he groaned. He thought he had his life in near perfect order. How things had changed! He tried to pull her closer but the console was the stumbling block. A tiny barrier yet it seemed insupportable. "We have to get out," he said very urgently, feeling the fine tremble in his hands.

"Hold on." She shook her head frantically, trying to whip herself back to some sort of control. "What *is* it you want of me, Matthew?" she pleaded. This man in some ways was as wild as a falcon.

He let out a shuddering breath. "You haunt me too much. I want to make love to you. Can't you just accept it?"

"No." If she did she would never be free of him. Her body began to arch and she held up her hands defensively. "I've been trying to convince you I could make you a good *wife* and you've been pushing me away. You refuse to take me seriously. You're a man who likes to keep control. I'm too—what do you say?—*exotic* to take a place in your life, but I'm plenty good enough to make love to."

"My God! You are," he rasped. "Actually, Cassandra, you're a first for me."

"You could tell me what that means. A first? You're not taken with the idea? Does it disempower you," she taunted.

Abruptly he reached out and gripped her shoulders. "Already you've got the power to wound." He sobered up at her small cry, softened his grip, apologised. "I didn't hurt you?"

"No." Her head fell forward with a mixture of helplessness and yearning. "There's nothing safe about us. *Nothing.*"

"Not from where I'm sitting." His voice was laced with self-derision. "There's no insurance we can take out."

Now she felt his hand on her long hair, fisting it, drawing it away from her face.

"Matthew." She began trembling, her hair spilling everywhere like silk, but already his mouth came back to hers, so passionate, so sizzling, she could feel her whole system turn molten, then…melt. He was willing her to risk everything, to move down to the beach, allow his hands and his mouth to race over her, her life's blood beating hot and wild beneath her skin. So easy to get her out of her clothes, so light, so fine. He was already slipping her voile shirt and her camisole top from her shoulder, baring it to his mouth that nevertheless spoke a kind of silent love.

"Matthew," she began again before things got totally out of hand.

"I'm so glad you call me that. I thought I would be Red for the rest of my days." He pressed his mouth into the hollow above her collarbone. "Damn you for making a fool of me, glorious Cassandra. Damn you for coming here looking like a princess on a royal visit."

"I really didn't have much say in it," she whispered. "It was Fate."

"So we don't know what we're up against? This could pass for you, Cassandra." He released her edgily and sat back in his seat. "Like a bout of fever. Once you're back in the city among your own kind. Not the least of it the guy in the office who's in love with you. I bet he considers himself among the high fliers. You could talk it over with Julie. Blame it on the tropics."

"That's absolutely wrong." She protested with her first real despair. Didn't he know she couldn't think of anything else *but* him? She drew away trying to straighten her shirt. "Maybe you should stick with a sweet little hardworking country girl, after all. A good cook with a green thumb. One who won't let it bother her you don't really love her. That's life. She answered an advertisement. She's not about to complain. There'll be babies, a home, financial security. She knows how to count her blessings.''

He nodded, indolently, looking unbelievably handsome and thoroughly arrogant. ''Well, hell, Cassie,'' he drawled. ''Any man in his right mind wants a peaceful life, not a woman who befuddles his brain and gets between his ribs and his heart. 'Course I didn't stay long at school. Never went to university. No money for that. We were very very poor. How's that for Jock Macalister's only son?''

Cassie shivered at the bitterness. All the deeply entrenched pain.

''Of course, he's the *only* one who's not certain of who I am,'' Matthew added.

''He'd know it in two seconds if he ever laid eyes on you,'' Cassie burst out, and wished more than anything she hadn't.

''That's a damn odd thing to say, Cassandra.'' He placed a finger under her chin and turned her face to him. ''Explain.''

''I told you. I met him once.''

''When you were a child?'' He raised his distinctive black brows. Macalister's brows.

''I was clever even then. Very observant.''

Still cupping her face with one hand, he ran a very shivery finger behind her silky ear.

''You wouldn't be lying by any chance?''

''No way,'' she said, colouring, glad of the glimmering dark.

''He could very well do business with your company,'' Matthew continued suspiciously. ''He's into everything. Real estate. Freight, oil, energy.''

''I met him once in my life.'' Cassie told the truth, still lacking the courage to reveal the rest. The scent of danger was all around the Macalister name. ''I told Molly I wouldn't be out long.'' She turned her face away, perturbed by her own passion and her slight control. ''Why don't you drive me home?''

''I guess that's best.'' What he felt for this woman was almost against his will, but still he asked, ''And our unfinished business?''

''Sleep on it, Matthew,'' Cassie advised. ''Weigh it up.''

CHAPTER SIX

HE DIDN'T contact her at all before she went home, knowing it was cruel; just as sure it was necessary. He wasn't quite ready to make the most important decision of his life realising his attitude was coloured by his own early sufferings.

Yet the thought, *What have I done?* raged constantly through his mind. For the first time he found it difficult to sleep, his work-weary body twitching in bed, often until dawn when the soft grey light streamed into his room and he got up to stare out the window. Even the sky reminded him of a pair of luminous eyes.

She would have made the journey back to Sydney thinking him a callous brute. This gave him tremendous concerns. If he was so disturbed, so, he was sure, was she.

But she had to return to her own life, friends and family, her own community, to view what had happened with any detachment. Everyone had heard of a holiday romance. People going on boat trips, having a fling. Flings weren't his nature. He'd had an eternity to ponder on what had happened to his mother. An eternity of bearing the brunt of a rash, ill-advised liaison. It was entirely conceivable once back among her own kind, Cassandra would come to believe their headlong attraction, so wildly at variance with their normal behaviour was just some powerful aberration to be put right. But then, a man of action, he had to *do* something.

It came to him during the night, so the next morning he rose early, got the men together, allocated them their respective jobs then organised a trip to Sydney. Maybe Cassandra wouldn't be thrilled to see him. Maybe she'd refuse to see him. It had been all of three weeks but he had learned something as frightening as it was thrilling. Right or wrong, he didn't want to live without her. She filled him with passion, with energy, a longing to carve out a great future. He knew he had it in him to give her a fine life.

Back in Sydney, Cassie had two priorities. To forget Matthew Carlyle. To keep her mind on her job. She was up for promotion. Julie's father waxed lyrical about her capacity for cutting to essentials, her coolness in tight situations. It was early days, she was a bit young for it, but she was a serious contender for Phil McKinnon's job now that he was moving up in management.

Cassie spent many long hours at her desk, tapping away at her computer, threading her way through innumerable facts and figures. All to prove her prowess. She was very good at tracking and cross-tracking numbers. It was a language she had got to know and understand. She didn't fare anywhere as well trying to forget Matthew. He smiled at her from behind her eyes.

Julie was shocked but relieved at her return.

"Obviously he was deeply attracted to you but he must have realised, Cassie, it would never have worked," she pointed out gently.

"Who the heck knows what is or isn't going to

work?'' Cassie fired back, upset and exasperated. ''There couldn't be an institution more subject to risk than marriage. Falling in love and getting married isn't a guarantee of bliss. It's like being infected by a fever. Neither person can run out and buy insurance.''

''I know. I know, but couldn't you love Nick?'' Julie pleaded. ''He worships the ground you walk upon. Even your father spent quite a deal of time talking to him at our Christmas party, don't you remember?''

Cassie made a dismissive gesture with her hand. ''Nick has mastered the knack of buttering up to V.I.P.'s.''

''True,'' Julie agreed with a wry grimace. ''But he was especially nice to your father for a reason. He's hoping to be looked on as a prospective son-in-law.''

''But it's over, Julie, and it can't be resurrected,'' Cassie said. ''It's Matthew who's captured my heart.''

A kind of despair settled on Julie's face. ''But he was always a wild card, Cass. And he has a very problematic background. What a fight you would have trying to get your parents to accept him.''

''Don't I know it.'' Cassie felt the old familiar knots in her stomach.

''Don't think my heart doesn't bleed for you,'' Julie said quietly, ''but the connection between your father and Red's. Did you ever tell him the *full* story?''

Anxiety seethed in Cassie's soul. ''I regret to say, no. I wanted to, but I couldn't. Matthew would have exploded if I'd said Jock Macalister was my father's *friend* as well as sometimes business associate. Anyway, what does it matter now?'' She sighed and picked up the phone to ring a client. ''Matthew completely rejected me.''

"I could kill him," Julie muttered darkly, seeing Cassie's deep hurt.

"That's okay." Cassie looked at her friend with shadowed eyes. "Given time, I'll get over it."

Cassie had dinner with her parents on the Saturday night, asking Nick along for company, because these supposedly quiet family dinners usually turned into a gathering.

Fourteen in all sat around the gleaming mahogany table, elaborately decked out with the finest china, crystal, silver, exquisite white linen and lace place mats with matching napkins. There were two low crystal bowls of white lilies flanking a filigree silver basket of luscious summer fruits and table grapes. Tapering candles in Georgian sterling silver candlesticks were placed meticulously down the table length.

The overhead chandelier was on the dimmer and candlelight threw a flattering light over the faces of the women. Everyone, with the exception of Cassie, was middle-aged but beautifully preserved through a strict diet and beauty routine. Cassie's own mother, in deep burgundy silk, could have passed for ten years younger, or as Nick put it outrageously on arrival, "I have to hand it to you, Mrs. Stirling. You look more like Cassie's sister with every passing day."

So what does that make me now? Cassie thought wryly. I must be showing the strain. In fact she looked beautiful in white silk crepe scattered with sequins, her mane of hair drawn into an elegant chignon and secured with a bejewelled clip the way her parents liked it. These dinners were invariably black tie. No backyard barbeques for the Stirlings. Her mother, in fact, would not have been caught dead in a pair of jeans.

Now Cassie looked down the table at her father, scrutinising him over the waxy petals of the lilies. He had a wonderful profile, his handsome head turned as he tossed off a joke to one of the women guests. He was a big man. Tall with broad shoulders but not heavy. He looked what he was: a rich, influential man, his personal wealth understated, not commented on.

He really needed a son to carry on the wonderful business empire he had built up, Cassie thought. A son in his own image. Not me. Women didn't really count to her father beyond the basic and obvious pleasure of their beauty, the charm of their conversation, the buzz of their admiration and artful flirtatiousness.

He turned, caught Cassie's eyes on him and raised his glass to her in a smooth, studied toast. She knew she was looking good. It was definitely about pleasing him. She was wearing the jewellery he had given her for her twenty-first birthday. A necklet of large South Sea pearls, with matching pearl earrings set in a basket of gold studded with diamond points. A glorious present as befitting the sort of patrician father he considered himself to be.

At least the gift had impressed everyone at the celebration when her mother had invited every young man she considered suitable for Cassie to fall in love with. That had included Nick. This was far from being his first time inside her parents harbour-side mansion.

Her father, who did approve of Nick, wouldn't like Matthew. She knew that in her bones. Even if Matthew weren't Jock Macalister's son. Her mother wouldn't hesitate to call Matthew uncouth. The fact was, anyone who didn't have money, dressed carelessly, or drove a battered car would be considered a boor. A terrible sense of loss continued to bear down on her. She had only known Matthew such a short time but he had captivated her utterly.

While the conversation eddied around her she absorbed the familiar scene, trying to place Matthew somewhere in it. Dressed in a costly dinner suit like her father's, his wonderful dark red hair brushed straight back from his wide brow, maybe an inch or so off it at the back, Matthew would easily eclipse any man at the table. Including her father.

No one had the blazing intensity of Matthew's blue eyes, that electric air. Matthew, she had found, could be witty, charming, clever. He mightn't have gone to university but she was prepared to bet he could hold his own in any discussion going on around this table. He was totally his own person. He was a true achiever. He was also the last man in the world her parents would regard as an excellent match.

"Where did you go off to?" Nick asked much later as he escorted Cassie to his car.

"Why make it sound like I've been orbiting Mars? I've been to too many of these rituals, Nick, I can't take a seat at my parent's table without grieving."

"About what?" Nick asked in genuine puzzlement.

"Family togetherness," Cassie said. It was the simple truth.

When they arrived outside Cassie's apartment block, Nick begged to come up. "I don't think that would help, Nick." Cassie pulled away from the hand that had moved caressingly around her neck.

"What's happened to you since you went away on holidays?" Nick demanded, his handsome face perplexed. "Where *are* you really?"

"Right here."

"Was it someone you met up there?" Nick persisted, a frown appearing between his brows.

"If I did, they turned me down," Cassie said in a wry voice, preparing to get out of the car.

"Are you serious?" Nick caught her arm, restraining her. "Let's get this cleared up. You met some guy and he turned you down?"

"They don't do that often," Cassie joked.

"So now you know what it feels like," Nick said. "I love you, Cassie."

"And I love you, too." She reached back and kissed his cheek. "But as a dear friend. Not someone I want to spend my life with. We've had all this out, Nicko."

"Ah, a *pal!*" He stared into her face. "That's not too bad for now. I'm going to give you time, Cassie, to get over your fantasies." Nick stepped swiftly out of the car and came around to Cassie's side, helping her out onto the street. "Marriage is a big step. We've both got plenty of time to think about it. A big thing I've got going for me is your father approves of me."

"What about *me?*" Cassie asked laconically.

"Your father is very proud of you. He told me," Nick said in a tender voice, but Cassie only smiled.

"I don't suppose you noticed I left home as soon as I was able. I think it was close to six months before anyone noticed. Anyway, thank you for coming with me, Nicko. You're always so supportive."

"Can't I come up for ten minutes?" he begged, the old desire pumping. "I promise I won't overstay my welcome." Nick reached out and tightly held her to him. Such a beautiful girl but so vulnerable. Of course her parents adored her. It was simply they led such a high-powered life.

Matthew, watching from the shadowed interior of a

hire car, was witness to this tenderly passionate scene. Now the guy was kissing her, his whole body language yearning. In the lights from the well-lit exterior of the swish apartment block, Matthew could see the man was roughly his own age, maybe a year or two younger, tall, dark-haired, dressed in an outfit Matthew had never worn in his life nor ever expected to. An expensive dinner suit. He wore it with easy grace. He couldn't stop kissing Cassandra and Matthew felt a momentary delirium, an intense rush of jealousy, raw and pure. The thought of another man touching her. He felt his hands clench on the steering wheel. His breathing stopped as he waited for the next move. He didn't care if it was right or wrong, he was going to stop it.

Cassandra broke away.

The relief he felt was so acute it actually hurt. She was shaking her head, saying something.

"'Bye-bye, Nicko," she called.

Then she was almost running. It was time for him to move. He'd been waiting in the visitors' parking lot for over two hours. He had found both her parents' address and hers simply from running a finger down the phone book. He got a recorded message when he rang Cassandra's phone, thrilling to the sound of her voice again, tongue-tied for a moment when it came time for him to speak after the beep.

He'd even driven past the Stirlings' mansion, impressed despite himself at its sheer size and imposing structure, the magnificent position overlooking arguably the finest harbour in the world. The mansion, one simply couldn't call it a house, was all lit up. Obviously some kind of party was in progress. Though the frontage was walled to a man's height, he could see several luxury cars parked around the driveway through the massive wrought-iron gates. Probably Cassandra was there, celebrating some event at the family home.

Finally he drove back to her apartment block and waited. And waited. That was hard. He wasn't a man for much waiting about.

Now here she was. He could feel the instant heat, the adrenaline rush, that flooded into his body. What's his name—Nicko—was back in his car, driving away.

Matthew acted, leaping a small beautifully manicured hedge to meet up with Cassandra before she activated the security door and went inside.

"Cassandra," he called once. Then louder. "Cassandra." This was what he preferred, action.

She turned and saw him, the shock registering on her beautiful face. She was wearing a white dress that sparkled, a dream of a dress, her wonderful hair drawn away from her face and knotted at the back. He could see some ornament that held the gleaming masses. Diamonds, crystals. It glittered.

Then he stood before her, a kind of anguish on his face, his high cheekbones flushed with the sudden torrent of emotion. "I need to see you," he said.

"What can you possibly want to say?" Anger and passion overlapped. Hadn't he put her through hell for weeks?

"Hello, beautiful Cassandra," he said, his vibrant voice a little unsteady. "It's wonderful to see you again."

"God, Matthew."

She struggled to come to terms with her warring feelings. Pride demanded she send him on his way.

"Let's go inside. Talk," he urged.

Such was his powerful fascination, Cassie let him in. "How did you know where I lived?"

"The phone book, what else?" He was desperate to touch her. Didn't.

"You didn't call Julie?"

"Let's keep Julie out of it." He only wanted to talk about *them.* "I even drove over to your parents' house. Be it ever so humble."

"I was there for a dinner party."

"With Nicko?" He had another powerful urge to sweep her into his arms, kiss her, but he didn't want to appear the reckless wild man. They were in the elevator that took them to the tenth floor where Cassie had bought her apartment with some of her inheritance from her maternal grandmother.

Every nerve in her body was jumping. She felt like she was being deliberately teased.

Matthew Carlyle.

They were inside the apartment that she had made as attractive as she knew how, listening on one level to Matthew saying how much he liked it, the English floral upholstery, the couple of beautiful antique pieces, the three remarkable paintings, all left to her by her grandmother. The objects, the porcelains, two bronzes of a boy and a girl she had loved as a child. Having her grandmother's things around her comforted her. She wished she had her grandmother now to give her advice.

"Would you like something?" she asked, dropping her evening purse onto one of the sofas, trying to ease the enormous mounting tension.

"Just to look at you." He had been standing admiring one of the paintings, a magical landscape, now he turned, his blue eyes ablaze against his copper skin.

"You look radiant. A goddess come straight down from her pedestal. Is Nicko the guy in the office?"

"Does it matter?" It shamed her to realise how very much she was in his power.

"He is, isn't he?"

"Are you going to tell me why you're here?" Irked, she almost snapped.

"Like I said. To see you." His eyes appraised the large lustrous necklet of pearls, the fancy earrings, the unfamiliar hairstyle. "I've never seen your hair like that."

"Classical style," Cassie explained. "My father likes it this way."

"So the dutiful daughter wears it like that." He came across the room and closed in on her. He put out his hand, freed her hair of the jewelled pin, then the clips that secured the chignon, dropping them into the top pocket of his jacket, a navy blazer which he wore over an open-necked sapphire-blue shirt and a pair of dress jeans. His body was simply so tall, so perfectly proportioned, so elegant, he looked like a Calvin Klein ad.

"I've missed you, Cassandra." He felt turbulent in an odd blissful way, revelling in the scented weight of her loosened hair.

She drew in a sharp breath, at the same time impaled by his hand. His fingers were moving against her scalp, gently massaging, dropping to her nape, encircling it.

"Don't be angry at me," he muttered, intense desire in his eyes.

"I am angry." She was, and furiously aroused.

"Of course you are. Why wouldn't you be?" He sounded shaken and humble.

"Why didn't you even come to the airport?" She said, a tear glittering along her lashes.

He couldn't bear to see her wounded. "Because I'm a stupid, stupid, man. I don't believe it now, but I wanted to make it as hard for you as I knew how."

"You brute!" Her face flamed with feeling and her mouth, rose-tinged and velvety, shaped an exquisitely sensual pouting cushion.

The crackle in his blood rose to a roar. There was no time for her to refuse him. He hauled her hard against him, plunging his mouth over hers, a wild beating in his ears while he waited for her to yield to his onslaught. He knew it was wrong to force her. He believed, he hoped, he would never do that, but this fever inside him was making him dizzy.

He had never wanted any woman like this. The sheer power of that want had come as a terrible shock.

Gradually under that rage of passion, the hand that had been pushing with such futility against his shoulder, now slid across his chest, her fingers finding a button, working it free. She was caressing his bare skin, her fingers moving through the tangle of hair plying that taut flesh. If she continued to do that, all his precious control would surely crumble. My God, he was so hungry for her. Starved.

They were kissing open-mouthed, desperately, avidly, as if each couldn't get enough of the other. His hands moved down over her body, skimming the beautiful white dress that clung like a second skin, cupping her provocative small bottom, holding her tighter against his own throbbing body. The pleasure was dazzling, driving him on. Cassie's knees must have weakened because she was sliding limply against him, an invitation for him to pick her up and carry her through to her bedroom. Overwhelming desire tore the breath from his lungs. He felt as fierce and focused as a caveman. This woman he wanted. She was unbelievably alluring to him, the long hair, the silky skin, the slender limbs. He could almost feel himself entering her beautiful body.

But what would happen then? He who prided himself on his judgement. He *cared* about her too dammed much. Blindly he broke away. He hadn't come prepared for a sexual encounter, and he realised she had gone beyond the point where she was strong enough to resist him. He wasn't playing the good guy. He was mad for her, his whole body one compulsive, powerful dangerous machine, but it was more than probable he could make her pregnant. He felt virile enough. Insatiable. Making her pregnant was something he wished for with all his heart, but she had to crave it, too. In her own time.

"Cassandra." He scooped her up and sank into the plush depths of a sofa. Her short skirt had ridden up, revealing her slender legs pale and gleaming in the sheerest stockings. Past the shimmering hem of her skirt was the apex of her heart-shaped body. To touch her there would be glorious and a potential disaster. She was so vulnerable, so vulnerable.

It took Cassie many moments to find her voice, sensation still shooting through her body making her limbs tremble. "You're good at making me lose my head." Her words were huskily given.

"I couldn't go any further." His voice was deep, agonised, intimate. "I had to stop."

"Why?" When she was desperate for him to devour her.

"Why?" He searched for the answer, amazed at his

control. "Because it's the right thing to do." His nerves were as tight as wire. "What sort of man do you think I am? A man like my father? A man who takes what he wants without a thought for the woman. I know what that sort of behaviour brought to my mother."

Cassie sobered, under a flood of understanding. "But I'm not your mother, Matthew. I'm not even like her. I'm one of the generation educated to looking after themselves."

"You're on the pill?" His fingers that were playing with agitation through her hair, stilled.

"Ask no questions, hear no lies." Cassie wasn't going to go into any detail. "I'm not sexually adventurous but I have taken it, yes."

"You had a relationship with Nicko? Is that right?" He slipped instantly into a jealousy that left him shaken.

She pressed her head back into his shoulder. "On and off for about two years. But it's long over. Does that shock you?"

He stared away, his eyes glowing like coals. "I wish it hadn't happened."

"But you've had relationships, Matthew." She felt and sounded upset. "I know nothing about them."

"They *were* nothing," he countered. "Nothing compared to you."

"Then it's the same with me. I thought I was in love with Nick. He means a lot to me as a friend, but my emotions lacked deep involvement. I tried but I could never see myself as his wife."

"Did you live with him?" Matthew fought to overcome this dark jealousy, so new to him. It was something he hadn't been prepared for.

"No. It wasn't best for either of us. Neither of our families would have approved, anyway. Marriage, yes. Live-in relationships, no. My own space has always been important to me. Up until now."

"But you still see him?" He wanted to learn everything about her. Discover her secrets.

"I *work* with him, Matthew," she retaliated. "Our romance is finished but he's still my friend."

His hand slid around her face, dangerously electrical, forcing her to meet his eyes. "Watching you, I thought he was a lot more than that."

"No." She gave a little distressed sigh. "Nick could kiss me a thousand times and it would never add up to one kiss from you."

He released her then, giving his heart-wrenching smile. "Fine. Can I talk to you now?"

"I want you to." She lay breathless in longing while he pushed a cushion behind her head.

His heart thudding crazily, he tried to repress the passion the sight and nearness of her aroused. For the first time it struck him his hands were terribly rough. Okay, so they weren't a bad shape, but the inside of his fingers and his palms were calloused.

Amazingly she took his calloused hand and held it to her breast. "We'll work it out, Matthew. Neither of us could say goodbye easily."

"I should never have let you leave." His fingers moved to link with hers. "Why don't you come back with me to Jabiru for a few weeks? I want you to experience Outback life at first-hand. Living in the middle of nowhere. Then we can both be certain it's where you're going to thrive. Too much emotion has happened to us too fast." His voice deepened as he looked very earnestly into her lovely face, sensing she was both excited and troubled.

"You're asking me to live at the homestead with you? The two of us alone?"

God, it would be *perfect*. An answering excitement was like a blaze within him but he tried to bank it down. No use being hard and hungry. This was a princess. "I'm not asking for a trial marriage, Cassandra, though it's a powerful temptation."

"But you're *human*, Matthew." Her eyes sparkled like diamonds.

"You're telling me! I'm no saint." His vibrant voice rasped. There was a swift rise of colour beneath her velvety skin, a sure indication of her imaginings, her lying spread out on his bed, him deep inside of her, fevered with desire, glorying in possession. "I swear I would never take advantage of you, Cassie, even if it kills me. I care about you too much to sabotage my chances. Obviously it can't be the two of us *alone*. If you agree, there's an old mate of mine, Ned Croft, who could play chaperone or something very like it. He'd be right there, at any rate. He'd love to come. Ned's a real character and a good person. You'll like him."

"So we play house?" Cassie's lips parted on a shaky breath.

"Don't you want to?" His blue eyes smouldered.

"Oh, yes." Suddenly all misgivings fell away. She reached up to link her arms around his neck. "It sounds great."

CHAPTER SEVEN

CASSIE lay in her narrow bed, the mosquito netting billowing around her, eyes closed but ears alert for the early morning sounds. This was her third day on Jabiru and she was settling in beautifully. Ned was a real sweetie, with eyes as bright and innocent as a baby's. They had taken to each other at once.

Ned was never happier than roaming the station doing little jobs here and there, drinking billy tea with the men. It seemed to Cassie he idolised Matthew, and Matthew clearly looked on Ned as family. It had worked out well. Ned had a droll sense of humour, as well, and he was well aware he was there to keep a "sharp eye" on the household arrangements as he once told her in his spare funny way.

It was decided, on Cassie's insistence, she would take over the cooking, something that appeared to make both men happy, so that meant she had to be up at dawn to make breakfast. And a full breakfast at that. Juice, fruit, steak and eggs, lashing of tea and toast. No hardship. Matthew and Ned appreciated her efforts and she was coming to realise she was quite domesticated.

She loved the early mornings. Especially the predawn. Picaninny dawn, the Aborigines called it, a time of magic, so wonderfully peaceful and still when nothing moved except the stars as they picked up their swags of diamonds and left the velvety sky one by one.

In a few more minutes the dogs would begin to stir, then Ned, who had his bunk out on a veranda silvered by the moon. Cassie opened her eyes, threw back the mosquito netting and got a little gingerly to her feet. Her muscles were a bit stiff and sore after so much riding. She had never been on a horse for such long periods in years. But she was loving it, riding between Matthew and Ned as they toured various camps on the station. It was an exciting life, so open and free, but she could see at times brutally hard and dangerous. Terrible accidents weren't unheard of.

Matthew came behind her as she was slicing paw-paw and mango into a bowl, bestowing a heart-stopping smile upon her, allowing himself the luxury of nuzzling her cheek.

"Sleep well?" The intimacy of his tone lent great charm to his voice. There was the pleasant scent of a herbal soap. More luxurious, the scent of *him*.

"Did you?" she parried, thinking her whole life had changed.

"Think of it this way, Cassandra," he drawled, "I'm a man on a knife edge. Rapture lies into the future."

"I'm thinking it will have to with Ned around!" Cassie answered, excited and amused. Ned took his job of chaperone seriously.

They ate at the big pine table, Ned contending he hadn't eaten so well for years.

"And here I was thinking you enjoyed my cooking," Matthew teased.

Ned nearly choked to set him straight. "So I *do*. I do, but it's lovely having a woman around. One as sweet and beautiful as Cassie. She's a man's dream."

"I think that earns you another cup of tea, Ned." Cassie got up to fetch the teapot.

Later in the morning she sat in the leafy shade of a paperbark with a marvellously textured trunk, watching Matthew, stripped to the waist, repair a section of fencing at the Twenty Mile. The cattle had trampled it down in their efforts to break out into the wild country. Now when time presented they would have to be brought back.

What a beautiful man he was! Cassie thought, feeling her heart thud. He could have posed for Michelangelo, some heroic work of young male virility. She began to fan herself with her cream akubra, trying to cool her blood. Such a play of muscle across his tanned back. He had the body of a natural athlete, wide-shouldered, tapering into a narrow waist, lean, long, muscled flanks, strong straight legs. He was, she had found, possessed of an enormous energy and the wonderful vitality of an absolutely fit and healthy man. Even after rain the earth was as hard as a rock, but he was wielding the crowbar and shovel like he was slicing through cake.

"That should do it," he called out sometime later, walking towards her with his elegant stride. The fan of hair across his dark copper chest cut to a narrow trail down his taut torso and disappeared into his body-hugging blue jeans.

Cassie's tensed fingers bit into her arms. "Well, you promised me a swim, didn't you?" Feigning casualness, she stood up and smiled.

"Absolutely right. I dreamt about you last night," he said very softly.

"Want to tell me the content?" Cassie stared back at him, mesmerised. This hands-off seduction focused every one of her senses. Sometimes, like now, unbearably.

"For some reason we were on a yacht together." His eyes drank deeply of her. "The Whitsunday's. Turquoise blue into cobalt water, a fifteen-knot wind strumming against the sails, you in a bikini."

"What colour?" she asked on a shaky breath.

"Yellow. I remember that distinctly. Yellow like a hibiscus." He placed his right hand so gently against her cheek she closed her eyes. "This is hell. And heaven," he breathed. "Arousal without ever cutting loose."

"It's not the *worst* experience of my life," Cassie told him in a wry, husky voice. It was sexual excitement on a short leash. Breathless with just a touch.

"What a super day!" a cheerful voice called to them, breaking the spell. Ned riding towards them. "Just great! I've got a surprise for you two lovebirds. While you have yourselves a swim, I'm going to cook the damper. Got the coals just right. We can wash it down with a panniken of tea. How's zat?"

Matthew smiled his beautiful smile. "We won't say no, Ned."

They rode light-heartedly towards the nearest billabong, a long curving sheet of water, surprisingly deep, watching a brolga flap its great wings in what appeared to be slow motion. Cassie hadn't as yet witnessed one of their stately dances. She had been told all about them, now she was hoping she'd be privileged to catch a performance. The water in the sunlight glittered a metallic dark green, jade in the shallows, with stands of water reeds and small cream lilies lining the banks, the whole framed by magnificent gums. It

was the most wonderful natural swimming pool remote from anywhere.

It was as Cassie was slipping out of her cotton shirt
and jeans—she was wearing her two piece swimsuit
beneath—that the brolgas arrived, flying low above the
chain of billabongs in a bluish-grey cloud. Thousands
of budgerigars flew above them, a bolt of emerald silk
against the burning blue sky.

"Oh, Matthew, look!" Cassie cried out in delight,
running down the sandy slope to join him where he
stood near the shallows.

"Quiet now!" Matthew turned quickly and caught
her around her hands' span waist. "If we make any
noise, they'll take off."

She rested against him, his splendid male body clad
in black swimming briefs, his arm ringing her as the
brolgas turned into the wind and began touching down
with a series of running steps like stones skimmed
across the water. "How beautiful!" Cassie was en-
chanted. Now the budgerigars flashed low in formation
over the water, their chittering filling the air. "Do you
suppose they'll dance for us?" Her eyes shone in anticipation.

"Not while we invade their territory," Matthew
said carelessly, himself well used to the spectacle.
"It's *our* turn for a swim after all that labouring.
There'll be plenty of time, Cassie, don't worry." He
clapped his hands and immediately the cranes took off
again, racing forward on their long spindly legs, they
gained enough buoyancy to spread their great wings.
The air vibrated with the swoosh of their flight. They
stood and watched the birds until their shrieks faded
and the quivering sheet of water became calm again,
the surface silvered by the sun.

"They'll move to another water hole further down." Matthew transferred his gaze from the cloudless blue sky to Cassie beside him. His heart juddered at the sight of her, near naked and beautiful. Her swimsuit, a tiny little bra and bikini pants, to his desire-drugged eyes barely seemed to cover her, the brilliant tropical print accentuating her smooth-as-satin skin. This woman…this woman…was the great revelation in his life.

"Matthew?" She felt her blood catch fire at the look in his eyes. "What are you thinking?" On impulse she fingered the cleft in his chin.

"Why don't we make love on the sand?" His voice was tauter than he intended. Hell, this was fabulous, but he was continually on the edge, his passion for her like a hurricane that could obliterate his moral stand.

Even Cassie's little laugh fizzled out. "I was thinking the same thing."

"I suppose Ned wouldn't look," Matthew said very dryly.

"He might consider it an infringement of our deal."

"I guess so." Matthew pulled a contrite face. "So, let's swim. Cool off."

Despite the crystal-clear coldness of the water, the heat between them continued to sizzle and spark. Taking her hand, Matthew tugged her into deeper water, beginning to kiss her with passion and a flicking tongue that licked the droplets of water from her open mouth and her flawless skin. He felt unbearably frustrated, the two of them curling their limbs together until they sank beneath the emerald waters still kissing with abandonment.

When they had to surface again for air, Ned was pacing back and forth along the golden sand. "Are you two okay?'' he yelled, gnarled old hands framing his mouth.

"Yes, yes.'' Cassie began laughing, scooping up handfuls of water and throwing them up in the sparkling winelike air.

"Gawd, you gave me a bit of a fright, that's all.''

"Sorry, Ned, my fault.'' Beneath the water, Matthew's hands cupped Cassie's small breasts, the silky tantalising flesh. The provocation to strip the bra from her was powerful but he had made a commitment. He had to be crazy. But then he knew beyond doubt. He loved her.

Time didn't seem to have any meaning for her. The days just flew, never enough time for all the jobs that had to be done. Matthew as the Boss worked like a Trojan, never asking more of his men that he was prepared to do himself. He needed more staff, Cassie thought, even though they all appeared to be tireless. Everyone on the station recognised her now and seemed to accept her. She was a good rider, getting even better, and wasn't afraid of a bit of hard work herself, though she always wore gloves to protect her hands.

Matthew, delighted with her interest and enthusiasm and confident in her organising abilities and intelligence, allowed her to organise choppers and cattle trucks for the current muster, and selling, giving her a sense of teamwork, of belonging. Ned took it upon himself to instruct her in the art of survival in remote country and how to recognise good bush tucker. Everything fascinated her to the extent she gloried in life. She and Ned were the easiest of companions, so much so, Cassie felt she had known him all her life.

That day was spent herding cattle along the Pardoo Trail which led to the highway and the cattle trucks after two days' drove off. Matthew's foreman and three of the aboriginal stockmen were to continue walking the cattle in, but Matthew had other priorities.

They were sitting around the dinner table relaxing after a long day when Cassie introduced a topic that had been in her mind. "What you really need is wings of your own," she told Matthew, her face bright and animated.

He smiled at her. "Don't I wish. But I can't come up with that kind of money, Cass."

"I'd be honoured to contribute," she burst out without thinking.

Of a sudden, Matthew's handsome face closed. "No, Cassie," was all he said, but it sounded absolutely final.

Ned licked his lips, a little dismayed by Matt's tone. He had great respect for this girl. If she was out here to prove herself, she was going fine. "Why not consider a compromise, Matt?" he suggested. "You could do with a helicopter. You could run the show from up there."

"I can't afford it, Ned, you know that. Not yet, at any rate."

"But Cassie has offered to help out. Aren't you two getting hitched?"

For a minute it looked as though Matthew was going to react hotly, but he laughed, an edgy sound. "I'm giving Cassandra a chance to make up her mind, Ned. I'm not taking her money."

"Face it, son, you're too proud for your own good." Ned scratched his head.

Matthew gave another grin. "That's the way I am, Ned, but it was very generous of Cassandra to offer."

Things were different now. Cassie stared at him. Back to *Cassandra* when he had slipped into the shorter Cassie or Cass.

"All right. Sorry I mentioned it." Cassie felt her mouth go dry. She hadn't intended to hurt or offend him. His fiery pride was explained in part by his damaged past.

Now Matthew abruptly changed the subject. "I've been wanting to talk about tomorrow. We start drafting the horses. The cleanskins have to be branded and the stallions castrated. It's not a job anyone who cares about animals enjoys, but it has to be done. You won't need to come." He shot a glance at Cassie's face. That beautiful bright light had gone out. He cursed himself for that, but he couldn't take money off her.

"But it's all part of station life, surely?" she protested with a renewal of spirit.

"Of course."

"Then you're on." She wasn't giving up even if he did look strung up.

Matthew went to shake his head but Ned intervened. "Ar, Matt, so far Cassie's acquitted herself well. She was great today, holding the line. I didn't expect her to be so good. It ain't pretty, I agree, but like you said, it's a job that has to be done. Besides, it gives the ringers a chance to show off."

"I'll think about it," Matthew clipped off, his eyes still on Cassie's lovely sensitive face. It was a source of some wonderment to him she had fitted in so neatly, like a piece of a jigsaw puzzle. A princess passing life in the bush with flying colours. But he was worried about taking her along to the draft. Tough as *he* was, he hated the spectacle.

"Well, I'd better get the washing up done." Aware of his withdrawal, Cassie rose from the table.

"Let me help you, love." Ned leapt up in his sprightly fashion, aware she was hurt.

"You have a bit of a rest, Ned." Matthew shook his head, reminded of Ned's age and their full day. "Cassie can wash, I'll wipe."

"Might have one little snort of whisky," Ned said gleefully. "Help me sleep."

"Go right ahead." Matthew walked around the table only to break into a mild curse as all the lights suddenly went out.

"Damn it, the generator."

Cassie was astonished by the blackness. It was total. "We're not out of fuel. I checked." Her voice sounded a little shaken.

"Probably a blockage in the fuel line," Ned guessed correctly.

"Gosh, it's pitch black." Cassie put her hand out uncertainly, feeling swallowed up in a dark canyon.

Even in the dark Matthew's hand closed around it. "Everything's okay," he said soothingly, his thumb caressing her palm. "Ned, the torch is just a few feet behind you. On top of the cupboard."

"I know. I know," Ned grunted as he stubbed his toe against the leg of the coffee table. "Got it."

A ray of light beamed through the blackness. "You stay here with Cassie, Matt, I'll fix it. Shouldn't take more than ten minutes or so."

"You don't need to do it, Ned. I can go." This when he wanted to pick Cassie up and carry her to his bed.

"That's okay. Cassie might be a little scared, I reckon. City folk are used to the lights." Ned sounded like he'd arranged the whole thing.

They stood in fraught silence for a few seconds after Ned had gone, taking the dogs for company.

"You're *not* scared, are you?" Matthew asked.

"Of course not. Not with you around. I'm a bit surprised by the degree of blackness, that's all."

"Come here to me." His arms reached out, made contact with her warm woman's body and encircled her. He was so hungry for her. In such need. But starkly aware of his power over her.

"I'm sorry if I offended you before. I feel terrible." She was aching for comfort.

"Offended me." He brushed that aside. "Of course you didn't, but I can't have you making those kinds of unbelievable offers."

"I do have money, Matthew. Money my grand-mother left me." She felt a fierce need to help him realise his vision.

"That's for *you*," he said in a voice that brooked no argument and seemed to put her in her place. A step behind him.

"Why are you so angry with me?" she demanded. Sexual hostility rushed through her blood. How could she ever aspire to be his wife when he wouldn't allow her to help him?

"I'm not angry with you," he repeated, realising his own voice was stormy.

"You are." She was every bit as aggressive as he when she was nearly fainting with desire.

"Because I'm half mad with wanting you. I'm sorry," he gritted his teeth, "people don't really do this, do they?"

"Do what?" she asked hotly, clutching at the front of his shirt. Her vision had adjusted somewhat. They were very close, touching, but he was just a towering presence in the dark.

"When are you going to sleep in my bed?" He hanked the ribbon that held the gleaming wealth of her hair at the nape, speared his hand into the freed masses. "I believe I'm doing the right thing. I'm certain it's best for both of us, but, God, there couldn't be anything worse." Furiously, the hand at her back hard and possessive, he began to kiss her in the intoxicating dark as though keeping his distance was far more than mortal man should have to tolerate. "Cassie, Cassie, I ache for you." He dragged his mouth from hers and moved it on a turbulent journey down to her breast.

"What do you think it's like for me?" Her whole body trembled violently under his plundering hands. But she wanted it. Loved it. "Just because I'm a woman doesn't mean the turmoil isn't the same."

"We can break our agreement anytime you want." His voice was harsh with the force of his passion. "Is that what you want? Just tell me." Her skin was hot, glowing. He could feel the tight, lovely buds of her breasts.

"I…" When it came to it, overwhelmed by the avalanche of pent-up emotions and the emotional cost of it, the words dried up in her throat.

"All right, then." His hands released her so abruptly she started to fall backwards and he made a grab for her, groaning in bittersweet regret. "I'm sorry, Cassie. It's my fault. I'm wild in more ways than one."

She had to wipe that slate clean. "No, you're a man

I trust absolutely. That's vitally important.'' Her voice was strained but steady.

"Even so, I make you frantic.'' He was an expert now at gauging her body's signals.

"Why not?'' She let her head drop forward onto his chest. "Why not!'' It was heartfelt.

"It might be better, Cass, if we cut short this experiment,'' he said a little harshly as knots of frustration tightened in the pit of his stomach. "I know it was my idea, but I'm not sure I can take it.''

"I need to know what you *think,* Matthew. Her voice had an edgy desperation to it. "Haven't I proved myself?'' She lifted her hands, tracing the strong bones of his face in the dark, blinking rapidly, as like a miracle the lights in the homestead came on again. Unnaturally brilliant. She wanted to retreat from them, wondering if she was anywhere close to convincing him she had found what she was searching for. This was a world previously unknown to her yet its wild beauty and grandeur brought peace to her soul. She wanted to make Jabiru her home. She wanted Matthew for her husband, for the father of her children. Even if the old secrets forced them apart, she would never forget this place or these few fleeting weeks. The understanding she thought had grown between them.

"Cassie,'' he murmured, drawing a lingering hand down over the soft curves of her breasts. "You have such strength inside you. But can you be strong enough?'' He knew because she had told him, her parents had been outraged when she had come up to join him. She had never, ever, done such a thing before, so they knew now the strength of the relationship. Both of them were feeling too much, wanting too much. It was a tremendous experience falling in love, but soon outside forces would begin to gather.

On the morning before it was agreed Cassie would return to Sydney, she rode with Matthew and Ned to one of the holding yards where several hundred head of bullocks had been mustered and penned. These were some of the biggest cattle Cassie had seen, big and wild from their long sojourn out in the scrub country. Four of the Aboriginal stockmen, wonderful horsemen, were on hand to release the bullocks through the yard gates into pasture, all riding good, sound, working horses, geldings of a nearly uniform bay colour. Cassie herself was on the beautiful little chestnut mare Matthew had selected for her to ride.

It all started off well. The bullocks were strong and frisky but a few looked positively dangerous. Cassie decided she wouldn't want to meet them in a bullfight. This was a big mob and it would take some time. "Steer clear of this lot, Cassie," Matthew warned her. "Stay on the sidelines." He wheeled his horse to ride into the throng.

"These are wild brutes, luv," Ned told her. "Some of them rogues."

Cassie wasn't about to argue. Her sweet-tempered mare was in fact dancing sideways as red dust rose from the holding yard and the bellowing of the cattle grew to an ear-splitting roar.

"You, too, Ned," Matthew had to shout over the noise.

"I'm not that stupid." Ned chuckled. "Some of those fellas are right bastards." He doffed his old battered hat. "Excuse the language, Cassie. Why don't we trot over to that ring of gum trees? Matt, he's a wonderful cattleman. Scared of nuthin'.''

They watched in a companionable silence for some time, admiring the skill of Boss and stockmen as they contained the beasts' rush holding them in line. Finally when all danger seemed past and only thirty or so head remained in the holding yard, they rode out to join Matthew and the men, taking up their place in the line. Cassie had tried this operation a number of times before and acquitted herself well.

Yet danger was the very stuff of life on a cattle station.

As one of the stockmen was momentarily diverted by a dive-bombing nesting bird, a huge bullock crashed out of the yard and thundered off at breakneck speed towards freedom. The same stockman, thoroughly disconcerted, wheeled his horse to go after the tearaway, leaving a break in their well-organised line. In a flash, the remaining cattle seized on the escape route so offered and started a stampede to get clear of the yard and out into the scrub.

Without even thinking, Cassie, next in line to the stockman who had broken ranks, made a desperate attempt to baulk the mad flight, oblivious to Matthew's agonised shout. ''For God's sake, Cassie!'' Matthew's blood curdled in fear and his heart began a hard pumping action as adrenaline flowed into him. This woman was precious to him and she was in terrible danger. Curse the mare! Though it was scarcely to blame. With good thoroughbred blood in her, the mare was not used to stock work and consequently startled easily. Now she was bucking with increasing vigour, ignoring Cassie's valiant attempts to control her. The men were desperate to get to Cassie, as well, but blocked by a heaving wall of bullocks. Matthew could have cheerfully killed the lot of them. As they picked up speed, Cassie was plummeted out of the saddle and momentarily disappeared from his sight in the great spewing clouds of dust.

For a split second all was chaos; not a one of them not sick with fear.

Don't let this happen. Don't let this happen, Matthew prayed to his God. With no thought for his own safety he plunged into the crushing throng, flailing his stock whip, cracking it over heads and backs. Finally he reached Cassie who had had the sense to curl herself up into a ball. While she cowered, fully conscious, he stood his big black gelding over her prone body, spitting hell and brimstone with whip and fierce shouts. The men, too, were closing, old Ned's tortured face filthy with red dust, all of them holding themselves together with great courage.

The mob, intimidated by Matthew's mounted figure and the thundering crack of his whip fanned out, their momentum broken, passing harmlessly with the blue sky above them full of nesting birds, shrieking in outrage at the tremendous din.

Matthew, grim-faced, was off his horse in a flash, handing it to Ned while he bent to Cassie huddled on the ground. It came to him with dread she could have broken bones, and he shook his head to clear it of confusion and the odd anger that gripped him now that the danger had passed.

"Cassie, oh, sweet Jesus," he groaned. No blasphemy, a prayer, half terror, half thanks. She looked so fragile, her narrow woman's shoulders, slender frame, her pale blue shirt and jeans coated all over with red dust, as was her face and beautiful hair.

"Cassie, are you all right?" He touched her shoulder as gently as he knew how, thinking if he had been robbed of her he would have been robbed of his life.

There was a moment of complete silence then Cassie straightened slowly, put out a finger and touched Matthew's beautiful mouth in the centre. "I reckon," she managed laconically.

Sick at heart a moment before, Ned shouted with laughter. "Good on yah, me little darlin'" he cried in trembling delight. "Good on yah. Yah a little trimmer."

But Matthew's frown was like a thundercloud. "That was the most foolish thing I've ever seen in my life," he reproached her, swirling the dust out of her hair. "I couldn't live if you got hurt. Here, let's have a look at you."

The men standing around with vast relief in their eyes, gave her the thumbs-up of approval. This Cassie was a regular bloke. She had acted instinctively as they all would have done. Only for the mare, everything would have been all right.

"You've got a bloody elbow there." Matthew sighed, and sighed again, unable to drive those moments of horror from his mind.

"And knee," Cassie observed, touching it gingerly. "I've torn a hole in my jeans."

"We'll get you another pair." Ned patted her like she was his favourite niece.

"Let me help you up," Matthew said, still in that taut voice that covered his agitation.

"Give me a minute." Cassie put a hand to her face and found it caked in dust. "Is the mare okay?" she hastened to ask.

"She's in disgrace," Ned told her cheerfully. "You put up a good fight, luv, before she tipped you off."

"A proper work horse would have made the difference," Cassie said in a matter-of-fact voice. "I'll never make that mistake again."

"You'll never get the chance," Matthew rasped, not looking up from his task of checking her limbs. This woman was his future.

"Don't get mad," she cajoled him gently, seeing inside him. "You couldn't have taught me better."

"All experience, luv." Ned was studying both their faces. Instinct told him Matthew's heart was badly twisted inside him. He really loved this girl. It had to work out.

"I'm going to take you back to the house and throw you in the tub," Matthew announced, getting his arms under her and lifting her like she was no more than ten.

"The outside shower will do. I won't have red dust all over the bathroom." She tightened her arms around his throat and looked into the blue flame of his eyes.

"So it's your bathroom now?" For the first time he found a quick smile.

"You saved my life, Matthew Carlyle. My home is your home. You can't get rid of me now."

CHAPTER EIGHT

AFTER that, there was no looking back.

Matthew returned with Cassie to Sydney, bent on speaking to her parents. "It's the right thing to do," he told her. "Your parents mightn't like me, but I'll have to take my chances. No sidestepping it. Just remember nothing and no one can come between us." It was said with such passionate conviction, Cassie felt the swift tears sting her eyes. She loved all of Matthew. His heart, his mind, his proud spirit, the sculpted face and body had left her weak at the knees. Here was a man strong enough to overcome every obstacle.

They were embarking on a life-changing journey, but she knew in her bones her parents' opposition would be the ultimate test of their love. Matthew had made the careful decision to stay in a city hotel. Both of them agreeing the celebration of their marriage and the ultimate union of their bodies would be the more wonderful for the wait.

"As long as it's damned soon," Matthew murmured into her creamy neck. He had almost become accustomed to battling the demons of desire but they had to cut the waiting time before he ran off the rails.

When Cassie rang her father at his office, shrinking a little at the severity and deep disapproval of his tone, he told her he was too busy to speak, he deplored what she had done, but if she wished to speak to him and her mother she should call at the house on Saturday afternoon. "At two."

How utterly predictable, Cassie thought. She was just another appointment. She had summoned up the courage to tell her father Matthew would be coming with her, but her father had already hung up.

Matthew, for his part, was quite ready to face the discord and get it over. Cassandra was a grown woman. She made her own decisions. Her parents had to accept that.

He hardly ever glanced at his own reflection, but that Saturday afternoon he took a good hard look at the man in the mirror. A strange face really. Very distinctive features.

He'd had his hair trimmed. Not much. The guy in the barber shop told him to stick with what he had. He'd always left it long to combat the burning rays of the sun on his nape, anyway.

He scarcely knew himself in the new clothes. Smart casual, they said. *Casual* at that price? Grey jacket with some sort of pattern in it, trousers a shade deeper, a blue shirt that felt incredibly soft against his skin. New socks, new shoes, the works. All for Cassandra. He smiled at the thought, catching the stark white flash of his teeth. Hell, he looked theatrical. To combat the feeling he gave a low growl in his throat.

Before he left the room he took a small green velvet case out of the top drawer of the bureau. He hoped with all his heart Cassandra would like it. Only one way to find out. Put it on her finger. Third finger. Left hand.

"You look wonderful," Cassie said when they met, so stunningly handsome he robbed her of breath.

"All for you, my magnolia love." She was wearing

an ivory silk shirt and a full skirt that set off her small waist, sandals on her feet, her long hair caught back with a turquoise silk scarf. She had such magnificent hair he wondered how anyone could possibly prefer it confined. He was shaken by the rush of fierce protectiveness. No one would ever hurt Cassandra. Not while he was around.

As they were nearing their destination, Matthew pulled over to a beautiful little park with an adjoining marina, helping Cassie out. The afternoon sun was dazzling, casting patterns on the ground through the light canopy of trees. Flower beds showed riotous displays of poppies and day lilies, a small boy was flying a splendid Chinese kite, watched over by his father, a young couple sat close together on a park bench beneath the welcoming shade of a blossoming gum. A truly peaceful scene.

Matthew took her hand, strolling to the water's edge. "The harbour is unbelievably beautiful," he said.

"We think so."

"Sure you won't miss it? Sydney has so much to offer."

"We can visit now and again."

"We can," he agreed. "And you can always take time to visit your parents and friends, Cassandra. I'm not going to keep you a prisoner." He reached out to brush her cheek. A shivery possessive gesture.

There was something immensely exciting about being Matthew's prisoner, Cassie thought.

"So much has happened," Matthew mused, his expression serious.

"I know it isn't easy for you, Matthew, meeting my parents."

He slipped a supportive arm around her waist. "I'm not concerned for myself. It's *you* I don't want to see upset. I don't know that I would take to that too well. You've given me a picture of what your home life has been like. But you're a woman now. In charge of your own life. Your parents will have to realise that."

"I hope so." The cold clear part of Cassie's mind told her that they wouldn't.

"What you need is an engagement ring." Matthew delved decisively into his breast pocket. "That will make a statement like nothing else can. Hold out your hand." His voice was low and rich with emotion.

Cassie's bones seemed to dissolve. She stood without moving, almost without breathing, a pulse beating heavily in her throat.

"I hope you like it," Matthew said, opening up the box to reveal an exquisite solitaire diamond ring set in gold.

Looking at the ring, a full carat or more, Cassie realised with a throb of anxiety how much it would have set him back. Could he afford it? But the eyes blazing into hers held only the realisation of a dream. "Matthew, it's so beautiful. I love it." She struggled not to cry. "Please, put it on my finger."

He took her wrist in one warm possessive stroke. "I want it to be a part of you. Of us. This reminds me of a star," he said with such brooding emotion it made her shiver. "Of your eyes. I want you to know before we speak to your parents, *you're* the star in my firmament. I want you to promise me for *always*." He slid the beautiful ring down her finger, lifted her hand and kissed it.

"*Always,* Matthew," Cassie promised with an answering depth of feeling.

* * *

Yet the afternoon that had started so brilliantly was to end badly. When they arrived at the Stirling mansion, a maid showed them through the luxuriously appointed house filled with magnificent furniture, paintings, antiques, so much it was impossible to know where to look first, to a large informal living room at the rear. It had a breathtaking view of the harbour. The whole area was flooded with light from the great expanse of glass and the French doors that led to a covered terrace with a deep pink bougainvillea climbing the columns. All this Matthew saw with a sense of appreciation not untouched with awe. It gave him a blinding perspective, too, on what Cassandra was giving up.

She had grown up in this splendid house when he and his mother had tasted real poverty in those awful years before they had found their way to North Queensland, where people like Marcy had reached out to help them.

The light was just so brilliant for a few moments he had only a dimmed view of three people seated very companionably on the boldly upholstered sofas on one side of the very large room. All heads were turned, two men and a woman. The men, tall, well-built, imposing in demeanour, stood up and for a split second Matthew thought he was going mad.

How could it be? As his eyes adjusted to the dazzling light it seemed to him the devil himself had materialised.

Jock Macalister.

At long last. Jock Macalister with a dazed expression on his damnable face. It matched his own, but Matthew felt only a terrible hush fall all around them.

Beside him, Cassie went white with shock. Couldn't

her father have at least told her Jock Macalister would
be there? But that was the curse of their family. There
had never been communication.

Her father started to speak, looking aghast. "For
heaven's sake, Cassandra, what *is* this?" For once his
voice had lost its customary aplomb.

Her mother was speaking, too, rushing in, unable to
believe her eyes. How in the name of all that was holy
was Jock Macalister's terrible secret right here before
them? With her *daughter*. She found it impossible to
understand. Was it possible Cassandra had done this
on purpose? If she hadn't been so shocked, Anita
Stirling would have been enthralled. The young man
of the dark red hair and blazing blue eyes was the
living image of the Jock Macalister in a portrait
painted long ago. It held pride of place in Macalister's
study at Monaro Downs. She had admired it many
times. Now the living, breathing double?

Macalister himself reached out for the back of an
armchair, clinging to it as for support.

"Cassandra, would you mind telling us the name of
your friend?" Stuart Stirling barked. As if he didn't
know. This was Jock's son. The astounding resemblance made it an uncontroverted fact.

"Don't tell me you don't know, Mr. Stirling?"
Matthew's vibrant voice challenged, resounded around
the room. His commanding physical presence was
such, he was impossible to not heed. "I go by the
name Matthew Carlyle. My mother's maiden name. I
never knew my father." This with a flashing glance
of contempt at the imposing, tawny-haired elderly man
who stood in an agonised silence, looking ill.

Stuart Stirling turned to Macalister with the face of
acute embarrassment. "Be certain, Jock, we had ab-

solutely no idea of a possible connection. Cassandra has given no hint of any such thing. We've never laid eyes on the young man.''

''Well, now, that makes all of you,'' Matthew drawled. ''My father never laid eyes on me, either.''

Until now.

He might as well have declared it from the roof tops.

Anita Stirling, looking whiter by the minute, closed the distance between herself and her daughter, her eyes wild. Stuart was bound to Jock Macalister in friendship and business.

''You'll pay for this, Cassie,'' she said in a furious undertone. ''I always said you were a very strange girl.''

''It was meant to happen.'' The gravity of Cassie's tone stole her mother's breath. Cassie was certain now it was so. She was as pale as her mother and all eyes. ''Don't you see, it was *meant* to happen. I had no idea. Father never said Sir Jock would be here.''

''Do you think I believe you?'' Anita Stirling gave a brittle laugh. ''Are you stupid, crazy?''

''While you're casting around for insults, Mrs. Stirling,'' Matthew interjected, disliking this thin, elegant woman on sight, ''I want to` tell you I would *never* have come here had I known the identity of your guest.''

Stuart Stirling moved to join his wife, anger leaping in his eyes. ''Look here, young man, don't expect us to believe that. Somehow you and Cassandra got wind of it. Sir Jock calls on us often when he's in Sydney. Many people would know. Her boss, for one.''

''You're good friends, I take it?'' Matthew gave Cassandra's father a hard smile.

"Twenty years and more, if it's any of your business," Stuart Stirling returned curtly. Arrogant young devil, but with the unmistakable stamp of authority.

"Why did you never tell me, Cassandra?" Matthew suddenly transferred his attention to Cassie, who was quaking inside.

"The moment was never right, Matthew." She lifted her head resolutely, feeling his trust in her begin to unravel.

Jock Macalister, who had been silent so long now, found voice. "I don't know if this means anything to you, Matthew Carlyle, but I've suffered for my wrongs." Carefully he walked across the room.

"You know nothing about suffering." Matthew stared back at him. "It was my mother who knew all about that."

The blood drained entirely from Macalister's face. "I swear one day I'll make it up to you."

"Don't try to be human, sir," Matthew warned, drawing Stuart Stirling's fire.

"I'd appreciate it, young man, if you'd leave my house," he said, throwing his head back angrily.

"No, no, Stuart, it's me who should leave," Macalister managed painfully. "Forgive me, Cassandra, my dear." He addressed her almost sadly. "What a beautiful young woman you've grown into. Could I ask where in the world you met...Matthew?"

"Ah, you know as well as anyone where we lived," Matthew broke in, full of a good, cleansing anger. "I bet you had us followed from place to place."

Macalister looked shaky and old. "And I've always been ashamed. So terribly ashamed. But in the beginning your mother simply disappeared."

"The hell with that!" Matthew spun on his heel. "May you live with your lies and your guilt forever."

Cassandra caught urgently at his arm. "Don't leave, Matthew, *please*."

He stood riveted. But only for a moment. This was the woman who had stolen his soul. Now she had betrayed him. Anger flooded him. Anger and outrage.

"I'm sorry, Cassandra. I'm shocked beyond words."

"I'll come with you." She drew closer, trying to align herself with him. Something that outraged her mother.

"Perhaps you can tell us first why you're *here?*" cried Anita Stirling, her voice ragged with dismay.

"Tell her, Cassandra." Matthew sounded indifferent to the reason.

"We came to tell you we're engaged," Cassie replied with dignity, lifting her hand and turning it so the light hit the sparkling solitaire diamond.

Her mother shook her head vehemently. "I've never heard such nonsense. Engaged? Why you only met this young man when you were on holiday, you've known him no time at all."

"Yet he's the man I'm going to marry." Cassie faced her parents with utter conviction.

"Good God!" Stuart Stirling's face went craggy. "This must be a terrible joke of some kind. None of this can be happening surely."

The heat and bitterness of Cassie's anger surprised her. "You've never taken much interest in my affairs, Father. I was trying to tell you on the phone but you were too busy to listen."

"Why don't you all sit down and talk this out?" Jock Macalister suggested, trying to contain the terrible damage. "Life is so strange. A man ought to see his only son before he dies."

Anita Stirling went to him, staring at him with anxious dark eyes. "Whatever are you talking about, Jock? You're a wonderfully fit man. How do we know he really is your son?"

"I know." Macalister spoke slowly, sorrowfully. "You didn't doubt it for a second, did you?" he challenged her in a quiet, pained voice. "He's the image of me as a young man."

"But you couldn't bring yourself to meet me?" Matthew said with profound scorn.

"You're not familiar with all the aspects of my life, Matthew, just as I'm not familiar with yours," Macalister answered.

"*Nothing* could excuse you."

"I can't forgive myself." Macalister bowed his head.

Matthew didn't respond, his handsome face carved in bronze.

"I'll see myself out, Anita," Jock Macalister said. "Maybe, Matthew…" he pleaded, his eyes seeking those of the young man with hair like dark flame. He saw the way it sprang from the wide forehead, the blue eyes, black brows, the chiselled features so exactly like his own.

For a powerful man, how uncertain he sounds, Matthew thought without pity. How miserable. Like a man who had sold his soul to the devil. "It's all too late." Matthew wheeled away, such a cold, prideful expression on his face. Terrified, Cassie went after him, but he put her away from him with his strong arms, anger exploding like an erupting volcano.

"I'm not ready to hear your explanation, Cassandra."

"You're not leaving without me?" Cassie was appalled at the turn of events.

He looked straight at her, his handsome mouth thinned to a straight line. "You know I fell in love with you, Cassandra. You watched me do it. You've been the greatest thing in my life, now hell, you probably set me up," he accused her heavily.

Cassie lost all colour. "No, Matthew, never!" She caught at his taut arm. "Can't you at least listen to what I have to say?"

"I believe not," he retorted curtly, removing her hand. "I'm pretty well disenchanted with your whole damned family."

He wasn't back at his hotel for hours and hours, causing Cassie to fret dreadfully. She had had the most terrible row with her parents and her head was spinning like a top. Where had he gone? She didn't know, but she was painfully aware in not being absolutely honest with him she had hurt and disappointed him, damaged her standing in his eyes. She had really come down from her pedestal. But then, she had never wanted to be on a pedestal in the first place.

Matthew's feelings ran very deep and his feelings were all centred around her. That was a big responsibility. Surely when he had time to think about it he would reject any idea she had set him up. Set him up for what? To bring a father and son together? It complicated matters dreadfully.

Jock Macalister was a millionaire a couple of hundred times over. Matthew surely couldn't believe she had connived to bring them together? But then neither could she forget his pride nor the way he had rejected her offer to help him financially out of hand. She felt sick with anxiety. One thing in her favour, he hadn't booked out of the hotel. She would just have to keep ringing.

Finally she went over to the hotel and waited, sitting in the lobby until she saw him alight from a taxi and swing through the entrance, a handsome vibrant force of nature. He didn't even see her, tucked away as she was, but made directly for the lifts. One of the desk clerks had given her the number of his room earlier, now she gave him a few minutes before she followed.

"Oh, God, please help me," she breathed. "Tell me how to handle it."

He greeted her at the door, stunning, raffish, jacket off, shirt undone by several buttons, a tumbler of whisky in his hand.

"Well, if it isn't my beautiful fiancée," he drawled in a deep slow voice.

"May I come in, Matthew?"

He gazed down at her, his eyes drinking in the poignant cast to her beauty. "As a matter of fact, no." He wasn't what he wished to be, totally in control of himself.

"I want to be with you," Cassie insisted, her heart in her eyes.

"I bet you do." His breath was warm, fragrant with the Scotch. "Maybe we can have a little adventure in bed?" He gave her a devilish wink.

"I thought we had a plan. A design for marriage?" Cassie said, realising this wasn't his first drink of the day.

"But you're a player now, Cassie, and you can spin

tales. I'm not sure I like that. Or whether I can forgive you."

"Please let me in, Matthew." She took another step towards him, for some reason feeling tiny against his swaying height. "I don't want to hover out here."

"Hell, is that what you're doing?" He put his head out of the door and looked around in an exaggerated fashion.

"Of course I am." With smooth deliberation she ducked under his arm, walked quickly into the room and stood near the small circular table and chairs.

"What do you need from me, Cass?" he asked her in a hard voice, shutting and locking the door.

"I love you, Matthew," she said quietly, standing her ground. "We became engaged today, remember?" Tears glinted like diamonds in her eyes.

"Ah, hell, no need to cry about it, sweetie." His vibrant voice was faintly slurred. He reached out and pulled her down on the sofa, wedging her into the corner with his lean powerful frame. "The thing is, Cassie—" he turned his face to her "—you did the worst, worst thing you could ever do."

"I didn't lie to you, Matthew," she said swiftly, but he put a finger to her mouth and brushed it across her lips.

"'Course you didn't, sweetheart. You just didn't tell me the whole truth. *Big* money. Is that why you tried to bring me and dear old Jock together?" He lifted a hand to his eyes and rubbed them fiercely. "God, Cass. I would give my life for you in a second, but that doesn't matter. The fact is I can't give you what you've always had. What you really want."

"You can't be talking about *money?*" She turned to him in extreme agitation.

"Oh, darling, *pleez.*" He kissed her forehead, kissed her cheeks. "That's one hell of an enormous house you were raised in. Chock-a-block with first-class paintings and antiques. On Sydney Harbour, for God's sake. Who the hell has a hope of living in a house on Sydney Harbour? Cassie, girl, you were born rich."

"So what?" Cassie was quivering all over, her whole body responding to being pressed against his. "It didn't make me happy. While my father was making so much money I was almost completely cut off from him. My mother lived for him and her social life. I might as well have been an orphan. Money isn't important to me, Matthew."

He smiled at her, a beautiful white sardonic grin. "No, darling, because you've never been without it." On a surge of anger he put a hand to her neck, and kissed her furiously on the mouth.

She couldn't seem to fight free of him. Didn't want to. He tasted wonderful when she had never had the stomach for whisky or spirits of any kind.

"Oh, for God's sake." He released her abruptly, turned away as if with self-disgust.

"Matthew, will you please let me speak?" she implored, her mouth pulsing from his kiss.

"Sorry, Cass." He shook his marvellous red head. "Right now I'm workin' on gettin' drunk. Would you like something yourself?" His eyes mocked her.

"No, I'm fine."

"Tell me, when did Macalister leave?" he asked in a harsh voice.

"Not long after you."

"Have you the slightest inkling what it meant having you drop him on me?"

She leaned into him and covered his hands with hers. "Matthew, for the last time, I had no idea Jock Macalister would be there, any more than my parents knew about your relationship to Jock. I simply didn't tell them as I wanted them to be free of preconceptions. Surely you can understand that? Even angry as you were, you must have registered their shock when we turned up?"

He laughed. "I thought you were all absolutely superb. Academy Award stuff. It's obvious to me, Cassie, your parents are manipulators of the highest order. All three of you could have set it up. All you needed was to bring Jock and his long lost illegitimate son together. For all I know, Macalister could be on his last legs. He didn't look too clever. Money always seeks to marry money. There can't be enough of it in some circles."

"I wonder why my father has threatened to disinherit me if I go ahead and marry you then?" Cassie asked.

"Ah, come on, Cass!" He lifted his glass to her and drained it to the last drop.

"I'm perfectly serious," she said.

"You poor little soul," he mocked.

Still, she persisted, loving him, forced to endure his distrust. "I feel terrible about not telling you the whole truth about Sir Jock and my father, Matthew."

"So what was your big problem?" he asked bluntly, his whole body emanating a tightly controlled anger. "You're not a teenager, Cassandra. You're not a poor little kid from the wrong side of the tracks. You're a princess. Hell, a Madonna. I'm half crazy to have sex, but I hold off. All for you. I want everything to be perfect for you, you adorable little liar."

"Oh, well, if you're not going to believe me." She tried to rise, her own temper flaring, but he held her down easily, without exerting any real strength.

"Enough's enough, Cass. Level with me and I might forgive you. You all thought marriage with me wouldn't be so bad if Macalister at long last acknowledged me. Better yet, felt moved to compensate me for a lifetime of rejection. I think he's worth around $300 million, isn't he? I'm sure I read that sometime back. It made me mighty mad. The distinguished Sir John Macalister, who kept his bastard out of sight, out of mind."

"I know how angry and hurt you are," Cassie repeated. "At him. At me." Without warning, overwrought and feeling the crisis of confidence she had created, she began to cry.

"You think that will make me soften?" His voice and eyes suggested he was losing control.

She twisted away from him and dashed her hand across her eyes. "I'm just beginning to realise you're a very hard man. I'm not a saint, Matthew. I'm a woman with flaws. I regret not confronting the issue of Sir Jock and my father, but all my life I've hated confrontations. I've had so many of them. With my parents...."

"Well, of course you were scared stiff of me." Angry, affronted, he cut her off.

"No, no." She shook her head. "But you're the one person in the world who would have made the telling hard, Matthew. Can't you understand that?"

"No. I'm not buying it, either."

"Do you want to break off the engagement?" she asked emotionally, her eyes sparkling with unshed tears.

"Listen, honey, I thought I made it very clear to you. You're *mine.*"

"Then you'd better reach deep inside you for the grace to forgive me," she countered with some spirit.

"Maybe I will. Sooner or later," he drawled.

"You're behaving badly, Matthew," she accused him, tossing her long hair over her shoulder.

"*I* am? That's splendid, coming from you." He was angry now. Really angry. Wanting to pull her into his arms. Punish her. Punish her.

"You have a dark side." She gritted her small teeth.

"We all have a dark side, Cassie," he informed her. "You couldn't look more beautiful, more luminous, or pure, but all along you've had an agenda of your own."

She wanted to hit out at him. Her captor. "You'd better stop that now, Matthew. I don't like it."

"Well, let's do something you do like," he said almost cheerfully, reaching for her in one powerful movement and dragging her across his lap, holding her so her head fell back and her long abundant hair fell across the arm of the sofa. He had the crazy illusion his blood was lava. "Come on, Cass. Wouldn't you rather make love than argue? How do you get to know so much about it, anyway?"

"About what?" she said furiously, trying in vain to get up.

"About turning a man on."

He sounded hopelessly cynical, but looked wonderful.

"Go on, you need to vent your anger on someone," she said shortly, vivid rose colour in her cheeks.

"You bet!"

He should have stopped there, but the tumult in his

blood was too fierce. One hand beneath her back, he raised her to him, his mouth closing over hers so voluptuously, so hungrily, he might have been eating her. Her sweet lips. He silenced her in a way she was never likely to forget. However much she had shocked him that day with her parents, the hated presence of Macalister, this woman was in his blood. He kissed her over and over until the breath was rasping in her soft throat.

"Matthew!"

"I'm here and I'll never let you go."

"I never lied to you."

"Hush." He spoke harshly but he wanted to believe her. Even her small struggles added to his sexual excitement. He wound his hand possessively into her long hair. Wonderful hair. Hair like a woman should have, thick, silky, fragrant. He revelled in holding her body against his in an intimacy she couldn't escape. She knew he was terribly aroused. Hot with hunger. He had talked so much about waiting for their wedding night. Hell, it was too far away. He was inflamed by a flood of desire so monstrous its power was taking him under.

She was wearing some skinny little top like a silk sweater. It outlined her tantalising small breasts. He rolled it up, pulled it over her head. Her bra was a scrap of lace. That went, too, as he fell into a mindless well of pleasure. Her breasts were beautifully shaped, spreading to his hand. He ran his calloused palm in quick friction up and down over her nipples, hearing her soft moans. Her face was so beautiful, eyes closed, mouth opened to her sighs, her expression akin to ecstasy. And agony. That was what it looked like. Her skirt was the same colour as the shucked-off top. The same intense violet-blue of the morning glory on Jabiru. He wanted to run his hands up and down her slender legs. Did. It was a matter of wonderment to him, the soft satiny feel of her skin. The exultation in him was growing fierce.

He was momentarily distracted when she cried out like a wild bird.

"Cassie! Who do you belong to?" he asked her tautly.

"Love me. Love me," she responded, her eyes intent on him but somehow unfocused as though she was centring her own overpowering desire, acknowledging it freely. "Now, Matthew. *Now.*" Her whole body was aflame.

He lifted her high in his arms and held her. "You want this, Cassandra."

"Yes, yes, a million times over."

"Then come to me."

CHAPTER NINE

OWEN MAITLAND showed no surprise when Cassie handed in her notice. He had in fact been waiting for it.

"So Jock has finally admitted Matthew is his son?" he asked, studying her with sympathy, seeing the sadness in her eyes.

"Yes, he did," Cassie answered huskily.

"It will all come out in any case, Cassie. You must be aware of that. Not that most people haven't heard the rumours anyway. They've been circulating for thirty years. I know Jock socially. Not half as well as your father. Jock's ruled over his empire with an iron hand, but to put it bluntly, in some respects Eleanor Macalister wears the pants. She's a Mondale, you know, which is to say, an aristocrat in her own eyes. Old money. Not a whiff of scandal has ever touched the Mondale family. As a matter of fact, Eleanor was considered to have married very much beneath her when she married Jock. He could buy and sell them now."

Cassie's expression was grave. "Are you saying Lady Macalister was the reason Sir Jock never recognised Matthew?"

Owen Maitland nodded. "Don't you think it highly probable? Eleanor Macalister is not a woman who could ever be taken lightly. She has a great stake in everything Jock does. He can have his mistresses. I'm sure he has done over the years, but he'll never leave

Eleanor. The alliances, the mergers. She knows where all the bodies are buried.''

"So he's a coward?" Cassie spoke like a woman who had weighed everything up carefully and given her decision.

"Coward?" Owen Maitland pressed against the warm leather of his arm chair. "No one could ever think that of Jock."

"Then what would you call abandoning Matthew and his mother?" Cassie challenged.

"I've never understood that." Owen Maitland frowned a little. "But I don't believe it was as simple as you think, Cassie. Jock might tell a different tale. Not that he's ever opened his mouth. But I do know he's carried a lot of unhappiness. I don't know the exact state of his marriage but I do know in many respects Eleanor cracks the whip. Many the occasion I've met him and I've come away thinking Jock Macalister's a very lonely man. Of course the terrible irony is, he's never had another son."

"It's very hard not to judge him," Cassie said. "Matthew is understandably bitter. Especially in relation to the treatment of his mother. He loved her. They were very close."

"I understand she died?"

"Yes."

"How sad. She couldn't have been very old."

"It was an accident," Cassie said, not wanting to be pressed.

"Julie told us Matthew has a fine property of his own?"

"Yes, he has." Cassie's eyes lit with pride. "Matthew's a fighter. He's had to triumph over a lot of obstacles. It's built strength of character."

"I would have liked to have talked to him," Owen Maitland said. See if the young man passed the test.

Cassie looked at her boss keenly. "I can arrange that. Everything has happened so quickly. In many ways its been overwhelming. We'll be married in North Queensland. I expect Julie has told you already. She'll be my chief bridesmaid. We have a mutual friend, Louise Redmond, I'd like to ask, as well."

"May I enquire what your parents think?" Owen Maitland uneasily awaited the answer.

"My father has threatened to disinherit me if the marriage goes through," Cassie said, apparently unfazed.

But Owen Maitland looked and sounded shocked. "Cassie!"

"He means what he says."

"Surely not," Owen Maitland exclaimed. "Parents often say what they don't mean when they're upset."

"Mr. Maitland, you know my father," Cassie pointed out gently.

Too well. Owen Maitland shrugged. "What exactly is it he's holding against you, Cassie?"

"The fact Matthew is Sir Jock's son." An irony when Matthew had briefly believed her father could have been party to the contrived meeting between himself and Macalister.

Owen Maitland gave a grim smile. "Whose side is he on anyway?"

"Not mine," Cassie said instantly. "Father believed if he offended Sir Jock or Lady Macalister in any way it would affect their business relationship."

"Well, yes," Owen Maitland was forced to agree, "it might, but it has to come down to *your* happiness in life, Cassie. You must love this young man?"

"With all my heart," Cassie said with such fervour Owen Maitland was touched.

At the same time Cassie was meeting with Owen Maitland, Stuart Stirling was moving on a plan to get rid of Matthew Carlyle from their lives. The whole point of being a rich man was that he could afford to buy out his opponents. Cassandra could have anything she wanted. *Except* Jock Macalister's illegitimate son. Getting rid of Carlyle was an imperative.

At home on Jabiru, Matthew worked himself to the bone so he and Cassie could have a clear ten days for their honeymoon on Angel Island, a small exquisitely beautiful island on the Great Barrier Reef with thirty private pavilions set in a magical rainforest garden, each villa overlooking the heavenly blue ocean.

Matthew, who had been there only once, remembered it as being the most romantic and tranquil place on earth. It had stood out like a beacon in his mind as he began planning this very, very, special wedding. He and Cassie had talked daily on the phone and they had worked out forty guests in all. The Maitlands had offered their luxury retreat for the reception, which was nice and supportive of them, but Matthew thought he needed to make it up to Marcy for all she had done for his mother and him.

He drove into town as soon as he was able, thinking it was high time to speak to Marcy about their plans.

Marcy spotted him as soon as he walked in the front door, greeting him with pleasure, throwing her arms around him and giving him a big motherly hug. "I've been expecting you to show up." She looked up at him, deciding he looked wonderful. Blazing with life and energy. "How's Cassie coping with all the excitement?" she asked.

"She's due here next week," Matthew told her with a feeling of powerful relief. "I can't bear her out of my sight. Now there's something I want to talk to you about, Marcy." Matthew took her by the arm and sat her down at an empty table. "You've been like a second mother to me."

"True." Marcy eased herself back in the chair, beaming with pleasure. "And I want to tell you right now, it's been an honour."

"I want you to handle the reception, if that's okay?" Matthew asked in a voice that hid a well of emotion. "Not a big crowd. I was hoping we could have it in the al fresco dining area, perhaps retract the roof. Around forty. Invitations are due to go out. The weather should be perfect so we could have it under the stars."

Marcy leaned forward and clasped Matthew's face in her ruddy hands, her mind working overtime. "This is going to be so exciting," she cried. "I know just what to do. You leave it to me, son. I'm going to give you and Cassie the best flaming reception this town has ever seen."

"I don't think we could ask for more." Matthew grinned.

"Oh, this is marvellous!" Marcy enthused. "By the way, luv," she suddenly remembered. "There's a guy looking for you. Arrived earlier this morning. Staying upstairs." She gave a jerk with her thumb. "City guy. Wears a tie."

"Name?"

"Simon Parker, on the register," Marcy said. "Seems a nice bloke."

"Never heard of him."

"You will now," Marcy pronounced. "That's him coming in the door."

Matthew shot the new arrival a quick look, feeling pinpricks of premonition. This was someone with something to say. Something he didn't want to hear about, he was sure of it. Nevertheless with a backwards word to Marcy he walked straight up to the stranger with his graceful fast-moving gait and held out his hand.

"Matthew Carlyle. Marcy tells me you've been asking for me?"

The man, middle fifties, dapper, overdressed for town, thinning dark hair worn straight back, smooth, intelligent face, nodded cautiously as though suddenly conscious of Matthew's ranging height and lean, powerful body. "Simon Parker, Mr. Carlyle," he introduced himself. "I'm here to represent my client, Stuart Stirling." He produced a card bearing the name of a major law firm above his own. "Perhaps we could find a quiet place to talk? My room, if you've no objections?"

"Why don't we just go for a walk?" Matthew suggested in a brisk voice.

It came to Parker he now dreaded having to say what he had been instructed to say to this dynamic-looking young man whose physical appearance had shocked him rigid. But his firm had been acting for Sir Jock Macalister for many long years.

They were outside in the brilliant sunshine, walking down the leaf-canopied main street of the picturesque little town, palm trees soaring, brilliant lorikeets flashing rainbows of colour from hibiscus, jasmine, oleander, bougainvillea. A village, really, on the edge of the rainforest but a prettier place it was hard to imagine. "This is very difficult for me, Mr. Carlyle," Parker admitted with a genuine feeling of regret, "but my client has instructed me to discuss a proposal he thinks might interest you."

"Fire away," Matthew said a little brusquely, understanding it wouldn't be good.

Parker did something he hadn't done in more than twenty years. He blushed. "What about if we sit down on that park bench over there?"

"You sound nervous, Mr. Parker." Matthew Carlyle gave him a half smile that nevertheless lit up his handsome face.

Parker shrugged. "I confess I am. You're not what I imagined."

"And that was? Some upstart cad trying to make off with the rich, snobby Stuart Stirling's daughter?"

"Something like that," Parker agreed, studying Matthew for a time, liking what he saw.

"Well, I'm happy to tell you, Mr. Parker, I love Cassandra. And she loves me. Stuart Stirling is just a damn big windbag."

Parker couldn't help it. He gave a whooping laugh which he quickly choked. "It has to be said that he and Mrs. Stirling have genuine concerns about the important step their daughter is taking."

"Indeed?" Carlyle looked down his fine straight nose in a manner that instantly brought Jock Macalister to Parker's mind. "I'm sure you've been told it has something to do with my family tree."

"Would I be impolite in saying you're the image of Macalister?" Parker managed, thinking it was a bit scary.

"I'm not completely happy with it." Matthew gave

an ironic laugh. "After all, he has disowned me from birth."

Or decided he needed a quiet home life, Parker thought. "You've never met Lady Macalister, I take it?" he asked.

"Sorry," Matthew said without a trace of regret. "He must be a real wimp to be dictated to by his wife."

"Lady Macalister is *Establishment*," Parker said as though that explained it.

"Better get on with it, Mr. Parker." Matthew flashed him a glance.

"Mr. Stirling is my client, Matthew. I hope I may call you Matthew," Simon Parker waited for the younger man's nod. "I'm merely acting for him. Passing on his proposal."

"I'm not dangerous."

But he could be under certain circumstances, Parker thought. Although he had a very engaging laugh. "To get to the point, Mr. Stirling has offered a sum of one hundred thousand dollars if you would ease yourself out of his daughter's life."

Matthew made a parody of scratching his cleft chin. "You're serious now?"

"Dead serious," Parker confirmed, thinking Stuart Stirling had a poor understanding of this young man's psychology.

"Have you ever done anything like this before, Mr. Parker?" Matthew shook his head in wonderment.

"I'm happy to say, no."

"Just how many hundreds of millions has Stuart Stirling got?"

"I'm sure you realise I'm not at liberty to say."

"Perfectly all right. It must be around three hundred, four? And he thinks Cassandra is only worth *one hundred thousand dollars?*"

Parker looked at him for a moment aghast. "Would you be wanting more? I have that amount in a cheque."

"I'm a gentleman, Mr. Parker, so I won't respond to that. May I see the famous—infamous—cheque?" The sunshine caught Matthew's dark red hair, making it flare. Like his temper.

"Why, yes, you can. As it happens I have it in my wallet." Parker stood up in a flash, delving into the pocket of his trousers. He withdrew an expensive light brown leather wallet, nicely engraved with his initials, S.A.P., Matthew saw with narrow-eyed amazement.

He smiled without humour. "Let's have it."

Parker sighed deeply. It was hard not to.

"What kind of a man is he?" Matthew asked quietly after a while.

Simon Parker shook his head. "A man who thinks his money can buy him in and out of every situation. Mostly it works."

"It's not working this time," Matthew said with disgust, and very neatly tore the cheque to shreds. "Take this back to Mr. Stirling and tell him that was a very bad move. Bad. Bad. Bad."

"I have to tell you I knew that the moment I laid eyes on you," Parker said.

"Why don't we go back to the pub?" Matthew suddenly invited, like that particular exchange was well and truly over. "Marcy does a great club sandwich. We could wash it down with a cold beer."

Stuart Stirling's envoy felt both relaxed and relieved. "Sounds great. Nice little town you have here."

Matthew looked down at him from his superior height. "You should come and see my place before you go. Cattle station by the name of Jabiru. I don't know what it's worth exactly these days but it's a hell of a lot more than one hundred thousand dollars."

Of course he said nothing about it to Cassandra when he spoke to her that night. One day he might, but for now he didn't want to add to the stress that all the inevitable changes to her life were creating. And yet, though he tried to put it out of mind, Stuart Stirling's plan to buy him off had inflicted yet another wound. Did Stirling really believe he was nothing more than an opportunist looking for a rich wife, or did he genuinely fear Jock Macalister, friend and business associate for so long, would desert him if Cassandra went through with the marriage. It was so easy to misread situations. Hadn't he done it himself until he came to his senses.

CHAPTER TEN

THE week before the wedding was a lot more eventful than Cassie ever anticipated. One morning when she answered the door of the Maitland hideaway where she was staying, she found Nick Raeburn, looking tired and haggard, staring back at her.

"I got your little letter telling me how you were going to get married," he said without preamble, as though accusing her of some crime.

This shouldn't be happening, Cassie thought. "'How are you' might work better, Nick," she returned a little hardily. She wanted to turn him away but he looked ill. On the other hand Matthew was driving into town to be with her and discuss final arrangements. She just knew he'd turn up before Nick could be persuaded to leave and, as she knew, Matthew had a temper.

"Is it possible you're really going to go through with this?" Nick demanded, far more aggressively than Cassie had ever heard him speak.

"Stop shouting, Nick, and come in." Cassie was satisfied now someone had got to him.

"This will kill your parents." Nick walked behind her while she headed to the sunroom overlooking the spectacular view.

"I didn't know my parents were your big favourites," she said with some irony.

"Lord, Cassie, why are you doing this?" Nick groaned.

"Would you believe I'm in love." Cassie turned to face him, indicating he should take a chair.

"You can't be, not like *this*." Nick sat down heavily on the sofa, looking utterly dejected.

"I'm sorry, Nick, I really am." Cassie spoke briskly. "We were over long ago."

"We weren't completely over and you know it," Nick protested hoarsely.

"I don't believe this." Cassie fell into the armchair facing him. "Your only excuse is you're not terribly well."

"Fatigue and shock." Nick gave her a disappointed look. "I feel as though I'm walking through glue. I've spoken to Julie. She explained the whole thing."

"That was decent of her," Cassie said dryly.

"I hope you know Julie loves you." Nick held up a hand. "She only wants what's best for you."

"Are you telling me that's *you?*"

"I *used* to be. Once." Nick pulled an unhappy face. "Honestly, Cassie, I can't believe this. It's not real. You of all people to respond to some damned silly advertisement."

"Julie told you that, as well?" Cassie felt somewhat disenchanted with her friend.

"No, not really," Nick said fairly. "It just sort of slipped out. Who is this guy crazy enough to advertise for a wife?"

"Someone who's serious and doesn't have a lot of time," Cassie tossed off. "Anyway, for whatever reason, I'm in love with him and we're getting married on Saturday."

"Believe me, you're going to regret it." Nick leaned closer.

Cassie put her hands over her ears. "No more, Nick,

please. A plane leaves around 2:00 p.m. I think you ought to be on it.''

''I'm not going until I get some answers, Cassie,'' Nick said stubbornly.

''It would be an awful pity if Matthew had to throw you out.''

''How could he?'' Nick squared his sagging shoulders. ''I'm pretty damned tough. Anyway, is he here?'' He whirled his head.

''I'm on my own, Nick, except for the caretakers, but Matthew is driving into town right now. If you think you're tough, believe me, he's tougher.''

Nick dropped his dark head into his hands. ''If anyone had told me only a short time ago you could do a thing like this, I wouldn't have believed them. Your mother and father are tremendously upset.''

''You've spoken to them?'' Why should it be a surprise?

''Your mother has been a wonderful support,'' Nick said gratefully.

''I bet.'' Anger leapt and flared. ''Did she advise you to come up here?''

Nick lifted his head to stare at her. ''She has every right to try to protect her daughter. The very first thing she said was, 'Nick you have to help me.'''

''You know how old I am, Nick?'' Cassie asked.

''Of course. You're twenty-four.''

''So stop talking to me like I'm under age.''

''I'm willing to do anything to stop you, Cassie, if you can't stop yourself. You're infatuated with this guy. Julie tells me he's really something, but hell, you've got nothing in common. What do you know about living in the Outback? You think it's going to be great? It'll be as lonely as hell. What about the cyclones? The floods? You know you've never had to cope with anything like that.''

"Think positively, Nick. I'll survive. Besides, I'll have Matthew.''

"I see this guy as a sinister figure,'' Nick cried. "He's taken you over like some damned Svengali.'' He was so agitated, his hand spearing into his wavy dark hair, it was standing in corkscrews. "I never thought I'd ever say this, but I feel like crying.''

"I wish you wouldn't.'' Cassie crossed to him and put her arm around his shoulder. "I'm very fond of you, Nick. I want us to remain friends.''

"You're just saying that to shut me up. Why, you didn't even invite me to the wedding.''

"Listen, it didn't seem like a good idea.'' Cassie gave him another hug.

"He needn't think he's getting a rich bride,'' Nick said tightly. "I hope you were able to convince him of that. There'll be *nothing* for you. Your mother made that perfectly clear.''

"And you agree with parents disinheriting their only child?''

Nick bit into his bottom lip. "If it's the only way to make you change your mind.''

"But I'm not changing my mind, Nick.'' Cassie shook her head. "Not for you. Not for anyone. I love Matthew. You don't know him.''

"Neither, it appears, does his own father,'' Nick retorted bitterly, burned up with jealousy.

"You've learned that, as well?'' Cassie sighed.

"Oh, yes. God, Cassie, you're not going to be able to keep it a secret,'' he groaned. "The whole thing's bizarre. This Matthew could be setting you up. He could have known all along your father and Macalister are business associates. Maybe he's having a crack at the big-time. You could be part of the master plan."

Cassie shook her head. "I'm sorry, Nick. Too many scenarios. Most of them wrong. Matthew despises Jock Macalister."

"Maybe so, but that doesn't stop him recognising a pot of gold."

"You don't know him, Nick," Cassie said in a clear voice. "If you did, you'd know what you're saying is all wrong."

"Don't count on it." Nick turned on her. "I hate the guy. He's not one of us."

"I see that as a bonus," Cassie said a little wearily. "I know my mother got you all fired up to come here, but she was only using you."

"Maybe." Nick's eyes stung at the thought. "But I still love you, Cassie."

"Lord, Nick." Cassie tried to straighten him as he fell forward and half collapsed against her. "I think you're coming down with something."

"I had a virus in Singapore. High fever, but the hotel doctor fixed me up. I'm all right, I'm over it. I just can't take this in."

"Why don't you lie down? You're not well." Cassie wasn't at all sure how to deal with this.

"Just let me hold you." Nick tried to clutch her.

"Listen, Nick, we can't sit here like this." Cassie was profoundly rattled. "Matthew could walk in."

"Don't mess up your life," Nick implored. He raised his head, his handsome face distorted. "I'm here to get you out of trouble. Take you home."

"Only one problem, she's not going," a hard voice behind them clipped off. "I don't know what in hell you're doing trying to hug my fiancée, but you've got half a second to stop.''

Cassie could have wept with relief. ''Matthew, I didn't hear you.''

''Obviously not.'' His tone was as dry as ash. ''I think you'd better introduce your pal. From where I'm standing you look like an old married couple.''

Nick rose a little groggily, gulping at the sight of Matthew Carlyle in person. ''I'm Nick Raeburn,'' he announced with as much self-assurance as he could muster. ''I've known Cassie for years and years. I'm her friend and I love her.''

''Wait up, here,'' Matthew grated, moving like a wildcat into the room. ''I can tell by looking at you you're none too bright, Nick. I'm Matthew Carlyle, by the way, Cassandra's hillbilly fiancé. We're to be married on Saturday. It is still Saturday, isn't it, Cass?'' He shot her a coldly dazzling glance.

In one springy movement Cassie was on her feet. ''Nick doesn't really know what he's saying. He's not well.''

''So?''

''I think he should lie down.''

''And what am I supposed to do? Carry him up to your bed?'' Matthew added with totally false affability.

''Don't be an idiot!'' Cassie flared.

''I'm no match for your friend.''

''I'll always treasure the lovely times Cassie and I shared together,'' Nick muttered mournfully.

''I just bet you will,'' Matthew said in a slow, deadly drawl.

''You're not going to hit him, surely?'' Cassie rushed to grab Matthew's arm but he fended her off.

"Go ahead," Nick invited stoically.

"I have never hit a defenceless man, but I could make an exception."

"Why, hello there, Red!" said an entirely different voice. It was Molly, who hadn't seemed to notice anyone else.

"The front door was open so I walked in." Matthew nodded to her.

"Molly, meet a friend of mine, Nick Raeburn," Cassie interrupted quickly. "A lightning visit, he's flying back to Sydney this afternoon."

"Actually I have time to put him on the plane." Matthew consulted his watch.

"Pleased to meet you, Molly," Nick said. "I'm trying to talk Cassie into coming back with me."

Molly gave a snort like a horse. "I don't see how that can be."

Nick reeled on his feet, hoping against hope his faintness would go away.

It was Matthew who caught him, taking his weight, pushing him back onto the sofa and lifting his legs so Nick lay back groaning. "Blessed if I've ever done that before."

"To hell with this!" Matthew exploded. "What's wrong with this guy?"

"I'd better get a doctor," Cassie said worriedly.

"No one can patch me up," Nick proclaimed. "Not now."

"Poor Nick!" Cassie took the wrong path to sympathy, not seeing Matthew's face darken.

"Get on to Doc Sweeney, Molly. Tell him Cassandra's ex-hero is suffering from a virus, exhaustion, whatever. Just get him here," Matthew ordered.

"I haven't had lots to eat," Nick said in a low, heart-tugging voice.

"You sound like a real asset, Nick," Matthew said, a dangerous light in his eyes.

"I've done a lot with my life." Nick looked up at the other man with a faint flicker of challenge.

"That's the go. But if you want to survive, you'll keep your nose out of my affairs. You see, Nick, it's quite simple. Cassandra loves me and I love her. You don't come into it. Understand? You're history."

"You're making a lot of people unhappy," Nick squeezed out.

"That's a shame," Matthew softly jeered. "Maybe if they were big enough they could change that."

Tom Sweeney finished examining the patient, then looked up at Cassie. "Nothing much wrong with him that good food and rest won't fix."

"Maybe I could stay for a few days, if that's okay?" Nick asked hopefully after the doctor had gone. He was soon jolted out of it as Matthew turned to look at him.

"You can't stay here, Nick, much as you were hoping to."

"Just for tonight perhaps?" The soft-hearted Cassie suggested.

For answer, Matthew took Cassie by the hand and propelled her out of the room.

"You're a lot of woman, Cassie." Matthew held her by the shoulders. "Tender. Compassionate. But having your old boyfriend stay over isn't on."

"But he seems to be heading for some sort of collapse, Matthew," she tried to speak reasonably.

"He's making that pitch, yes, but *I'm* making the decisions here. It's not a good idea."

"Heavens, Matthew, you don't think I *want* him here, do you?"

"You'd never guess when you're in your comforting mood," he answered tautly.

"You can't be jealous?" Her eyes went huge. Matthew was everything to her.

"I'll be damned if I'm going to allow your old flame to sleep over. If you're not going to protect yourself, I will. You're my girl. Hear that and hear it well."

"But this is absurd," Cassie said, looking straight at him. "It's only a kindness."

"Is it?" There were vertical lines between Matthew's black brows.

"And general stupidity on your part," Cassie said, with a little answering huff of anger. "I was just feeling sorry for him."

"It's one helluva step from your point of view to mine." Matthew slid his hands from her shoulders to her waist. "Raeburn goes."

"Okay. Fine. You're the boss."

"And what's he doing here, anyway?" Matthew was shocked by his own jealousy. "Apart from trying to persuade you to go back to Sydney with him?"

Cassie's anger turned to an ache. "It's mainly my mother's fault," she sighed. "She spoke to him. Got him all riled up."

"So who *else* is going to run interference?" Matthew flashed. This was to have been a wonderful day together, not playing nursemaid to Raeburn.

"What do you mean?" Cassie stiffened instantly.

"Ah, forget it." There was self-disgust in his eyes and he tugged her close.

"The hell I will!" She broke away. "You were going to say something, Matthew. Who *else?*"

Off balance, he exploded. "Your father sent one of his legal guns to buy me off."

"No." It caught her like a blow.

Matthew recovered, appalled. "Me and my big mouth," he groaned. "I wasn't going to say anything at all."

"You were going to keep it from me?" She fisted one small hand and punched it into his hard muscular chest.

"I didn't want it to hurt you, Cass." He caught her hand and held it still against him.

"When *was* this?" She felt furious.

"A few days ago. Before you arrived." He reached deep inside him for calm, wanting to kiss, to soothe.

"It's just the sort of move Father would make," she said bitterly. "How much was I worth?"

Matthew was determined she would never know. "I could name my own price."

"Why didn't you take it?" she lashed out in humiliation.

That rocked him to the core. He hauled her back into his arms. "You dare to ask me that?"

The tenderness and passion he had felt turned to steam. His strong arms trapped her so she couldn't move. She shouldn't be thinking of anyone but him. His mouth came down over hers, hard and furious, persuading it into a ragged surrender so her petalled lips opened and he could taste the seductive velvet of her tongue. No one could make him feel like this. His need for her had grown even keener, wilder, since he had so eagerly consummated their love. Capturing her in one long, rapturous night when all the love he felt for her came pouring out like a torrent. Could he ever forget it? Hell, he loved her so much he couldn't think straight. Now, damn it, she had insulted him.

Cassie had already come to realise it with distress. Frantically she tried to make amends, responding with a passion that matched his, running her hands possessively over the taut muscled ridges of his wide back, straining to give him what he needed.

"I didn't mean what I said, Matthew," she gasped between kisses, pulling her head back.

"I can't get enough of you. Hell, I can't even get close to you." He pressed his mouth to her neck.

"Soon." Cassie's voice shook with emotion. "Soon we'll be together again."

Irresistibly, her mind, like Matthew's, raced back to that one fabulous time they had come together in a delirium of passion. A night that still fuelled her dreams and made her desperate for him to claim her again.

"I want it to be Saturday *now!*" Matthew groaned in frustration. "When you're mine forever."

"Our wedding day." Joy welled in her.

"I don't want anyone else loving you," he muttered, putting a hand to her breast. "No one but me."

"There's never been anyone like you, Matthew," she answered him.

"So, Raeburn has to go?"

"God knows, I didn't ask him." Cassie rose to him and kissed his mouth. "Why don't we both take him into town? Marcy can keep an eye on him."

"Why not?" Matthew gave his first laugh of the

morning. "Marcy's had a lot of experience taking care of people."

Back in Melbourne at the old Mondale mansion, Eleanor Macalister was sitting in her father's study, a dark-panelled room full of leather-bound, gold-tooled books, waiting for her husband to arrive. Eleanor spent most of her time here now, to be near her grandchildren. She had inherited the very large house from the father she had adored. Now the home was used as a grace and favour residence by their eldest daughter, Tessa, her husband, Graham Downes, a young Liberal M.P., and their two children, Amanda and Laura. Beautiful children. But all girls, girls ran in Eleanor's family.

Hardly a matter of concern for loving parents and grandparents, Macalister thought, but there was no male heir for the cattle empire he had built up. He couldn't die before putting that straight. His daughters wouldn't be resentful as long as they got their share of the money. None of them, husbands, either, were born to the land. They wanted the glamorous city life. Only Eleanor would stand firm against him. As she had done from the beginning.

It occurred to him, iron-fisted cattle baron he was purported to be, he was bracing himself for the coming ordeal. Damned if Eleanor couldn't make him feel perpetually in the wrong. She was five years older than he. Thirty-five when he had married her without anyone else asking for her hand despite her father's wealth and social standing. Not that she was plain. Then or now. It was her autocratic manner that put most people off. Not him. He had always been an adventurer. And wonder of wonders, she had fallen in love with him.

It wasn't a love match for him, of course. But it suited him well. At the time. He had places to go. Eleanor would help him.

There she was waiting for him in her father's favourite wing-back armchair, beautifully dressed as she was every day of her life, fully made up, a handsome woman with sharp refined features, an immaculate snow-white coiffure and piercing light grey eyes, her thin hands glittering with diamond rings. The immense emerald-cut diamond that had belonged to her mother, the lesser rings, still very valuable, he had given her through the years. His engagement ring at the time, a modest sapphire, had been put aside many long years ago as unworthy to join the collection. Which in fact it was. Seventy-five this year and Eleanor was still as sharp as a tack, her hearing acute, her vision excellent. She enjoyed splendid health. She would see him out.

"Well, Jock, what have you to tell me?" A stern mother to a naughty boy, he thought tiredly. Eleanor didn't beat about the bush. She had her spies. Just like him. She knew how he longed for that son of his. She knew of their meeting in Sydney at the home of Stuart Stirling. She knew all about the bitter quarrel that had caused Stuart Stirling to disinherit his child.

"I think it's time, Ellie, we confronted the fact I have a son," he began sadly, taking a seat opposite her. He was longing for a cigar, the very poison that was killing him, but Eleanor for many years now had never permitted him to smoke in front of her.

"*You* have a son, Jock," Eleanor returned icily, "*we* do not. I will never acknowledge your bastard in any capacity until the day I die. You have a family. Your daughters and your beautiful grandchildren. Isn't that family enough?"

Macalister drew a deep, harsh, rattling breath. "To put it bluntly, my dear, *no.*"

Eleanor glared at him. "I know what's on your mind, Jock, but you can't bring disgrace on us all. I won't have it. Not now. You've ignored the boy's existence for the last thirty years. Why this pitiful last stand?"

He actually laughed. "Because I'm dying, Ellie. You know that."

She stared at him, never forgiving him for that terrible defection, but still loving him in her way. "You've got years left in you yet."

"No one better than you, Ellie, for hiding your head in the sand. You've been a good wife to me." Another wry laugh. "You've always stood by my side, but you came between me and my son."

"How do you know he's your *only* son?" Eleanor demanded, her voice as sharp as a knife. "Are you going to search the countryside for them, too? I know how many women you've had in your bed."

"Ah, Ellie. That mightn't have happened if you hadn't hated it so."

She had the grace to blush. "You know I did everything you wanted in the early days, Jock."

"I know you always found sex awkward," he answered her, almost kindly.

"Well, it *is.*" She frowned. "Why you had to get mixed up with a child, that nanny, I'll never know."

"So long ago, but it doesn't seem like that," he said. "I've never forgotten."

"How dare you say such a thing, Jock," Eleanor said through clenched teeth. "It's water under the bridge."

"It's the most shameful thing I've done in my

whole life,'' Macalister answered with enormous regret. ''You threatened to ruin me, Ellie. Well, maybe I deserved it. But you can't stop me now. I'm honour bound to make amends before I die.''

Eleanor Macalister looked shaken and aghast. She had wielded considerable power in her own right. Now *this!* ''The press will pick it up, Jock,'' she warned. ''You realise that. A disgraceful scandal and that Stirling girl involved.''

''They've threatened to disinherit her.''

''They couldn't do better.'' Eleanor leaned back in her chair and closed her eyes.

''You're a hard woman, Ellie.''

The ice-hard eyes flew open. ''Of course you would say that. I have standards, Jock. My whole life has been devoted to you, though I know I was only a ticket to where you wanted to go. But you have daughters. Do you think they will permit you to bring this young man into our midst?''

''Their half brother, Ellie, but he won't want to come. Wild horses wouldn't drag him here. He's proud.''

''I know human nature all too well.'' Eleanor tried to rally but she was in shock. ''He's after the money.''

Macalister sighed. ''You *all* are. It's my intention to leave Monaro Downs to the boy, together with two or three other stations in the chain. He'll need them. But there's not going to be any knock-down, drag-out fight.''

Eleanor who never cried was almost in tears. ''We'll fight it after you're dead, Jock.''

''Fight all you like and stop looking like you'll all be out on the streets. The one who decides to contest the will stands to lose their inheritance." Now he sounded tough and grim.

"You'll never get away with it, Jock," Eleanor warned.

"I think I will." Calmly, with finality, Jock Macalister stood up and walked to the door. "This is one fight, Eleanor, you're not going to win."

Cassie remained absolutely motionless with shock when she saw Sir Jock Macalister approaching her in town. For a moment she wondered if she was hallucinating. The sun that had been flooding the world so brilliantly seemed to slip behind a cloud. She'd finished her shopping and now she was enjoying a quiet cappuccino at an outside table of the local coffee shop.

"Sir Jock, what a surprise!" It fact it was like a blow.

"Wonderful to see you, Cassandra," he answered courteously, tipping the grey akubra he wore. "May I sit down?"

"Please."

He seemed to be out of breath and even thinner than the last time she had seen him, but still a man of immense presence. Already customers at the other tables were whispering quietly behind their hands. Everyone knew who he was. Sir Jock Macalister, the cattle baron. Maybe he was about to put an end to all the rumours.

"You look enchanting." Macalister gave her a smile that was still dazzling.

"Thank you." It was impossible not to smile back. Besides, it was Matthew's smile even to the heartbreaking quality. "Was it Matthew you wanted to see?"

"Ah, Cassandra, you've read my heart."

This was Matthew's chance to reject him. Cassie found herself shaking with nerves. "You know we're getting married this Saturday?" Nothing must mar the great day.

"I've heard." Macalister nodded. "As far as I can make out, the whole town is jumping for joy."

"It's wonderful." Cassie's smile trembled. "Everyone's treating our wedding as a grand occasion."

"Which it is," Macalister said warmly. "The most important step of your life." His own marriage mocked him now.

"You know my parents haven't replied to our invitation," Cassie told him, glancing away.

He touched her arm. "That makes no sense."

"My father is a very stubborn man. He has strong notions about what's right and wrong."

"And he thinks it's wrong for you to marry Matthew?" Macalister's voice hardened, but he stopped himself.

"He thinks it will cause a great deal of trouble."

"He surely couldn't think it would offend me?" Macalister frowned.

"What you think is very important to him," Cassie told him quietly.

Macalister considered that with a lurch of the heart. "How ironic! As it happens, Cassandra, I'm absolutely delighted you're to marry my son."

"So you admit it? He *is* your son." Cassie mourned for Matthew, all he had lost. Now it was spoken. Ineradicable. "You've never acknowledged him before."

The ghost of Matthew's mother rose before Macalister's eyes. "To my eternal shame. I can't bear it anymore. I can't bear Matthew's anger and hatred of me.''

Cassie couldn't speak for a moment, then she murmured, ''I'm sorry. I can see you're very unhappy. But there are such reasons for it, Sir Jock.''

Macalister moved the jar of raw sugar slightly but deliberately, as if he were making a chess move. ''Of course. No excuses from me. It was a one-time encounter with Matthew's mother, Cassie. She was so sweet, so pretty, so loving, I simply lost my head. The next time I visited the out-station she was gone. Just like that. Disappeared like the wind blew her out of my life. It was a few years before the rumours began to reach my ears.''

''You didn't follow them up?''

''Oh, yes.'' A sick look came into his eyes. ''My wife learned about them, as well, and threatened to walk out on me and take the children. She and her family wouldn't tolerate a breath of scandal. But the real trouble was, Ellie knew everything that went on behind the scenes. You understand? The deals. She struck a hard bargain. I deny my son, or she'd ruin me.''

''You really believed she would?'' Cassie was dismayed.

''I've never been more certain of anything in my life. None of which excuses me. With your help, Cassandra, I have to meet Matthew again. I look on this as my great mission.''

''You make it sound as though Matthew's eating out of my hand,'' Cassie said in a distracted way. She recognised this could cause trouble.

''Isn't he?'' Macalister replied simply, thinking at least his son was a lucky man.

"Matthew is his *own* man. He loves me, as I love him, but he makes his own decisions," Cassie declared. "I don't think I could persuade him."

"All I want is a half hour," Macalister was reduced to begging. "Just long enough to beseech him to forgive me."

Surely he deserved that chance. "Sir Jock, I *want* to help you," Cassie began, "but I can't promise anything. I feel bound not to upset Matthew before our wedding. Matthew feels very strongly about this."

Macalister said nothing at all for a few moments as a hard dry cough racked him. "If you could just intercede, Cassandra," he implored when he had recovered. "It means everything in the world to me." I don't want to face my Maker with this on my conscience, he thought. He had decided not to speak of his failing health let alone the unvarnished fact he had six months at the most. "I need to reconcile with my son, Cassandra. To offer him my deepest remorse."

His appearance and the way he was speaking told Cassie a good deal. She stretched out a sympathetic hand, looking into Macalister's suffering eyes. "Let me speak to him. He's very proud. I'm sure you saw that."

"There's compassion there, too, Cassandra," Macalister insisted. "If it's at all possible I'd like it to be today. If you'll come with me, I'll organise a helicopter flight. That will save the long journey and a lot of time."

Cassie couldn't raise Matthew despite several attempts, so in the end she agreed to their taking the helicopter to Jabiru on the other side of the purple range. She was acutely conscious of Sir Jock's exhaustion. He seemed so tired, as if this was his last chance. She only hoped Matthew would understand. Sir Jock needed her beside him. She was sure of that.

The landscape seen from the air was an eternal green. The miles and miles of cane fields, the great crop of the tropics, then as they crossed the rugged spur of the Great Dividing Range that ran the entire length of the east coast, the vast savannas, home of the great Queensland cattle stations, the biggest holdings in the world. Macalister himself controlled a chain that stretched from the Channel Country in the far southwest, through Outback Queensland into the Northern Territory. Now they could see the glittering lakes, the great flights of birds that banked sharply over the water. Thousands and thousands of them. An astonishing sight.

"Here we are, Jabiru." The pilot lifted his voice above the noise of the rotor and pointed below.

Cassie's stomach lurched as they dropped altitude.

"I'll try for a landing close to the homestead."

On the ground the heat assailed them and the pilot grabbed Sir Jock's elbow, speaking cheerfully. "Steady as you go, Sir Jock. Let's get you into the shade. Reckon Matthew will have heard the chopper. In fact, if I'm not mistaken, that's a puff of dust."

The puff of dust materialised into a rider on horseback, covering the ground at a full gallop.

Even with sunglasses on, Cassie cupped her hands against the glare, staring at the horseman until his image became clearer.

It was Matthew. No mistaking his topnotch riding style or the set of his lean, wide-shouldered body. He stopped only a few feet away, his beautiful bay mare trembling ever so delicately. Matthew dismounted, his expression so tight nothing was revealed of his feelings.

"Hi there, Matthew." The charter pilot waved, walking down the steps towards him, holding out his hand. "How's it going, mate?"

A few words were exchanged and the pilot moved off to the yellow helicopter a small distance away. He had a call in the region. It had been arranged he would come back for Macalister and Cassie in a little over an hour.

As the pilot lifted off in a flurry of dust, Cassie stepped down from the veranda and out into the sunlight. She ran towards Matthew, holding out her arms.

He caught her. Held her. His quietness more daunting than anger. He wore his normal working gear, blue denim shirt and jeans, red bandanna around his neck, high riding boots, a black akubra pulled down over his eyes.

"Cassie," he said, his voice clipped hard. "What's Macalister doing here?"

He stared over her head to where Sir Jock was standing in the shade of the veranda, a portrait of dignity.

"I tried to reach you several times," Cassie said with a quick, frustrated shake of her head.

"I've been out since dawn," he told her, raising his chin in a high mettled gesture. "He approached you. Of course he did."

Cassie laid a placating hand against his chest, feeling the strong pump of his heart. "Matthew, he's a sick man. I'm sure of it."

"And how does that piece of information justify his presence here?" His eyes were stormy.

"He wants a chance to speak to you." She appealed

to him for understanding. "Won't you allow him the opportunity?"

Matthew shook his head. "I really don't think so. If my mother had lived, maybe. Not now. Why is he bothering us? Can't he leave us in peace?"

"He has no peace himself, Matthew, don't you see?"

Matthew's handsome mouth compressed. "He's never spoken a word to me in my entire life, now he's here wanting some sort of forgiveness?" He gave an angry, baffled laugh.

Cassie's breath came on a long sigh. "I want you to give it to him for me. It's a big ask, Matthew, but I think he's been punished enough."

His gaze softened. "You know what? You're compassionate to a fault."

Cassie swallowed on tears. "It's *you* I want to see at peace, Matthew."

He studied her lovely upturned face, torn between his love for her and the tremendous hostility he felt towards his father. There were tears in her beautiful eyes that bothered him. Cassie won. He looked towards the tall man standing on the veranda. There was a slump to the fine head and shoulders, as though a once powerful persona had lost his great vigour.

"Only for you, Cassandra," Matthew said quietly, "only for you. I really love you."

Her lips curved with the most beautiful smile. "Oh, thank you, my darling Matthew." Cassie felt a wonderful calm. "Let's put an end to all the long years of bitterness and pain. Reach out to him. I fear the life force is slipping away from him."

Matthew didn't really understand it but he felt a sudden tightness in his chest, an odd pity. He raised his hand, acknowledging the man who was his father.

CHAPTER ELEVEN

IT WAS one of those glorious blue and gold days just made for a wedding, the world flooded with sunshine and soft breezes that spread the perfume of the beautiful heady tropical flowers and lifted the heart. Cassie woke early after the most wonderful of dreams. All she could think of was by the end of the day she would be Matthew's wife.

Matthew's wife! It filled her with such joy and excitement. She didn't feel in the least nervous, rather her sense of anticipation was like a bright light inside her, causing her whole body to glow.

Her dress, made by a Sydney designer, was a ravishing sheaf of delicate white silk lace, the long skirt forming a slight train. The sleeves were long, too, to show off the exquisite beauty of the lace, the gossamer confection worn over a slender white silk slip. She and Julie, when they had shopped for it, had thought it perfection and wonderfully appropriate for her rainforest wedding.

Her hair she was wearing full and loose, long strands woven with tiny orchids, a delicate headdress of seed pearls and crystals worn like some medieval fantasy diadem down on her forehead with her hair streaming around it. Her bridesmaids, Julie and Louise, were to wear delicate, summery, silk gorgette dresses, Julie in a misty green, Louise in a soft gold. All three would carry a simple spray of lilies and orchids.

Matthew's two attendants, best man and grooms-
man, she had only just met. Cattlemen like Matthew,
one the son of a Northern Territory pastoralist, the
other managed a large Central Queensland property.

Matthew, Cassie knew, was wearing a cream linen
suit with a Nehru-style jacket, as were his attendants,
the difference being different coloured shirts with the
same stand-up collars. With eyes like Matthew's, his
had to be sapphire blue. Matthew had arranged that
they would spend their wedding night in a suite at the
very beautiful Port Douglas Marina Mirage, leaving
the next day by helicopter for one of the most magical
places in the Great Barrier Reef, the secluded Angel
Island, a guarantee of romantic bliss.

Cassie felt like she was drowning in pleasure. She
hadn't heard from her parents. She simply had to accept it. Just as she was planning to get up, the bedside
phone rang.

"I have to see you," a vibrant voice murmured into
her ear.

"You can't wait for this afternoon?" She lay back
against the pillows.

"It has to be *now,* my darling bride," Matthew said.
"Not at the house. I want you to come down to the
beach."

"You'll have to give me five minutes," Cassie said.
"I'm still in bed."

"You'll have me right beside you tomorrow."

"You don't know how good that sounds."

She was out and running in just under ten, willow
slender in a tight pair of jeans and a mulberry camisole
top. Matthew was waiting for her at the base of the
long winding stairs to the beach, looking so vital, so

handsome. God, so beautiful, she threw out her arms to him in an ecstasy of love.

"My beautiful Cassandra, my delight and pride." He caught her to him, whirling her about in a circle as though her weight was no more to him than a child's.

The pleasure was so heady, so sweet. She went to speak, but he slid his arms around her and bent his head, kissing her with such heart-rocking desire Cassie felt humbled. At last, at long last, someone to love her as she loved him. Someone with whom she could realise her dream.

"Matthew!" Dreamy-eyed, she stared up at him. "The gods have smiled on us."

"I know exactly how you feel."

He smiled and reached into his breast pocket for a small package wrapped in tissue paper. "I'd love it, Cassandra, if you could wear these today," he said in a low intense voice that throbbed with emotion.

"Here, let me see?"

"They belonged to my mother," Matthew explained. "The only things she had of value. I'd like you to wear them in memory of her. It seemed to me they would suit beautifully."

Cassie touched the long pendant earrings with a reverent finger. "Oh, Matthew. They're lovely." Her eyes filled with tears at the association.

"My mother would have loved you to wear them, too, Cassandra." Matthew battled his own deep feelings. "Do you want to try them on?"

Cassie blinked to free her long lashes of teardrops. "Of course. They'll be perfect with my dress."

"And I can't wait to see you as my bride." Matthew watched as she swept her hair back from her face, screwing the earrings to her small earlobes. She wasn't wearing makeup, not even lipstick, and she looked as beautiful as a magnolia. There was no other word for her. That perfect matt creamy skin, the very soft mouth he loved to kiss, a natural velvety rose. The earrings were "family," his mother had told him. He had only seen her wear them on special occasions. Now they were swinging from Cassandra's ears, a delicately worked combination of silver, corals and pearls.

"They're Victorian, mid-Victorian, I think," Cassie said with interest and pleasure. "How do they look?" She tossed up her head for his inspection.

He was shaken by his love for her. The force of it leaping out of his eyes. "Perfect."

All at once she was back in his arms, mouth on mouth, both of them murmuring passionate endearments between kisses. Temple. Cheekbone. Chin. Oh, the mouth!

"My goodness, you two," a laughing voice called down from the overhead terrace, causing them to at last break apart. "Can't you stop kissing?"

"This woman is mine!" Matthew shouted exultantly, locking Cassie in his arms.

"You've got a great way of showing it, Red." Julie felt their deep emotion as if she could catch it on the breeze. "Come on up. Molly is making breakfast. The wedding day has started."

On the edge of the rainforest, a beautiful bright and sunny place, myriads of butterflies greeted them, flitting around and between the bridal party like a fairy tale. Even the breeze blew showers of confetti from the great billows of lantana interwoven with bougainvillea that grew along the rainforest borders, attracting these flying kaleidoscopes of colour.

Permission had been given for them to enter the rainforest, everyone moving delicately along a track carpeted with fallen leaves. The procession was led by a young girl barely into her teens but already a fine musician, playing the flute for them. Flowers garlanded her head and she wore a floating ankle-length dress of cream organdie. It was like having a head full of the most wonderful singing birds, Cassie thought.

Eventually they reached the spot she and Matthew had chosen. A small clearing before a magnificent rainforest giant with buttresses soaring some fifteen feet high, creating deep, woody caverns. Luxuriant masses of intertwining vegetation ringed them round, heavy evergreen crowns of the forest trees formed an interlocking canopy a hundred and fifty feet and more over their heads.

On the forest floor it was like a mysterious luminous jade-green twilight as quiet and calm as a cathedral. There was barely any breeze but it was beautifully cool, the air redolent of mosses, ferns and herbs, the magnificent cycads, the staghorns, the elkhorns and the orchids that grew from large clumps high up in the trees, sending down cascades of richly scented flowers in colours of cream, gold, deepest pink, coral and deep mauve. The air was like incense as befitting Nature's great cathedral.

The celebrant, a woman dressed in silver brocade, waited until everyone was assembled. Then the marriage service began, the celebrant's expression serious but entranced as were they all by the beauty and power of this most ancient place.

Cassandra's headdress, delicate as a silvery spider's

web, sparkled in the green light as did her lovely pendant earrings and the white-gold bracelet set with two pave diamond hearts that encircled her wrist. Matthew's gift to her. She turned to him, so heartbreakingly handsome, a loving smile curving that beautifully shaped sensuous mouth. Softly she made her responses, her voice flowing like music. The wonder of it! It was flawless. She would remember every moment down to the tiniest detail. Once she put her hand briefly to her throat as emotion threatened to overwhelm her, but in truth she had never been happier.

Matthew, for his part, wanted to shout his love for his Cassandra to the treetops, hearing it echo through the forest, scattering the brilliantly coloured birds that were feeding on the starbursts of flowers across the canopy. It seemed to him life had been aimless until now.

The marriage ritual over, Matthew bent his head to his bride for their ceremonial kiss, sweeping her slender lace-covered body to him, both of them drowning in the magic of the moment. Now they had joined forces to face the world. Mr. and Mrs. Matthew Carlyle.

But the deepening forest had one final surprise for them. As bride and groom turned to face their guests, the great canopy appeared to split open, allowing a momentary single ray of light to enter this wonderful, mystical, luxuriant terrain. It seemed to enfold Matthew and his bride like some marvellous beneficent force before vanishing like a bright puff of smoke.

"Maybe it was your guardian angel," Ned whispered to Cassie later. ''Whatever it was, it was most extraordinary.''

The street barbecue was already in progress by the time they were all driven back to the reception. Seemingly everyone in the town, including tiny babies, cheered the wedding party as they arrived, offering their best wishes. It wasn't the grand, sophisticated affair Cassie knew her parents would have given for her had she married a suitable man of their choice, but it was so wonderfully friendly and heart-warming.

Marcy and her team had made the al fresco dining area as romantic and celebratory as possible, flowers everywhere, a combination of cream, white, and dark green foliage, luxurious big cream silk bows tied to the chairs dressed with cream slip covers. The tables were covered with sugar-pink linen cloths over full-length cream, with matching napkins, the tables topped by posies of white orchids interspersed with feathery green twigs of baby's breath and tiny white roses. The bride looked like an illustration from a fairy story, her attendants like moonbeams.

As Matthew and Cassie walked into the reception room, delighted and grateful to Marcy for all her hard work, their eyes were instantly drawn to three people who stood before the long bridal table draped in cream linen and tulle. All looked resplendent in their wedding finery, Sir Jock Macalister, grey-suited with a white flower in his buttonhole, beside him delivered by his private jet, Cassie's mother and father, their expressions for once, anxious and a little torn.

''Matthew!'' Cassie whispered, her hand tightening within her husband's clasp. No matter what, these were her parents. She wanted them here.

"Go to them, darling," Matthew urged, his own happiness opening his heart. "It's what's called absolution."

Weddings are times of high emotion, of hope and reconciliation. This was no exception.

Many hours later while the wedding celebration continued into the night, Cassie and Matthew arrived by limousine at the luxurious Port Douglas resort. They were shown immediately to their suite, the sitting room scented with the incomparable perfume of two dozen velvety red roses. Champagne in a silver ice bucket waited, two crystal flutes beside it.

"Twelve o'clock, the witching hour!" Cassie began to twirl in pure pleasure, stopping to look out on a night made radiant by a huge silver moon. "Time for bed," she cried, causing Matthew to burst into a rapturous laugh.

"I'll turn back the covers, shall I? I can toast my little mail-order bride between the sheets."

"You can toast her *after!*" she called.

In the dressing room she quickly removed her chic little going away suit, then, in her lace bra and briefs, creamed off her makeup before the mirrored wall in the spacious bathroom. This was it! Their Shangri-la.

Everything had gone so splendidly but now they were alone. They had earned it. Under the shower she let the perfumed foaming bubbles slide all over her satiny-smooth skin, her excitement intense. She felt alight with desire. Her body dry from a big fluffy white towel, she rubbed her favourite body lotion over her breasts and limbs, imagining Matthew's caressing hands. Next her nightgown that had cost almost as much as an evening dress. The softest, tenderest, pale peach, thin as a veil, with tiny empire sleeves, the ruched front secured by tiny pearl fastenings. She reached for a brush and dropped it in her excitement then let her hair crackle and stream over her shoulders. The way Matthew liked it.

Matthew!

In the bedroom with its huge king-sized bed, she found him. His pintucked blue shirt was undone to the waist, and her bones seemed to melt.

Matthew turned and saw his bride with the light from the dressing room behind her. It streamed through the exquisite nightgown he had heard so much about, clearly illuminating the beautiful naked body beneath. At least he got to see her in it before it would fall in a pool at their feet.

Slowly, tantalisingly, he walked toward her, his eyes gone darkest blue. ''I'm going to make love to every little inch of you,'' he warned in a voice so thrilling it made her heart hammer. ''Every bone, every bend, every curve, every crevice. Right down to the last little atom.''

Cassie trembled, ravished by anticipation, her body arching in delight as Matthew began to undo the tiny pearl buttons...one by one....

Marion Lennox has had a variety of careers – medical receptionist, computer programmer and teacher. Married, with two children, she now lives in rural Victoria, Australia. Her wish for an occupation which would allow her to remain at home with her children and her dog led her to begin writing, and she has now published a number of romances both for Medical Romance™ and Tender Romance™.

Look out for Marion Lennox's latest book:
STORMBOUND SURGEON
Out next month, in Medical Romance™!

DR McIVER'S BABY
by
Marion Lennox

CHAPTER ONE

DR ANNIE BURROWS seemed to spend her life avoiding Tom McIver's dogs and Tom McIver's women. Tripping over Tom's baby was the last straw.

The baby must have arrived just before midnight, but neither Annie nor Tom had heard it come.

Annie had sat up until twelve, doing medico-legal letters. Then she figured she'd have to sleep some time — and if she wanted any sleep she'd have to knock on Tom's door and tell him to keep the noise down.

There was sound-proofing between Tom's apartment and the hospital wards, but not between Tom's and Annie's apartments. A woman's laughter was making Annie wince, his stereo was playing too loud and one of his dogs was barking at the rising moon.

'Shut up, Hoof. Or Tiny. Whoever you are,' Annie muttered to Tom's out-of-sight dogs as she walked out into the darkened corridor.

And then her foot caught on something soft, and before she could recover Annie sprawled heavily over a bundle, lying in Tom's doorway.

Annie wasn't hurt. She was just plain furious.

For more than ten seconds Annie lay full length on the linoleum floor and swore. Swore at bachelor doctors who left their belongings strewn in the hallway. Swore at the woman who was still giggling inside. Swore at Tom's dogs who were both now barking hysterically on the other side of the door.

'I'll murder him! If this keeps up I'll commit real violence!'

Maybe she'd have to leave Bannockburn. She couldn't stand Tom McIver much longer.

The thought made her even angrier. Annie didn't

want to leave. Bannockburn was lovely. It was a tiny south Australian town, nestled in a coastal valley. The twelve-bed hospital needed two doctors to run it, and the doctors were Tom and Annie.

Tom McIver was a GP surgeon, a skilled clinician who concentrated one hundred per cent when he was working. He also concentrated one hundred per cent when he was playing — be it with his pair of huge Great Danes or his various women. It seemed to Annie that there wasn't a pretty face in the district Tom McIver hadn't been seen with. Tom's startling good looks had the valley girls smitten, and Tom made the most of it.

And Annie?

In her mid-twenties, Annie was seven years younger than Tom and had only been in Bannockburn for eight months. She studious and quiet — a GP with anaesthetic and paediatric skills. Tom had obstetric training so in tandem they worked brilliantly. It was only personally that Tom drove Annie nuts.

So Annie lay sprawled in the corridor and thought dark thoughts about her future — and even darker thoughts about Tom McIver. Then the bundle lying under Annie's legs moved.

Annie sat up as if she'd been burned. The package was alive! In one swift action she scooped the bundle into her arms. It was warm and moist and, as Annie lifted it, from the depths came a plaintive cry that told Annie this was no puppy or kitten.

This was a human child.

Tom's dogs had heard the sounds of Annie falling and the cry of the baby. The barking on the other side of Tom's door reached a crescendo.

The door burst open and a stream of light slashed down over her. Tom McIver stood in the doorway while his two damned dogs launched themselves at Annie, attempting to lick her to death. Somewhere behind him a woman was trying to peer round Tom's broad shoulders.

'Tom, what is it? Is it a prowler?'

'It's Annie,' Tom said blankly. 'Annie, why are you sitting on the floor?'

Annie didn't answer. With one hand she was fending off Tom's huge dogs, and with the other she was desperately trying to see what lay underneath the cloth. She'd fallen hard. Had she hurt it? She bent her body over the child in an effort to protect it, and then Tom was stooping beside her.

'Are you hurt? Annie, what is it. . .?'

And then he saw what she was holding.

'What the hell. . .?'

'Get the dogs off,' Annie snapped. 'Now.'

She'd hardly finished saying it before the dogs were gone. When Tom moved, he moved fast. Annie had never been able to fault Tom as a doctor, and in an emergency there was no one she would prefer to work with. Now, suddenly, the corridor light was on, Tom's dogs and his woman were behind his closed door and the baby on Annie's lap had all Tom's attention.

'What's wrong? Annie, what is going on here?'

'I don't know,' Annie muttered. She was peeling away layers of blanket. The child was dressed in a simple white towelling suit. Its tiny face was screwed up in anger and, as it started to cry, its legs and arms moved with an ease that told Annie there couldn't be major damage. The layers of woollen blanket had protected the child well.

'Everything seems OK,' Annie said, her hands running swiftly over the little body. 'I'll get it somewhere warm and undress it. . .'

'Annie. . .' Tom sat back on his heels and stared at Annie as though she'd lost her senses.

'Yes?' Annie flashed him a glance and then turned back to the baby.

Tom was looking decidedly dishevelled. His deep brown curls were tangled, he was wearing old jeans and a shirt which was undone to the waist—revealing far too much chest—and there was a trace of lipstick

on his collar. The sight of Tom's body had the power
to unsettle Annie. It always did. Now, as always, her
defence was to concentrate on her work.

'Annie, would you mind telling me just what the hell
is going on? Who is this?'

'I don't know,' Annie said simply. She undid a button
on the baby's towelling suit and took a peek under the
nappy. 'It's a girl.' She looked up at Tom and pressed
her lips together. 'Dr McIver, this baby was lying on
your doorstep. Does she belong to your friend in there?'

'You have to be kidding!' Tom smiled, with the magnetic laughter in his deep brown eyes that made him
an instant hit with each of his women in turn. And
unsettled Annie no end.

'Do you think we'd let the dogs in and leave a baby
outside?' Tom demanded of Annie, his ridiculous sense
of humour obviously caught. 'For heaven's sake. . .'
Then his smile faded. 'Where did you say the baby
was lying?'

'On your doorstep. I tripped over her.'

Tom's smile disappeared completely as he heard the
concern in Annie's voice. 'You tripped over her. . .'

'If she doesn't belong to your friend then she's been
dumped,' Annie said slowly. 'She's only about two
months old. She can hardly have crawled here by herself.' She looked down at the tiny bundle in her arms
and she felt her heart twist. The little girl was sobbing
her heart out. Who on earth would dump a child
like this?

She looked up and Tom's expression matched hers.
The laughter had faded completely as the seriousness
of what was happening hit home. Soundlessly, Tom
held out a hand and helped Annie to her feet. Annie
rose and let him steady her, and as she did a folded
piece of paper came loose from the child's wrappings
and fluttered to the floor.

Tom swooped and had it unfolded before Annie had
even straightened. She nestled the child into her arms,

crooning and rocking it until the child's distress eased. Then she looked back at Tom, and found his face had lost every vestige of colour.

'Tom?'

Tom didn't answer. He was staring at the paper as if he were staring at a nightmare.

'What is it?' Annie's voice was gently insistent, and it cut across Tom's shock. He lifted his face and stared at her—but he wasn't seeing Annie.

Which was nothing new. Annie was a diminutive five feet four inches tall. She kept her soft brown curls knotted severely back from her face. Her clear grey eyes were well hidden behind glasses, and her face showed more determination and honesty than loveliness. Compared to the willowy beauties Tom McIver favoured, Annie was plain, and the first time he'd seen her she'd known he saw only a doctor who could reduce his workload. Nothing more.

Which she shouldn't mind at all, she told herself ten times a day. From childhood people had thought of Annie as plain, and they'd told her so. Bluntly.

She should be used to it.

And she shouldn't be thinking of it now when this little one was in such trouble.

'Tell me what the note says, Tom,' Annie asked again. She could have taken it from him. By the blank look on Tom's face she knew his fingers could hardly grasp a thing, but Annie's arms were full of baby.

Finally Tom pulled himself together, and focused on something other than the note.

'I'll show you. . .show you soon.' Tom took a ragged breath and visibly squared his shoulders. 'Annie, she'll have to be checked. You take her down to Children's Ward and examine her. I'll get rid of. . .I'll say good-night to Sarah and be with you as soon as I can.'

'You're sure this isn't Sarah's baby?' Annie asked, and Tom stared at her blankly.

'No. No. . . Melissa. . .'

Tom put a hand up to his eyes and the impression of nightmare deepened. 'No,' he repeated. 'It's not Sarah's. Just. . . Just check her, will you, Annie? I'll be with you. . .I'll be with you when I can.'

Annie's paediatric skills weren't called for. Medically, the baby was just fine.

Bannockburn Hospital was quiet tonight, with four of its twelve beds empty. There was no one in the two-bed children's ward, but Helen, Bannockburn's more than capable night sister, bustled in soon after Annie arrived to see what she was doing. She stayed to help, and together they checked the baby completely. Annie didn't tell Helen what she was looking for and, apart from a couple of sideways looks at Annie, Helen didn't enquire.

The result? One healthy six-week-old baby girl. Well cared for. Great set of lungs. Just starting to smile, with a lopsided grin that went straight to the heart. Just starting to fuss about her next feed. Helen made up formula while Annie dressed the baby in dry hospital clothes. She cuddled the baby close, smiled down at that infectious grin and thought of what to do next.

'So, who is she?' Helen asked as she handed over a prepared bottle. Annie hadn't told her anything. She wanted to see Tom's note,before announcing publicly that the child had been dumped.

'Tom asked me to have a look at her,' Annie said ambiguously. She hitched herself up on the examination table, her denim-clad legs swinging. Then she took the warmed bottle from Helen and popped it into one eager little mouth. The baby's eyes widened in amazement — as though she hadn't expected anything as wondrous as a bottle — and she attacked the teat as if there were no tomorrow.

Annie looked down and found herself smiling into the baby's wide brown eyes. Some baby!

Helen gazed at Annie, her kindly eyes speculative.

In the few months Annie had been at Bannockburn Helen had taken Annie under her wing. The senior nurse had a kindness for the new young doctor — and she seemed to have a knack of knowing what Annie was thinking.

Helen's eyes said she knew there was something going on — something Annie knew and Helen didn't.

'Do we know her name?' Helen asked.

'No.'

'But. . .' Helen's tone was thoughtful. 'Dr McIver's asked you to take a look at her — and Dr McIver's not on duty tonight.'

'I think. . .' Annie hesitated. 'Well, maybe I'd better not say what I think,' she said at last.

'I see.' Helen was momentarily baulked. She looked at Annie and sighed in exasperation. And launched into the grievance she threw at Annie on a weekly basis.

Or daily.

'Dr Burrows, when are you going to do something about your clothes? You could be so attractive if you tried — but, sitting up there, you look about fourteen years old!'

'You think so?' Annie returned Helen's smile, swung her legs some more and allowed herself to consider. Maybe Helen was right. Maybe she did dress in clothes that made her look young. Maybe jeans and oversized checked shirts weren't dignified enough for a doctor.

So. . .should she wear slinky clothes like Sarah? Annie's smile faded. Ridiculous. Clothes like that weren't meant for the likes of Annie Burrows so, if Helen thought jeans and T-shirts weren't dignified enough, maybe she should stick entirely to sensible skirts.

Ugh!

Annie tried a glare at Helen, which didn't quite come off. There was no way Annie could come the dignified, autocratic doctor over Helen. Helen was fifty-something and had been night charge sister here for ever — or maybe longer. There was little round here that Helen didn't see. She was looking at Annie now with eyes that saw far too much.

Well, maybe Helen could be put to use — instead of letting her stand and speculate on thoughts inside Annie's silly head.

'Helen, do you know a Melissa?' Annie asked. 'Are there any Melissas who live locally?'

'There's Melissa Fotheringay. She's five.'

'Wrong age.'

'What age are we looking for?'

'Someone who might be this one's mum.'

Helen's face stilled.

Silence.

Helen stared from the baby to Annie's face — and then back to the baby.

'You mean. . .?' She frowned. 'You mean you really don't know who the mother is? Does Dr McIver know?'

'I don't know what Dr McIver knows,' Annie admitted. 'Helen, keep this to yourself,' she begged, 'but think of Melissas for me.'

'But there's no other local Melissa. The only other Melissa I know — or knew — was Melissa Carnem.' Helen's forehead furrowed in thought. 'Melissa Carnem was a nurse here. She came from Melbourne and left just before you arrived. But. . .'

'But?'

'Well, she's long gone. And Melissa's blonde and blue-eyed and fair-skinned. This little one has such brown curls and lovely brown eyes. . .'

'So she has,' Annie said thoughtfully, and a muscle twitched at the side of her mouth. 'But maybe. . . Helen, maybe she's very like her father.'

Annie's candid grey eyes met Helen's. Woman to woman. A message passed between them that was unmistakeable.

Helen stared incredulously down at the baby, and she saw then what Annie saw.

'You don't think. . .' Helen's eyes had grown so wide they practically enveloped her face. 'Annie, you can't think. . .'

'Helen, were Melissa and Dr McIver. . .friends?'

Helen almost goggled.

'Oh, my dear!' Helen couldn't tear her eyes from the baby. 'Melissa went out with Dr McIver a few times. But. . .'

'Why did Melissa leave?'

'She went to Israel.' Helen was staring at the child with a disbelieving daze. 'Melissa lived in a soap bubble. Full of plans that changed almost daily. In the end, she decided she wanted to live on a kibbutz. Find herself or something. She'd come here because she'd thought living in the country would be wonderful, but she was bored after a couple of months. And she's been gone. . . she's been gone almost ten months.' Helen's eyes fell again to the baby and both women were silent.

Ten months. . .

The silence was broken by the sound of a bell. It took a huge effort for Helen to respond, but the bell rang again and finally she did.

'I'll have to go. That'll be Robert Whykes, needing more pain relief — or more reassurance.'

'The physio's coming tomorrow,' Annie said automatically. 'Tell him that should help.'

'I already have,' Helen told her. 'But the only thing Robert's interested in is an instant cure. He doesn't want to know a damaged disc in a neck can take months to settle.' Helen turned to the door, and then hesitated. 'And, by the sound of it, here comes Dr McIver. Oh, my dear, I'm busting my stays to know what's going on here.'

'You're not the only one,' Annie confessed. 'I think my stays bust about half an hour ago.'

Tom walked in and further conversation was cut short. Helen cast him a curious glance as they passed, tried a smile which didn't quite come off — and retired fast.

He'd entered the room with his customary long stride, but he stopped dead when he saw Annie who was still perched on the couch at the end of the ward, legs swinging. Nestled in Annie's arms, the baby had almost finished her bottle. The child's deep brown eyes were wide open and looking about her with avid intelligence as she sucked.

The likeness was startling!

'It took you a while to tear yourself from Sarah,' Annie commented.

As always, Annie was ignored. To Tom, Annie had kid-sister status. He walked slowly forward, his eyes on the child in her arms.

This was the dearest little baby, Annie reflected, watching Tom's face work through a gamut of emotions. Some babies only a mother could love. This little one, though. . .

The child was perfect. She had lovely dark skin without a blemish, a halo of deep brown curls, bright eyes that gazed up at the world with interest and a tiny, rosebud mouth that sucked at her bottle for all it was worth. And, even when drinking, her eyes seemed to be constantly dancing.

Life was good, her eyes said, and this bottle was fantastic!

Tom stared down and the silence went on and on. The only sound was the slurping sucks made by a hungry baby.

There was only one way to break the silence. Ask the unaskable. Ask what she was aching to know. What had to be voiced some time.

Annie's voice gentled. 'Tom, is this your daughter?'

He heard her then, and took a fast step back. The step put distance between him and the baby — but his eyes stayed on the child in Annie's arms. It was as though the man were seeing a miracle.

'No!' he muttered blankly. 'I mean. . .'

'Can I read the note?'

Tom put a hand to his shirt pocket — and then let it fall again. He looked helplessly at Annie. Tom's face — strongly boned, lined with laughter and intelligence — usually reflected confidence. It was the face of a man at ease with his world. Out to enjoy every moment. But now. . . Annie had the feeling if she reached out and pushed he'd fall right over.

With sudden decision, she slid down from her perch, stepped forward and placed the little girl into Tom's arms.

'Take her.' Her voice was insistent. She lowered her hands so that Tom was forced to grasp the bundle of baby. The milk bottle sagged to one side. The baby gave a last suck at the empty bottle, then turned her gaze up to Tom McIver's face — and smiled.

The resemblance was unmistakable. Carved in stone. And Tom McIver looked as if he'd been punched in his solar plexus.

He stared down into the smiling little face for a long, long moment. The baby smiled and smiled and, despite his shock, the corners of Tom's mouth twitched in response. He couldn't resist her. Who could? And they were matching smiles. . .

A tiny miracle — and she was all Tom's.

She had to know.

Annie lifted the note from Tom's shirt pocket. Tom was too pole-axed to argue. She flicked open the single folded sheet — and stared.

I have a friend who had a baby and went to live on a kibbutz, and it sounded fantastic — a dream. So I conned you into making me pregnant. But then I found it was stupid because kids tie you down and I've met a great guy who doesn't want a baby. So if you don't want her adopt her out. If you want things signed — adoption forms or anything — my mum will forward them. Her address is below.

I haven't named her — it seemed stupid when I didn't want her. They're pressuring me into registering her now so you name her if you want. I know I tricked you into making me pregnant so I doubt if you want anything to do with her but Mum said I had to give you the choice.

Melissa.

Annie read and re-read the note. Then she looked into Tom McIver's face. He was shocked to the core. In his arms the tiny mirror image of Tom gurgled and chuckled at this delightful world.

Despite the gravity of the baby's situation — despite the sheer irresponsibility of the unknown Melissa's actions — for the life of her, Annie couldn't keep the muscles at the corner of her mouth twitching in response.

Tom saw.

'Dr Burrows,' Tom McIver said, his voice dangerously quiet as he looked across his tiny daughter at his partner. 'Dr Burrows, I believe that if you so much as smile I shall wring your neck!'

'Who's smiling?' Annie pressed her lips tight together as she fought for control. 'I mean, who could laugh at this?'

Who, indeed? Certainly not Tom McIver. His daughter was, though. Well fed, warm and content, the baby was chortling with pleasure.

'Annie. . .'

'I'm sorry, Tom.' Annie forced her features into something resembling gravity. Tom was right. This was a nightmare situation. But for the whole eight months Annie had been in Bannockburn it had been Tom who had been in absolute control, and a reversal of roles was something Annie had ached for.

Tom McIver had run the Bannockburn hospital since

it had been built six years before, and he pulled every string. Annie had been brought in to cope with the work he didn't want himself, and to give him time to enjoy himself.

He enjoyed himself all right—but not with Annie. Annie soon discovered why Tom had chosen her for the job. It was because he could treat her as a hard-working doormat. A kid sister with a medical degree. Plain, hardworking and useful. Nothing more.

'She's competent and ordinary,' Annie had overheard Tom telling someone the first week of her time in Bannockburn. 'If we're lucky, she'll grow to be a great old-maid doctor. She's not the sort to give trouble. The town will get its money's worth.'

Annie had darn near walked out on the spot when she'd heard that. Only the thought of how lovely Bannockburn was, and how much she wanted this job, had made her stay.

Well, not quite only. . .

There was also the knowledge that, despite his penchant for women who looked as if they'd stepped off the cover of *Vogue*, Annie had been head over heels in love with Tom McIver since the first time she'd seen him.

Stupid, stupid, stupid. . .

She should never have come. But she had, and over the months, as Annie worked whenever Tom wanted a social life and studied at night while Tom McIver entertained his stream of beautiful women, she'd started to smoulder. Tonight things had come to a head. Tonight she'd been close to handing in her resignation.

Now her anger had been diffused so fast she couldn't believe it. For once in his life, Tom McIver was totally at a loss.

'I gather you didn't know of this little one's existence,' Annie managed, getting a grip on herself with a massive effort.

'No!' There was anger in Tom's clipped response.

And then he looked down again at his daughter's face —
and the anger faded again to wonder.

'I see.' Annie compressed her lips again, swung herself up to her perch and considered father and child
from a height. 'So. . . What will you do with her?'

What, indeed? Tom stared helplessly down at his
child. His mouth twisted into a grimace.

'I haven't the faintest idea.' Tom shook his head.
'You've checked her? She. . .she looks lovely. Is she
healthy?'

'She's perfect,' Annie said softly. 'Great little body.
Well nourished. No nappy rash or any other sign of
neglect. No problems with her hips or anything else, as
far as I can see. I'd say she had a fairly trauma-free
birth, and she's been well looked after since then.'

'By Melissa's mum, I'll bet,' Tom said savagely,
unconsciously holding the baby tighter. 'It won't have
been Melissa. She doesn't care for anything.'

'You don't like Melissa?'

'No, I do not!'

'Well, pardon me for asking,' Annie said mildly, 'but
why did you make her pregnant if you don't like her?'

Then, as anger grew to near apoplexy on Tom's face,
Annie jumped from her seat and crossed to the door.

'I'm sorry, Tom,' she said softly. 'Of course, it's
none of my business. I'm off to bed now. Goodnight.'

'*Annie*!'

It was a roar of rage, and the baby in Tom's arms
jumped and blinked. Then she smiled again.
Great game!

Annie raised her eyebrows.

'Yes?'

'Annie, you can't just leave me.' The rage was being
supplanted by panic.

'Is there a problem?'

'Of course there's a problem. I can't look after
a baby.'

'You can't look after your own daughter?'

Silence. Annie raised her eyebrows in mild enquiry — and waited.

'*My daughter.*'

Tom said the words slowly, and as he spoke his anger faded. So did his panic. What was left was absolute incomprehension.

'She is your daughter,' Annie said gently. 'I guessed even before I saw the note. Sometimes resemblance between parent and child is so marked that it's unmistakable. It is in this case. Unless you're absolutely sure you can't be the father, I wouldn't waste time DNA testing.'

'But it was only the one night.' Tom groaned and shook his head — shaking off a nightmare. 'I guess... it must have been after the Bachelors and Spinsters Ball. I hadn't had a night off for ages and I'd finally managed to find a locum. I drank too much. Melissa had some damned liqueur she kept insisting I drink. She drove me home and then...'

He broke off, his expressive face working overtime. It showed doubt, then confusion, and finally — anger.

'Hell,' he swore. 'It was Melissa who... She must have meant to get pregnant. She set me up...'

'You can be as angry as you like with Melissa,' Annie said gently, 'but it doesn't alter the fact that the little girl you're holding is your daughter. Whatever her mother's done, Tom, it's not the baby's fault. Now you need to decide what to do with her.'

'Do...' Tom looked down and he groaned again. 'I don't know what to do. *You'll* have to do something. Admit her into the ward here, Annie. I can't look after her.'

'Why not?'

'Because...'

'All she needs are feeds and nappy changes,' Annie said bluntly. 'And I'm rostered on call tonight so you won't be called out. Of course you can look after her.'

'Admit her *here*!'

Annie shook her head 'Tom, she's not sick. The hospital's quiet. There's no one else in Children's Ward and you know, with the layout of the hospital, as soon as we admit a child we have to call an additional nurse. Do you expect Helen to roster on another nurse — wake someone after midnight and ask them to work — just to look after your baby?'

'She's not my baby!'

'Whose baby is she, then?' Annie demanded. She removed her glasses and met his look head on. 'You're the only parent this little one seems to have, Dr McIver.'

'*Annie*. . .' It was a roar of anguish. 'You have to look after her.'

But even doormats have their limits.

'Tom, I'm going to bed,' Annie told him, hardening her heart. 'Helen will give you enough formula and nappies to last the night. I know something about adoption procedures and fostering so if you'd like to talk to me about that I'll meet you after morning ward round. We'll discuss it then.'

'Annie, stop it,' Tom demanded, his anger flaring. 'Stop it this minute. You're not my damned doctor!'

'No?' Annie looked at him thoughtfully. 'What am I, then, Dr McIver?'

'You're my friend, dammit!'

'And, as your friend, you'd like me to take your daughter and care for her overnight — or until you can figure out what to do with her. You'd like me to take over responsibility for her.'

'Yes.' Tom sighed and his shoulders sagged. 'That's just what I would like, Annie. You've done some paediatric training. I haven't done anything.'

Should she?

No!

For once, common sense prevailed. There was no way Tom McIver was involving her in this, Annie thought bitterly. He didn't think of her as his friend. He thought of her as his doormat. And the doormat had just revolted.

'Yes, you have, Tom,' Annie said gently—inexorably. 'You've fathered a child. This little one doesn't need a doctor. She needs a daddy—and you're it. Welcome to fatherhood, Dr McIver. Welcome to responsibility. Yours. Not mine. Yours.'

'But, Annie...'

'Goodnight, Tom.' Annie set her face and hardened her heart. 'Good night. You take care of your daughter. I'm going to bed.'

CHAPTER TWO

IT WAS all very well to say the baby was Tom McIver's responsibility, but it didn't stop Annie worrying. In the few short minutes she'd held her, the baby had melted Annie's heart.

She took her time going to bed. Annie undressed slowly, then sat before the bedroom mirror and stared.

What had Melissa done? Seduced Tom and then tossed away his daughter as if she didn't matter? Her love affair with him had been so casual that she was moving on to the next man without a backward glance. 'I conned you into making me pregnant. . .'

If Tom had made love to Annie. . . If Annie had been privileged to bear his child. . .

Annie closed her eyes — and then opened them again to stare at herself with brutal honesty. What hope would someone like her ever have against the likes of someone like Melissa?

She was too short. Her grey eyes were too big for her face. Annie's nose was snub and there were definite freckles scattered over her nose and cheeks. 'Let's face it,' she told her reflection harshly. 'Compared to Sarah, you're just plain ordinary.'

'So what?' Annie made a face at herself in the mirror and hauled the pins from her hair. Released from its knot, her hair curled round her face in an unruly mass. A brown mass. Mud brown, her mother called it, and sighed every time she saw her.

'I don't know how I came to be stuck with such a drab daughter,' she'd told Annie from her childhood on. 'You take after your father. Thank heaven your sister takes after me. Oh, my dear, your skin. . . And your nose. . . For heaven's sake, just wear plain clothes and have a career where looks don't matter. And dress plainly or you'll make yourself ridiculous.'

Annie made another face and stuck out her tongue at her absent mother and sister. It didn't help. They still had the power to hurt. Her mother was right. Sexy clothes were for the Melissas and Sarahs of this world.

As was the man she loved. Tom McIver.

And Tom's baby.

What would it be like to have such a little one of her own?

Fat chance she had of ever finding out. She was the worker. The sensible, plain one. The doormat. She should block out all thoughts of Tom.

But the baby's smile stayed with her, and she couldn't help worrying, so Annie tossed and turned and listened to the sounds next door all through the night.

First she heard two large dogs being ejected from their master's bedroom. Tom's voice was apologetic but firm.

'I'm sorry, guys. I know you like sharing, but three of us in the bed is crowded and four is ridiculous.'

A few anxious whines — then the whines escalated.

And Tom's voice.

'Look, one day you'll make a couple of nice bitches happy — and your world will fall to pieces, too! Until then you'll just have to accept that women and children come first. Before dogs.'

The dogs weren't in the least impressed. They made their displeasure felt in full chorus, and Annie grinned as she heard Tom placate them with food.

'And you needn't think this is the start of a new routine! It's just for one night. One night!'

What did Tom think would happen tomorrow?

Then Tom tried to put his daughter to sleep while, on the other side of the wall, Annie kept right on listening.

'It's two a.m., dammit. Babies your age are supposed to sleep twenty hours a day.'

Tom's daughter obviously used a different rule book.

From what Annie could hear, the little girl seemed happy as long as Tom held her. It was only when he put her down that she started to cry.

Five times Annie heard Tom say, 'Now sleep!' Then the sound of light being clicked off. Five times she heard fussing, followed by Tom's muffled curses. Gradually the baby's fussing turn to a full-throated roar, the dogs howled in sympathy, the light clicked on again and Tom's distinctive footsteps stomped back and forth. Over and over again.

Finally, at about four, Tom fed his daughter again. In the peace while the baby suckled Annie fell into an uneasy sleep and left them to it.

When she woke the next morning there was silence. Even the dogs were quiet.

Eight o'clock. Today was Saturday and there was a ward round to be done before clinic at ten. Annie dressed for work in a sensible skirt, blouse and white coat — doormat clothes, but at least they made her look older than her jeans — and went to see what the rest of the world was doing.

It wasn't doing a lot. The hospital was Saturday morning quiet. The day nurses weren't busy and the news of the baby's arrival had already spread through the hospital.

Robbie, the hospital administrator — or 'matron', as he jokingly called himself — stopped her as she walked past.

'OK, Annie, what gives?' he growled, and at her look of incomprehension he took matters into his own hands.

Robbie was six feet three, built like a tank and his face was almost hidden by a vast red beard. He was gentleness personified with patients — but when he decided that Annie should talk to him she didn't have much choice. Now he physically lifted her off her feet and set her in his chair.

'Dr Burrows, I can get nothing out of anyone and I

am going nuts,' he growled. 'Did Melissa Carnem really dump a baby on our Dr McIver last night?'

'Rob, it's none of your business.'

'It's none of your business either, but you know. And Pete, my cousin who works at the garage, knows. And Helen. Everyone except yours truly. So give!'

'Hmm.' Annie tried to rise — and got nowhere. 'Rob, I thought nurses were supposed to respect doctors. You know how it's supposed to work. I expect tugging of forelocks and the odd bow and scrape. Pinning the doctor down until she reveals confidential information isn't in any nursing manual I ever read.'

'Well, grow, then,' Robbie ordered. 'I'm damned if I can be deferential to a five-foot-four scrap of a girl who refuses to tell me what I want to know.'

Annie grinned. In medical situations Robbie snapped straight back to being one of the best nurses Annie had ever worked with, but now. . . Well, one of the reasons Annie liked working in Bannockburn was the informality of the excellent staff. The lines between nurses and doctors — so clearly drawn in her big training hospital — were so hazy in Bannockburn you could hardly see them.

'So, what do you know?' she asked cautiously as Robbie glared.

'Melissa filled her car with petrol before she came to the hospital last night,' Robbie explained with exaggerated patience. 'My cousin works the pumps. He recognized Melissa, saw the baby in the back seat and asked what was going on. And she told him. Brother, did she tell him! And my cousin's been shooting his mouth off ever since.'

So, by now, the whole district would know.

'Is Melissa still in town?' Annie asked slowly.

Robbie shook his head.

'Not according to my cousin. She told him she was catching a plane overseas this morning. And Helen wouldn't tell us anything — even when I pulled rank.

And she's bigger and older than you. If I threaten her
with physical violence she rings my mum. But. . .'
Robbie shook a bewildered head. 'Annie, has she really
left a baby with Doc McIver?'

There was no point in dissembling. Robbie had to
know sooner or later.

'Yes,' Annie said bluntly. 'She has.'

'And is it his?'

'You'll have to ask Dr McIver,' Annie said primly —
and then she watched as Robbie's broad face broke into
the broadest of smiles. As the father of three, if there
was one thing Robbie loved it was a baby and he
reckoned the whole world just ached to be parents.

'Bloody hell!' He stroked his beard and thought
things through. 'Where's the baby now?'

'With Dr McIver, of course.' It was hard to suppress
a chuckle as Annie watched Robbie grin. 'Where else?'
She forced herself back into medical mode with a
supreme effort. 'Now, suppose we take a look at Mrs
McKenzie's ulcer, Robbie? If it's not looking better
today we'll need to consider a graft.' She lifted her
patients' case notes from the desk and then, as an after-
thought, she collected Tom's as well.

'And I'll take a look at Dr McIver's patients as I go,'
she told the bemused Rob. 'He might just be busy this
morning.'

'If it's really his baby, he might just be busy for life.'
Robbie chortled. 'Oh, boy. . . The valley's going to
love this!'

There was an hour's gap between ward round and morning clinic. Annie tried to talk herself into reading the
newspaper or doing bookwork — but finally she did
what she most wanted. She made a mug of hot, sweet
tea and carried it to Tom's apartment.

There was no answer to her knock. Not even the dogs
seemed interested in a visitor this morning.

Annie hesitated, then pushed the door wide and went right on in.

The dogs were in the living room. They rose with the reluctance of two weary canines. They'd had a hard night, their exhausted eyes said. Pacing the floor with a baby must be hard work. It was as much as they could do to give their tails perfunctory wags. They were far too tired to be watchdogs.

As they slumped back on their mats Annie crossed to the bedroom door and knocked.

Nothing.

She opened the door just a crack.

Tom and his baby were fast asleep.

Tom's bed was huge. Just plain vast. There was a hospital crib beside the bed but the baby wasn't in it. The little one was right where she wanted to be, sleeping peacefully in the crook of her father's arm. Right against his naked chest.

Annie's heart missed a beat at the sight of them.

As always, Tom McIver had the power to take her breath away. The first time Annie had seen him she'd been a fifth-year medical student and Tom had been giving a guest lecture on country medical practice. He'd only just started in Bannockburn then, and had been brought in to tell the students what they could expect.

His talk had held the lecture theatre enthralled. Even medical students with no intention of working outside a city in their lives had come away enthusiastic.

Tom had talked of his ideals.

He'd talked of the concept of whole care — of taking responsibility for the health of a child at birth and seeing that child grow into adulthood. He'd talked of knowing the ills and troubles — and the joys — of whole families. Being with them in good times as well as bad. Of being part of their lives, and them being part of his.

Tom's talk had convinced Annie that country practice was for her, and Tom's charismatic, caring personality had stayed in her heart ever since.

Now his personality showed through. Tom McIver might be irresponsible — might have sired a baby in ignorance — but now it was impossible for him not to care. It would have been impossible for Tom to put his child in another room last night and let her sob herself to sleep. It would have been against. . .

Against all the reasons why Annie loved him.

Annie stared down at father and child, and she felt the old familiar longings surge through her stronger than ever. If only. . . If only she could be Tom's Melissa. The mother of his child.

'In your dreams, Annie Burrows,' she muttered fiercely. 'In your dreams.'

Tom McIver opened his eyes and stared straight at her.

Annie managed a shaky smile.

'I brought you a cup of tea,' she told him, her words spilling out a shade too fast. 'I thought you might need it.'

'Annie, you're an angel!' Tom pushed himself up on his pillows and held out his free arm. The covers fell completely away, revealing him to be naked to the hips.

Annie blinked — then took three steps forward to thrust the tea into his hand, and three fast steps back.

'I won't bite,' Tom said mildly, and Annie flushed.

'I came to ask what you want to do,' Annie told him, monitoring her voice to keep it emotionless. She kept her eyes on Tom's face — not his magnificent body. 'If you want me to contact social workers it'll be easier if I do it now. After midday on Saturday it's impossible to find anyone.'

'Why would I want you to contact social workers?' Tom asked slowly.

'To look after the baby.'

Tom cast an uncertain glance down at his daughter. 'Yeah, well. . . I've been thinking. Maybe I don't need to. If you look after things here for the weekend I'll take the baby to Melbourne. Find Melissa and sort things out.'

Annie shook her head. 'Not possible.'

'Why not?'

'Because Melissa's catching an international flight this morning. She may already be out of the country.'

Tom stared. 'Says who?'

'Says Robbie's cousin at the garage. He saw her last night and she told him what she was doing.' Annie hesitated, but Tom had to know the worst some time. 'Tom, it seems Melissa told Pete everything. About you and the baby. Everything.'

'I see,' Tom said slowly, in the voice of someone who doesn't see at all. 'So. . .if Pete knows. . .'

'Then the whole valley knows,' Annie confirmed gently. 'They know Melissa brought your daughter here last night. There's no escaping it.'

'I suppose not.'

Tom set his tea aside and sank back onto his pillows, his daughter still tucked against him. The baby didn't stir.

'Well, I know Melissa's mother won't take her,' Tom said bleakly, thinking aloud. 'I met her once. She's a hard-headed businesswoman with a life of her own. I can't imagine her taking on a grandchild.'

'Your own parents?' Annie said gently, and winced at Tom's harsh laugh.

'You have to be kidding!'

'OK.' Annie took a deep breath. 'So it's you or adoption.'

Tom's eyes flew open. 'I guess. . .' He glanced uncertainly down at his daughter. She'd snuggled into him, her tiny body curved into his chest. She looked. . .

She looked as if there was no power in the world that should drag her from where she was.

'It wouldn't be so hard if she didn't look like me,' Tom said slowly.

'I don't suppose it would.' Carefully noncommittal,

Annie stood back and waited. In her brief paediatric training she'd seen this before — the awful gulf facing a parent giving up a part of themselves. And Tom had only just learned that this new little part existed.

Tom shifted again and took a mouthful of tea. He looked up at Annie and then took another mouthful. And another. As if he were gaining strength from the hot, sweet drink. Finally he put the empty mug down. And stared at the ceiling.

'You know the adoption procedures?' he asked flatly.

'You've never had a patient go though it?'

'Never — thank God! Have you?'

'Yes. If you decide. . .' Annie faltered to a halt. She looked down at man and child. They looked so right, the two of them. A matched pair.

Some decisions were just too hard for anyone to make.

'Once you've decided on adoption I'll call in the social welfare people,' Annie said finally. 'They'll arrange foster care. That can be done now, if you like, if I ring before midday.'

'Foster parents? Why not adoptive parents straight away?'

'There's a six-week cooling-off period,' Annie told him. 'You and Melissa must both state you want the child adopted. Then she goes to foster parents and waits. After six weeks you need to re-state your wish for adoption. It'll take longer than six weeks if Melissa's overseas. The forms will be sent there.'

'It seems a lot of trouble.'

'Babies are,' Annie said gently. 'They have to be. They're people and this little one has as many rights as you have, Tom McIver. Despite what Melissa's done, your baby deserves better than just being dumped.'

'I just meant. . .' Tom sighed wearily and finally looked at her. 'There's no need to get on your high horse, Annie. I'm not looking for a quick fix here.'

'Aren't you?'

'Well. . .' Tom sighed again. 'I don't know,' he said honestly. He looked down at the baby in the crook of his arm, and touched her gently on the nose. Then he looked up again at Annie and his face was almost pleading. 'Are you telling me, Annie, that *my daughter* has to stay with foster parents for six weeks?'

My daughter . . .

Annie blinked. The way he said it. . . There was pain behind the words — the pain of impending loss.

'Foster parents are special people, Tom,' Annie told him, her voice gentling even further. 'You know that. They're carefully chosen to take good care of her.'

'Yeah, but. . .' His voice trailed off to silence.

Tom's baby was still deeply asleep. She hadn't stirred as Tom had pushed himself up on the pillows to drink his tea. She'd slept as he'd touched her and she slept on now. Tom stared down at her for a long, long moment, and the expression on his face was one Annie had never seen there before.

'Annie, she hasn't even got a name,' Tom said bleakly, with an ache behind his voice. 'She's six weeks old — and my daughter hasn't even been given a name.'

'Then maybe it's up to you to name her.'

'But if I do that. . .'

'If you name her then you're laying claim to her.' Annie still kept her voice carefully noncommittal. She was trying desperately to keep herself objective. Unemotional. 'Tom, I know this has been a shock, but you either have to dissociate yourself and pass her on fast to people who'll love her — or you have to start making decisions.'

'Decisions?'

'Like whether you want to name her. Whether you want access to her as she grows up. Whether you want her to know you as her father.'

'If I have access she'll know I didn't want her,' Tom said bitterly. 'What sort of father would I be, demanding access? She'll know I didn't even want her conceived.'

'She'll know that, anyway,' Annie said bluntly, 'if she's adopted.'

Tom stared up at Annie for a long moment — and then slumped wearily back down on his pillows. Cradled in his arm, his tiny daughter slept peacefully on. She'd probably sleep all day now, Annie thought ruefully, and then wake up and socialize again tonight.

It didn't have anything to do with Annie. This baby was *not* her responsibility. So why was she feeling exactly like Tom?

She had to get out of here. She must. . .before she walked over and lifted the baby from Tom's arms and burst into tears.

Which wouldn't help anyone.

'Tom, I must go,' she faltered. 'I've done ward rounds of your patients as well as mine but there are people waiting in clinic. There's no need for you to work today. I can cope on my own. Do you. . . Do you want me to ring the social worker now — or wait until Monday?'

Tom glared and his hold on his daughter tightened. As if Annie was threatening to take her away.

'Thank you for doing my rounds — but I haven't decided.'

'OK.' Annie nodded. 'Are you prepared to look after her for the weekend?'

'I don't know whether I can.'

Annie bit her lip. 'Tom, if you want her to go to foster parents today then the latest you can leave it is eleven-thirty. Let me know before then — OK? You know where to find me.'

With one last uncertain look at the tiny child nestled against her father's chest, Annie walked out and left Tom, staring after her. His face was a picture of absolute confusion.

And, if anyone had seen her as she walked down the corridor, so was Annie's.

*   *   *

Annie was removing plaster from Henry Gillies's foot when Tom made up his mind. He burst into Annie's surgery, causing both Annie and the elderly Henry to jump.

'Annie, she's staying!'

Annie lowered Henry's foot carefully onto the examination table and turned to face Tom. Dressed now in tailored trousers and neat shirt, newly shaved and his hair almost ordered, Tom McIver looked much more civilized than the last time Annie had seen him.

But no more in control.

'Would you like me to come out and talk to you?' Annie offered, directing a pointed look down at the all-too-interested Henry.

'No.' Tom shook his head. He strode forward and gazed down at Henry's foot with interest. 'The whole valley must know what's happening by now, and Henry's a mate. Rebecca told me you had Henry in here, Annie, so I knew you wouldn't mind me interrupting. What have you been doing to yourself, Henry?'

'A blasted cow stood on me foot,' Henry told him. 'Happened last week. You were out with some damned woman or other so Doc Burrows shoved plaster on it for me. Now she says this plaster's gotta come off and she'll stick more on. If you'd done it you would have stuck on some that'd last, wouldn't you, Doc?'

Tom smiled down at the elderly farmer. His smile was engaging and mischievous. The old Tom McIver.

'Don't you trust our Dr Burrows?'

'Well, she's all right,' Henry said grudgingly. 'For a woman. But this bloody plaster. . .'

'Has to come off.' Tom lifted Henry's foot and inspected the old plaster with care. 'Dr Burrows is right, Henry, and I'd have done nothing different. The bruising to your foot takes ten days to go down, and when it does the plaster becomes too loose. You'd be wiggling your toes no end if we left you in it.'

'Yeah, well—they itch,' Henry growled.

Then Henry saw what Annie was lifting from the bench. His eyebrows hit his hairline and he visibly recoiled. 'Hell's bells, girl! I dunno about that. A circular saw for a plaster. . . What happens if you get carried away?'

'I fix your itch for good!' Annie chuckled and relented. 'It's OK, Henry. The saw might look vicious but it doesn't spin. It simply vibrates and shakes the plaster apart. If it touches your skin you'll hardly notice.'

'Hardly notice as my foot falls off. I see.' Henry had the look of a man appalled. He cast a look of appeal at Tom. 'You trust her with that?'

'Absolutely.'

'Bloody hell!' Henry shook his head in disgust. 'Women and power tools! What next?' He sighed. 'Go on, then. Take the bloody thing off. And if the foot comes off with it, well, I've got another one after all, and I'm not a man to grumble.'

He put his hands behind his grizzled head and, blocking out the thought of Annie behind a buzz saw, looked up at Tom in resignation. 'So what are you saying, lad? That you're keeping this baby I've been hearing about?'

'Well. . .just for a short while. Are you right to start, Annie?' Tom cast Annie a sideways glance, then held Henry's foot while Annie positioned the saw. 'Just for the six-week waiting period until I can get her adopted.'

Annie was concentrating on what she was doing so she was halfway into the plaster before she thought about what Tom was suggesting. Then she had to raise her voice above the noise.

'You mean — keep her here instead of sending her to foster parents for six weeks?' she asked.

'That's right.'

'And then get her adopted straight away.'

'It'd be simpler.'

'Then, no,' Annie told him bluntly. 'No way.'

'No?' Tom's brows snapped up.

'Hold the foot still, Dr McIver,' Annie rebuked him, smiling down at Henry. 'Even though Henry has two feet he probably wants both of them.'

'That's told you, Doc.' Henry grinned broadly, relaxing. 'She's a good 'un, our Doc Burrows. Bet none of those painted dolly-birds you take out have the guts to tell you off.'

'Thanks, Henry,' Tom said dryly, frowning, but he did concentrate then. They didn't speak until the plaster fell away. Tom started cleaning the leg while Annie fetched bandages and prepared the new plaster.

'What's wrong with her staying here?' Tom asked, his tone almost conversational. 'I've thought it out. She can stay in Children's Ward and I'll personally pay for an extra nurse if there's no one else in. That way she doesn't have to go to strangers.'

'Tom, to your daughter you're a stranger.'

'She's used to me already.' Tom grinned and there was a hint of pride in the smile. 'When I handed her over to Cook just now she cried.'

'Lucky Cook.'

'The hospital's quiet,' Tom said firmly. 'Mrs Farley doesn't mind.'

Mrs Farley wouldn't if Tom asked it of her, Annie thought bitterly. No woman would. All Tom had to do was smile. . .

Well, someone had to say no to him.

'Tom, it's not on,' Annie told him. 'If you want your daughter adopted then she has to go to foster parents. There's a six-week cooling-off period and that cooling-off period can't start until you no longer have custody.'

'You mean. . .if I keep her here for six weeks then there still has to be six weeks of fostering after that?'

'That's right.'

'OK.' Tom dried Henry's leg and dusted it off. Automatically he took the bandages from Annie and started winding. 'We can get round that, I reckon. If she's admitted here then I don't have custody.'

Annie stared. 'You're saying you'll admit her here
and then tell the social workers you're not caring
for her?'

'No.' Tom shook his head. 'I can see they wouldn't
come at that. But if you admitted her, dearest Annie. . .
If she was in your charge. . .'

And he flashed her that all-persuasive smile.

His 'Annie-the-doormat' smile.

'He's wheedling you, girl,' Henry commented dryly.
'Don't you let him talk you into what's not right, Doc
Burrows. Doc McIver does the best wheedle I've ever
been privileged to hear. He even talked Bert Humphrey
into giving up the fags!'

'He does, doesn't he?' Annie agreed, glaring at Tom.
'It works a treat — most times. But now. . . Tom, you're
asking me to lie to the social workers to get you what
you want.'

'Not lie. . .'

'The six-week cooling-off period means no access.
So I'll be lying unless you promise not to have any
access at all to your daughter,' she told him bluntly.
'That means not even standing on the other side of the
observation window and looking.'

'Annie. . .'

'I won't do it, Tom,' Annie told him. 'Wheedle all
you want.' She stared across at him, troubled. Half of
her would really like to see this man grow attached to
his small daughter. But the other half was the doctor
in Annie, who'd gone through the adoption procedures
with patients and knew the heartache on all sides. . .

'Tom, as soon as the cooling-off period begins the
welfare people start the process of finding adoptive
parents. Those parents may have been waiting for a
baby for years. They'll be told about your daughter and
asked whether they want her. They'll be told there's
still a possibility you'll change your mind, but if nothing
changes in six weeks then the baby is theirs.'

'So what's wrong with that?' Tom's hands still

wound Henry's bandages, but he was working totally on automatic. He stared up at Annie, a trace of defiance on his face.

'Because the reason the welfare people have stirred up so much hope — have told a desperate couple there's a baby — is that they'll believe you've taken the hardest step of all. You've relinquished your daughter. And unless you have, Dr McIver, then it's just not fair. So don't ask it of me, Tom. I won't do it.'

Tom's face darkened. 'What is this, Annie? Some sort of moralistic punishment?'

'I'm not punishing anyone,' Annie said strongly. Dear heaven, she hated saying this. But it had to be said. 'Tom, I can't punish some childless couple who'll want her desperately.'

'You're saying there's a possibility I won't give her up in six weeks?'

Deep breath.

'If you keep seeing her I believe you may not.'

'Well, that's nonsense. Of course she has to be adopted.'

'So why won't you give her up now?'

'Because I've only just met her,' Tom said harshly. 'Hell, Annie. . . Six weeks. . .'

'You want to get to know your daughter better?'

'Yes, I do. Is there something wrong with that?'

'You'll get to know her — and then give her away?'

'Yes.'

'Oh — ho. . .' Henry broke into their conversation. The elderly farmer was lying on the procedures trolley with the look of a man thoroughly enjoying himself. 'If you think that then you don't know babies, Doc McIver. When mine were born they were so ugly I pretty near had a palsy stroke but, ugly or not, they pretty soon wind themselves round your heart like a hairy worm.'

'Henry, this is —'

'No matter about sleepless nights,' Henry continued,

watching Tom's bewildered face and sweeping aside protest. 'The house'll be chaos. The wife and every other busybody in the neighbourhood'll be clucking over seven pounds of squawking sog. You can't get a word in edgeways. Cooked meals are a thing of the past.

'Then the wife says, "You hold her for a bit," and the kid looks up at you and you see your eyes in her eyes. And she smiles. And they tell you it's wind but you know for sure it's nothing of the kind. She's grinning at her old man — and she's got you hooked for life.'

Henry's eyes crinkled and he chortled in pure delight.

'And I wouldn't mind betting it's happened already,' he said slowly, watching Tom's face. 'What do you reckon, Dr Burrows?'

Annie took a deep breath — and somehow managed to avoid Tom's eyes as she looked back down at Henry. Henry was a wise old farmer who saw a lot. And she saw it, too.

There was nothing else to do but to tell it to Tom like it was.

'Well, I reckon. . .I reckon you're absolutely right.' Annie managed a smile. 'I think Doc McIver needed to hear that, and it's better coming from a man. Like women can operate power saws without chopping off toes, you men can fall in love with your babies.'

A sideways look at Tom's thunderous face made Annie decide her best bet was a fast retreat.

'Henry, I have people in the waiting room and, seeing Dr McIver's free, I can leave you safely with him.' She gave Tom an uncertain smile. 'I've finished with the power tools now, Dr McIver. It's safe for you to take over.'

She walked out the door before Tom could say a word.

CHAPTER THREE

ANNIE worked steadily through a stream of patients all morning and didn't see Tom again for hours.

In fact, her patients were all suffering minor ills, but consultations were lengthened by every single patient's enquiries as to what was going on with Dr McIver's baby. In the end, Annie was starting to suspect there'd been hasty assembling of symptoms just to grill her!

Every time there was a knock on the door she looked up, expecting Tom to burst in and tell her to contact the welfare people. There was no Tom — and by the time Annie saw her last patient it was two o'clock and she knew that Tom would be spending the weekend with his daughter.

'He's not admitting her into the hospital under my bed-card,' she told herself firmly. 'If he thinks he can talk me into caring for her. . .'

Feeling uncharacteristically crabby, Annie bade farewell to Rebecca, her receptionist, and turned her thoughts to lunch. It had been a long time since breakfast. In fact — looking back — Annie couldn't remember breakfast at all.

Drat Tom McIver and his emotional high jinks, she thought bitterly. He had her on an emotional roller-coaster. She wished the man would just go away! She stomped crossly around the back of the hospital to her apartment, opened the door — and saw Tom McIver in her living room.

So was his baby.

The cot was fair in the middle of the room, and Tom's daughter was soundly asleep under the covers. Tom had just emerged from the kitchenette, carrying a bowl of salad.

Annie stared down at the table. Two places were beautifully laid on a linen tablecloth. There were wine glasses and wine in an ice cooler. Crusty bread rolls. There was a smell of something cooking in the kitchen that made Annie's nose wrinkle in appreciation. Beef. Bacon. . .

Good grief!

'Whatever you want, you can't have it,' she said, and watched Tom's face crack into a grin.

'Annie, you are the most untrusting woman. . .'

'I know you, Tom McIver.' Annie stalked back to the door and held it wide. 'Out. No, no and no—and out!'

'Annie, I need to talk to you.'

Yeah. He wanted her to be a doormat. She just knew it.

'Then organize a meeting in the clinic.'

'Annie. . .' Tom plonked down the salad bowl in the middle of the table and walked toward her. He placed two hands on her shoulders and held her at arm's length.

Only Annie knew what the feel of him touching her did to her.

But Tom was oblivious. He was intent on something—but Annie didn't know what. She only knew she didn't trust him one inch.

'Annie, this is the first taste of my new domestic self,' he told her. 'Hannah and I have been to the butcher's and the greengrocer's and we've spent the rest of the morning cooking.'

'Hannah?'

'Hannah.' For the first time a trace of uncertainty crossed Tom's face. 'I. . . I've named her Hannah. After my grandmother.'

'It's pretty, Tom,' Annie said gently—and somehow she managed to wrench herself from his hold and take two steps back. 'Do you want it to be a permanent name?'

'I guess. . . The adoptive parents will be able to change it, I suppose.'

'They can,' Annie agreed. 'But. . .you're not agreeing to separation yet?'

'Monday,' Tom told her. 'I figured if you wouldn't agree to keeping her here longer then I'd at least have her until then.'

'I see.' Annie met his look head on. There was still something going on. Something Tom wanted. 'So, what do I owe lunch to, then, Tom?'

'It's a goodwill gesture.'

'No.'

'What do you mean —no?'

'Meaning, no, I don't believe you,' Annie said flatly. 'What do you want?'

'At least have a glass of wine before I ask.'

'No again. I don't drink when I'm on call.'

'One glass won't hurt.'

'And I especially don't drink when someone's trying to con me into something against my better judgement,' Annie said ruthlessly. She shrugged off her white coat and tossed it onto a chair. 'So tell me.'

Tom stared at Annie for a long moment and then a faint smile played at the corners of his eyes. 'No, Annie, I won't,' he told her firmly. 'I've taken a great deal of trouble to set this up so the least you can do is to eat my lunch. And it's delicious,' he said persuasively. 'You wouldn't want Tiny and Hoof to have it all.'

Annie glared, glared again and finally caved in.

She was hungry. It did smell good. And she knew enough of Hoof and Tiny to know, once offered, her meal would be gone in seconds.

'I'm making no promises. I owe you nothing.'

'Just shut up and eat like a good doctor,' Tom said blandly. 'And then we'll see!'

So Annie sat and ate a magnificent casserole and enjoyed every minute of it, but all the time her eyes demanded to know what he wanted. She loved being with Tom. She always did. But she didn't relax for a minute.

Finally Tom pushed his plate back and sighed.

'You're a very unrestful woman, Annie Burrows.'

'If I rest then I'm taken advantage of,' Annie said darkly. She glared across at him — and then relented enough to smile. 'OK, Tom. You've fed me well and I've enjoyed it. If I can help I will — but not in looking after your daughter for six weeks.'

'Just for tonight.'

Silence.

'Tonight?' Annie said blankly.

'It's the hospital ball, remember?' Tom said. 'And Sarah's expecting me to take her. And you're on call, anyway.'

'You want me to babysit Hannah tonight?'

'Well. . .sort of.' The rat had the grace to look embarrassed.

'If I'm on call I can't look after a baby.'

'No. But I've talked to Robbie and there's a nurse willing to cover Children's Ward. Chris. So all you have to do is say yes.'

'Tom, you only have your daughter for two more nights.' Annie shook her head, confused. 'And you want to spend one of those nights going to a ball with Sarah?'

'I can't cry off. Sarah's already fed up with me,' Tom admitted, 'because of last night. . .'

'I don't see why she should be,' Annie said waspishly. 'She had a good enough time before midnight.'

Tom gave Annie a strange look. 'Annie. . .'

'What?' Annie's crabbiness, having receded a little in the face of Tom's food and infectious smile, flooded back in force. This man was asking her to babysit his daughter so he could take another woman to a ball!

Dear heaven. . .

How could she keep living in Bannockburn? She was crazy to stay. Crazy — when she was head over heels in love with a man who didn't even know she existed.

Except as a medical partner-cum-baby-sitter!

'Annie, I can't afford to get Sarah offside,' Tom said slowly. 'She's a lovely girl.'

'Lovely, all right,' Annie flung at him bitterly. 'With the brains of a cotton-wool ball.'

He gave her another strange look. 'She's a school teacher, Annie.' Tom looked at her steadily. Under his gaze, Annie felt herself blush.

Well, OK. Maybe she was being unfair. It was only the woman's laugh that went right through her. And the fact that Tom thought she was lovely. She swallowed. 'You're. . .you're serious about Sarah, then?' she asked in a small voice, and winced inside as Tom nodded.

'I think I am.'

'I see.' Annie rose and carried her plate to the sink. Then she stood with her back to him. Asking questions like this was like probing a raw wound, but she had to ask. 'It was someone else last week, though, wasn't it? Sarah's new on the scene.'

'Yes, but. . .'

'But?'

'As I said, Sarah's a school teacher,' Tom said softly. 'She's good with children. Maybe if I could persuade her. . . Maybe she'd take Hannah and me on.'

Annie wheeled round, her face incredulous.

'You're thinking of setting up a family?'

It was Tom's turn to blush. 'Well, yes. It did occur to me. I thought. . .if I could spend some time with Sarah tonight. . . Think about it. Get her to think about it. I mean. . .' Tom spread his hands helplessly, rose and walked over to his sleeping daughter. He stared down at the baby for a long, long moment — and then looked back at Annie.

'She looks like me, Annie,' he said tightly. 'Hell. . .I can no more look after a baby than I can fly — but Henry's right. She's got to me.' He shrugged. 'Look, call it a crazy idea but I have two days to think about this. Two days. So. . .I already know I'm starting to love my daughter. Now I need to spend some time with Sarah.'

'But. . .you don't know whether you love Sarah?' Annie was striving for all she was worth to keep her voice casual.

'Well. . .' Tom considered. 'I don't think one loves a wife like. . .well, what I'm starting to feel for Hannah. I mean. . .it's different, isn't it? I've always thought the bit about romantic love was overrated. If you're wise you choose your marriage partner sensibly.'

'And Sarah's sensible?'

'I think so.'

'And beautiful, to boot.' Annie grimaced. 'Very sensible, Tom McIver. Poor Sarah!'

'Hell, Annie. . .' Tom's face darkened in anger. 'What am I supposed to do?'

'I have no idea,' Annie snapped. 'No idea at all. I'm sure what you're intending is very sensible and you'll all live happily ever after. So don't let me stop you. OK. Tonight I'll take responsibility for your daughter while you go and sweep the lovely Sarah off her feet and talk her into a life of domestic bliss.'

'There's no need to be a cat.'

'No!' Annie hauled herself up to her full five feet four inches and glared for all she was worth. This man was so blind! How could he not see he was tearing her heart out? How could he stand there and say there was no such thing as romantic love—when Annie was so in love with him she was even agreeing to his crazy schemes for finding a wife?

'No, there's not,' she agreed, 'so I'll go back to being a doctor. Sensible, hardworking, plain Dr Burrows, who's always there when you need her. And who's crazy enough to say she'll take responsibility for your daughter. For tonight and tonight only!' She stalked over to the door and held it wide. Tom was looking at her as if she'd taken leave of her senses.

Maybe she had.

'You'd better...you'd best leave me to study in peace before the next call comes,' she faltered, 'because I need space. But, yes, I'll take responsibility for your baby, Dr McIver. Once only. But as for the future...'

She shook her head and couldn't go on — and her face grew bleak.

Who knew what the future held? Bannockburn and Dr McIver. Dr McIver with Mrs McIver and their child? Living next door for ever?

No and no and no! She'd have to leave.

'As for the future, your future is up to you,' Annie said dully. 'Your future with your baby has nothing to do with me. *Nothing.*'

She held the door wide until Dr McIver and Dr McIver's baby were gone.

Saturday night started quietly.

Annie was reinserting a failed drip in the next-door ward when Tom and Sarah brought Hannah to Children's Ward. They made a stunning couple — Tom tanned, self-assured and impossibly handsome in his dinner suit, escorting a vibrant Sarah. Sarah with legs that went on for ever and blonde hair that swung down in a silken veil. The figure-hugging crimson dress she wore — slit to the thigh to reveal miles of leg — was simply stunning.

They were enough to take an onlookers's breath away, smiling at each other as they stood holding hands over the crib as they admired the sleeping Hannah — and then sweeping off to the ball.

While Dr Annie Burrows — Cinderella Burrows — stayed behind and tried hard not to turn into a pumpkin.

'Don't they look just so lovely together?' Chris, the night nurse on children's Ward, sighed romantically as she watched them go. 'They're made for each other. Oh, Dr Burrows, if only I looked like Sarah...'

'Yeah, well, that makes two of us, dreaming for the moon.' Annie dug her hands deep in the pockets of her white coat and surveyed the empty corridor with gloom. The lovely, laughing pair had left and the emptiness in the little hospital without Tom's presence was almost tangible.

Annie wrinkled her nose, readjusted her glasses and managed to grin at Chris. 'Well, we can't all be Snow White. And we're not exactly the ugly sisters. It's only that Sarah's so gorgeous she'd make Sleeping Beauty look seriously in the looking-glass.'

'Boy, you know your fairy tales,' Chris said in mock awe.

Annie shrugged and smiled, her natural good humour surfacing. 'Well, I guess there's an up side here, Sister. With most of the town at the ball, we should have a nice peaceful Saturday night. And you have a whole night of looking after a children's ward with one only healthy patient.'

'Isn't it great?' Chris chuckled and hauled a romantic novel from her apron pocket. 'And I know just what I'll do with it.' She sighed and sank into an easy chair beside Hannah's cot. 'Bother fairy tales. I've something better. Bliss! Off you go and enjoy your quiet time, Dr Burrows, and don't find me any patients to spoil my peace. I'm up to page one hundred and twenty and if Jack doesn't fall into Kimberley's arms tonight he may never!'

He didn't.

Half an hour later Murray Ferguson, aged eight, was brought in, suffering a severe asthma attack. Chris's romance was put good-naturedly aside, and she and Annie worked solidly for two hours, stabilizing the little boy's breathing.

Then Ray Stotter was admitted with chest pain. Annie and Helen were fully occupied for another two hours while they ran a full barrage of tests on the old man, decided he was most likely suffering from severe angina, started him on glyceryl trinitrate and reassured his terrified wife that, while Annie was fairly sure that the pain was not from a heart attack, she was keeping him in overnight to be safe.

In the end, Annie spent more time with Martha Stotter than she did with her husband. For once Helen's soothing presence didn't work, and it was Annie the elderly lady clutched as she sobbed out her fears.

It was one in the morning before Annie ended up back in Children's Ward to check Murray's breathing. Murray was asleep but Hannah was awake and starting to fuss.

Chris was walking the baby back and forth across the ward, soothing her and watching Murray's fitful sleep at the same time.

'She won't settle,' Chris told her. 'There's nothing wrong, but every time I put her down she sobs her heart out. Maybe she's missing her mum.'

'I suspect she's just worked out a routine where nights are for play,' Annie explained wearily. 'Maybe that's what pushed Melissa into abandoning her.' Annie stared down at the tiny baby in Chris's arms and her heart wrenched. Maybe that was the explanation—but how could a woman walk away from her own child? Walk away and leave nothing but a note, disclaiming all responsibility?

'Poor little mite.' Chris cradled the little one closer, echoing Annie's thoughts. 'She's such a lovely baby, and she looks so much like. . .' She shook her head. 'Well, I always thought Melissa was an air-head and now I'm sure of it. And heartless as well. Meanwhile. . .'

'Meanwhile we just keep one baby as happy as we can until the grown-ups in her life sort out the mess,' Annie said sadly, and Chris nodded.

'Well, she's fed and happy enough now—as long as I don't put her down. I don't want Murray to wake. He's terrified.'

'The worst of his asthma attack seems to be past now, but it must be dreadful, not being able to breathe,'

Annie agreed. She frowned at Chris. 'Can you cope here?'

'Of course I can,' Chris assured her. 'I can cope with two patients with my hands tied — and while one of them's asleep it's a cinch.' She grimaced and then grinned. 'Pity about Jack and Kimberley, though.'

'They'll still be just as passionate tomorrow night.' Annie returned her smile. 'The good thing about a hero in a book — you can shove him under the bed until you're ready for another spot of passion. Much tidier than real life romance.'

'I wouldn't know,' Chris said darkly. 'I've a feeling romance'd be more fun as a hunk of fabulous male who refuses to be shoved anywhere!' She looked at Annie thoughtfully. 'Anyway, Dr Burrows, I've been dying to ask. I have the odd romantic fling — though usually it's so odd I retire to my romance novels fast — but you. . . You haven't been out with anyone since you came here. Don't you want to?'

Annie shrugged. 'I'm busy,' she said. 'I don't have much time. . .'

'You're pretty, though,' Chris said, considering. 'If you got rid of those glasses. . .'

'Then I couldn't be so fussy about choosing males.' Annie grinned. 'I couldn't see them.'

'Yeah, well, that might be an advantage,' Chris said gloomily. 'The problem with working in this hospital is that you keep seeing Dr McIver, and every other male pales in comparison. Don't you think he's gorgeous?'

'Gorgeous.' Annie's voice was flat and devoid of expression — and Chris's eyes widened.

But in her arms Tom's baby stirred and fretted, and with one last long look at Annie's mounting colour Chris resumed her walking.

'OK, miss,' she told the baby. 'You just shut up and listen to Aunty Chris tell you the story of her love life. That'll put you to sleep if anything will.' She grinned at Annie and carefully forbore to comment on Annie's flushed face. 'Just don't find me anything else to do, huh?'

Of course, Annie did.

Ten minutes later, just as Annie was climbing into bed, the phone on her bedside table went.

Helen.

'Annie, there's a car accident coming in,' Helen said briefly. 'I don't know the details but ETA is ten minutes.'

'I'm on my way.'

There was no more to be said. Annie was already moving. She dressed quickly. This was the worst time. The ambulance officers rang as soon as they received a call, but they wouldn't know yet what the damage was.

And if it was bad. . .

Trauma in a place like Bannockburn could be even more of a nightmare than it was in the city. In the city there was specialist back-up on call. Here. . . Well, it was thirty miles by ambulance to the nearest major hospital. There was only Annie and Tom.

In Bannockburn there were no strangers. Road victims weren't statistics. They were the people you passed every day in the street. Friends.

'Let it be minor,' Annie breathed as she dressed. 'Please. . .'

Two minutes later Annie was dressed and hurrying down the hospital corridor to Sister's station. Helen was replacing the phone as Annie arrived, and her face was grim.

'It's bad,' Helen told her, her fingers already flicking through the phone lists of nurses on call. 'It's Rod and Betty Manning and their little girl, Kylie. Rod and Betty had been to the ball, and they collected Kylie from the babysitter on the way home. Then they hit a tree.'

'They're alive?'

'Yes. But Rod and the little girl look grim. Betty has facial lacerations. That's all I know. Dave says Rod was unconscious at first and now is screaming in pain, and Kylie's leg was caught. They've had to cut her free. Dave sounds really churned up.'

Annie nodded. Dave was one of the valley's team of volunteer ambulance drivers. He'd done basic training but the few times he'd been called out hadn't been enough to give him a thick skin against trauma.

'Staffing?' she asked. Helen knew staff availability far better than Annie.

'I'll need Chris as back-up in Theatre,' Helen said, thinking aloud, 'and I've called in Susan to take over the wards. I'll call in Elsa to help in Children's Ward — she's done SRN training and should be able to cope with Murray's asthma. I don't know, though. . .' Helen's face clouded. 'Tom's baby's still awake. Maybe I should ring Robbie — but he's tired and he's on tomorrow.'

'We don't ring Robbie because of Tom's baby.' Annie frowned. 'But you're right. Elsa can't cope with the baby as well as Murray.' The thought of the easily flustered Elsa trying to calm Murray as well as care for a sobbing child made her wince. Told to sit by Murray's bed and monitor his breathing, Elsa would be fine — but Annie didn't want her distracted by a baby. 'Is Tom back from the ball yet?'

'He came in a few minutes ago.' Helen cast a dubious look at Annie. 'I think he and Sarah are in Tom's apartment. But. . .' Helen looked doubtful. 'I was about to phone Tom. We'll need him here, won't we? He won't be able to look after his. . .the baby.'

'Yes, we'll need him,' Annie agreed. 'But Tom told me Sarah was good with children.' Annie managed a wry smile. 'I guess. . . Well, there's no choice. Let's see how good!'

Annie wheeled Hannah's cot straight round to Tom's apartment. Tom took two minutes to open the door to Annie's knock — and there was lipstick on his collar again.

Annie shouldn't notice such trivia, but she did. She couldn't help it.

Forget the lipstick, she told herself dully. Concentrate on what matters. Annie pushed the baby inside the apartment before Tom had a chance to protest. Both Tom and the dogs stood back, stunned.

'Dr McIver, you're needed in Cas.'

Tom blinked. And so did Annie.

Sarah was there. She stood in the middle of the living room, her lovely blonde hair dishevelled, and on her face there was the dazed look of someone who'd been. . . Well, someone who'd been doing what Annie longed to do. Why did it hurt so much? Why couldn't she be impartial and unemotional and. . .and *sensible*?

Just do what had to be done, say what had to be said and get out of there. She pushed Hannah's cot forward until it was in front of Sarah.

'We need you too, Sarah,' she said. 'Tom needs you to look after his baby. It's an emergency. I hope you don't mind.'

'Emergency?' Tom's eyes creased into swift concern. Sarah might look dazed, but Tom's mind was razor sharp and clicking fast into medical mode.

Annie turned to face him. Look at his face, she told herself. Not the lipstick.

'Car accident,' she said briefly. 'Three—two adults and one child. ETA about now. I have to get back.'

'I'm on my way.' Tom was transforming from lover to doctor with the speed of light.

'But, Tom. . .' Sarah's voice was a wail of dismay. 'Tom, you invited me back for coffee. Can't Annie cope by herself?'

'No,' Tom said bluntly, and Annie knew he'd hardly heard Sarah's wailed protest. He was concentrating only on what lay ahead.

'Not with three badly injured people, I can't.' Annie relented a little at the look of dismay on Sarah's face. What she was doing wasn't fair, Annie acknowledged. Even though she couldn't help calling Tom away, how would Annie feel if she'd been Sarah. . .in Tom's arms. . .?

Some wish!

'I'll take over by myself again as soon as I can,' she promised the disappointed woman. 'If the injuries aren't severe Tom can come back. . .'

'But —'

'But I'll be a while, Sarah.' Tom was hauling off his dinner jacket and tie as he spoke. In a sense Annie knew that Sarah had already been abandoned. Tom's thoughts were no longer here — with this woman — but concentrated solely on medicine. His capacity to block everything else out when he was needed — to devote himself absolutely to the job at hand — was one reason why Annie loved him, but Sarah saw it as no virtue.

'Well, I'll go home, then,' Sarah said sharply. She hitched her handbag over her naked shoulder with an irritable flounce. 'There's no point in me hanging about.'

Annie looked from Tom to Sarah and back again. Tom was hauling on his white coat, and Sarah was looking petulantly at Tom. Neither of them was seeing the cot.

Both of them had to face it. Both of them had to face the responsibility of one small baby. If this was an embryo family then the time to start was right now.

'Sarah, Tom needs you to babysit,' Annie managed, and she was pleased that her voice sounded firm. 'Tom, you know we can't spare staff to look after a well child. Hannah will scream the hospital down if she's unattended. So. . .'

Annie looked from Sarah's beautiful, discontented face to Tom's blank one.

'So someone has to look after your child, Tom.' And somehow she forced her eyes to stay steady.

After all, it wasn't up to her to find babysitting answers here. It was Tom's job. It was his baby. And Sarah was his intended bride.

Annie had made a suggestion, and that was all she could do. She was needed elsewhere.

'Come as soon as you can,' she managed, and Annie turned — like the coward she was — and left them to it.

Give her car accident injuries any day!

Annie didn't know how he sorted it out. She didn't ask. By the time Tom arrived in Casualty — about three minutes later — Annie was drowning in work. So were the three nurses. Tom walked to the casualty entrance and involuntarily recoiled.

Annie breathed a sigh of relief as she saw him. Kylie Manning, five years old and terrified, needed more doctors than just Annie. Annie checked the saline drip, gave the child's hand a squeeze of reassurance and straightened.

'OK, Helen,' she told the charge nurse as Helen moved in to take her place beside the child. 'Dr McIver's here. Could you and Dr McIver get Kylie into X-Ray?' As Annie spoke she walked swiftly to another trolley, where Chris was trying to stop a distraught woman from rising. 'It's going to be fine, Mrs Manning.' Annie pressed the woman's shoulders gently onto the pillows. 'There's no need for distress. We're looking after Kylie and she'll be OK.'

Then Annie's eyes sent an urgent message to Tom — a message that sent him straight to the child's stretcher. Get the little one out of here, Annie's eyes said. Annie wouldn't be able to settle the mother while the child lay blood-spattered and semi-conscious within sight.

'Are you right with everything else?' Tom asked rapidly, his eyes taking in the three trolleys in quick succession before he focused on the child.

Annie wasn't. Mrs Manning was bleeding from a deep and ragged laceration on her forehead and was obviously in shock. On another trolley her husband was writhing and moaning with pain. Dave, the ambulance driver, had his work cut out to hold the man still.

'I'll settle Mrs Manning and then I'll see to her husband,' Annie reassured Tom, but her reassurance was meant mostly for Mrs Manning. 'Kylie's broken her leg, though, Dr McIver, and she'll need an X-ray. . .'

Once again Annie's eyes met Tom's. They'd always worked brilliantly together, intuitively understanding what was needed and reacting in tandem with the ease of partners of years. Now a flicker behind Tom's dark eyes showed he understood. Helen lifted the sheet covering the child's leg for Tom to see. One look, and Tom's face tightened.

There was little circulation below the knee. A compound fracture had cut off the blood supply. If Tom didn't move fast the child would lose her leg.

'But Rod. . .' The woman Annie was holding sobbed in distress, tears mingling with blood. She tried to push Annie away. 'My husband. . . He's worse than me. Can't you see. . .? Can't you hear. . .?'

'Rod has a broken arm,' Annie told her. 'We'll stop the bleeding from this cut first —'

'But —'

'We say what comes first, Mrs Manning,' Tom said briskly, his voice cutting across her husband's moans. 'Dave is looking after your husband. I suggest you lie back and let us get on with our jobs as fast as we can.' And, with a long, hard look at Rod Manning, Tom wheeled the child out of the room.

'I'll be with you as quickly as I can,' Annie murmured after him, knowing Tom needed her now. The child needed two doctors but successful triage — sorting of priorities — was impossible.

Annie couldn't go while Betty was bleeding so badly. And her husband? One brief inspection had shown a broken arm, but Dave said the man had been fleetingly unconscious. That meant he needed a more thorough examination.

So, although Kylie was number one, only one doctor could be spared for her as yet — and Tom's fast actions said he agreed with her. Blessings on Tom. There was no one Annie would sooner hand the child on to.

'OK, now, Mrs Manning,' Annie told the young mother, gently wiping the blood from her face and checking the pressure pad over her wound. 'You know Kylie's in the best of hands. Dr Tom will take good care of her. She has a broken leg and that's the worst of it, as far as I can see, so we'll tend to you next. Let's get you into our procedures room and stop that face bleeding.' She lifted the pad over the woman's forehead and winced.

Mrs Manning looked fearfully up through shocked and pain-filled eyes. 'You're sure. . . You're sure my little girl. . .'

'Tom won't let Kylie die of a broken leg,' Annie said firmly, and watched the fear fade out of the woman's face. And then the fear flooded straight back as Betty looked over to her husband.

'But what about Rod?'

'Apart from a fractured arm, I don't think there's anything major wrong with your husband,' Annie told her. 'And it seems a simple break.' It was hard to keep harshness — the censure — out of her voice.

If what Annie suspected was true. . .

If she was right then she couldn't set his arm tonight, nor could she give him much in the way of pain relief. Annie motioned to the nurses and ambulance officer. 'Susan and Dave will look after your husband. Then, as soon as you let me stop your face bleeding, I'll see to him. So what about lying back and letting me give you something for the pain so I can get on with my job? You agree, Mrs Manning?'

'OK. You'll tell me if anything. . .'

'We'll tell you what's happening every step of the way,' Annie said strongly. 'Promise.'

Thirty minutes later Annie was free to join Tom. He and Helen had Kylie in Theatre. As Annie pushed through the doors Tom looked up from injecting anaesthetic, and his face cleared at the sight of her. His old-maid partner.

'Great. We're losing the little circulation we have. I was just about to make do with Helen.'

'And double great.' Helen sighed her relief. In an emergency Helen could give an anaesthetic—coached every step of the way by either Tom or Annie—but she'd only been called on to do it twice and she'd hated every minute of it. Now she stepped back from the head of the table and made way for Annie.

'The leg. . .' Annie's voice was fearful. If the artery was torn there was little hope. It took the air ambulance two hours to make a return trip to Melbourne to the nearest vascular surgeon.

'The artery's not torn. There are bone fragments kinking the artery and a small amount of blood is still getting through. I may be able to manipulate the leg back so the artery can do its job.'

Annie looked doubtfully at the leg. Dear heaven, it was a mess. If Tom could do that. . .

'How are things out there?' Tom lifted his hands and Helen slipped surgical gloves over his long fingers as he snapped the question at Annie.

Annie didn't answer straight away. Her first priority was the anaesthetic. First she checked Kylie's general condition. The child was already deeply asleep and intubated. Her vital signs were OK—as well as could be expected in a child as shocked as this. The monitors were attached and everything looked fine to go.

'Better,' she told Tom finally, signalling him to go ahead. 'Rod's been X-rayed. I'm pretty sure the only thing wrong with him is a broken arm—radius and ulna—and a few bruises. He's confused and is still making a heck of a fuss, but he's been lucky. Chris is specialling him.'

'And Betty?'

'She's lost a lot of blood, mainly through that gash

on the head. It's taken a bit of stitching to stop the bleeding and I'm afraid my handiwork will be temporary. She'll need repair work by a plastic surgeon. I've sedated her now. Susan's watching her but I think she'll sleep until morning.'

'Which leaves Kylie,' Tom said grimly. 'Two have been lucky. Let's see if we can make it three out of three.' He stared down at Kylie's leg. 'Hell. I could use an orthopedic surgeon here.'

They certainly could. Annie stared down at the fractured mess that was Kylie's knee and knew the child was in for major reconstructive surgery.

The time for that would be later. A skilled children's orthopaedic surgeon would take over where Tom left off—but if Tom couldn't establish a blood supply now there'd be nothing for the surgeon to reconstruct.

'OK, Dr Burrows,' Tom said steadily. He looked at Annie, meeting her eyes and demanding her full concentration. Whatever else had happened tonight—whatever drama was in Tom's life and whatever other patients waited for them outside—this was the time to focus totally.

To commit themselves to saving one little girl's leg.

CHAPTER FOUR

IT WAS an hour before Tom was sure he'd done it. He'd lifted fragments of bone, shifted the leg, applied traction and watched. Three times the blood had surged into the lower leg — only to slowly cease. And Tom had sworn softly and started again.

It was a further half-hour before he stood back from the table, wiped sweat from his forehead and said in a voice where exhaustion dragged, 'That's it. The best we can do. Let's hope it's stable enough to hold.'

Annie looked down to where the child's feet — untouched and unharmed — lay side by side. Completely normal — until Annie looked higher and saw Tom's massive dressing around the knee. . .

'There's circulation now,' Annie told Tom gently. 'You've done the best you could do, and I doubt a skilled orthopod could have done better. But she'll need an artificial kneecap and months of physio.' She hesitated. 'Will we send her on to Melbourne tonight?' She took the reversal injection from Helen and carefully inserted it, then watched like a hawk as the child's muscles came into play. Any minute now Kylie would try to breathe on her own.

'Let's keep her tonight and stabilize her as much as we can,' Tom said wearily, as Helen moved to take his tray of instruments away. 'I don't like the idea of moving that knee one bit.' He looked down at the little girl's face, his eyes concerned. 'She's got a hell of a road ahead of her.'

'At least she has a chance of full recovery.' Annie watched carefully as Kylie's chest heaved. The reversal taking effect, her body retched in rejection of the breathing tube and Annie slid out the hose. Two ragged, painful breaths. . .three. . .and Annie relaxed. Job done.

Thank God!

Annie wasn't the only one glad it was over. Tom's face was grey with exhaustion. The surgery he'd done had required every ounce of his skill and a lot more. He looked absolutely drained.

This was the Tom McIver his women never saw, Annie thought. The Tom who gave every inch of his dedication to his patients. A lesser doctor would have put Kylie in an air ambulance tonight and not tried. . . Not tried because the chances of success were slim. But Tom had fought and Kylie had a good chance of keeping her leg because of it.

Tom was some doctor!

Some doctor. Some love. . .

Dear heaven, she loved him so much. It was as much as Annie could do not to walk over and place her hands on his face and smooth away the lines of exhaustion and pain. Tom did feel this child's pain, she knew. This was the reason she'd fallen so deeply in love with him. He felt his patient's pain like his own and she wanted. . . oh so badly. . .to take his pain and to share it.

She couldn't. Of course she couldn't. It wasn't her place. Annie was part of Tom's medical life — but not a part of his private life at all.

'I'd better go out and see how Rod is.' Unaware of the gamut of emotions tearing at Annie, Tom sighed and crossed to the sink. 'If he's still making a fuss. . .' Tom turned on the taps and let the water flow over his wrists, as if drawing strength from the flow. 'I gather you're not suggesting we set his arm tonight, Dr Burrows?'

His eyebrows rose, and Annie nodded.

'I don't think I'd be game to give him an anaesthetic. I'm guessing as yet, but it's my bet his blood alcohol's somewhere over point one,' Annie told him. 'Maybe a lot higher. I can smell beer and the police asked that I take a blood sample.'

'Have you?'

'I'll do it now.' Annie shrugged. Taking blood samples for the police wasn't one of her favourite jobs but she had no choice. 'I didn't have time before but they're insistent, and when I said they'd have to wait they seemed happy enough. The sergeant says he doubts a few hours' delay will drop him to the legal limit. The tree Rod hit was beside a straight stretch of road, and Sergeant Grey says the wheel marks are all over the road. He must have been drinking heavily at the ball.'

'I didn't notice him,' Tom said shortly.

Annie nodded. Of course he hadn't. What man would notice anything when he had the lovely Sarah in his arms?

Tom wasn't thinking of Sarah now, though. He stared down for a long moment at the child on the operating table and when he turned back to the sink his face was dark with anger. He hauled the tap further round with a force that sent water down so hard that it splashed over onto the floor. Tom didn't notice.

'Bloody fool,' he said bitterly. 'Idiot! To drink himself stupid, and then put his family in the car and drive. . .' He shook his head. 'The man doesn't deserve a daughter.'

'He nearly lost one,' Annie agreed.

Helen had taken the used instruments into the sluice room. Now she came back and looked at Tom, her face creased in concern.

'But you'll treat your daughter better than this, Dr McIver?' the nurse asked gently, and Annie almost gasped. It was a question that had been playing at the edges of her own mind, but she'd never have voiced it. Not in a million years. The redoubtable Helen, however, had no such qualms.

Tom looked up and stared at Helen, but his stare was blind. It looked straight though her.

'I. . .' He shook his head, as though clearing a fog. 'I won't have a chance. My daughter's being adopted.'

'So you say,' the nursing sister agreed equitably. 'Well, let's hope she's lucky enough to end up with parents who don't drink and drive.'

'That's ridiculous. The adoption criteria are rigid.' Tom's voice was curt. He was holding himself under control with a visible effort and Annie could sense his tension growing by the minute.

The pressure of tonight's operation had come on top of almost overwhelming personal pressure, Annie realized. In the moment it took to dump a baby on his doorstep Tom's life had been transformed — and Dr Tom McIver was taking his transformation hard.

'She'll get good parents,' he said tightly.

'Adoptive parents don't come with any guarantees. No parents do.' Helen's voice was implacable. She glanced at Annie, as though seeking silent support for what she was saying, and kept right on talking. 'Rod Manning would pass adoption criteria. To the outside world he's a model citizen. There are whispers that he gives Betty a hard time, but she won't admit that and there'll be no official record that he drinks too much.'

'What are you saying, Sister?' Tom demanded angrily, and Helen spread her hands.

'Just that it's in the lap of the gods who gets your daughter once she's up for adoption, Dr McIver,' she told him, her voice flat and definite. 'And whoever adopts her will have absolute control. You'll have none. No say at all.'

Helen paused — and then shrugged and continued. In for a penny, in for a pound, her body language said. And Annie watched, spellbound.

'Dr McIver, since last night I've been thinking about your little daughter most of the time and. . .well, I've four children myself and I'd find it impossible to hand that responsibility to anyone. It's incredible that Melissa has — and I find it even more incredible that you should.

'You think about it well before you hand your daughter over for life. You'll spend the rest of your days not knowing what's happening to her. If you can't offer her a decent life then you don't have a choice — but you're a grown man with a stable life and. . .' Helen took a deep breath and glanced at Annie. 'And your pick of lots of ladies who'd love you and love your daughter. Some who I bet you haven't even thought of yet.'

Then, as Tom's brow snapped down and he opened his mouth to retort, she cut him off. 'I'll take Kylie out to Recovery and watch her,' she told both of them, and she turned her back on Tom's anger. 'But, Dr McIver. . . if I were you I'd think long and hard over what you're doing. Adoption's a final step — and she's so much your daughter. . .'

Helen directed a shamefaced grin at Annie — as though she suspected she'd had no right to say what she had, but was willing to stand by her words anyway — and she wheeled Kylie to the door.

'Oh, and, by the way, Dr McIver,' she added kindly, turning once more to face him as the door started to swing closed behind her, 'I'd turn off that tap! Your feet are getting all wet.'

Tom and Annie were left alone.

'Hell!'

Tom stared at Annie for a long moment and then, finally, turned his gaze to the tap. The water had been spraying up and over the bench while Helen spoke. The overboots on Tom's shoes were soaking and there was a pool of water around his feet that was spreading by the minute. 'Hell!' said Tom again, only louder, and turned off the offending tap.

'It is, isn't it?'

Annie didn't look at him, concentrating fiercely instead on unfastening the ties on her gown.

Tom stood stock-still and glared. 'How would you know?'

It was an angry demand — and Annie blinked. Tom was glaring straight at her.

'I beg your pardon?' she managed, confused.

'You heard,' Tom snapped, lashing out. 'What the hell would you know, Dr Burrows? You just march into my life and dump my daughter on me and then expect. . .'

Annie took a deep breath and finally met his eyes.

'I dumped. . .?'

'You dumped,' Tom threw at her. 'If it weren't for you. . .'

'I didn't dump,' Annie gasped. 'Melissa dumped. If it weren't for me, your daughter would be lying in a hospital corridor waiting for you to stop making love long enough to find her.' Annie tilted her chin and glared. 'Of all the arrogant, rude —'

'You enjoyed dumping her on us yesterday. And again this evening. . .'

'Enjoyed! What was I supposed to do?' Annie put her hands on her hips and let her temper sail sky-high. A part of her knew Tom's tension was so great it had to explode. Part of her was offended, but part of her relished rising to his bait. The relief of a successful operation — of averting what could have been a tragedy — was having its effect, and a good shout would do her good. So. . .a good shout was what Tom got.

'We needed every nurse tonight, and you know it,' she flung at him. 'And your baby didn't need a nurse. I hardly had time to advertise for babysitters.'

'You could have tried.'

'Oh, sure,' Annie snapped. 'Mrs Stotter's here, staying the night with her sick husband. Maybe I could have woken her and asked her to look after your daughter. Is that what you wanted, Dr McIver? Or did you expect me not to interrupt you — to let Kylie lose her leg — because you wanted to spend the night with your precious Sarah? Well, unfortunately, Kylie only has two legs, Dr McIver, and she needs them both — and you have your whole future to spend with Sarah.'

Unexpectedly, Tom's face fell. The anger went out of him in a rush.

'No.'

But Annie wasn't prepared to let her temper go. Not yet. She was actually enjoying herself.

'I don't know what you mean by that, Dr McIver,' she snapped. 'You and Sarah seemed to be getting on like a house on fire when I interrupted you.'

'Yes, and we might have. . . You stopped us. . .'

'Stopped you from ending up in bed?' Annie demanded crudely. 'Well, maybe I stopped you making another baby, Dr McIver. Bully for me and the birth control movement.'

'No,' Tom snapped. 'You stopped me asking Sarah to. . .' And he didn't continue.

Silence.

Annie knew instinctively what he'd been going to say. She could see it in his face.

She knew.

'I stopped you proposing?' Annie asked at last. And her temper somehow faded, too. Just when she needed it most. Dear heaven. . .

'That's right.' Tom's hands ripped through his dark hair and his look of fatigue deepened. 'I had it all planned.'

Annie bit her lip. She mustn't care. She mustn't!

'Well, now's your chance again, then,' she managed, forcing her voice to stay light. 'I can cope by myself now. I'll contact the air ambulance and have them collect Kylie and her mum in the morning, but meanwhile I can hold the fort until dawn. You go back to your. . .'

She stopped as the word hit her, but then she forced herself to say it. The sensation was like biting down on a broken tooth. 'You go back to your family, Dr McIver. Your. . .your family. They're waiting for you.'

'They're not my family.'

'No?' Annie shrugged. She was very close to tears but she was holding them back somehow. Somehow. . . 'Dr McIver, you have a fiancée and a baby. That sounds like a family to me.'

'They're damn well not a family!' Tom lifted a towel and started drying his arms. He looked over at Annie and his normally confident face held a plea for help. 'I tell you, they're not! Annie, what the hell am I going to do?' he demanded. 'What the hell. . .'

Annie stood immobile where she was. If she crossed to the sink. . . If she took one step nearer Tom McIver she'd be compelled to place her arms around his neck and comfort him. . .kiss away the worry and tiredness and uncertainty in his eyes.

She'd told herself over and over that she couldn't even think of such a thing. It wasn't her place!

'Tom, go and ask Sarah to marry you,' she said dully. 'A delay of a couple of hours won't make a difference. If that's what you've decided.'

'That's what I *had* decided.' Tom's voice was as flat as her own. 'It made sense a couple of hours ago. But, then, when you left Hannah with us. . .'

What had gone wrong? 'Sarah wasn't very happy, was she?' Annie asked gently, and waited. And waited. While Tom's tired face grew dark.

Finally he threw the towel on the floor in disgust.

'She wasn't,' he told her. 'Sarah said she spends all day every day with children and she didn't expect to be dumped with my kid on a date. She said. . .she said you were a manipulating little vixen, just trying to separate us.'

Annie blinked. Sarah was. . .jealous?

That was ridiculous.

'Yeah, well, you told me it was my fault you got landed with Hannah,' Annie said mildly, and watched Tom's face crease in disgust.

'Hell, you know I didn't mean that, Annie,' he said. 'You know I was just letting off steam. And you weren't really offended. You never seem to mind. I don't know. You understand. . . But. . .' He shook his head. 'Sarah said you were out for the main chance. . .out for me. . . As if these last two nights haven't been anything other than a disastrous coincidence that's made you interrupt us. She said you were trying to split us up.' He shook his head as though the idea was crazy.

Which it was, Annie thought bleakly. As though Sarah could possibly think Annie could be any competition.

'Maybe Sarah was upset, too,' Annie said softly, and heaven alone knew the effort it cost her to be nice. 'Maybe. . .'

'Maybe,' Tom said wearily. 'Maybe, like me, she was just ripping back in frustration. She agreed to babysit Hannah in the end and she'll be back in the flat when I finish here. But. . .' Once more, his hand ripped through his dark hair. 'But it's made me see one thing. I certainly don't know Sarah well enough to marry her. Hell, Annie, I know you better than I know her. I could as soon marry you. . .'

He gave the towel a ferocious kick that sent it flying out to the sluice room, then cast Annie one last unhappy look — and walked out of the door.

Back to Sarah, and back to his baby.

I could as soon marry you. . .

The words echoed round and round the empty theatre, and it was all Annie could do not to weep.

'But you certainly wouldn't want to marry me,' Annie said gloomily to the empty room. 'No way, Dr Tom McIver. Not in a million years.'

Not ever.

She closed her eyes — and then she started cleaning up and getting on with the rest of her life.

The air ambulance took Kylie and her mother to Melbourne at seven the next morning, and Annie was asleep five minutes after the plane took off. The night shift was over. Tom could take over medical duties for the day. Annie didn't care whether Hannah had kept him awake or if he'd spent the night making love to

Sarah — she was so tired she could hardly hold her head up, and from seven Tom was officially on duty.

She hit the pillows and didn't wake until one. Until someone knocked on her door.

Still mostly asleep, Annie fumbled her way to the door. Tom stood in the corridor, holding his daughter in his arms. He took a step back as Annie opened the door, an expression of almost sheepish apology on his face.

'I thought you'd be awake.'

'I wasn't,' Annie muttered, and folded her arms over her breasts — a gesture of pure defence. Tom was fully dressed in his casual trousers and shirt, and Annie was anything but fully dressed. Her nightie was too flimsy by half and she'd been too tired to do it up properly when she'd fallen into bed. It was too late now to retreat and find a dressing-gown.

Tom was staring. His apologetic expression was changing to one of interest. As if he was watching a frog that had just changed into a princess, or a pumpkin into Cinderella. . .

'I've never seen you with your hair down,' Tom said slowly, his gaze raking her from her bare toes up. Annie's soft brown hair was a cascade of curls around her breasts and her wide grey eyes seemed huge without her normal barrier of glass and tortoiseshell rim.

She blushed crimson and took a hasty step back inside her apartment. She grabbed her glasses from the top of the bookcase and shoved them down on her nose.

Shield up!

'Why don't you wear contact lenses?' Tom asked curiously — and then looked more closely at her glasses. 'They're not very thick. Do you need to wear them all the time?'

Annie's blush deepened.

'Yes, I do need them — and I don't see the point of contact lenses. What do you want?'

Tom's face lightened into a grin. 'Just to annoy you,

of course,' he told her. 'And I'm good at it. I seem to make you cross, without even trying.'

'Not true,' Annie snapped, glaring. 'How can you say "without even trying" when you are very, very trying?' She glanced at her wrist-watch and her glare deepened. 'Tom McIver, the agreement today was that you'd do the work from this morning and I'd take over again tonight. So go away! Unless there's an emergency, I'm not working today and, no, I'm not babysitting.'

'Why do you always attribute my motives to anything but altruism?'

'I didn't think you even knew what altruism meant,' Annie said bitterly. 'Consideration for others is hardly your strong point. And now you appear at my door, holding a baby.' Annie glowered. 'It's enough to make anyone suspicious.'

'Well, I'm not asking you to do anything,' Tom retorted, with the air of a man much maligned. 'The hospital's dead quiet again. You got Kylie and her mum off OK with no problems. I assume if there were any worries you would have woken me.'

'Mmm.' Annie recrossed her arms and wished again for a wrap. Standing in her doorway with bare toes and a nightgown that was way too thin was making her extremely uncomfortable. She wanted her sensible clothes, a white coat and any other defence she could muster. 'There was a doctor on board the air ambulance so they were in good hands. I did think of waking you but —'

She broke off. She'd thought of waking Tom, but the thought of disturbing him. . . If Sarah was still there. . .

She didn't know if Sarah had stayed the night and she didn't want to know. Such knowledge was more than Annie could bear. Anyway, she could hand over patients and histories as well as Tom could. Surgical notes could be faxed later if required.

'You should have.'

'Yeah. . .' Annie put her hand pointedly on the door-knob. 'Was that all you wanted to say?'

Tom ignored the gesture. 'You decided not to send Rod with his wife and daughter?'

'I did.' Annie tilted her head and glared, sensing criticism, and Tom's smile deepened.

'All right, Touchy. I'm not being critical. I just wondered whether he'd wanted to go. He's belligerent as all heck now, and threatening to sue if anything happens to his wife and daughter.'

'He was vomiting as the plane left,' Annie told him. 'Moaning and vomiting at the same time. I gave him as much prochlorperazine as I dared but the alcohol is just going to have to wear off itself. His nausea would have kept the plane's staff from Kylie and Mrs Manning. Mrs Manning needs a plastic surgeon. Kylie needs an orthopaedic surgeon and Rod needs to dry out. The drying-out can be done here.'

'You think it might take a while?'

'The way his body's reacting, his blood alcohol content must be sky-high.' Annie shrugged. 'The police will have a field day with the results of his blood test, but I can't help that. Also, with that level of alcohol on board, his arm will have to wait until tomorrow to be set. Unless you're prepared to give an anaesthetic?'

'No way.' Tom shook his head. 'I'm with you.'

'When he recovers from drunkenness Rod Manning is going to feel really sorry for himself,' Annie said sadly. 'As soon as the result of his blood test comes through the police will take his licence, and there's no way he'll get it back before a court case. He'll be visiting his wife and child courtesy of bus travel, and Kylie's going to be in hospital for quite a while.'

'Months, at a guess.' Tom's smile faded completely. He stared at Annie — and then looked down at his own daughter. 'Fool. . .' He looked back at the girl holding the door open. 'Anyway, Annie, I didn't come to talk to you about work. I came to ask you to go on a picnic.'

'What — today?'

'Today.'

'You're on duty,' Annie said flatly, still deeply suspicious. Tom McIver didn't ask Annie for dates. He asked her for favours.

'Not a far picnic,' Tom explained patiently, 'a near picnic. It's just. . .' He checked Annie's look of stunned incredulity and grinned. 'Hell, Annie, I'm not asking you to fly to Africa or indulge in a spot of illicit drug-running — or even go to bed with me! It's just a picnic.'

Annie's eyes narrowed.

'But why?'

'Does there have to be a reason?'

'Yes.'

'I've told you before — you have a suspicious mind.'

'It's the only protection I have,' Annie said bluntly. 'And I'm keeping it suspicious. You propositioned me with lunch yesterday then asked me to babysit, and now you're offering me food again. What do you want this time, Tom McIver?'

'Not to waste a picnic.'

Annie took a deep breath and watched Tom's face. 'I. . .I see. Sarah. . . Sarah doesn't want to go?'

'You could say that.' Tom sighed. 'Annie, there's a great spot where the river runs into the sea, not much more than a mile from here. If the hospital beeps me I can be back in three minutes.'

'Your favourite seduction site, in fact.'

Tom's eyes narrowed. 'Annie, why the hell are you so aggressive? You sound a real little moralist.'

'Yeah, well, maybe I am.'

'It's what you look like in your nice, sensible clothes with your hair hauled back and your glasses on,' Tom said. 'But you can't sound like a moralist as you look now. Did you know the buttons over your breast are unfastened almost to your waist?'

She didn't.

Annie's blush turned to fire-truck red and she grabbed

the door. Tom prevented her closing it by simply shoving his foot in the crack.

'I'll collect you in fifteen minutes,' he said firmly. 'Wear your bathers under your sensible clothes, Dr Burrows. I dare say your neck-to-knees will look pretty bulky under your knee-length skirt and straitlaced blouse, but Hannah and I will turn a blind eye.'

'I am not going to lunch. . .'

'But —' Tom threw in his trump card ' — we have a whole lobster.'

'A whole. . .' Annie gasped and was silenced.

The local lobster went straight to the Japanese export market and the Japanese, with their strong yen, seemed to eat more lobster than Australians did. It was now priced ridiculously high.

'A whole lobster,' Tom said again.

'But. . . Tom McIver, do you know how much lobsters cost?'

'I ordered it yesterday,' Tom said sadly. 'I'd never proposed before — and it seemed like the right thing to do. If things had gone according to plan I'd be an engaged man by now.'

'And you'd be eating lunch with your fiancée.'

'That's right.'

'So. . .I'm a fiancée substitute.'

'You make a cute one.' Tom grinned, unabashed. 'I hadn't realized how cute until now. And, instead of offering you half my worldly wealth, I'm offering you half my lobster.' His amazing smile — never absent for long — flooded back in force. 'Take it or leave it, Annie, but there's champagne as well, and vol-au-vents with Atlantic salmon, avocado salad, chocolate éclairs. . .'

'That's not a seduction scene for one fiancée,' Annie gasped. 'You'd get a whole harem for that.'

'We don't want a harem, do we, Hannah?' Tom said morosely to his daughter. 'We just want Annie.'

'You want me because there's no one else available.'

'Yeah, well, we thought that, didn't we, Hannah?'

The man was at least honest. An honest toad! He looked back at Annie — and his smile twinkled out again. 'But that was before we saw the undone buttons. And what's underneath them. Very fetching! But, if you like. . .if you like, we'll try very hard to forget what we've seen and we'll have a very chaste lunch on the beach. A business lunch, if you like. A business lunch with lobster and champagne. I wonder if I can claim it as a tax deduction. What do you say, Annie Burrows?'

What did she say?

She knew darned well what she should say. She should slam the door hard and go straight back to bed. She'd had six hours sleep and it wasn't enough. And it wasn't the least bit sensible to go anywhere near this man on a social level.

But Annie looked up and saw the twinkle lurking behind Tom McIver's eyes — and she also saw a hint of panic. Tom's life was changing dramatically and he couldn't cope. Not on his own.

And she couldn't refuse.

'OK, Tom McIver,' she faltered. 'I'll. . .I'll be your substitute fiancée for the day. But that means I drink champagne and I eat your lobster and I sunbake. It does not mean I take any calls for you, or babysit your daughter. Or do anything at all for your dratted dogs. Right?'

'Well. . .'

'Right, Tom McIver?'

'I've never had such an ungracious acceptance to an invitation,' Tom complained, and Annie wrinkled her nose and grinned.

'Well, this is what you get! Me! Suspicions included. Take me or leave me, Dr McIver, but I come with conditions. No medicine, babies or dogs. Now, do you want me — or not?'

Tom looked at her with a very strange expression in his eyes, an expression that said he was seeing someone he'd never seen before. Annie Burrows without her defences.

'I rather think I do,' he said slowly. 'And maybe... maybe with or without conditions.'

CHAPTER FIVE

AS PICNICS went, it was a picnic to die for. Tom had packed everything possible for a magnificent engagement celebration.

The only thing was...it wasn't quite your standard romantic scene. Annie checked out Tom's car and she could see why Sarah had whisked herself back to her schoolroom. Tom's Rover was packed high with food and drinks, rugs, cushions, baby capsule, nappy bag — and two huge dogs squashed somehow one each side of the baby capsule.

'They had to come,' Tom told Annie warily, interpreting her look of astonishment. 'I've kicked them out of my bedroom. I can hardly kick them out of my life.'

'I can see that.' The dogs had their dopey heads out of the back windows. Their tongues were almost down to ground level and they were clearly bursting with anticipation. 'Does Hannah like dogs, then?'

'Who could help but like my dogs?' Tom said smugly. 'They're great guys.'

'Yeah, well...'

'You don't like them?' Tom sounded astonished.

Annie considered. The dogs' huge heads were bobbing up and down like sprung toys. Their tails were thumping on the car roof and their tongues were leaving a series of damp trails on the paintwork.

'I have to say I've seen brighter dogs,' Annie admitted at last, smiling to take the edge off her criticism. 'These two seem... Well, the lights are on but maybe no one's home?'

'Hey, Annie!' Tom's face grew shocked. 'Hell, they'll hear you. What a thing to say about my beautiful boys! I'll have you know their pedigree's impeccable.'

'But are they trained to do anything but bay at the moon?' Annie demanded, and Tom gave a reluctant grin.

'Well. . . They eat on command.'

'I'll just bet they do.'

'And they're house-trained!'

'You mean they know how to sleep on your bed. It's a wonder there's room for you. Honestly, Tom, why didn't you buy yourself a couple of chihuahuas? Let's face it—doorstops would be more useful than these two. Also, they'd eat less.'

'I didn't buy these two,' Tom confessed. 'One of my old patients died last year and Hoof and Tiny were his. They were going to be put down if I didn't take them, and they. . .well, they looked at me. . .'

They looked at him.

That silenced her.

They'd looked at him and Tom had been lost. Of course.

Did Sarah know this side of him? Annie wondered. The side Annie had seen the first time she'd met the man—the side of his nature Annie recognized almost intuitively.

Tom McIver appeared to the world as hard and capable and. . .and womanizing. Inside he was pure marshmallow. Any wife of his would have to be prepared to open her house and heart to all sorts of waifs and strays.

So. . . Where did that leave Tom now? How could Tom give his beautiful daughter up for adoption to strangers when all two stupid, overgrown dogs had to do was look at him?

They hardly spoke as Tom drove the short way to the sea. They couldn't. The dogs barked with joy the moment the engine started and didn't stop until they reached the river mouth.

Once there, the dogs burst out of the car to chase gulls and Annie rubbed painful ears. Tom lifted Hannah's borrowed baby capsule onto the river bank, then produced so many things from the back of his car that Annie figured this was a conjuring act.

'Whew. . .' Annie stared down at the ice cooler, holding French champagne, and then gazed up at Tom in stupefaction.

'This is some seduction scene,' she said slowly, as she sank onto the pillows Tom had spread over the rug. And then she looked up at him suspiciously. 'Are you sure you want to waste it on me?'

'I don't know.' Tom bent to prise open a container holding lobster. He placed it before Annie and then he straightened. The lobster cast its distinctive aroma upward and Annie's nose twitched in appreciation.

Tom stood beside her, his denim-clad legs splayed, the warm, sea breeze ruffling his tousled brown hair and his strongly boned face showing uncertainty as he looked down at the slight girl at his feet. 'I thought I did,' he said slowly, 'but now I'm not sure.'

Annie was hardly listening. The sight of Tom's body standing right above her was doing strange things to her insides — but her attention was almost diverted. Lobster! She leaned over, lifted a morsel and bit. Mmm. . .

'Well, you can't change your mind now.' She smiled up at him, then grabbed the lobster container and held on like grim death. 'At least, not until I've finished this lobster. And why should you, I'd like to know?'

'You like lobster, then?' He grinned.

'Offer me a lobster or a Rolls Royce and I'm the one sitting on the road stuffing her face.' Annie returned his smile and cracked some shell. 'But you can have half. Did you bring scales so we can make it fair?'

Tom's smile faded. He stood, looking down at her and considering, and Annie knew he wasn't thinking of lobster.

'Annie, will you tell me why you're wearing those clothes?'

'What do you mean?'

'Annie, this morning I thought inviting you on a picnic was a sensible idea.' Tom shook his head, confused. 'Then, when I saw you in your nightgown with your hair down and your glasses off, I thought inviting you was a fantastic idea. But now. . . Now it just seems sensible again. Annie, why are you wearing your jeans and baggy T-shirt? And you've hauled your hair back too tightly again. It's like. . .it's like you're deliberately hiding yourself.'

Annie flushed. He was right, she supposed. They were an ill-matched pair. Tom looked like a hero straight out of a romantic movie, but Annie didn't fit the bill as a heroine.

She was a doctor. Not a lover!

'It's the way I like it.'

'But your hair's beautiful out. Gorgeous.' He bent to touch it but Annie flinched. She concentrated fiercely on her lobster and tried hard to ignore him.

'Tom, this lobster's fabulous. Eat some before I forget the half deal.'

But Tom's attention was not to be diverted. For the first time in eight months he was seeing Annie as a woman, and now he was checking her out from the toes up.

'You know, jeans and floppy T-shirts are for kids. Especially when you're asked out on a date.'

Annie bit again and glowered. 'You decide what you wear, Tom McIver,' Annie said crossly. 'Leave me to wear what I want.'

'But. . .why don't you wear something attractive? Dresses and things. Or. . .even jeans and tops that fit!'

Annie shook her head, her courage slipping. Good grief, after all these years she should be immune to comments on her appearance. She started to lift another piece of lobster, but her fingers trembled. And Tom saw.

He stooped and took Annie's fingers in his. The perplexity on his face deepened.

'I've upset you, Annie. Why?'

'You haven't upset me.'

'Liar.'

'Tom. . .' Annie hauled her hand back from his. Tom released it, but he knelt on the cushions before her and watched her with eyes that were suddenly concerned.

'Annie, I haven't seen it before but. . . There's something wrong, isn't there? Something that makes you wear what you wear. Something that makes you wear your white coat and stethoscope as a shield. Or your awful T-shirts. Something that makes you afraid.'

'There's nothing wrong,' Annie said flatly. 'I like jeans and T-shirts, that's all. And as for something being wrong. . . It's you who has the problem. Remember?'

'But my small problem's sound asleep in her baby capsule.' Tom motioned to where Hannah slept soundly in the shade. 'My daughter's working up energy for tonight. So. . .now I can concentrate on you.'

'I don't see why you should do that all of a sudden,' Annie said crossly. Tom's interest was throwing her right off balance. 'I've been working here for eight months and you've never shown the least interest in me before.'

Tom's eyebrows snapped together.

'Yeah, well, maybe I've been remiss.'

'Or maybe you want something now.'

'I told you, Annie, I don't want anything.'

'Then why am I here?'

'Because dirty nappies scare the socks off me and she's due,' Tom said promptly — so promptly that Annie was forced to smile. Tom laughed with her, a deep chuckle that echoed out over the sand-hills around them.

Annie found herself smiling into Tom's eyes — and suddenly she found herself relaxing a fraction. Just a fraction, but it was enough. Maybe. . .maybe this could be fun. Maybe she could enjoy her picnic. She let Tom pour her champagne and then raised her brows in mock disapproval as he poured a glass for himself.

'OK, OK. I know I'm on call,' he told her, meeting

Annie's censorious look with laughter. 'But it's fine to have one glass. A glass of champagne just makes me feel intelligent.'

'More intelligent than you normally feel?' Annie teased. '*Wow*!' She smiled up at him, relaxing even more. It was hard to stay tense in such a place — on such a day — and she was far more comfortable when she could slip into the teasing banter she and Tom always used with each other. Brother and sister stuff. . .

Only she didn't feel like Tom McIver's sister.

Tom started talking about Robert Whykes's bad back and the problems he was having, coming to terms with long-term recuperation, and that helped. Immersed in her medicine, Annie could relax completely with this man — just savour his competence and caring. She put in her two bits' worth every now and then, but for the most part she was content to listen.

She lay back on her cushions, ate her lobster, sipped her champagne and tried as hard as she could to feel like Tom's kid sister. Or like a medical colleague and nothing else.

Impossible task! The champagne went straight to her head, and Annie started feeling weird. Nice — but weird.

This setting was magic. They were lying under gum trees on a bed of moss where the river rippled peacefully down to the sea. Fifty yards from where they lay the moss became sand and the sand sloped gently down to the beach. The faint wash of surf provided a sleepy background whisper. The dogs were chasing crazily after gulls — too far away to disturb them. Sunlight dappled through the leaves above their heads and Annie relaxed, ate, drank and let the peace of the day wash over her.

While Tom watched.

'You should go to sleep,' Annie told him, opening one eye to find him watching, and flushed under his gaze. 'I'll wake if the mobile phone rings, even if you don't. And you needn't worry. If you're called I'll wake you up fast enough. Considering how peaceful they are, I'll even let you leave Hannah and the dogs with me if you need to go back to the hospital. Just leave the left-over lobster when you go.'

'Generous to the bone!' Tom smiled but his smile was different. It was confused. As if he suddenly didn't know who he was with any more.

'Annie. . .'

'Hmm?' Annie was curled up on her mossy bed, her head on a mound of pillows. She'd drunk two glasses of champagne, her fingers were sleepily popping strawberries into her mouth and she was feeling indescribably happy.

Stupidly happy.

'Tell me about yourself.'

Annie considered while she ate more strawberries. It was a strange question — but, then, it was a strange day. A day out of the box.

'You know about me,' Annie said slowly, without opening her eyes. 'You read my résumé when I applied for the job.'

'I read your qualifications,' Tom told her. 'They're impressive. One of the youngest ever graduates from medical school. A year's rotational residency and then a year each of anaesthetics and paediatrics. Impeccable references from everyone. It was as if you were specifically training yourself for this job! But since you've been here. . .well, you don't seem interested in anything but medicine.'

'My medicine's important,' Annie told him. 'It's the most important thing in my life.'

'But. . . Annie, I do other things. Are you inferring my medicine's not important to me?'

Annie blinked — and then flushed.

'No, Tom,' she admitted, not meeting his look, 'I wasn't inferring you weren't dedicated. But. . . Yes, I'm committed to medicine. I thought that was what you wanted in a partner.'

'But you have room for outside interests, too — it's just that you don't want them.'

'That's right.' Annie shrugged, trying to shake off the memory of Tom's hurtful, overheard words: 'She'll work hard. If we're lucky, she'll grow to be a great old-maid doctor.' Tom McIver had employed her because she didn't seem to want outside interests. And now he was waiting to know why she didn't want them. 'I haven't been qualified long,' she managed. 'There's so much to learn.'

'With medicine, there's always so much to learn.' Tom poured coffee from a vacuum flask and handed her a mug. 'The trick is finding a balance.'

'Which you have?'

'Which I have,' Tom agreed. Then he glanced uncertainly across at the sleeping baby. 'The balance might just have to change now, though.'

Annie nodded. She drank her coffee and laid her empty mug carefully on the moss. As the champagne became diluted her dreamy haze cleared a bit. She thought through what he'd said, and moved the topic of conversation carefully away from herself.

'Tom, are you seriously thinking you might keep your baby?'

'Maybe.' Tom stared out at the beach to where his dogs were racing in crazy circles. They definitely were a sandwich short of a picnic, Annie thought. Dingbat dogs!

'Maybe meaning yes?'

Tom nodded.

'I'm starting to think so.' The laughter was gone from Tom's voice now. 'It's been a shock,' he said slowly, talking almost to himself. 'But I spoke to Melissa's mother on the phone this morning. Melissa arrived home from Israel eight and a half months pregnant, with the idea of having the baby adopted and then getting on with her life as fast as possible. The man she's currently fallen for is climbing mountains in Nepal and that's where Melissa wants to be. She doesn't give a toss about her baby. Our baby.'

He shrugged. 'So that leaves me — and I'll admit I'm finding it hard to be dispassionate. Objective. Maybe the best thing for Hannah is adoption. But. . .but I'm starting to think I want to keep her with me. I just can't bear not to. If only I could just figure out how.'

'Do you know anything about rearing children?' Annie asked, watching his face, and Tom grimaced.

'You know I don't. I don't know a damned thing, Annie, and that's the truth. But. . .' He shook his head and his eyes clouded. 'I know what it is not to be wanted. My parents never wanted me. My father tried to talk my mother into an abortion and she would have had one if she hadn't been afraid of the medical procedures.

'They made no bones about telling me I'd messed up their lives. I had teenage nannies until I was five and then my parents talked my grandmother into taking me. I hardly saw them after that. I was sent to boarding school soon after and, apart from my grandmother, I had nobody. The thought of my daughter being the same. . . The thought of her not being wanted. . .'

He closed his eyes and when he opened them again they were full of pain. 'I've been thinking and thinking,' he said harshly, 'and I don't think I can bear it. What Helen said last night. Not knowing who's looking after her. Not knowing what she's wearing — what she's doing. Knowing my daughter's alive in the world *and I'm not there*.'

His words were full of pain. Annie looked up at him. Tom's eyes were intense and brooding, as though he were looking back at a childhood full of rejection. And Annie's heart stirred in recognition.

'So. . .how about you, Annie?' Tom demanded, as if reading her thoughts. 'Did you play happy families all your childhood?'

'Who, me?' The switch of subject made Annie jump.

'Who else?'

Who else, indeed? Annie flushed and tried to make herself answer. She shouldn't mind the question. It was just. . .it was just that Tom's query was so personal — so exposing — and Annie wasn't used to people getting close.

But Tom had told her of his rejection. Told her about the loneliness of his childhood. And, by the look in his eyes, Annie knew he didn't confide often. She knew he'd spoken of something that still hurt.

And. . .maybe the only way to ease hurt was to share it. When sharing with Tom was something she'd wanted to do for so long. . .

'My dad walked out when I was tiny,' Annie admitted. 'And. . .my mum didn't want me either.' Annie shrugged. 'I have an older sister who's beautiful. My mum didn't know what to make of me.'

'But you're beautiful.'

It was a flippant remark. Stupid. He couldn't mean it. 'Tom, don't. . .'

'Did you spend all your childhood being told you were plain?' Tom asked incredulously, and the silence that greeted him was answer enough.

Annie flinched inside.

It sounded stupid now — that it had hurt so much. But Annie's mother was an ex-model who valued people solely on looks, and Annie's sister was long and willowy and. . .and just Tom's type.

When she was fifteen, a boy in senior school had asked Annie to go to a ball. He'd been a hunk, she remembered, and Annie had been astounded that she'd been chosen. She'd spent two months' clothing allowance on a dress she'd thought was fabulous.

Well, Annie's mother and sister had taken one look at Annie dressed up and had hooted in derision. And then the boy had come to collect her, and he'd met her sister. . .

End of story.

So Annie had given her dress to charity, put on her
jeans and baggy T-shirts and told herself she was made
for working. The boys she'd dated after that had been
those who'd lived and breathed study and work.

Until she'd met Tom, that is. Since Tom, somehow
she'd had trouble dating anyone. And how stupid
was that?

'You hide all your lights,' Tom said gently, and by
his voice Annie could tell he'd seen unhappiness wash
over her. 'Annie. . .'

'Tom, don't. . .'

Annie put her hand up to prevent him — but not fast
enough. Tom's fingers reached out and lifted her glasses
from her nose. And laid them aside on the rug. Before
she could realize what he was about, his skilful fingers
found the clip at the back of her hair — and lifted it to
let her curls fall free.

And then he sat back and looked at her as her soft
curls tumbled down about her shoulders.

'Don't ever let anyone tell you you're not beautiful,
Annie Burrows,' Tom said gently. 'Don't ever believe
them. If they say that then they're liars.'

That was a bit much! 'Tom McIver, how can you
say that? When for the last eight months you haven't
so much as looked at me. . .'

'I haven't looked past your defences until now,' Tom
said softly. 'And maybe I've been a fool.' He raised
his hand and pushed a wispy curl back behind her ear —
and Annie flinched as if she'd been burned.

'What's wrong?' Tom asked.

'I don't like —'

'You don't like me touching you?'

He had to be kidding! All Annie wanted him to do
was touch her. But she still didn't trust him. She was
here as a Sarah substitute, she thought desperately. A
fall-back position because Sarah had let him down.

Hold onto that thought.

'Tom. . .it's time to go.'

'It's not time for us to go,' Tom said firmly. 'Rob will call us if he needs us. Murray's asthma is subsiding. Mr Stotter's angina has settled. Rod Manning will be sleeping off his hangover. We can't set his arm until his alcohol level is right down and all he'll do if we come near is abuse us. There's nothing else that needs doing. It's Sunday afternoon and Bannockburn's asleep.'

'Then we should be sleeping too,' Annie muttered. 'Tom. . .what if we're up again tonight?'

'Then we'll worry about that tonight. Annie, why are you afraid?'

'I'm not afraid.'

'You mean. . .' Tom stirred on the cushions and moved closer to look directly into her frightened eyes. 'You mean, if I kiss you, you won't flinch?'

'You don't. . .you don't want to kiss me.'

'Yes, I do.'

'Tom. . .'

But Tom wasn't listening. His hand had come out and caught the back of her head and pulled her face forward—forward so that his lips could meet hers in a first gentle kiss of exploration. And it was done so suddenly that there was nothing Annie could do to prevent it.

If she'd wanted to.

So Tom kissed her. And it was the kiss that Annie had dreamed of all her life.

It was a kiss of questions. A kiss of wonder. A kiss that held a faint astonishment on Tom's part that he'd wanted to do such a thing. He'd never thought of Annie Burrows as a woman before. And yet. . . And yet here she was before him, and her face was soft and her eyes were huge and wondering. . .

And when his mouth met hers the kiss slammed home the knowledge that Annie was every inch a woman. As desirable as any Melissa. . .or Sarah. . . Or any other woman. . . As desirable, or more desirable. . .

Because, as their lips met, it was like two halves of a whole fitting together — two pieces of a shattered coin being joined again after years apart. Each slot and niche and fold fitted into itself with a certainty that couldn't be argued with.

Tom's body stiffened in shocked recognition. His mind stilled as his mouth tasted the girl he was holding.

Quite suddenly, nothing in his life had ever felt so good before — or so right.

And Annie. . .

For a moment Annie's mouth didn't move beneath his. She didn't respond at all. And then, as though moved by a force stronger than self-control — stronger than anything she'd ever known — Tom felt a desire to respond overwhelm her. He felt her lips move softly beneath his — then part — and open themselves to him as a flower welcomes summer rain.

As a woman welcomes her man home.

Dear God. . . Something was happening here that was stronger than both of them.

Tom's hands fell to pull Annie's body against his — to feel her soft curves yield so that her breasts pressed against his chest. His kiss deepened, as did the wonder. His mouth devoured hers, tasting her — finding her inner being and wanting more. . . Wanting to know what this wonder could be that he was finding in such an unexpected corner of his life.

This woman under his hands was like no woman he'd ever thought he'd wanted.

Annie wore no make-up. She looked up at him with eyes that held no hint of the coquette. Annie had been a colleague and a friend for eight months and secretly, in her inner being, she'd held this wonder — the capacity to make his soul ache with a need that was almost overwhelming. It was a need that he'd never known he had.

And, in his shock, it was Tom who withdrew — who

pulled back and gazed at the girl before him with eyes that were dark with passion and with shock.

'Annie. . .' Tom's voice was a husky whisper.

'No!'

For a long, long moment they stared at each other in stunned silence, and then somehow Annie managed to pull away — to rise from Tom's cushions and his pillows and to haul herself out of his dangerous range.

'What. . .what do you think you're doing?' she faltered, white-faced and trembling. 'Tom. . . How dare you. . .?'

'Annie. . .' Tom made to rise but Annie took two more hasty steps away.

'No.'

'Annie, it was only a kiss. . .'

'I know.' She couldn't keep her voice from shaking. 'That's all. A kiss. . .'

Nothing, she told herself savagely. A kiss meant nothing!

'You toad. . . You toad. . .'

'You wanted to be kissed as much as I wanted to kiss you,' Tom said mildly, watching her face. 'It's not such a crime.'

'It is!'

'You're not telling me you've reached twenty-five without being kissed!'

'No! No! But it means more to me. . .'

Annie was practically in tears. How could she explain to this man that his kiss — this one kiss that meant so little to Tom McIver — had transformed her life?

Before this moment she'd known she was in love with Tom, but she'd also known that such a love was crazy and senseless and she could live her life here, knowing she was being stupid.

But how could she go on now?

Tom stood motionless, watching her across the clearing. Annie had all the signs of a frightened deer, ready to bolt for cover. 'Annie, I'm sorry — but I wanted to kiss you badly,' he said softly.

'Well, I don't know why you should,' she managed, and there was even a trace of crossness in her voice. 'Unless it's just because I'm female.'

'Meaning I'll go after anything in a skirt.'

'*Yes!*'

Tell it like it is!

'I see.' And, damn him, the laughter was flooding back into Tom's eyes.

'It's true, isn't it?' Annie felt confusion give way to anger. How dared he make her feel like this — how dared he! 'How many women have you gone out with in the valley since I've been here?' she demanded. 'I must be pretty much the only one you haven't asked. Does that pique your pride, Tom McIver? One woman left untouched. . . Is that why you're trying to make love to me?'

'It's not true.' Tom was almost as off balance as Annie. Despite the laughter, there was still confusion in his eyes.

'I'm no scalp to be added to your belt.'

Tom rose and took two long strides off the rug to where Annie was standing. Strong hands caught her shoulders and held her. He looked down into her face long and hard, searching behind the defiance.

And what he saw there made him draw in his breath.

'Annie, you're no scalp,' he told her strongly. 'Don't ever think I'd do that to you, Annie. Don't!'

'But. . .'

'You're afraid.'

'I'm not! Why should I be afraid?'

'I won't hurt you, Annie.'

'I know you won't hurt me,' Annie snapped, trying desperately to haul herself free. 'You won't hurt me because I won't let myself be hurt. Last night you kissed Sarah. Now you kiss me. And you say I'm not another scalp!'

'You're different from Sarah.'

'I'm different to the lot of them,' Annie said harshly. 'You don't want me, Tom McIver. You're just filling in time until the next Sarah flies into your orbit. Or the next Melissa. Or whoever. . .'

And then, at the sound of a tiny whimper behind her, Annie gave a sob of relief. She hauled herself away from him and reached into the baby capsule to retrieve his daughter. She lifted Hannah into her arms and held the little girl before her defensively.

'Tom, stop playing games,' she said, and her words were pleading. Her wide eyes looked up at Tom and her words tumbled out too fast. 'You must. . .you must get your life in order. Going from woman to woman. . . Living the life you do. . . Tom, you have to stop. . .stop this. . .play-acting. . .if you're serious about giving this little one a home. . .'

Tom's eyes were dark and fathomless. 'It's not play-acting, Annie. And I *am* serious.'

'Really?'

'Really.'

Silence.

And Tom stood motionless, staring at the girl before him. Annie stood, slight and confused, with her bare toes curled into the moss and her arms holding his daughter against her breast. Woman and child. . . Tom took one more step forward—and then he stopped, stunned.

He looked like someone who'd been hit by a vision. Or a lightning bolt.

Annie tightened her hold on Hannah. Reassured by Annie's arms that adults were present and her food supply hadn't been cut off, the baby ceased her whimpering, nestled happily in Annie's arms and cooed. While Annie stared up at Tom in bewilderment.

'Tom, what is it?'

'I've just had a thought,' Tom said blankly. 'It's. . . Annie, it's. . .'

'What thought?' Annie said impatiently — exasperated. 'Tom. . .'

'It's something Helen said to me before she went off duty this morning. I thought she was crazy, but now. . . Annie, she was right and I think I must have been crazy not to see it. She was right all the time.'

'What. . .'

'Annie, will you marry me?'

CHAPTER SIX

ANNIE gaped. And gaped some more.

Then Tom finally recovered some of his equilibrium. After all, he'd had two whole minutes longer than Annie to get used to the idea.

'Close your mouth, Annie,' Tom said at last, his ridiculous laughter surfacing again. 'You'll catch flies.'

'Tell me what you just said,' Annie managed faintly, and Tom smiled.

Of course he smiled. The man treated life as a permanent joke. Only this joke was sick. Cruel. But. . . Tom didn't sound as if he was joking. Only the words he was saying weren't making sense.

'I'm asking you to marry me, Annie,' Tom said gently, still smiling. 'There's no need to look so dumbfounded.'

Annie took a ragged breath—and steadied herself.

'Oh, of course,' she muttered, gathering strength as well as indignation. Some joke! 'Of course,' she repeated, her anger growing. 'No need at all to look surprised! Good grief, Tom McIver! On Friday night Melissa hands over *your* baby. Saturday night you tell me you're marrying Sarah. And now. . . Now you kiss *me* and ask me to marry you. Totally logical, really! Why didn't I expect it? It's a wonder I didn't rush out this morning to buy a wedding dress.' She lifted her eyes to his, and her eyes flashed with fury.

'Do you have an engagement ring for me, Tom?' she demanded. 'And is it my size? Or is it Sarah's? Or Melissa's? Or does it fit someone I haven't even heard of yet? Tomorrow's lover.'

'Annie. . .'

'Don't mess me around, Tom,' she snapped. 'You

can make sick jokes with all your other damned women — but not with me. I thought I was a doormat — but now I see that it's all your other women who are the doormats. You use women, Tom McIver, *and you're not using me.*'

'I don't. . .'

But Annie was no longer listening. 'I'm walking home,' she snapped. 'You can just stay here and try and think of some other lover you can add to your stupid list. Some other doormat.'

And before Tom had a chance to reply she whirled round and hiked off as fast as her legs could carry her — over the sand hills to the beach beyond.

She would have headed for the road, but Tom was in her path to the road and there was a way home along the beach.

Annie forgot one thing.

She forgot she was carrying a baby. Tom's baby. Fifty yards across the sand hills, when she suddenly realized Hannah was still in her arms, it seemed impossible to turn, to go back and hand over Hannah. By that time Tom was already moving after her.

To run while carrying a baby in her arms was well night impossible. If Annie had stomped off any faster over the soft sand she would have tripped and fallen. Even so, by the time Tom caught her — by the simple expedient of moving quickly past her and then turning to block her path — Annie was out of breath and out of places to run.

She'd headed straight for the sea. Now she stood just where the waves reached in their incoming rush, and the wet sand oozed up through her bare toes. Baulked, she stood still and glared as Tom placed his hands on her shoulders. And in her arms Hannah gurgled her delight at all this action.

'Can I have my daughter back?' Tom said mildly, and Annie glared some more.

'You don't deserve her, you womanizing toad. . .'

'I'm not a womanizer.'

'Oh, no?'

'Look, Annie, I don't sleep with every woman I go out with!' Tom sounded exasperated.

'How very discriminating!' Annie was almost past speaking. Fury was threatening to choke her.

And, in her arms, Hannah chuckled.

Tom gave his daughter a sideways grin—and then focused on Annie again, as if politely assuring her of the importance of what she was saying.

Patronizing. . .arrogant. . .

'Annie, it may come as a surprise to you, but you're the very first woman I've ever proposed to.'

'Oh, really? How very kind of you! And I'm supposed to go down on bended knee with gratitude?'

'Well, a bit of common courtesy might be nice,' Tom said bluntly. 'I don't see what I've done to have you react with anger. Honestly, Annie, think about it. Helen said if I was serious about finding a wife I should look no further than you. I thought she was crazy and then, when I kissed you, I suddenly saw she was right. It would be sensible.'

'Sensible?' Annie's voice was rising fast to a squeak. 'What could be sensible about marrying you?'

Tom gave his daughter another grin, and then transferred his smile to Annie. 'Annie, we could be a family. The three of us.'

'Oh, yeah?' Annie managed in between angry gasps. 'Three? There aren't just three, though, are there, Tom McIver? There's a whole menagerie. Me and you and Hannah, and your two idiot dogs—and every other unattached woman in this town. And probably even a few attached ones as well.'

Tom sighed. 'Annie, I am *not* a womanizer!'

'So you keep saying. Pull the other leg. It plays *Jingle Bells*.'

'Annie. . .'

'I'm going home!'

'Would you like to give me my daughter back first?' Tom asked mildly. 'You know possession's nine tenths of the law. If you keep her she's yours.'

Annie glared. 'You'd like that, wouldn't you?' Annie said bitterly. 'A nice convenient mother for your child. Knock a hole between our two apartments and push Hannah through to me whenever you're entertaining one of your —'

'Annie, I am offering you a serious marriage proposal.' Tom's smile faded as his voice rose in exasperation. He lifted his daughter from her arms and then glared straight back at Annie, anger meeting anger. 'I'm serious, Annie. I do mean it when I say we could be a family. And families mean faithfulness.'

'Oh, sure,' Annie jeered. 'You'd be faithful to me — as payment — while I care for you and your daughter and your two dogs.' She paused as the sound of the dogs' barking reached a crescendo, the noise momentarily — blessedly — distracting her. 'And if you don't stop your dogs chasing birds, Dr McIver, I'll report you to the RSPCA. They're killing something.'

'The birds are enjoying their exercise,' Tom retorted. 'If you think any bird stands in danger of being caught then you don't know Tiny and Hoof. Look, Annie. . .'

But Annie was no longer listening. She'd turned blindly to watch the birds — to see anything but Tom McIver's face — and she hadn't seen any birds. What she saw. . .

'Tom!'

Tom stopped in mid-sentence at the sudden urgency in Annie's voice. Annie was staring along the beach where the dogs were barking themselves frantic. Instead of their bird-chasing, though, the dogs had transferred their attention to something along the beach where the river met the sea.

'Tom, they're not chasing birds,' Annie said urgently, her own attention changing direction as swiftly as the dogs' had done. 'Tom, there's a boat in trouble!'

'A boat. . .' Tom stared blankly up the beach. 'Annie. . .'

'I saw it,' Annie said faintly. 'Upside down in the river mouth. The waves are washing over it. It's under now but watch!'

Hannah was unceremoniously thrust back into Annie's arms as Tom swivelled round. 'I can't see. . .'

'It's under water now. Tom. . .I think I saw someone. . .just for a minute. . . But I think he was washed off when it went under.'

But Tom was no longer beside her. He was already running up the beach.

So, what *did* one do in an emergency when one was left holding the baby?

Annie stared down at Hannah's tiny face while her mind clicked into gear. OK. First things first. Call for help and find somewhere safe to put Hannah.

Then, forgetting to fret about stumbling, she ran almost as fast as Tom, but in the direction of the car and mobile phone. One fast phone call to the ambulance.

'Dave, a boat's hit rocks at the river entrance. It's upside down and someone's in trouble. I don't know any more.'

'I'll contact the lifeboat crew and be with you in five minutes,' Dave growled and shoved the phone down.

Done. What next?

Dear God, don't let Tom try to rescue someone on his own. . .

Annie grabbed the emergency bag from Tom's luggage compartment. What else? A rope. . .if there was one. . . Blessedly, there was. A coil of rope lay with Tom's car tools. Annie looped it round her neck, put Hannah back in her baby capsule and set off again at a run, capsule at one side and medical bag at the other.

The bag and baby capsule combined weighed a ton. At the end of this Annie's arms might have been stretched six inches longer, but now her burden hardly slowed her at all.

Hannah must wonder just what sort of crazy life she'd tumbled into, Annie thought wryly as the baby jogged up and down at Annie's side. She lay back in her baby capsule and gurgled and watched and enjoyed every minute of this new experience. She was some baby! She was Tom's daughter in every way.

There was a rocky outcrop where the river met the sea, a bank of sorts, providing a sheltered entrance at low tide. But it was high tide now and the water was crashing over the edge. From where they'd stood on the beach Annie had been able to see over it, but closer she couldn't.

'OK, Hannah, you're on your own,' she muttered as she reached the rocks, the thought of Tom fighting his way through the water on the other side of the bank making her priorities easy. Hannah would be safe enough—much safer than Tom!

Tom's two great dogs were standing on the bank. Their barking had stopped and they were wearing identical expressions of dog-like concern. They looked as fearful as Annie felt.

So. . .

So Annie placed Hannah above the high-water mark on the sand, checked that the baby was facing away from the sun and then clambered up the bank to see. And drew in her breath in horror.

The boat was almost submerged. Whoever was in charge of the boat had headed in when the water had been too high to make the entrance safe. Annie had been warned of this place when she'd first moved here.

'The entrance is safe when the water's low across the rocks, but as soon as the rocks are submerged there are all sorts of currents and cross-waves that'll crash a boat into the wall. If you go out at low tide, make sure you get back in before the water rises.'

Annie had never been tempted to try, but this time. . .

Whoever was in the boat had tried and failed. The boat had smashed into the rocks. Annie could see a mass of shattered wood that was the sinking hull, but the man Annie had thought she'd seen was nowhere in sight.

Tom was. Just.

He was swimming strongly across the current, and Annie caught her breath in fear at the sight of him. Tom was a strong swimmer but the waves were breaking over the rocks, sending spray over the ledge Annie had climbed, and the sea inside the river mouth was a maelstrom of white water.

He couldn't make it. . .

Dear God. . .

There was nothing she could do. Annie stood uselessly on the bank, clutching the doctor's bag like a talisman, watching. She never took her eyes from Tom.

He reached the upturned hull. There were waves hitting it from both sides. The man must have been an idiot to try and come through. In these conditions, the only safe thing to do was to wait for low tide. He couldn't have known. . . And now he was putting Tom at risk.

Annie allowed herself a fierce glance around, willing the surf lifeboat to appear from the ocean or the ambulance from the landside. Of course it was too soon. There was nothing—only Tom. And then Tom disappeared, diving under the hull.

The world stopped. Ten seconds. Twenty. Thirty. . .

Annie was counting in her head. Thirty-two. . . Thirty-three. . . How long could he hold his breath?

And then Tom's head broke the surface, and in his grasp he had what he'd been searching for. The body of a man. . .

Annie dumped the bag on the ledge, wedging it so that it couldn't be swept away, and scrambled down to where the waves broke over her. She went as far as she dared into the water, keeping a fierce toe-hold on her rocks. Before Tom could drag the man anywhere near her she was looping her rope and spreading her hands, trying to work out when she could reasonably throw it.

The currents were swirling round in shifting patterns. It was past high tide now and the bulk of the water was moving out to sea. Tom swam on his side, concentrating fiercely on keeping the man's head out of water. He was making no headway at all—and he was being slowly swept out to sea.

Now! Her brain screamed the word at her, even though she knew she could hardly reach him. But if she didn't throw it now. . .

Annie wedged the end of the rope under her foot, eighteen inches under water. Then, holding the loop as wide and high as she could, Annie threw with every ounce of strength she possessed.

It landed four feet short.

Sobbing in terror, Annie hauled the rope back in, but Tom had seen what she was doing. He looked fleetingly back at her—and then Annie knew he was kicking himself toward her with superhuman strength.

He couldn't make it. It was up to her.

She looped—and threw.

Tom let one hand loose from his burden, grabbed—and held.

Annie hauled for her life—and two minutes later Tom was scrambling up the rocks, with Annie helping him drag his lifeless burden after him.

'Mask. . .' Exhausted beyond belief, Tom was hardly able to speak as he dragged himself out of the water. 'I've got him. We can't. . . Oh, God, get the mask, Annie. . .'

Annie was already moving, fighting her way out of the water to reach the bag.

It was a dreadful place to try resuscitation. On dry sand it would have been difficult enough, but there was no time to carry him to the beach. Instead, Tom and Annie used their bodies to block the wash of water as they fought desperately to find some response.

'Breathe, damn you. Breathe.' Tom pumped rhythmically on the man's chest as Annie worked the mask. Tirelessly they worked, knowing the man had a chance. If Annie had seen him above the surface then he couldn't have been under water for more than five minutes.

Breathe... And finally he did — a raw, choking splutter that turned into a vomit of sea water. And another.

And then the man's eyes opened and he looked up in a haze of bewilderment.

'Wh —' He couldn't speak. The word spluttered into a cough and he fell back.

'You're safe. Take it easy.' Tom held the man's head slightly raised. There was still urgency in his voice, though. He'd thought what Annie hadn't dared to think. 'But tell us whether there was anyone else on board. Was there anyone with you? We need to know *now*!'

Silence.

Annie was scarcely breathing herself.

Blessedly, the man shook his head.

Dear God...

And then, suddenly, there were people everywhere. Dave and his partner were racing across the sand with oxygen and a stretcher, and out to sea the lifeboat appeared around the headland, with its captain shouting through a megaphone.

Annie squatted back and felt like bursting into tears.

'Don't do it, Dr Burrows,' Tom said gently before they all arrived. 'It'll destroy your reputation as a dour lady doctor.' He reached out and touched her gently on the face. 'And your hair is still hanging free and you're minus glasses and you've just saved my life... And you look...you look...' He broke off, but not before Annie heard the raw emotion in his voice.

She didn't deserve what he was saying.

'I did not save your life,' she whispered. 'You did it yourself...'

'We would have been swept out onto the rocks on

the reef. . .' Tom shook his head and then smiled down at the man, still struggling to catch his breath. 'Take your time, mate. Thanks to this lady, you have all the time in the world.'

'Thanks to you both. . .' The man choked, gasped and fell silent.

After that, there was little more for Annie to do.

The lifeboat went disconsolately home, the boys irked that it wasn't them who'd done the rescuing, and the ambulancemen loaded their patient onto a stretcher. Tom set up an oxygen mask over the man's face, trying to get some colour back into him.

There was now no trace of the boat.

'I'll go back with the ambulance,' Tom told Annie quietly. 'He's still not breathing well and I'm not sure it's just shock. I need to check his lungs.' He hesitated. 'Can you bring the car back?'

Annie managed a smile. 'I guess. . . If you don't mind a soggy backside on your driver's seat.'

'You can put your soggy backside anywhere you please.' Tom smiled at her in a way that made Annie's heart do a back flip. 'Thank you, Annie. That's the best lassoing job I've ever seen. It seems a bit rough now to land you with my daughter and dogs.'

'I don't mind. Only this once.'

'Mmm.' Tom checked the mask again and then turned to give Annie one last smile.

'OK, that's it. Go and find yourself some dry clothes. We'll continue our picnic at some later date.'

'Tom. . .'

'Don't think I'm letting my really good idea rest in peace, Annie,' he told her, and his voice was dead serious. He put a hand up and pushed his sodden hair back from his eyes. 'The more I think of it the more I like it, Annie Burrows. All you have to learn is how sensible it is.'

Annie sighed and turned away. 'Don't! Tom, your

proposal...your proposal is about as sensible as your two dogs!'

'And my two dogs just found a man who would have drowned if he hadn't been seen,' Tom said, and his tone was dead serious. 'Sense is where you find it, Annie. Think about it.' His smile deepened. 'And, by the way, look at my dogs now.' He motioned to the beach where Annie had dumped the baby capsule.

Hannah was in good hands. The dogs had taken themselves back to where the baby lay and they stood like two stern sentinels, one on either side of the capsule.

'She's ours,' their body language said. 'We're on guard. Touch her if you dare!'

'As sensible as my two dogs?' Tom reached out and gripped Annie's hand in a gesture that was hardly more than a fleeting touch — but was as intimate as any caress. 'I happen to think that my dogs are very, very sensible. And so is my proposal.'

Hannah was taken out of Annie's care as soon as she reached the hospital. Mrs Farley, the hospital cook, fussed out as soon as she arrived back.

'You go and change, dear. The ambulance is here and we know all about it. You must be exhausted. I'll look after this one. She's such a little pet — and, by the way, I've had a really good idea about who else would love to help look after her.'

So Annie showered and changed — and then tried to figure what to do with the rest of her afternoon.

Tom didn't need her.

Albert Hopper, the boatman, was recovering. His lungs were clear enough. Rob had told her when she rang the nurses' station so Annie was free to avoid Tom as much as she liked.

It wasn't easy. The hospital was too small.

She tried to work but no one needed her. The little hospital was quiet. The only patient not asleep or knee-deep in visitors was Rod Manning, who abused her so thoroughly when she approached that she retired in haste.

'You gave that sample to the cops, you bloody bitch. Do you know what that'll cost me? You had no right. I'll sue! Just let me get out of here and get to my lawyers. And why can't you give me anything else for the pain. . .?'

Annie couldn't defend herself in the face of his fury. She boosted his painkillers as high as she dared and took herself out of range of his invective.

She tried doing paperwork in her office — but she could hear Tom moving about the little hospital. She could hear his voice giving orders, and he and Robbie laughing at a joke she couldn't hear. She couldn't work at all.

Finally she shoved her beeper on so she could be contacted in an emergency and took a sheaf of paperwork out under the gums at the back of the hospital. She found a spot where no one could find her — and settled down to dictate letters.

She couldn't stay there for ever.

She went for a long walk at dusk, and came back well after dark. Then she had to listen to Tom all over again. She heard him give Hannah her late feed. She heard the baby fuss and then settle.

After ten minutes of holding her breath there was a knock on her door which she didn't feel like answering.

What she needed here was a bit of resolution.

'Go away, Tom. It's late, I'm tired and I don't want to see you.'

Her voice echoed from the walls and Annie winced as she listened to herself. Her words sounded petty.

'Why not?' Tom's voice was bland — smooth as milk. 'Are you afraid? Is your hair still down?'

'No!' Annie snatched up her glasses and shoved them hard on her nose. Shield up! Her defences still felt fragile.

'Annie, let me in.'

'I'm too tired.'

'And I'm too tired to talk through a closed door. If I yell any louder I'll wake up patients. Come on, Annie. I need to talk.'

'What about?'

'Medicine.' Tom's voice assumed a note of pious duty. 'Annie, it's your professional duty to open the door.'

'Very subtle!' Annie glared at the closed door. 'I'll bet the big bad wolf never tried that line at the pigs' house. Why don't you just huff and puff, blow yourself out and then go away?'

'Annie, this is stupid. We need to talk.' Tom sighed heavily on the other side of the door. 'Don't you think you're being just a tiny bit paranoid?'

Annie glared some more.

'Annie?'

OK. OK. She knew she was being petty. Or just too scared for words.

Taking a deep breath, she swung the door wide and Annie's personal wolf grinned in triumph — and marched right in.

Straight through to her kitchen.

'Where do you think you're going?'

Annie stood by the door and glared. Tom was considerably dryer than the last time she'd seen him. He was wearing his white coat over clean trousers, his stethoscope swung from his neck at a crazy angle and his curls didn't look like they'd been combed after his shower. And one look at him was enough to make Annie's heart do back flips.

She had an almost irresistible urge to straighten his stethoscope — and comb his hair. Or just touch it!

'I'm making coffee,' Tom told her, ignoring her hostility. 'God knows, I need it.'

'Why don't you make coffee next door?' For some reason it was hard to make her voice work.

'Because my sink is full of bottles that need steriliz-

ing and pans from making formula. I need a
housekeeper.'

'Yeah, so you said.' Annie was talking to his back
as he filled her plunger with coffee grounds and ran
water into her kettle. 'And I'm supposed to be it.'

Tom swung around from the kettle and his face
stilled.

'Annie, I didn't ask you to be my housekeeper,' he
said gently, meeting her gaze with calmness and honesty. 'I asked you to be my wife.'

'So what's the difference?' Annie's voice was bitter,
but that was the way she was feeling. Bitter as all heck!
It was all very well for this man to throw marriage
proposals in her direction. It didn't turn *his* life
upside down.

'Hey, Annie. . .' In a few swift strides Tom crossed
back to where she still held the door open. He seized
her arms and hauled her close against his chest. Behind
her, the door closed with a thump. 'Annie, that's a crazy
question.'

Annie held herself still. The feel of Tom's chest
against her breasts was making her heart thump. Somehow, though, she had to make herself say it.

'You. . .you mean you want me for sex as well as
housework?'

Silence.

Carefully Tom let go his grip on her. He stood for a
long, silent moment, staring down at her troubled face,
and then he turned and went back to his coffee.

'Let's start this again, shall we?' he said politely,
concentrating on the coffee. 'Can I make you a drink?'

'I don't want one. I want to go to bed.' Annie was
being as rude as she could, but she didn't seem to have
a choice. Her heart felt as if it were shrivelling inside.
Tom was offering her something she'd dreamed of for
years, and she was thrusting it away as worthless.

No. It wasn't true.

Tom wasn't offering her her dream. Tom was offering her marriage. And what Annie wanted — all Annie wanted — was Tom's love. One without the other didn't make sense at all.

So now she did what she'd always done in times of distress. Retired into her work.

'How's Albert?' she asked, and crossed the room to sit on a kitchen chair. The chair was hard and she sat stiffly upright. Her body felt as if it were about to snap.

'He's not good.' Tom's face snapped down in a frown, following her lead back into medicine as he carried his coffee to the table.

'His lungs are clear enough, and he'll recover from shock, but his ego's taken such a dent it'll take a while to mend. If it ever does. He's fished that entrance so many times he reckons he knows it like the back of his hand. His wife came to see me tonight and says he can hardly speak to her. . . Can hardly look at her. . . And his boat wasn't insured.'

'Oh, no. . .'

Tom shrugged. 'Albert's lectured local kids time and time again on the danger of the bar. The fact that he broke the rules — and nearly lost his life, doing it — will take some living down.' He met her eyes and managed a smile. 'Familiarity breeds contempt, they say. Maybe it's true. Like me and you, Annie. I was so familiar with you I never saw what was before my eyes.'

'Tom, don't.' Annie flinched and stared at her hands. She stayed silent while Tom drank his coffee — and while he quietly watched her.

'Shouldn't you be getting back to Hannah?' she murmured as he set down his empty mug.

'She's just through this wall, and I can hear every whimper. It's no different to being in the next room. Now, if we knocked a door between us. . .'

'No!'

'Annie, why the hell not?'

'Tom, I won't go knocking holes in walls — and I won't be getting married just because you need a babysitter.' Annie's breath was coming in painful gasps. 'I won't. And, besides. . .'

'Besides?'

'I don't know whether you've considered, but marrying me wouldn't solve your problems. In an emergency we're both needed. You're much better off marrying someone like Sarah.'

'I don't want to marry Sarah.'

'Well, keep looking for someone else.'

'I don't want to keep looking either,' Tom said softly, watching Annie so steadily that colour started sweeping across her face. 'Unless it's at you. I've decided you have the cutest nose of anyone I know.'

'You're not telling me you've fallen in love with me since this afternoon?' Annie's words were practically a jeer. Her whole consciousness was twisting in pain.

'Well, no. . .'

'There you go, then.' Annie stood up so fast that she jolted the table and made Tom's mug slip sideways. 'End of story.'

'Are you saying you'll only marry if you fall in love?' Tom stayed exactly where he was, his voice calmly meditative. His calmness made Annie's pain worse.

But somehow she made her voice stay calm to match his. 'Tom, I doubt if I'll ever marry.' The pain of Tom's words in her first week at Bannockburn swept over her in bitter memory. 'And I thought. . .I thought an old-maid doctor was what you wanted here.'

'Who told you that?' Tom's face had stilled.

'I heard it,' Annie said bitterly. 'I heard you say it the first week I was here. That's what you wanted — but now you think I might be more useful as something else. A little domestic appendage. . .'

'Annie, stop this!' Tom rose, kicked his chair out of the way and came round to Annie's side of the table. Her white face told him exactly how distressed she was.

'Hell, Annie, I might have said that once — but I didn't mean to hurt you. . .'

'Well, you have.' Annie's voice was a jagged whisper.

'Then I'm sorry, but let's leave it.' Tom reached out to hold her again, his hands gripping her shoulders and his head tilting so he could look into her pain-filled eyes. 'Let's leave it as something I might have thought before I knew you. Annie, don't look so upset. I'm not asking you to marry me tomorrow.' The irrepressible grin burst out. 'Next Saturday's fine. That's six whole days to sort yourself out.'

'Tom. . .'

'I know. I know.' His smile became placating, affectionate, intimate. 'I'm pushing. In fact, there's a four-week waiting period before we can legally do it. But it does seem like a great idea, Annie.'

'Great for whom?' Annie made a huge effort to make her voice work properly. She glared up at Tom and found his eyes inches from hers. Too close by half. 'What's in it for me, Tom?' she managed. 'You stand to gain a babysitter and a dogsitter and a domestic convenience. What do I stand to gain?'

'Well, I beat a hot-water bottle!'

It was said so fast — so blatantly — that Annie gave a startled jolt within Tom's hold — and stared. Despite her confusion, the sides of her mouth curved into laughter.

Toad!

'I prefer a hot-water bottle that doesn't take half the bed.' Somehow Annie fought her insidious laughter back and she shook her head. 'No, Tom. The idea's crazy.'

'It's not crazy, Annie. Think about it.' He stood back from her, but his eyes didn't leave her face. 'Annie, we've both come from backgrounds where we've learned that romantic love is for the birds. Your dad walked out and my parents were dysfunctional, to say the least. We've had a rough deal with our families.

'Maybe. . .maybe a marriage that's based on common sense and friendship might be ideal. And I know we could be good together. I felt that in one short kiss. And you felt it, too. We pack a powerful punch, Annie Burrows, and we could have a very satisfying long-term partnership.'

They could. Or, rather, he could.

Romantic love is for the birds. . .

Tom's hands were holding hers now, making her feel wanted and cherished and all the things she could never be.

Solid, sensible Annie. . .

How would Tom McIver cope with such a marriage when he realized his wife was absolutely, totally in love with him? Annie wondered dully. She was so in love that if Tom treated her as a useful friend and nothing more it would tear her heart in two.

Oh, God, why did it have to be so hard?

Why couldn't she just say, 'Yes, I'll marry you.'

Because. . .because she wanted such an announcement to be met with joy. With a love and commitment to match her own.

If she said it now — said, 'Yes, I'll marry you' — Tom would just as likely give her a perfunctory kiss of satisfaction and take himself to bed. To *his* bed. On *his* side of the wall.

Bargain sealed. A nice satisfactory contract. He'd have found a steady, sensible mother for his daughter.

Well, Annie wasn't it!

'I'm not marrying you, Tom,' Annie told him, and only she knew the pain her words were causing within her heart. 'I'm not marrying anyone.'

And she knew what else she had to say.

'And I can't stay here,' she added, and she watched as Tom's eyes widened. 'Not now. Not. . .not with this between us. I'll stay until you have the chance to find another doctor for the town. But consider that I've handed in my notice.'

'I'm leaving, Tom. I wish you the best of luck with your daughter. With your life. But. . .but I don't have any part in it.'

CHAPTER SEVEN

SOMEHOW Annie got some sleep that night—but not very much. She woke, feeling as if she'd been run over by a train, and her face, when she worked up enough courage to look in the mirror, told her too much the same.

Her mother and sister would have too much sense to cry themselves to sleep, she told herself crossly. Showered and dressed, she made a dive out to the dispensary to find eye-drops. They made her eyes feel better but they didn't reduce the swelling.

'So. . .it's clinic in dark glasses this morning,' she muttered, and headed out to face the world through green-tinted frames.

'Dr Burrows, why are you wearing sunglasses inside?' The first nurse she saw asked the question when Annie wasn't two feet inside the hospital corridor. She muttered something about hayfever and felt like bolting for cover.

It was worse when Robbie saw her. The nursing administrator checked out Annie's glasses and said nothing at all.

'I have hayfever,' Annie said defiantly. Robbie just nodded.

And pigs fly, his look said.

Then Tom came out of a side ward and the urge to bolt became almost overwhelming but, mercifully, Tom was acting as though nothing at all was between them.

'Dr Burrows, we need to set Rod Manning's arm this morning,' Tom said briefly, ignoring her glasses. 'The sooner we get the thing set and get him out of here the happier I'll be.'

'You mean he's still furious?'

'His temper hasn't subsided with his alcohol level.'

Tom grimaced with distaste. 'I've been in touch with Melbourne this morning and they say Kylie's leg will be fine. She'll have a little residual stiffness but, with luck, she may well walk again without a limp. And the plastic surgeon is happy with Betty's face. I've told Rod, but he acts as if everything is our fault.'

'I guess he can't accept that the fault's his.'

'No.' Tom sighed. 'I'm afraid he has it in for you, Annie. I can't get it through his thick head that you were legally required to provide the police with a blood sample. Anyway, he's been nil-by-mouth since midnight, and I've given him a pre-med to quieten him down before you anaesthetize him — but you're still in for some invective. I'm sorry.'

'I can handle it.' For heaven's sake, Rod's temper was the least of her problems. 'When do we start?'

'Half an hour.'

'I can do that.' And she set her face and proceeded with her ward round.

Annie discharged Murray, and checked the rest of the patients before Robbie pounced, and pounce he did. She might have known there was no keeping him at bay.

'Am I imagining it, or is there an atmosphere of tension in this hospital this morning?' Robbie demanded as she returned to the nurses' station to fill in Murray's discharge notes. 'And. . . Dr Burrows, are you intending to operate in sunglasses?'

Annie hauled off her glasses and glared at her notes. 'No.'

'So. . . Are you going to tell Uncle Robbie what's wrong?'

'Double no.'

'How about if I pick you up and put you on the filing cabinet and refuse to let you down until you tell me?'

Annie glared.

'You're the nurse, Robbie McKenzie. And I'm the

doctor. The handbook says I'm the one that's supposed to be bossy.'

'Yeah, but I'm still bigger than you.' Robbie smiled down at her, his kindly face sympathetic. 'And, as of this minute, I'm on coffee-break. That means that I'm your friend. Come on, Annie. I can tell you've been having a howl. Ignore the beard and treat me as a mother substitute.'

Annie took a deep breath and looked up at Robbie. He wouldn't leave it, she knew. He had to know some time. Only. . .there was no easy way to say this.

'It's only. . .I'm leaving.'

'Leaving?' Robbie stared. 'You mean. . .leaving Bannockburn?'

'That's right. As soon as T — As soon as Dr McIver can find a replacement.'

'And why would you be doing that?' Robbie's eyes carefully and slowly perused Annie's ravaged face. 'Has our Dr McIver being upsetting you, then?'

'No.'

'No?'

Annie bit her lip. She picked up a patient chart and then put it down again. Chris — the nurse who specialled in romance novels — came into the station and started checking medication sheets. Her ears almost visibly flapped.

And Robbie watched.

The problem with the nurses in this hospital was that they were just too darned good, Annie thought desperately. Tom hand-picked them for their caring natures and their perception, and here it was in force — caring and perception.

Robbie wasn't about to be fobbed off with a half-truth, and neither was Chris. Chris might pretend to be reading medication charts, but Annie knew she was as concerned about Annie's sunglasses as Robbie — and just as determined to know the cause.

So. . . So the truth, the whole truth and nothing but the truth!

'Dr McIver's asked me to marry him,' she said bluntly, and watched two face freeze in shock.

'Bloody hell!' Robbie's jaw dropped a foot or so.

'Oh, Annie!'

'Well. . .' Annie took a deep breath and burrowed her hands deep in the pockets of her white coat. 'You must see how impossible it is for me to work with him after that. So I'm leaving.'

'That's ridiculous.'

'It's what I'm doing.' Annie took a deep breath, grabbed her patient charts and headed for the door — to find her way blocked by Robbie's massive shoulders.

'Are you seriously telling us you'd leave Bannockburn rather than marry our Dr Tom?' he demanded incredulously.

'Rob, don't. . .'

Robbie wasn't listening. A chair was suddenly under Annie. Chris had pushed the swivel chair forward, it had caught Annie under the knees and she'd sat down hard. She was stuck, with two nurses standing over her. Each had one hand on her shoulders — Robbie on one side and Chris on the other — like secret service interrogators.

'Tell us all,' Chris gasped. 'Now! I thought Dr McIver was in love with straw-brained Sarah.'

'He might well be,' Annie said bitterly. 'I wouldn't know. Love's got nothing to do with what he's offering. Can I get up now, please?'

'Not until you've told us everything,' Chris demanded, she and Robbie pushing Annie down again in unison. 'Oh, Annie. . .you and Dr McIver. Wouldn't that be wonderful? Robbie, think about it. . .'

'We could knock the two doctors' apartments into one again.' Robbie grinned his pleasure at the idea. 'They were one big house originally, you know. We had a hell of a time splitting them in two. The bedrooms become one huge living room that looks right out over the river.'

'But. . .'

'And as you have more kids. . .well, we could put an intercom between here and there. Another ward maid to cover the extra work, or a permanent nurse in children's ward. . . Annie, it's perfect.'

'Robbie. . .'

'Oh, and think of the wedding!' Chris looked over at Robbie with stars in her eyes. 'The romance I'm reading now. . . The heroine marries on the beach. . . Bare feet and a simple white dress and her hair hanging free. And the dolphins come in. . . And their two hearts become one. . . Oh, Annie, that's what you should have. A beach wedding. Just like that.'

'I dunno about the dolphins,' Robbie said dubiously. 'I don't think they come to weddings on command. But the rest. . .' His broad face broke into a grin of pure delight. 'Hell, I could even be matron of honour. Just wait until my wife hears about this!'

'Will you two cut it out?' Annie was practically yelling. 'I am *not* marrying Dr McIver!'

One of the domestic staff, scuttling past on early morning collection of menus, cast a startled glance at the trio and scuttled even faster toward the kitchen. Her eyes were as big as saucers.

The news was definitely out.

There'd be no silence in the kitchen now, Annie knew, but there was silence here. Annie sat, wedged between her two interrogators, and glared for all she was worth. Chris and Robbie looked at each other — and took a step back.

'Oh, my dear, of course you are,' Robbie said softly, but there was understanding in his voice as well as pleasure. 'It's such a good idea.'

'For whom?' Annie said bluntly, and Robbie had the nerve to grin again.

'For us, of course. If Dr McIver marries Sarah I'd

imagine he'll live off the premises, and it's much more convenient for us if he lives here.'

'And we don't like Sarah,' Chris said honestly. 'She gives herself airs now. Can you imagine her as the doctor's wife? And if you think any of the other hair-brained twits he's taken out have been any better. . .'

'He picks 'em for their bodies,' Robbie said sagely.

'Well, he didn't pick me because of my body.' Annie rose and backed to the door. 'He picked me because I'll be a good, sensible mother for the family he's envisaging. Our Dr McIver suddenly has a daughter and he realizes it's going to be inconvenient to play sole parent. So. . .so he thinks he'll share the load.'

'Is that how he put it?' Robbie said doubtfully. 'Bloody hell. . .' Clearly he was starting to see where Annie's problem lay.

'So marry him and ask questions later,' Chris said blithely. 'That's what I'd do if someone as dishy as Dr McIver asked me.'

'Yeah, well, no one's likely to because you're a flea-brain,' Robbie said bluntly. 'Annie can't marry him if all he wants is a babysitter.'

'If all he wanted was a babysitter he could have me. Or any one of fifty girls within calling distance.' Chris grinned. 'Annie, I know the paperback romances talk about love and stuff, but honest by. . . Does it really happen in real life? I mean, all the heroes in my books have pecs bigger than footballs — and everything else to match. In real life I've never met any guy like that unless they were out of their brains with steroids. Even Tom McIver has pecs within the normal range. We girls have to take what we can get.'

'But. . .I fell in love with my wife,' Robbie said dubiously, and he reddened under his beard. 'Just like in the books. . .'

'Of course you did.' Annie glared at Chris. 'See? It does happen. There's no earthly reason for me to marry

Tom — and him asking me is an insult. I can't work
with him. . .'

'You can work with us, though,' Robbie said, and
his voice was suddenly bleak. As if he realized the
force of Annie's argument. As if he knew Annie would
have to go.

'Oh, of course I can.' Annie's eyes filled with sudden
tears and she blinked them away with a fierce effort.
She rose and gave Robbie a swift hug, then turned away
before her eyes could fill again. 'Or I could until this
happened. You're the best workmates. But. . .but I
have to go.'

She blinked and made her way down toward Theatre
as fast as her legs could carry her.

Tom was already scrubbing.

'So, where's Hannah?' Annie asked as she donned
theatre gown and mask. She wasn't about to look at
him, but it was hard not to.

'With my housekeeper,' Tom said blandly, and Annie
blinked.

'I beg your pardon?'

'You heard,' he told her.

'You didn't have a housekeeper when I went to bed
last night,' Annie said cautiously, and Tom grinned
behind his mask.

'Nope. I advertised fast.'

'I see.' She didn't see at all. Who was it, then? Sarah?
Or the next in line?

'Don't look so suspicious, girl,' Tom complained.
'Cook found her. Edna Harris is fifty-five years old and
a happily established widow. Edna intends to grieve
placidly for her hubby for the next thirty years. She's
not interested in men — but she loves babies. So you
haven't been supplanted in my affections.'

'That's amazing,' Annie said dryly. 'I was Sunday's
bride. I thought for sure you'd have Monday's edition
by now.'

'Annie. . .'

'Rod's ready to go,' Annie said severely, motioning through the open door to where Chris was wheeling in the trolley. 'Maybe we could concentrate on our work?'

'Maybe we could defer this conversation for an hour or so,' Tom agreed. 'But it isn't going to go away, Annie. No matter how hard you try to avoid it.'

The procedure was trickier than expected, for which Annie was profoundly grateful.

First Annie had to anaesthetize Rod — an unpleasant task as he berated her until he lost consciousness. Because Rod Manning was overweight and a smoker, he was tricky to intubate. Then she had to stand not four feet from Tom while he carefully positioned the broken limb, and concentrate on something that wasn't him.

All the time Chris, as theatre nurse, watched Tom and Annie with bright-eyed interest, and Annie knew every look — every nuance — between Tom and herself would be reported happily from one end of the hospital to the other.

Tom had destroyed their working relationship, Annie thought savagely as she finally reversed the anaesthetic. It was finished. She couldn't work with him. It was going to take a superhuman effort to stay here until he could find someone else.

'I'd like you to advertise at once for a replacement,' she told him as Chris wheeled their recovering patient out of Theatre. 'You shouldn't have any trouble getting someone.'

'Your contract is for a year.'

'I'm breaking my contract,' Annie said brusquely. 'If I thought you'd have trouble finding someone then I'd worry, but you won't. So sue me, if you must, but I'm leaving anyway.'

'You don't think your reaction might be just a bit over the top?' Tom said mildly, watching her face. 'I've asked you to marry me, and you've said no. Why the histrionics?'

'I'm not indulging in histrionics.' Annie hauled her theatre gown off and threw it into the laundry basket with more violence than it deserved.

'Annie, I haven't offered you an indecent proposal.' Tom's voice was a study in patience. Experienced doctor coping with hysterical patient. 'I've offered you a sensible and respectable position. It's hardly enough to make you run.'

No. It wasn't. Annie acknowledged the truth of what he said with an inward grimace. But how could she tell him why she was running. . .? She couldn't say, 'It's because I love you, Tom. I can't marry you because I love you. For me, the marriage is no sensible and respectable position. I can't be sensible when I'm near you. And I can't stay here because I love you.' She couldn't.

Instead, she shook her head and headed for the door.

'Annie. . .' Tom caught her wrist and held it. His eyes were suddenly concerned. 'Hell, Annie, what is it?'

'If you don't know. . .'

'Don't know what?'

'That most marriage proposals have the power to change lives,' Annie whispered. 'They change relationships. I can't stay here with you now, Tom. Not now. Not when you've messed everything up. . .'

'By giving you a sensible proposal?'

'How is it sensible?' Annie managed. 'You hardly know me.'

'I do know you, Annie,' Tom told her, and his voice was suddenly dead serious. 'I do. I accept that I haven't seen you as a desirable woman—until yesterday, that is. But I've seen you as a colleague. And what I've seen I like. You're clever. You're kind. You're dedicated to your work and to this hospital. You think about other people and you have a habit of keeping me on the straight and narrow. You're the only woman I know who questions what I do —'

'It sounds like I'd make a great governess,' Annie burst out. 'Not a wife.'

'Maybe I should be the judge of that.'

'I see.' Annie was dangerously close to tears. She fought them back and stood her ground. 'And. . .what sort of husband would you make, Dr McIver? What are you offering?'

'I told you. . . I'd be faithful.'

'I'll adopt Tiny and Hoof if I want faithfulness,' Annie retorted. 'And company. They come with a better track record.'

'Are you offering to take on my dogs?' Tom's ready laughter sprang into his eyes, and Annie backed to the door.

'No way. I'm just saying they'd be as good as you. Better.'

'They eat more. And they snore.'

Was he never serious? Annie winced and reached behind her to open the door.

Chris was still outside in Recovery, standing by Rod's trolley. Her ears were tuned straight to 'receive'.

'Annie, don't go.' Tom stopped her, walking forward and shutting the door on Chris and the outside world again to prevent her leaving. Then he leaned against the door, his long frame dwarfing her and his twinkling eyes looking down with a smile which was nearly her undoing.

'Annie, I'll be a good husband,' he said gently. 'I promise you that. It's true I'm not marrying for romantic reasons. I need. . .I need a mother for my daughter. I need a family. I've suddenly realized that, and I know you haven't made that same decision.

'But I believe a family might suit you, too. It could give us both a stability that's been missing in our lives. I'd be a friend, Annie. Your friend. Someone batting for you. I'd be in your corner — and I'd be in your corner for life. I think that's an offer worth considering.

I know I want you in my corner, Annie, and I'd like to be in yours.'

Annie looked blindly up at him, and it was all she could do not to let her head fall against his chest and hold him tight. . . But he wanted no such thing.

Tom was looking down at her with a look that was earnest, rather than intense, serious, rather than loving — business like.

It was more than Annie could bear.

Somehow, blessedly, anger came to her aid. How dared he put her in this position? She shoved past him with a determination that came of desperation. She had to get out of sight before she thoroughly disgraced herself and slapped his rotten, smiling face — or howled.

'I have three house calls to do this morning,' she said desperately, 'and you have morning clinic. Leave me alone, Tom McIver. Just leave me alone. I suggest we get on with our work — and forget this nonsense ever happened.'

Brave words!

How on earth could Annie forget what had just passed? She hadn't a snowball's chance in a bushfire, she acknowledged as she drove on her morning rounds.

It was just plain impossible. especially as news seemed to travel round Bannockburn even faster than the telephone wires could transmit.

'Is it true?' her first patient asked. Annie had called to check a troublesome ulcer, and Mrs Elder was so excited she was leaning on the front gate, waiting. Normally bed-bound, the old lady was agog.

'They say Melissa Carnem's dumped a baby on our Dr McIver, and now he's decided you'll make a nice wife for him,' the old lady said excitedly as Annie helped her hobble inside. 'Oh, my dear, is it true? My daughter-in-law rang me up not fifteen minutes ago.'

Good grief! It had been a whole two hours since Annie had told anyone! This valley was impossible.

'My dear, I do so hope it is.' Mrs Elder patted Annie's arm and settled back into her chair while Annie unwound the bandages. 'You're such a nice couple — made for each other, I'd say — and it's time that wild young man settled down.'

She smiled at Annie with such affection that Annie blinked.

Oh, dear. . .

The valley might be claustrophobic. There might be solid reasons why she had to get out, but she knew she would desperately miss these people when she had to leave.

She fobbed off Mrs Elder's interest as best she could, and made her way to her next patient. Kirstie Marshal's three-year-old son had earache. Kirstie had six-week-old twins and found it impossible to get to the surgery. She was just as excited as Mrs Elder.

'Sue-Ellen rang and told me,' she said, balancing a twin in one arm and her sad little three-year-old in the other. 'Sue-Ellen's husband delivers the milk to the hospital and they told him this morning. Oh, it's lovely. I can't think why we didn't see it coming. It's such a good idea!'

'You mean it'll settle him down?' Annie asked dourly. She smiled at Kirsty's toddler and lifted him from his mother's grasp. 'Come here, young Matt, and let me see your ear.'

'Well, it can't do any harm.' Kirsty smiled in reminiscence. 'Believe it or not, my Ian used to be a right tearaway. And you should see him now! A nice, steady dad.'

As her 'nice steady dad' chose that moment to stomp through the kitchen attached to muddy gum boots, the second twin started wailing and Matt realized Annie meant business with the auriscope there was little more conversation, but Kirsty and her Ian beamed at her all the way back out to her car.

The valley had wedding bells on the brain.

At least Margaret Ritchie wouldn't be thinking wedding bells, Annie thought, and then grimaced at her thankfulness. That was a small mercy and one she would gladly have done without.

Margaret had terminal bone cancer, and her farmer husband was taking care of her at home. Annie had visited Margaret on the previous Friday and she'd been weak but comfortable, but now Neil Ritchie met her at the back door — and the look on his face was dreadful.

'She's in so much pain. . . Oh, Doc. . . I've given her as much morphine as I dared and now I don't know what to do. We didn't want to trouble you, but we were so glad you were coming. . .'

'What's happened, Neil?'

'I don't know. She got up to go to the bathroom and suddenly she just crumpled. I lifted her back into bed but the pain's something fierce all down her leg.'

'When was this?'

'An hour or so ago.'

He stopped, distress choking his voice. Annie gave his hand a silent squeeze, and made her way swiftly inside.

She stopped in the doorway, recoiling in dismay.

On Friday Margaret had been sitting outside in the sun, but Friday suddenly seemed a long time ago. Now the woman was huddled in her bed like an old, old woman, and her face was contorted in pain. Every few moments a spasm seemed to catch her and her whole body became rigid. Margaret's eyes looked up wildly, pleading for help from anyone — anything — and then she fell back exhausted. She pushed her face into the pillow again, as though trying to hide. . .

'How long has she been like this?' Annie asked, appalled, as she moved swiftly to the bed. 'Oh, Margaret. . . Did you say an hour?'

'Yeah. A bit more,' Neil told her. 'I rang half an hour ago to check you were still coming and they said you were on your way.'

'Neil, I told you to beep me directly if you needed me.' Annie lifted Margaret's wrist and winced at the weakness of her pulse. 'I would have been here in minutes. . .'

'Yeah, but we knew you had others waiting. . .'

That was often the way. The patients who needed help least were the most demanding, and the urgent cases kept their humble place.

'You've given her a boost of morphine?'

'Twice. Ten milligrams an hour ago and another ten just before you arrived.' Neil wiped tears from his face and struggled to make his voice work. 'I wasn't game to give her more.'

'Twenty in all.'

Annie bit her lip in indecision. Tom was in control of Margaret's treatment, and Annie had little experience in the management of cancer pain. Margaret had a syringe driver set up — a mechanism which fed morphine into her body gradually so she didn't suffer the highs and lows of four-hourly injections. Annie lifted the chart and stared. Tom had the driver set at 240 milligrams a day. She did quick conversion into the dosages she was accustomed to — that was forty milligrams every four hours!'

Annie stared helplessly, down frantically trying to think what to do next. Margaret's pain was in her thigh and it didn't take much skill to imagine the probable cause. Annie had seen Margaret's recent X-rays. There was a tumour in the bone. In all probability, the bone would have simply given way and snapped.

The pain was clearly unimaginable.

An ambulance trip to hospital to set it? Yes, but not yet. To move her in such pain was unthinkable. But what else could she do? More morphine? Surely they were at peak dose now, Annie thought bleakly. Any more morphine and Margaret could die under the needle, but as she looked down Annie knew Margaret would count death as a blessing.

And yet. . . Although the cancer in Margaret's bones made her weak and would cause eventual death, she was enjoying the life she had left to her. When Annie had called three days ago, Margaret and Neil had been reading the papers in the sun — gossiping and laughing. Annie had thought Margaret could have up to a year more, please, God. Not like this, she couldn't.

She wouldn't want to live another hour with this pain. In fact, if it wasn't controlled soon she'd go into shock and that alone could kill her.

But the morphine wasn't working.

Why not?

Annie didn't know. She needed help here and she needed it fast. She needed a specialist oncologist or palliative care physician. Or an anaesthetist to block the pain. Or at least a damned good text book. . .

But whatever she needed she needed it now!

'Hold her hand, Neil,' Annie said urgently. 'Tight. Make her aware that help's here. Tell her I'm organizing drug doses. Tell her the pain will stop soon, and tell me where the phone is.'

'And, please, God, let Tom have an answer that I don't,' she said under breath as she headed for the phone. 'Please. . .'

The fact that two hours ago she'd never wanted to see Tom again was forgotten. Now she needed him fast.

At least Tom was available. Rebecca, their receptionist, was fielding calls while Tom conducted Monday clinic. She put Annie straight through and Tom answered on the first ring.

'Hey, Annie.' Tom's voice was strong and warm and welcoming. 'Have you done any reconsidering?'

'Tom, don't. . .' On those two words Annie paused, and by the immediate, listening silence she knew Tom's flippancy was over. As always, when she needed it, she had Tom's instant professional attention.

'What's up?' Tom's voice was suddenly hard, clinical and blessedly steady.

'Margaret Ritchie. . .' Swiftly Annie outlined the problem, and Tom was silent when she finished. Annie didn't question his silence. Her own mind was turning over plan after plan, and she knew Tom's would now be doing the same. He had seven more years medical experience than she. Please let him have an answer.

He did.

'Give her another dose of morphine, Annie,' Tom snapped. 'Now. Thirty milligrams. Do it while I look something up and then come back to the phone.'

'But. . .' Annie gasped. 'Tom, that's almost a hundred milligrams she'll have on board.'

'It won't narcotize while it's working against pain,' Tom explained. 'We can go higher if we have to. Just do it.'

Annie moistened suddenly dry lips. She was being asked to put total professional dependency on Tom here. If Margaret died. . .

She trusted Tom — and there was no choice. Silently she put the phone down and went to do as he said. When she came back to the phone Tom was waiting.

'Two things,' he snapped. 'My oncolgy text says that sometimes with bone cell cancer morphine isn't as effective as other drugs.'

'But —'

Tom was answering her next question before she got it out. 'Naproxen by mouth or rectally if you must — and Panadol as well,' he barked.

'Naproxen. . .'

Naproxen was a non-steroidal anti-inflammatory drug. How would that work if morphine didn't?

'Try it and see, Annie,' Tom ordered. 'I know it's guesswork but, by the sound of it, you have no choice and the text I have is definite. Stay with her and, if you must, give her another dose of morphine. Another thirty milligrams. . .'

'Tom. . .'

'You won't kill her,' Tom reassured her. 'I promise.

Shock from the pain's more likely to kill her. It's only when it's not combating pain that the morphine becomes dangerous. So do it! I'll ring a palliative care physician in Melbourne and check what else to do, then finish here and bring the ambulance out.'

And the line went dead.

Naproxen and Panadol. . .

Annie stared down at the receiver. What a cocktail! On top of that much morphine! A normal, healthy person would die with that combination of drugs.

She had to try. She had no other answers. There wasn't a choice. But if Tom was wrong. . .

With a heavy heart she headed for the car to get what she needed.

It worked.

Just occasionally, in medicine, it was possible to produce a miracle. A really nasty infection pulled up short by antibiotics still had the power to astonish Annie. And this. . . Ten minutes after the first thirty milligrams of morphine was injected, the spasms of pain started losing power. The pain was still bad so Annie took Tom at his word and injected more. Within an hour the naproxen and Panadol started to do their work.

Margaret's body sagged in exhausted relief and, still clutching her hand, Neil Ritchie burst into tears.

'Oh, girl. . . Oh, Doc, you've done it. Dear God, I thought I was losing her.' He slumped back into a chair and put his head in his hands.

'I think Margaret intends sticking round for a while yet.' Annie smiled, almost dizzy with relief herself, and took Margaret's thin hand from Neil. 'You agree, Margaret?'

Margaret stared speechlessly up at her, exhausted beyond belief, but her frail fingers gripped and held.

'How goes it?'

Annie spun round to find Tom in the doorway. Her relief was so great that if Margaret hadn't been holding her hand she could have crossed the room and kissed him! Or agreed to marry him on the spot.

'Here's the man we have to thank,' she whispered, her voice almost as shaken as Neil's. 'Dr McIver told me what to do. Tom, it worked! How on earth. ..? I just don't understand. ..'

'It's just getting the right cocktail mix — and I've spent years of my life studying cocktails.' Tom grinned and carefully placed what he was carrying — one baby capsule — on the floor beside the door. He smiled at them all, and crossed the room to grasp Neil's shaking shoulders in a strong grip of comfort.

'Hey, Neil, you look sicker than your wife. Take it easy.' Then his eyes met Annie's, warm and strongly reassuring. 'Morphine works against most pain but occasionally it doesn't. According to my text — and the physician I rang backs it up — bone pain is one thing it can sometimes not be effective for. Luckily, when it doesn't work naproxen usually does. I gather it's been effective.'

'You can't imagine,' Margaret whispered weakly.

'I think I can.' Tom looked from Annie's face to Neil's and then back to Margaret. 'Bone pain is just bloody! Annie, have you done an examination yet?'

'No.' Annie shook her head. 'I didn't want to stir any more pain. I'd guess the leg's broken but we'll need to do an X-ray.'

'I'm not going to hospital,' Margaret said fiercely, and Tom smiled.

'Not even for a quick visit? All we'll do is X-ray your leg, and if it's fractured — as we suspect — then we'll pin it. That's the long-term solution for this fierce pain.'

'The long-term. ..?'

'You're not going to die on us yet, Margaret,' Tom said gently. 'I think the time's come when we need to look at a wheelchair, but the modern wheelchair is a wonderful thing. You'll be able to round the cows up

with Neil, no sweat!' His smile faded. 'Margaret, Annie
said you'd been in pain for over an hour before she
came. Why didn't you and Neil call us?'

'We. . .we didn't want. . .'

'To bother anyone.' Tom finished the sentence for
her and crossed to sit on her bed. He took the hand
that Annie wasn't holding, linking the three of them
together.

'Margaret, you and Neil have decided to cope with
your illness at home. That's great. You should have
months — maybe years — of peaceful life before you.
And Annie and I agree that whatever treatment you
need will be given at home. But it's conditional,
Margaret. Our help is conditional.'

'On. . .on what?'

'On you calling us when you need us. The minute
you need us. On you treating us as if we're no further
than the telephone and we're sitting idle and waiting
for your call. If you don't do that, Margaret, then it
makes it impossible for you, impossible for Neil and
impossible for us.'

'But. . .'

'Look at Annie's face, Margaret,' Tom said sternly.
'And look at your husband's. They both look like
they've been through the wringer. When you suffer we
suffer, and if you don't let us help then it punishes
us. It doesn't inconvenience us if you call. It hurts if
you don't.'

He squeezed her hand and rose. 'Dave's outside with
the ambulance, and we'll move you now and get this
leg fixed,' he told her. 'By the look of you, you're close
to sleep, and there's nothing to stop you from sleeping
through the next couple of hours while we X-ray and
pin the leg, if we need to. Sleep, and we'll do our work
while you're sleeping.' He smiled. 'But before you drift
off. . .I brought someone to meet you.'

Margaret was so exhausted she was almost past

speaking, but her eyes moved instinctively from Tom's face to the floor by the door.

'You brought. . .'

'I brought my daughter.'

Tom walked to the door and scooped up his little girl from her capsule. Hannah was fast asleep, her tiny body limp and peaceful in Tom's big hands. Tom lifted the baby high in a gesture of love and pride that made Annie gasp.

It seemed at long last that Tom McIver was falling in love — with his tiny daughter.

Annie watched, tears pricking behind her eyes, as he carried the baby over to the bed and laid her on the coverlet. He stood back as Margaret reached to touch the tiny, sleeping face.

'Oh, Tom, she's so like you,' Margaret whispered, and her face which, minutes before, had been contorted in pain relaxed in pleasure. 'And she's perfect. . .'

'Isn't she?' Tom scooped up his daughter again, cradling her against his chest. He looked down into the baby's sleeping face and his eyes reflected his pride. 'Sleep now, Margaret — but I sort of hoped you might like to see her.'

He'd thought this through, Annie thought in amazement, intensely moved. Tom must have checked his texts, talked to the physician and decided Margaret's pain could be alleviated — and then he'd thought to what lay ahead. Now, instead of sleeping with the thought that the pain might return — that something else might break — Margaret was being given something new to think about. There could be no better ending to a morning of terror than the gift of new life.

'If you like, from now on we'll bring her whenever we come to see you,' Tom told Margaret. 'Either Annie or I. . .'

'It's true, then?' Margaret was fading fast toward sleep, whispering with her eyes almost closed. It was all Annie could do to hear her. 'Ellen Elder rang — just

as things were getting really bad — and said you and
Annie were getting married.' Her eyes closed completely. 'I can't think. . .I can't think of anything I'd
look forward to more. The marriage of two people who
deserve each other. . .'

And she drifted off to sleep.

CHAPTER EIGHT

'THE WHOLE VALLEY thinks it's a good idea,' Tom said plaintively. 'You're the odd man out.'

'They do not!' said Annie. 'Have you asked Sarah?'

'That's hitting below the belt.'

'Have you?'

'I don't know why Sarah should object. Sarah doesn't want to marry me.'

'Neither do I. Now could you concentrate on what you're doing or we'll have Mrs Reilly suing us for removing the wrong bit.'

Tom chuckled, unmoved.

'She wouldn't miss anything. Mabel Reilly hasn't seen anything below the waist since she hit sixteen stone many years ago. I doubt she'd notice if we whipped off a leg and attached a wooden one instead. She'd only complain that the floors sound noisy.'

Chris giggled from the other side of the table. The young nurse was thoroughly enjoying what was happening between Annie and Tom. The whole of Bannockburn was enjoying it! Chris handed Tom a suture and beamed.

'I think it's about time you two sorted things out,' she pronounced with authority. 'We all do. It's been two weeks, Dr Burrows, and you haven't given the man an answer.'

'I have given the man an answer,' Annie said darkly. 'It's just not the one he wants.'

'It's not the one anyone wants.' Chris gave Tom a conspiratorial grin. 'Dr Burrows, Dr McIver's right when he says everyone wants you to marry him.'

'Would I be marrying Dr McIver — or the valley?'

131

'The valley,' Chris said promptly. 'You couldn't leave then.'

'And you'd all have a nice, steady doctor for years.' Annie concentrated on her dials with a ferociousness that a simple gallstone removal in a healthy fifty-year-old didn't warrant. 'I just wish everyone would get off my back. Especially you, Dr McIver.' She managed a speedy glare between scrutinizing dials. 'And I know you haven't done the first thing about advertising my position — but I'm leaving at the end of the month, whether you've bothered to find a replacement or not!'

Tom just gave an infuriating grin — but Chris gasped. 'You can't mean that?' Chris sounded outraged.

Annie lifted a syringe and had to collect herself before she plunged it home with more force than it deserved.

'I do,' she pronounced savagely. 'The whole valley's blackmailing me into this marriage — and I can't see a single thing in it for me. Nothing!'

'You can't mean it.'

Chris's question was repeated when Helen found Annie that night, sitting in Children's Ward beside a little boy suffering from a spider bite. The spider was a white tail, which meant there was little danger to the child's life but that particular spider's bite had a nasty habit of making the skin around the bite die if it wasn't treated with care.

The child's parents were dairy farmers and hadn't been able to come in tonight so Annie, with time on her hands, had sat with him until he'd slept.

'I can't mean what?' Annie was a million miles away. Now she stirred, and turned to find that the night sister had obviously been watching her for a while.

'Chris says you don't believe there's anything in this marriage for you.'

'That's right.'

'No.' Helen hauled up a chair and sat down beside

her, with the air of a woman ready to sit it out. 'It's wrong. Annie, maybe it's time you and I talked.'

'Talk all you like,' Annie said bitterly. 'The whole valley's talking. They've been talking of nothing else for two weeks.'

'They have, you know,' Helen said gently. 'They've been talking of the change that's come over Dr McIver since his baby arrived. They've been watching as he carts the little one around like a man who's been granted something he never thought he'd have. He has his housekeeper, but his little girl's spending more time with her daddy than with Edna. Dr McIver's been knocked sideways by his little daughter, and you must see it.'

'I suppose. . .' Annie shrugged, grudgingly conceding the point. 'I suppose he has.' She thought back to the Tom she was seeing around the hospital. 'I guess he seems more peaceful.'

'He does that.' Helen smiled. 'The man's been like a coiled spring since I've known him. Filling every moment with activity. This evening when I came on duty I found them both out in the hospital garden — Tom and his daughter — lying under the gum trees waiting for the evening star to appear. Tom was explaining the heavens to his daughter. They didn't see me and I wouldn't have intruded for the world — but, oh, my dear, it made me feel lumpy inside to see it.'

'Yeah, well. . .'

'It makes you feel like that, too, doesn't it?' Helen asked softly, and when Annie didn't answer she put a hand on hers.

'You love him, Annie.'

'I. . .'

'Don't lie to me,' Helen told her. 'I've watched you. I know you love Tom McIver. That's why I told him he should marry you.'

'You. . .'

'The night of the accident,' Helen told her. 'He was

wandering round like a stunned mullet, trying to figure out just what he should do. He was still talking about marrying Sarah. I told him that if he wanted someone who'd turn him into part of a family he shouldn't look past you.'

'Yeah. He didn't even think of it himself,' Annie said bitterly, and Helen gave a sad little smile.

'He couldn't. Something happened in the past that makes him wary of commitment. That's why he's gone from one unsuitable girl to the next. That's why. . . that's why he has to marry with his head — and find that love will come later.'

'Helen. . .'

'He thought the idea ridiculous when I told him,' Helen went on, ignoring Annie's interruption. 'But then. . .halfway through your picnic he said he suddenly saw what I'd been seeing all along. That you're true and kind and loving — and you'd make him a much better wife than any of these nincompoops he's been escorting. So. . .'

'So he made a decision with his head.'

'That's right.' Helen's voice firmed. 'He has. And you love him. So it's up to you to marry him and teach him to love you back. You can do it, Annie. If I didn't think you could I would have shut up in the first place. But I think this marriage has a far better chance of working than many where the only thing the bride and groom have going for them is romantic love. You love the real Tom McIver, Annie. And he's worth the risk!'

'Helen, I can't. . .'

'You can, you know,' Helen said gently. 'And I wish you would.' She stood. 'But, meanwhile, Mr Whykes is unsettled and I need an order for diazepam — if it's OK with you, Doctor?' And her request was so meek that Annie burst out laughing.

'I don't believe you need doctors at all in this hospital, Sister. Just signatures. You organize us all.'

'I try,' Helen said meekly. 'You and Dr McIver first. Chris next. She's on my list.'

'Poor Chris.' Annie rose and looked down searchingly at the sleeping child. 'Bobby won't wake until morning. I'll come and see Mr Whykes. Does he need sedation? He's been much more settled.'

'I know. But Robbie said one of his sons brought in the farm books this afternoon for him to go over. He thoroughly enjoyed telling them all how badly managed the finances had been since he'd been in hospital. He spent too much time with pen and paper and is now paying the consequences.'

Helen put a hand on Annie's shoulder and pressed her back down onto her chair. 'There's no need for you to come. Verbal order and sign later. You sit there — and think about what I've just said. Think, Annie. Because if you don't take this risk — if you don't marry the man you love — you may just regret it for the rest of you life.'

'Marry him, dear.'

Margaret Ritchie was lying on a settee on the verandah when Annie called the next day. And, as per orders, Annie had brought Hannah. The baby gurgled and chirped on Margaret's coverlet and then subsided into delighted silence as Annie produced a bottle.

'Do you take her with you often?' Margaret asked, and Annie shook her head.

'Only here.' She smiled. 'Tom takes her everywhere. His dogs are too jealous for words.'

'Will they be jealous of you, do you think? When you marry him?'

'Margaret. . .'

'Don't tell me.' Margaret reached out and touched Annie's hand. She was pain-free now and the lines around her face had softened and eased. This lady would face death with dignity and courage when her time came — but her time was a long way off yet. 'Don't tell me you're not brave enough.'

'Margaret, he doesn't love me!'

'But do you love him?'

Silence. Neil had left them alone. There were only the two women in the soft afternoon sun — and one feeding baby.

The answer lay between them as clearly as if it had been spoken.

'I see,' Margaret said gently. She looked down at the sleepy Hannah. 'And this little one. . . Do you think you could love her, too?'

Annie looked down at the tiny cluster of brown curls on Hannah's head, and she felt her heart twist. It was strange. She'd never thought she'd have children. Tom's vision of her future — as an elderly spinster doctor — was pretty much how Annie had seen herself. But this little one. . . Somehow Hannah had twisted her way round her heart, and Annie knew she had feelings for her as she had for no other.

Maybe it was because she was so much a part of Tom. . .

'And what about his dogs?'

Margaret's voice was insistent, and for the first time Annie found herself smiling.

'Tiny and Hoof. . . What woman would be crazy enough to take them on?'

'I think you would,' Margaret said softly. 'I think you should.'

'Margaret, he doesn't love me.'

'He doesn't know what he wants,' Margaret said. 'It might take a bit of age and experience to see that but, in a way, I think Tom McIver is as confused as you are. And with this marriage. . .' She shook her head.

'Annie, life isn't a dress rehearsal. Look at me. I'm not quite sixty, and it's almost over. But I've had my Neil, my children, my farm and my life — and there's not one thing I've done that I've regretted. I've made mistakes but I've taken every opportunity that's come my way — grasped it with open hands — and I'm so glad

I did. Sure, Tom McIver might cause you heartaches, but what's the alternative?'

'Margaret. . .'

'Marry him, dear!'

Marry him. . .

Annie spent the rest of the day working on automatic pilot. She did her afternoon clinic and was fortunate that there was little except coughs and colds and the odd sprain or stitch. After dinner she took herself for a long walk on the beach. She returned after dark and sat alone in her flat, listening to Tom talk to his baby and his dogs.

As Hannah settled, Annie took her courage in both hands — and walked the few steps to his door.

Tom answered on the second knock, and his dogs tumbled out behind him to greet her. Two dogs and one doctor. Three males, almost as big as each other. All with the same silly grins.

'Annie. . .'

'Can I talk to you?'

Tom's grin faded. He shoved his dogs back inside and closed the door.

'What is it, Annie? What's wrong?'

Annie took a deep breath. And then another one.

'I've decided,' she said at last, in a voice that trembled. She stared down at the floor. 'If you still want me to. . . Tom, if you think it's a good idea, I'll marry you.'

Silence.

And then, very slowly, Tom pulled her into his arms.

'That's great, Annie,' he said, and she could feel his breath against her hair. 'That's fantastic. You won't regret it. Between us, I think we've made a really sensible decision.'

CHAPTER NINE

SENSIBLE!

That was the last word Annie would have used to describe her decision, and it was the last word she *could* use to describe the way the valley reacted to the news. The valley erupted into something that wavered between hysteria and delirium, she decided, as her request for no fuss was met with blank rejection.

'No way,' Chris declared.

'If I can't be matron of honour, I quit,' Robbie announced. Margaret Ritchie even sent off to Melbourne for a new dress.

'Because I won't miss your wedding for the world, my dear,' she told Annie. 'No one will. If we're not invited I think you'll have every head in the valley poking in the church windows and singing along with the hymns.'

'Oh, you're invited,' Annie said, and she couldn't quite keep a note of panic from creeping into her voice. 'I want you to come especially, Margaret, but you'd be coming, anyway. Tom's invited everyone from here to Timbuktu. If you've ever been on a mailing list or in a telephone book then you're invited.'

'Annie, stop panicking.'

Tom found her in her office later that afternoon. She'd fled there to escape the wedding buzz around the hospital.

Legally there was a four-week waiting period for marriage, but Tom would wait no longer than he had to. So. . . They'd been engaged for two weeks, there were two weeks to go before the wedding and Annie didn't see how the fuss could get any greater.

In the hospital kitchen there were pink and white rosettes being made instead of cakes for the patients' supper.

'It won't hurt the patients to have bought biscuits until the wedding,' Cook informed her. 'Everyone understands.'

They surely did. There were even a couple of patients tying pink and white ribbons.

Annie retreated to Intensive Care, only to find that Chris was sitting by Mrs Christianson's bed, checking monitors and stitching her bridesmaid's dress at the same time.

So she'd fled.

'The whole hospital's mad,' Annie muttered, bending over her work. 'Tom, this is crazy.'

'Annie!' Tom leaned over her desk and put his palms flat on her prescription pad, effectively stopping her writing. 'If we're going to get married we might as well have the works. I only intend to do this once in my life. Besides, it'll mean you have to take your jeans off for the day.' And he kissed her on the top of her head.

Yeah, great! He was still treating her as a kid sister. Would he always?

Annie looked up doubtfully at the man before her and, as always, she felt a lurch of something she could never understand. Tom was white-coated, professional and self-assured. The full medical bit. He looked like a medical colleague, but there was no way Annie could see him as such.

She was so full of doubts, but it seemed there were no doubts for Tom. Tom McIver was in charge of his world again, and ever since Annie had agreed to marry him he hadn't stopped grinning.

'Tom, it seems stupid. To have the full romantic bit when we're not—'

'We're not what? Romantic?' Tom kicked the door closed, seized her face and gave her a light kiss on the lips. 'We can be as romantic as you like. So. . .how romantic would you like to be?'

With an effort, Annie pulled herself free.

'Don't be silly, Tom.'

'I'm not being silly.' He didn't mind her pulling away, though. He dropped into a chair on the other side of her desk and watched her with complacency. Tom had her where he wanted her, and he wasn't pushing his luck. 'Speaking of romance, though. . . How about a honeymoon? If I get a locum, shall we take ourselves to Tahiti?'

'What, with Hannah and Hoof and Tiny?' Annie hauled another patient's file towards her and flipped it open. 'You go on a honeymoon, Tom McIver. I'm too busy.'

'You sound crabby.'

'I feel crabby.'

'Why?' Tom asked blandly — and Annie had to find an answer.

'Because I'm being bulldozed into white lace and confetti.'

'You really, truly, don't want it? A proper wedding?' Tom folded his arms and fixed her with a look.

And Annie couldn't say no. She couldn't. She stared at the paper in front of her and thought of saying what she really thought — that a full bridal and a honeymoon with Tom were things she'd dreamed of for years and now she'd gone this far she couldn't pull back, but that the dream wasn't complete.

But, of course, the words couldn't come. If they had Tom would walk away right now, she thought sadly. She'd scare him silly. Tom wanted an independent partner. A sensible match. Not some clinging vine. . .

'I. . .I had a letter from Rod Manning's solicitor,' she managed finally, retreating back to medicine as fast as she could.

'Rod. . .' Tom frowned, blessedly distracted. 'What does he want?'

'He wants a copy of his treatment notes.' Annie rose to look out the window. Tom at her desk was, well, he was too close for comfort.

'Why?'

'I think Rod's trying to figure a way he can sue me,' Annie said heavily. 'He hates me.'

'Surely not.' Tom's frown deepened. 'The man must be reaching paranoid stage. It's more than a month since the accident. He should be coming to terms with it by now.'

'I don't think so.'

'And he's upsetting you? Is that what's wrong?' Tom rose, walked around to where she stood and placed his hands on her shoulders. Against her better judgement, Annie felt herself lean back against him. His body felt so good. It felt so right. 'Annie, I'm sure there's no need to worry. I agree, the solicitor's letter demanding the notes is ominous, but he might have some other reason for wanting them. Maybe insurance. . .'

With an effort, Annie managed to keep her voice working. The way he was holding her. . .she could almost imagine herself cherished. 'I don't. . .I don't think so.' She sighed, giving in to the feel of Tom's hands.

'Kylie and Betty are OK —but gossip says Betty's asking for a divorce. It seems the accident was the last straw. Rod's been drinking heavily and knocking her around. On the night of the ball Betty knew he shouldn't be driving —but he was so abusive that she went with him against her better judgement. So now. . . Rod hasn't just lost his licence. He's lost his family.'

'I see.' Tom was kneading her shoulders gently and Annie's body had started to do strange things. She was growing warm from the thighs up. 'His world has been blown apart —and it's easier to blame you than himself.' Tom's voice was as gentle as his hands, infinitely comforting. 'Annie, none of that is your fault. Rod did it to himself.'

'I guess I know that. I rang medical defence and asked them to check my notes, and they're happy I acted properly. I had no choice but to give the police the blood sample so I've sent the notes on to Rod's lawyer. With luck, his lawyer will tell Rod the same story — that I didn't have a choice in giving the police the blood sample — and that'll be an end to it.'

'I don't like it, though.' Tom pulled her tightly against him, her back curved into his chest. He was becoming more possessive — more patriarchal — by the minute. 'Rod has a violent temper. You keep out of his way.'

'Yes, sir. . .'

It was a mocking rejoinder but it made Tom hold her tighter.

'You're my future wife. As of Saturday week. No one threatens my family.'

'No.' The word was a faint, bleak little reply that no one could understand except Annie.

She was being stupid, she told herself. Tom was offering what most girls would kill for. He was offering her his name and his protection.

And he'd love her — in a way. She knew that. It was already happening. He'd love her as he loved Hoof and Tiny — he'd love her because she was part of the family he was creating. But what that love lacked had everything to do with the dull ache around her heart.

He'd have loved Sarah if he'd thought she was suitable. Or Melissa. Or someone else. . .

Annie just wanted him to love her for herself, sensible or not. For her. For Annie.

It was stupid wish. Fairy tales happened between the covers of books. They didn't happen to Annie Burrows.

Tom kissed her on her nape — a kiss of light affection. 'OK, Annie, as long as you stop worrying I'm off. I'm taking Hannah and the dogs to the beach so I'll see you later.'

He kissed her again lightly on the cheek—a kiss of affection and farewell—and he left her.

Annie was left staring at a closed door. And the panic welled up all over again.

Tom was taking Hannah and the dogs to the beach. He was taking *his family*. But he wasn't taking Annie.

He hadn't thought of asking if she wanted to go, and there was no reason why he should. Tom had done his courting. He had what he wanted.

But. . . The hospital was quiet. If they took the mobile phone there was no reason why Annie shouldn't go to the beach with them. If they'd wanted her.

It was her own fault, she thought sadly. She'd consented to be his wife. There was no need to court her any more. No need at all when one essential element to a marriage was missing. Tom's love.

Annie slumped down in her chair again, despair rising within her. Dear God, what was she letting herself in for?

The wedding was perfect.

It didn't have a choice. Every person in the valley contributed. Even Tiny and Hoof were groomed to canine perfection. They stood to attention on either side of the entrance to the chapel, and they hardly needed the children Tom had assigned to hold them.

Annie had been right in her guess at numbers. Every person in the telephone book was there—plus a few more!

Much to Chris's disgust, they had a traditional church wedding.

'Beach weddings are fine when you only have young, healthy guests,' Tom said definitively when Chris told him her plans for sea and dolphins, 'but I want the whole valley to come. Grandmas and grandpas and people with prams and—'

'You really are making a public statement that you're starting something big,' Chris said curiously, and watched Annie's face. Annie had been growing more and more quiet as the day approached.

And on the day itself she was almost dumbstruck.

Chris and Helen dressed her in a gown made by Chris's mum — and Annie gazed in the mirror and hardly knew herself.

A vision flashed through of the girl she'd seen once before. The student who'd worn a ball gown for the first time and had been derided by her family for being ridiculous.

As soon as they'd opened their mouths, that was how she'd felt. Ridiculous. Well, neither her mother nor her sister were here today. Her sister was overseas on a modelling assignment and her mother was taken up with some new man.

But their words stayed with her.

'I don't. . . Helen, I can't. . .'

'Of course you can.' Helen twisted her around so that Annie was staring straight at the mirror. 'You must. If you think we can waste this. . .'

Annie stared. This wasn't Annie.

The gown was deceptively simple — soft silken organza with a sweetheart neckline, tiny sleeves and a bodice that curved around her breasts as if it was moulded to her. As, indeed, it was. The front of the dress was simplicity itself, but at the back silk lacing ran from where the neck scooped low at the neckline to where soft folds billowed out from her tiny waistline to fall in soft clouds to the floor.

There were no frills. The dress was designed to show Annie as she really was — not some designer version of what a bride should be. Chris and Helen tumbled her shining curls softly around her shoulders and a wreath of tiny white rosebuds drifted through her hair. In her hands Annie held a posy of the same white rosebuds. Her eyes were huge in her face, and it was a face Annie had never seen before.

'Oh, I wish Hannah was old enough to be a flower

girl,' Chris breathed. 'Not that you need one. Annie, you're quite beautiful.'

'I'm not beautiful.'

'If you don't think you're beautiful then you must be blind,' Chris retorted. 'And don't tell me you are blind. You know you don't really need those awful glasses, and why you wear them. . .I think I'll toss them into the river now we've finally got them off you.' She linked her arm in Annie's. 'Enough. Helen and I have decided there'll be discussion on this subject after you're safely hitched, but for now. . . For now, Dr Burrows, Matron Robbie is waiting to give you away. And if anyone catches your bouquet except me, I'll just *die*.'

And then events overtook them.

There was so little of her wedding day Annie remembered.

Snatches.

A chapel bursting with people. The dogs, smirking as if they'd planned the whole thing. Tom's housekeeper, coming forward with Hannah—beaming her pleasure and placing the baby in Annie's arms for a brief photogenic moment before she went into church. Flashbulbs popped everywhere, and afterwards there were pictures of Annie, holding her new little stepdaughter, pinned on walls all over the valley.

Hannah gurgling up with pleasure as if this new arrangement was entirely to her satisfaction.

Margaret Ritchie in a wheelchair just inside the church, reaching forward to grip Annie's hand before Rob led Annie proudly down the aisle.

'My dear, this is the best thing. . .for you both. . . Savour every moment.'

She couldn't. She couldn't even think.

The wedding march blared forth.

And then Annie looked ahead, to find Tom smiling at her like the proverbial Cheshire cat. He looked impossibly handsome in his black dinner suit, his eyes on hers — as if he sensed her panic — impossibly gentle and kind.

How could she not want to marry this man? He'd asked it of her, and she could give him this one thing. Give him herself.

Only. . .

Tom wanted just a part of her. He didn't demand the part she was longing to give.

She took a deep breath, and then Rob was leading her forward. The smile on Robbie's face matched Tom's. The valley had made this match, Rob's grin said, and the valley folk were seeing it through.

Annie let him take her forward until another hand came out to claim her — and she turned to become Tom's wife.

Day misted into night. There was a feast to end all feasts, and dancing out under the stars.

As the night grew old Tom pulled his bride into his arms and held her close.

'OK, my lovely, lovely Annie. Time to leave this lot to enjoy themselves. Time for bed.'

'Bed?' Annie flashed a look up at him that was half-scared — the rest of her was just plain terrified. 'Tom. . .'

'It's customary, you know,' he teased. 'The best of couples do it on their wedding night. I know we decided against a honeymoon, but for tonight, well, there's two of my doctor mates who are currently dancing their legs off with Chris and Sarah, but they've promised to look after medical emergencies. Edna's caring for Hannah. And I've even boarded out Hoof and Tiny. What greater sacrifice can a man make?'

What, indeed?

Annie looked helplessly up at him. She was way out of her depth — scared stiff of crossing boundaries she could hardly see. There were no rules for the game she was playing.

How to love a man and yet not love him.

How to need him so much that her heart was dissolving at the thought of him needing her — and yet not let him see her need.

And how to cope with the fact that she was a sensible wife. A wife of necessity.

'Don't worry, my Annie,' Tom whispered, pulling her into his arms and holding her close. He misunderstood the reason for her panic entirely. 'I won't hurt you. I'll never hurt you.'

But will you ever love me like I want to be loved? Annie thought longingly, as Tom wove his way through the dancers, holding tight to his bride at his side and laughing a goodnight to their guests.

Will you, Tom?

He made a good start.

Annie woke to bliss. There were no words to describe how she felt. She lay curled in the protective line of Tom's body, his arms holding her close, and she thought if she could die now there could be nothing more she could ask for.

She might be a wife of necessity — but last night she had felt truly loved. Tom had taken her to him as something of infinite worth. She had felt beautiful and wondrous and cherished, and her body had melted into Tom's as if they'd been made for each other.

Her husband. . .

She looked up into his face and she felt her heart stir with overwhelming love. Maybe this could work. Please. . .

He opened his eyes and looking down at her, and his eyes were as gentle and loving as she could possibly hope. And possessive. She was his wife, his look said. His. 'Awake, my Annie?'

'Mmm.'

He kissed her on the forehead — and then bent to kiss her full on the mouth. Annie felt her lips tremble under his, and as his kiss deepened heat surged through her body as she responded to all the love inside her. Like a bud unfurls to the sun, she responded to this man. Her love.

She put her arms around him and held him close — his naked body against hers — and just for this once she let all her pent-up longing explode into aching need. Her body arched into his and she felt his body react with disbelief — and then with absolute delight.

'My God, I've married a wanton. . .'

'Wanton. . . Wanting you. . .'

'I didn't hurt you last night, did I?'

She'd surprised him, she knew. He'd expected her to be as reluctant as the look of panic she'd worn on her face when he'd led her to bed had suggested. Only. . .the panic wasn't that he'd love her. The panic was that he wouldn't.

Would I be coming back for more if you'd hurt me?'

'Are you coming back for more?' He kissed her again.

In answer, Annie's fingers drifted downward. . . down. . .until they found what they were seeking. And there was no mistaking what she felt.

He did want her, her fingers told her. Love her or not, for this moment she was his woman — his wife — and he wanted her in the age-old way a man had loved a woman from the beginning of time. If she had to be content with that then so be it.

She'd made her bed and now she'd lie in it. She'd take what she could get, and fight for more.

'Oh, yes,' she breathed, and she let her fingers do her pleading for her. 'If you'll have me, Tom McIver, then I'm yours.'

It couldn't last.

Their honeymoon came to an end mid-morning when the rest of the world broke in. Tom's medical mates had to return to the city, and without them Tom or Annie was needed. There was a hospital to run.

The farmer who'd cared for Tiny and Hoof drove by and released them in the hospital grounds. He obviously hadn't given them breakfast and they were displeased. They signalled their return by attempting to scratch Tom's door down.

Edna rang to say she'd run out of formula and would they like her to bring Hannah home?

Tom had a fast shower, while Annie lay in his bed and tried to come to terms with her new status. Her new life. She watched through the bathroom door as Tom showered, marvelling at his wonderful body — the body that held the promise of pleasure to come.

'You look like the cat that got the cream.' Tom smiled down at his wife as he hauled his shirt on. Annie lay still under the sheets, sated and drowsy. Holding onto this moment for as long as she could. 'But the cat had best stir. The world calls.'

'The world's coming right in if you don't open that door,' Annie retorted, smiling back at her love. 'Tiny and Hoof between them are a match for any barricade.'

Then she hesitated, thinking of nights to come. If she stayed here. . . She was sleeping in Tom's bed. There was no separate bedroom in his apartment for Hannah, or for the two dogs.

'Tom, do you want to do something about the apartments?'

'What?' Tom looked around his bedroom as if he were seeing it for the first time. 'What's wrong with it? Do we need a bigger bed, do you think? This is about as big as they come.'

'I mean. . .' Annie hesitated, searching for courage. 'Tom, Robbie suggested, we knock down the wall between the apartments. Make them into one big house.'

Silence.

Tom carefully buttoned his shirt, hauled on his pants and sat on the bed to put his shoes on. He didn't look at her.

'Let's wait, Annie,' he said at last.

'Wait?'

'Well, I agree we should put a door between us. But one house. . .'

'You don't like the idea?'

'Well, it's just that we're two independent people.' He shrugged, then leaned back and lifted her curls, tumbling over her pillows. 'I don't say that I'll get tired of you, Annie, but. . .well, there may be times when we do want to be apart.' He kissed her on the nose.

'I see.'

'You agree?' He was looking at her as if she couldn't help but agree. After all, it wasn't as if she was in love with the man—was she?

'Of course.'

Flat. Sensible. The return to earth of Annie Burrows.

'Fine, then.' Tom took himself off to the mirror to comb his hair.

The world calls. . .

Annie swung her legs over the side of the bed, hauling the sheet with her, and Tom watched her in the mirror and laughed.

'Modesty? Where was that an hour ago?'

When I was pretending that you really wanted me as your wife. Annie thought her reply, but she couldn't say it.

'There's work to be done, Tom McIver. If you spend any more time preening in front of the mirror I'll have to take over your patients as well as mine.'

'Preening?' He winced. 'Ouch.' He shook his head. 'Annie, once a day, whether I need it or not, I stand in front of the mirror and do my hair. Also I shave. Your definition of preening. . .'

'Preening,' she said flatly, half-teasing. 'Sheer vanity!'

'Well, maybe it's time you learned about vanity.' With a grin of pure mischief, Tom stalked out into the corridor and into the apartment next door. She heard him moving round in her bedroom—and then he marched right back. In his arms he carried the entire contents of her wardrobe which he proceeded to dump on the bedroom floor.

'Watch,' he told her firmly.

Then, while Annie stared, dumbfounded, he marched out to his kitchenette and came back with two large bottles. Before Annie could realize what he intended he'd upended them over the lot.

Annie's jaw dropped about a foot.

'You. . .' Annie stared speechlessly. 'Tom. . .' She made a dive for the pile but Tom was before her. He swept her off her feet, her sheet slipped sideways and he dumped her naked body back on the bed.

'No, you don't,' he told her kindly, his eyes dancing with wickedness. 'If you knew how long I've been aching to do that. . . The big bottle was soy sauce and the bigger one's bleach from Theatre. Double strength. Let the bleach do its job. Ten minutes and even *you* won't wear them.'

'You have no right!'

'I'm your husband.' He grinned. 'In days gone by I could have bumped you on the head with a club and dragged you back to my cave by the hair. Or installed you as wife number eight and made you pregnant fifteen times.

"I've thought it all out. I'm doing none of those things because I'm a civilized male — and because, of course, we're equal. But this once, Annie. . .this one time. . .I figured I don't want a wife in old T-shirts two sizes too big for her, and the only way to avoid that is to be ruthless.'

'Ruthless. . .' Annie hauled her sheet back around her and glared up in fury. 'Tom, if you don't like my clothes then you didn't have to marry me.'.

'But you fit my criteria in every other way.' He smiled, and the dangerous twinkle that had been Annie's undoing gave her a message of pure sensuality. A look to make her toes curl! 'And very exacting criteria they are, too. Annie, you are a truly beautiful woman and yesterday you took my breath away. So. . . Helen and Chris and I. . .'

'Helen and Chris. . .'

'I like being wicked in a team.' Tom chuckled. 'Then I can say it was all their idea.'

'Was it?'

'No. I decided —'

'You decided what?' Annie could hardly speak. Her nice, controlled world was tilting on its axis at such a crazy angle she was in danger of falling off.

'I decided that from this day forth you could come out of your hiding place and stay out.' He hauled a large suitcase from the top of the wardrobe. 'And in case you're wondering what to wear. . . Chris and Helen took themselves to Melbourne last weekend and had a buying spree.'

'I'll kill them. . .'

'Look what they bought you before you kill them.' And he tipped the contents of the suitcase over the bed.

Annie was effectively silenced. She sat stunned, surrounded by a mound of tissue and ribbon, and her new husband sat down on the bed and started opening parcels.

He didn't say a word. Just silently held up one garment after another.

Helen and Chris had started from the skin out.

There were tiny, frothy pieces of lace that Annie recognized — but only just — as a far-flung relation to the sensible cotton knickers and bras that she wore.

There were silk slips and sheer, slinky pantihose.

There were nightgowns — two — and Annie blushed just to look at them. She would never have bought herself anything like this — not in a million years.

She looked up at Tom — and then looked away quickly. The toad was having a ball.

He was lifting each garment for inspection and then

solemnly laying it before her — as though she'd really accept them!

There were two dresses — short and summery. Far too short! And skirts that were possibly meant for work, only they were tiny and cut to fit revealingly around her thighs. They'd had her measurements, of course, Annie realized. Chris's mum had made her wedding dress, and Annie had wondered at the time why she'd had to measure *everything*.

It went on. Three blouses — fine silk and soft, embroidered lawn. Tailored pants, and a lovely linen jacket that Annie was almost tempted to reach out and touch.

Almost. Not quite.

'Well, now you've unpacked it you can just pack it all back up again, Tom McIver,' she said in a tone that was dangerously quiet. 'None of this is the sort of thing I wear.'

'That's just it. It should be.' Tom lifted a tiny wisp of lace and held it up in awed admiration. 'Not that you'll get to wear it long. Not now I'm your husband.'

'Tom. . .'

'You don't have a choice, Annie. There's nothing else.' He motioned down to the floor. The mess of bleach and soy sauce had done its job well. 'I agree — you'll need more clothes so in a week or so maybe you and Chris could go back to Melbourne and choose some.'

You and Chris. . .

A quiver of doubt crept into Annie's daze. *You and Chris. . .*

Not *you and I*.

Somehow she made herself concentrate on what was important. 'Tom, I liked my jeans and T-shirts.'

'No.' Tom shook his head, leaned over and took her face between his hands. He kissed her gently on the lips. A feather kiss. A kiss of reassurance. A kiss of friendship.

Again she felt that quiver of doubt.

'If I thought you really liked them I wouldn't have done this,' he told her. 'But you hate your clothes, Annie. You've married me, and my marriage is a gift. I now have a wife and a mother for my child. I tried to figure out what I could give you in return, and this is what I came up with. You're beautiful, Annie, and somewhere in the past someone's taken that image away from you. I'm giving it back. You're beautiful and I'm proud of you, jeans or no jeans. Now, though, in these the rest of the world can see the Annie I'm seeing.'

'Tom. . .'

'Not another word.' Tom straightened as a knock at the door outside sounded over Tiny's and Hoof's frantic scratching. 'I think the family's back.'

He walked over and opened the door, and his family surely was back. With a vengeance!

Tiny and Hoof burst in and flung themselves straight through into the bedroom to their very favourite place — Tom's bed. They landed right in the middle of Annie's lingerie, and by the time Edna Harris carried Hannah into the living room Tiny was turning wild circles around the living room, barking in full voice — and wearing a pair of silky crimson knickers on his head.

Edna stopped dead.

'Well. . .'

But the best was yet to come.

Hoof grabbed a wispy bra between his teeth and headed after Tiny. Annie made a frantic grab at Hoof as he headed out of the bedroom, and missed by a mile. She sprawled onto the carpet. Stark naked.

There was nowhere to hide. Hoof knocked the bedroom door wide open as he charged back through to the living room, and Edna looked straight in at Annie. The good lady's jaw sagged so fast that Tom took Hannah in a hurry in case she dropped her.

'Thanks, Mrs Harris,' Tom said blandly over the barking, and only the faintest tremor in his voice showed he was aware of anything unusual. 'We're grateful to you for looking after Hannah last night, but we'll be right now. We're a family.'

Annie lay on the carpeted floor in her birthday suit among dogs and knickers and chaos, and couldn't figure out whether to laugh or cry.

Her married life had begun.

Maybe her doubts were futile. Maybe it could work.

'You don't need to worry about us,' Tom was saying as he gently propelled Edna out of the door. 'We have all we need.'

But did they?

CHAPTER TEN

AFTER two months of marriage they might have been married for years, but Annie's doubts, rather than fading, just grew.

In a way, her life changed dramatically. She took her courage in both hands and wore the new clothes, and even bought more. They certainly made her feel different.

In other ways, nothing changed at all.

It was as if they'd been married for thirty years, she told herself. Tom treated her as a dear, familiar thing — a partner and friend and, at night, a lover. But only at night. During the day they were two very separate people.

The hospital ran as smoothly as before. Maybe more smoothly because Tom was around more and there were no women to distract him. Certainly Annie didn't distract him. His free time he spent with Hannah, and Annie wasn't invited. Annie had free time when Tom was on call, and when he had free time she was on duty.

It was a strange marriage!

At least they didn't fight, and at night, unless their work called them away, Annie could snuggle into Tom's arms and pretend he really was her husband.

Only he wasn't. In the morning he was back to being friend and colleague, and the pretence faded to bitter reality.

She wasn't his wife in the true sense. She wasn't his love.

It was as if he'd opened his bedroom to her — as if he knew that sex was what marriage was about — but he hadn't figured what else was involved. Or even realized that anything more was required.

Annie didn't have the courage to teach him. She held herself back, fearful of being too pushy. Of making him tired of her. If he found her presence cloying then maybe in time he wouldn't even want her in his bed.

It should have gradually become better, she told herself. That was what she so desperately wanted. But although she was falling more deeply in love with her husband by the minute — and although Hannah and the dopey Tiny and Hoof had become such a part of her life that she knew she could never leave them — Tom still held himself apart. He talked to her about Hannah and he talked about their work, but he didn't talk about what he himself felt.

That one day by the beach when he'd spoken of his childhood had been a rare glimpse inside the man, Annie thought, and she started to fear that a glimpse was all she would ever get.

'Give him time, dear,' Helen told her, seeing a look of pain wash over Annie's face on the anniversary of two months of married life. Annie was gazing out of a hospital window to where Tom had Hannah down by the river. Tom was floating a tiny wooden boat in the shallows, the dogs were racing along to catch it in the current and Hannah was crowing her delight in her father's arms. Annie was so jealous she could weep.

Time . . .

'He just doesn't know what marriage is about.' Helen looked again at Annie's face and sighed. 'He'll learn.'

'Will he?'

'Why don't you go down and join them?' Helen suggested. 'I'll call if I need you.'

Annie shook her head.

'He wouldn't want me.'

'But. . .'

'Oh, he'd act pleased to see me,' Annie said sadly. 'He'd smile a welcome — and then wonder why the hell I came. And next time he still won't think of inviting me. He. . .he still needs his personal space.' She shrugged and turned away — and Helen watched her with troubled eyes.

At least there was still work. The work she loved.

She looked along the corridor to where Kylie Manning was practising walking with her crutches.

'You're going beautifully, Kylie,' she called, and wandered up to talk to Kylie's mother. Anything was better than staring out of that damned window.

Kylie had been back at Bannockburn for a week, having been transferred from the Melbourne hospital where her knee had been reconstructed. In another few days she could go home. Once Betty was organized.

'I've just walked out of my past life,' Betty Manning told Annie, as Kylie proudly navigated the hospital corridors. She fingered the angry scar running from cheek to temple. 'I can't bear to move back. I guess. . .I guess I'm too scared of what might happen. I'm moving into a flat in town.'

'Does he hit you?' Annie asked, and as the colour washed out of Betty's face she didn't need an answer.

'You know, if you had legal advice you could possibly ask Rod to leave and let you and Kylie stay in the house,' Annie told her diffidently. The Mannings lived in a huge house, set on thirty acres of prime grazing land. They had stables of beautiful horses. Two cars and five garages to put them in. Swimming pool and tennis courts. . .

'I don't want it.' Betty's voice was flat. 'It's mortgaged to the hilt and I've always been uncomfortable living somewhere that I owed so much money on. No.' Betty shook her head, her eyes on her injured daughter. 'Rod can keep his house and his lifestyle. I hope. . .I guess I hope it'll make him less bitter this way — if I ask for nothing. A bit more likely to accept what's happened and not to take his anger out on Kylie.'

'You'll ask for nothing at all?'

'Nothing.' Betty sighed. 'I've taken a few things that belonged to my mother but otherwise — well, you know

I have a part-time job in the local real estate agent's office. Mr Howith's offered to put me on almost full time. He's lovely. He says I can have school holidays off. He and his wife helped me find the flat, and with their help we'll survive.'

'It's a hell of a change for you, Betty.'

Both Annie and Betty started. Unnoticed, Tom had entered the hospital. He was cradling his daughter in his arms, there was river mud on his shoes and his jeans were wet to the knees — hardly professional at all — but his tone was richly sympathetic and Betty gave him an uncertain smile.

'I know, Dr McIver. But. . .' She shook her head. 'Rod's been frightening me for years. Yes, he's hit me — and he's hit Kylie. It only happens when he's drunk and he's always sorry afterwards, but he's been drunk too often. There's nothing left between us. I used to think that things — material possessions, appearances — were important, but I've finally decided that anything — *anything* — is better than a loveless marriage.'

'Hmm.' Tom cast a curious glance at Annie and then looked away. 'And will Rod have access to Kylie?'

'If he wants it. But he hasn't. . .he hasn't even visited us. Not once. I had to find him when I got out of hospital and tell him what I'd decided. It's hard. I don't want Kylie to grow up without a father but. . . If he wants access I'm asking for a court order that he can't drink when he has her.' She hesitated.

'Well, maybe if I'm not around to annoy him he won't drink so much anyway. He's charming to his friends. A real gentleman. So I can only hope.' She gave them a bright smile — a smile of courage.

'Anyway, Kylie and I have something we've been meaning to ask you,' she continued, smiling at Tom. 'Kylie's coming home from hospital — home to our new little flat — next Friday, and the following Saturday it's her birthday. She's six. We thought we'd have a party

to celebrate. Not much. Just. . .just a few friends with
their children. Bread and butter and hundreds and thousands, little red sausages and red cordial.'

Betty's smile deepened as her daughter finally made
it back to her side, and her hand came out to tousle
Kylie's bright red curls. 'But Kylie and I would love
it if you could bring Hannah. We thought it'd be an
honour — a house-warming gift to us — if we could have
Hannah at the very first birthday party she's ever
attended.'

'I see.' Tom chuckled and stooped to address Kylie.
'Well, Hannah would consider it an honour to attend
your sixth birthday party, Miss Manning,' he told her,
as his boots squelched river water onto the hospital
corridors. Matron Robbie would have a fit! 'I'll bring
her myself. What time would you like me to come?'

Me . . .

The word hung in the air, and Betty looked uncertainly at Annie.

'I thought you all. . .' she faltered.

'Annie's on call on Saturday afternoons,' Tom
told her.

'But. . .don't you ever go out together?'

'We don't. . .'

'Annie can't. . .'

Their answer was spoken in unison, and Annie found
herself staring at the floor. Anywhere but at Tom.

'Saturday's busy,' Tom explained. 'Sports
injuries. . .'

'But I have the phone on and it's only two minutes'
drive from the flat back to the hospital.' Betty was
staring in bewilderment from one to the other.
'Unless. . .unless you don't want to come, Dr Burrows.'

'Of course I'd like to come,' Annie said stiffly.
'Tom's right, though. There are sports injuries on
Saturdays. I'll come in my own car in case I'm
called away.'

There. She'd go separately. And once there she'd

have a celebratory glass of red cordial and slip away before she cramped Tom's style. He wasn't used to having a wife by his side.

'It'll be better if you all come,' Kylie confided, slipping her small hand into Tom's. 'We've invited my dad and we hope he comes, too.' Her small face puckered. 'I *need* my mum *and* my dad — and I bet your baby does too. She's just not old enough to ask yet.'

My mum and my dad. . . That was what Annie and Tom were supposed to be. A family.

Betty Manning's eyes blinked back tears — and it was as much as Annie could do not to join her.

'Why don't you want me to go with you?'

Annie and Tom were sitting over roster sheets — a task Annie found infinitely depressing. It was getting worse. *You work Saturday, I'll work Sunday. I'm taking Hannah out to Dave McCrae's farm on Wednesday so can you cover me here? If you're going to Lisa Myrne's kitchen tea then I'll work.*

If you'll be here then I'll be there. And vice versa. Portrait of a marriage.

'Go?'

'To Kylie's birthday party,' Annie said bluntly. 'Why don't you want me to go with you, Tom?'

'I do.'

'No.' Annie shook her head. 'You don't. It sticks out of a mile. Even Betty could see it and she thought it really strange. It's like. . .now we're married you're uncomfortable when I'm around. As if you don't know how to treat me.'

'That's not true.'

'I guess it is,' Annie said sadly. 'Tom, the valley is expecting you to treat me as a wife — and you still treat me as a medical colleague.'

'I do treat you as a wife, Annie.' Tom's hand reached out to grasp hers and she pushed herself back from him. 'No.'

'Annie. . .'

'You don't understand, do you, Tom?' she said slowly, and all at once it was unbearable. What he was asking of her. 'You don't understand that I've put myself into an almost impossible situation.'

'OK,' he said, his eyes watchful. 'I *don't* understand. Explain.'

Explain. . . How on earth could she explain?

'I thought. . . Well, I talked myself into believing that this could work.' Annie rose and looked down at him. Looked down at her love. 'I wanted it so much, you see. But I didn't count on how you made me feel. . . how going to bed with you would change things.'

Tom's dark eyes met hers and searched, trying hard to follow what she meant. That was the trouble, Annie thought bitterly. He was so damned kind. So understanding. If there was a right thing to do then Tom McIver would do it.

But he couldn't do the right thing now. How could he understand the role Annie wanted him to fill when that role was so ill-defined that Annie was hard put to explain it to herself.

'When I go to bed with you I give myself to you,' Annie told him in a voice that wasn't quite steady. She hauled her white coat around her as if she were cold. 'And every morning you expect me to take myself back. It's sort of like there's two of me. The night-time Annie — and Dr Annie Burrows, colleague. But I'm one person, Tom. I can't do it any more. It's tearing me in two.'

Tom ran his hand through his hair in a gesture that Annie knew and loved. He used it when he was tired. Or worried.

He was worried now.

'Hell, Annie, I'm trying. Trying to make this marriage work, I mean. I don't know what else you can ask of me. I know it's hard, putting up with me and Hannah and the dogs. . .'

'That's just it, Tom,' Annie said sadly. 'It isn't hard. But I want more. You don't ask enough. I want to give more. And if you don't understand what I want to give. . .'

'You're talking in riddles. . .'

'No.' Annie took a deep breath. Helen had counselled patience, but Annie had run right out of patience. Run out of sanity. She couldn't keep going like this.

'I've fallen in love with you, Tom McIver,' she told him, and the whole world stilled as she said the words. She'd sworn never to say them, but here she was, breaking all her promises.

He still didn't understand. Tom's face softened instantly and he stood to take her hands.

'But, Annie. . . That's great. Hell, I love you, too.' She knew he didn't.

'Tom, I'll bet you have old sweaters you love just as much as me.'

'That's not —'

'Quite true?' Annie shrugged and deep inside her heart she turned to ice at what she was doing. 'It is, you know. You love me because I'm your wife and you're supposed to love your wife. Well, maybe. . . maybe I'm dreaming of something out of the pages of one of Chris's romantic novels, but my ideal of someone who loves me is someone who welcomes me always. Sure, lovers can be apart. Married couples can be apart. But, if they really love each other, when they come together they fit like two halves of a whole. Whereas you and I. . .'

'We do.'

'No. We don't. I come into the room and you're polite and kind and welcoming — but you don't really relax until I leave again.'

'Annie, we're good together.'

'Only in bed.' Annie shook her head, and even though she knew what she had to say it was all she could do to get the words out. 'And I can't. . .I can't keep

sleeping with you. Not now. Not now I've told you.'
She sighed, her heart dull with aching loss. To lose him
at night as well. . .

There was no choice. She was starting to feel that at
night she could be anyone. That he turned off the lights
and loved her body. Loved a woman. . . But not her.

'Tom, you want a wife. Well, you still have one. The
wife you wanted. The wife you married me for. I'm
not asking for a divorce. I'll stay here and we'll keep
the door between our apartments open, and I'll be as
much a mother to Hannah as you'll let me. But. . .but
I won't sleep in your bed, Tom. I won't be half a love.
I don't see how any woman can be.'

'Annie, this is crazy.'

'It is, isn't it?' she said dully. 'I was crazy to believe
it could possibly work. But now. . . All I'm asking is
that you keep to your side of your door at night, as well
as by day, and I'll keep to mine. And we'll go from
there. Please, Tom.'

He stared at her, baffled.

'I don't know what the hell else I can do, Annie.'

'No, you don't,' Annie said sadly. 'And that's just
the trouble.'

It was the hardest decision Annie ever made. It was
even harder sticking to it.

At eleven that night, just after she'd crawled between
the sheets in her own bleak bedroom, Tom came through
to find her. He knocked first, as he always did when
he came to her side of the wall. As if she might have
something to hide — like a lover tucked under the bed.

'Annie, I need you.'

She needed him, too.

But she knew from his voice that it wasn't his love
life Tom was talking about. She sat up in bed, hauling
her trusty sheet after her.

'What for?' Her voice was laced with suspicion and
Tom flicked the light on and sighed.

'Not for your sweet self, Annie.' It was odd how his voice sounded dull and flat. Tired. 'But old Mr Howard needs a catheter.'

Jack Howard. . .

Jack Howard was a nursing-home patient and had been for the whole time Annie had been in Bannockburn. He was in care because of 'confusion', but it was Annie's guess that the confusion was assumed. Certainly he was bad-tempered and irrational, but by all reports he'd been that way his whole life.

Jack lorded it over the nursing-home staff. He seemed to enjoy living here much more than living under his daughter's care. Certainly his confusion escalated every time the hospital board thought of sending him home.

'Why does he need a catheter?'

Annie pushed tousled curls from her face and tried to focus on medicine — on something other than Tom, standing at the edge of her bed. Good grief! It hadn't even been twelve hours since she'd told him she wouldn't sleep with him, and already her body was aching with loss.

'He's got a blockage of some sort. Urine retention. It'll have to investigated, but meanwhile he's yelling in pain, his bladder's full to bursting and he won't let me near him.'

Annie grimaced. Jack, with a real reason to complain. . . Oh, dear!

'So. . .'

'I know it sounds stupid,' Tom said wearily, 'but Helen and I have tried all options. He's convinced we're trying to rape him.' The sides of his mouth quirked into a smile. 'Well, maybe he's not convinced, but he's certainly enjoying telling the world that's what we're doing. What he's saying. . .well, it's just as well you're a married lady.'

Tom's smile faded as he looked down at her. 'He needs intravenous sedation, Annie, before he wakes the whole hospital. Can you do it? I've already turned the intercom on between Hannah and Children's Ward.'

It was an arrangement they'd made that suited them. Children's Ward was always staffed at night now so both Annie and Tom were available if needed.

'Of course.' Annie swung her feet out of bed. And then remembered she'd gone to bed as she'd gone to bed for the last two months — with nothing on at all. Her gorgeous nightgowns had proved totally useless. She hastily retired to her sheet. 'You. . .you go ahead. I'll be there in five minutes.'

'Three,' Tom said harshly, and his face was bleak. 'The pain's bad, and your modesty takes second place.'

It was a tricky procedure. Inserting a catheter was simple in a compliant male, but Jack certainly wasn't compliant. By the time Annie reached the ward he was roaring like a stuck pig and Annie couldn't decide whether it was from pain or indignation.

Mostly indignation, she guessed. Pain made people weak, and there was no weakness behind the old man's protests. The social workers had been in the day before, Annie remembered, trying to talk him into returning home. Therefore, if there was something wrong with him he'd play it up for all it was worth, and if there was a fuss to be made Jack would make it. They hadn't a hope of making him see reason. When Jack saw Annie he reacted with the fury of an active volcano.

'Bloody woman! Get the hell away from me. You leave me private parts alone. And you. . .' He jabbed a finger up at Tom. 'You oughta be ashamed of yourself. Let a man alone.' Then a spasm of pain caught him and he left out a roar of indignation that life could treat him with so little dignity.

If he hadn't been hurting Annie could have almost found it in herself to smile. And if she hadn't been hurting. . . Tom's voice cut across Jack's moans. 'Jack, we're here to stop your pain. Nothing else. Now shut up and let us get on with it.'

'You young b—'

'Jack, shut up or I'll pack you home to your daughter first thing tomorrow.'

Annie blinked at Tom's bluntness, but the bluntness seemed to help. The old man stared up in speechless indignation, and stayed still long enough for Tom to hold him—no mean feat in itself—while Annie quickly administered a sedative. The bluster started again as Jack felt the prick of Annie's needle, but by then it was too late.

The bluster died, allowing Annie to get a word in edgewise.

'Mr Howard, I've given you something to stop the pain and let you sleep. Just relax and let it work.'

The fast-acting drug was already taking hold, and Jack Howard's eyes showed real confusion now.

'I'll make it long-lasting. It's no use settling him if he rouses just as angry as he is now,' Annie told Tom, as Jack slumped back on his pillows. 'He'll haul the catheter straight out again.'

Jack wasn't quite finished.

'Bloody women just want a man's body. Bloody sexpot. . .' And he drifted peacefully into drug-induced sedation. Sexpot! Yeah, right! There was a certain irony in being called a sexpot when she'd just sworn off sex for life.

Think of something else.

'Why has he blocked?' Annie asked, as Tom carefully inserted the catheter into Jack's penis.

'His prostate's enlarged,' Tom told her, concentrating on what he was doing. 'I was hoping it wouldn't cause him problems, but it has now. We'll have to do something about it, but can you imagine doing a prostate operation on Jack?'

'No,' Annie said bluntly. 'Thank God I'm not a urologist.'

'That makes two of us. He'll have to go to Melbourne for the operation, and heaven help the urologist who has to examine him first. There!' Tom stood back from the bed as the urine bag started to fill. 'Whew, see the pressure. That pain wasn't assumed. The poor old coot must have been in agony.' He shook his head. 'We'll transfer him to Melbourne tomorrow and see if we can get him operated on by the weekend.'

'His daughter won't like it.' Annie knew his daughter well. She was forceful, tough, thoroughly unpleasant — and furious that her father didn't show the least sign of dying. She'd tried to have him certified totally incompetent so she could assume control of his farm, but Jack's confusion magically lifted every time he saw a lawyer.

The sooner Jack died and let his daughter get hold of his farm and money the better pleased she'd be, Annie knew. If he went to Melbourne for an operation Jack was likely to demand a single room and every expensive extra he could get. Which meant less money for his daughter later on. She would be furious.

'She's said no medical intervention at all.'

'Yeah, well, she'll have to lump this,' Tom said grimly. 'Jack's not going to die of an enlarged prostate but it'll make his life miserable. If I must, I'll get permission from the public trustee.'

'She'll fight. . .'

'I can fight, too.' Tom looked grimly at Annie as Helen came into the room to keep watch on the old man. Annie gave Helen directions on Jack's care, but Tom didn't speak again until they were out in the corridor.

'I can fight for what has to be fought for,' Tom reiterated, and his voice was flat. 'Annie, I want you to come back to my bed.'

'Why?'

'Because we both want it.' He managed a smile. 'Tiny and Hoof are missing you.'

'It's midnight on the first night,' Annie snapped. She was dangerously close to breaking. 'They can hardly be pining already. And I'll bet you anything they ate their dinner as if nothing at all was wrong.'

'If they stop eating, will you come back?'

'No!'

'What about if I do?'

'Tom!' Annie stopped dead and turned to the man by her side. 'Tom, why? You don't really want me.'

'I do.' He reached out and grasped her hands in a grip that was sure and strong. 'Annie, I love you in my bed.'

It had been the wrong thing to say.

I love you in my bed.

He did, Annie knew. And that was the whole problem!

'I love you in your bed, too, Tom,' she whispered, and her voice was filled with desolation. 'But I love you all the time. All the time, without stopping. And I've finally figured it's all or nothing. So. . .unless you can figure out what that means. . . Unless you want me always you can't have me in your bed. Because it's like taking a piece of me, and by cutting that part out the rest of me can't survive.'

CHAPTER ELEVEN

WHAT followed were bleak and lonely days.

Luckily the hospital was busy. There was little time to sit and mope. In her free time — the time when Tom was neck-deep in work because he'd pencilled in Annie as absent — Annie took the dogs to the beach or carried Hannah down to the river and played with her.

She could leave. She could get a divorce.

But when she held Hannah. . .when she sat by the river and held her so her tiny feet kicked the water. . . when she watched her face crease into Tom's delighted smile. . . Annie knew she could do no such thing.

Tom had invited her to be a part of Hannah's life and now she couldn't walk away from that. She'd fallen head over heels in love with two people — with Tom, and with his little daughter.

Despite the yawning gulf between Annie and Tom, she knew she could still be a mother to this little one. Watch her grow. . . She couldn't leave Hannah for reasons that were purely selfish.

And, good grief, she even loved the dogs!

The two crazy mutts were swimming in the currents. Now they lunged out of the water past Annie and stopped just long enough to shake the water from their fur and soak her to the skin.

'Ugh. . . Horrible dogs. I don't love you. I don't!'

It wasn't true. She did love them, and once again it wasn't just because they belonged to Tom.

Annie held Hannah close and put her lips in the baby's soft curls. She didn't know what on earth she was going to do.

But, whatever it was, she couldn't walk away.

*   *   *

It was Saturday. The day of Kylie's party.

Annie was on call. She spent the morning seeing patients at clinic, was caught up with a gashed leg, followed by a fractured arm, and at two in the afternoon she went to find Tom — only to discover he'd left without her.

'He told me to say he'd meet you there, as he knew you wanted to take your own car,' the nurse on duty told her.

Fine.

Annie had intended to discuss a gift with Tom but there hadn't been the opportunity. She'd chosen a pretty wall frieze covered with cartoon characters, intended as half house-warming gift and half birthday present.

Would Tom think of taking a gift himself? If so, they'd be taking separate gifts.

Surely not? If it happened it'd be the talk of the valley but, then, sharing a gift would never occur to Tom. It would never occur to him because they weren't a couple. They were two separate people, with only love for one baby, two dogs and medicine in common. And nothing else.

The party was well under way when Annie arrived. Betty's new apartment was at the back of a big, free-standing house, and Annie could hear children's shouts and laughter from out on the road. A bunch of balloons tied to the fence told her she was in the right place, and so did a tribe of children who came whooping round the side of the house.

'You've come!'

Kylie's crutches weren't cramping her style at all. Gorgeous in party pink, Kylie was moving nearly as fast as her friends. She grinned happily up at Annie, words tumbling out in excitement.

'Dr Annie, this is my new party dress that Grandma made me. My grandma's my mum's mum and she visited me all the time I was in hospital. While my leg was in tr-traction she sat by my bed every day and

sewed embroidery on the front and talked about the day
I'd wear it. And now it's finished. Do you like it? I think
it's beeyootiful. . . And you're my second-last guest, Dr
Burrows.'

'I love your dress,' Annie said warmly, stooping to
give her a hug. 'And I'm sorry I'm late, but an old lady
hurt her arm and needed me. Who else is late?'

'Daddy.' Kylie led the way to the door, her crutches
leaving neatly patterned holes on the lawn. 'Mummy
says he mightn't come, but I know he will. It's my
birthday.' Her small face puckered. 'And he must *know*
it's my birthday.'

She shoved the door open with her shoulder, and
then, with chameleon emotion, her grin returned.

'Hey, I'm opening my presents now,' she yelled.
'Want to watch?' And the children crowded in around
her, leaving Annie to bring up the rear.

Tom was already there. He was sitting on a bean-bag
on the floor, with Hannah sleeping in her cocoon
nearby. When Annie entered he gave her a transient
smile which Annie thought looked strained, and then
went back to talking to the cluster of adults with Betty.
Annie stopped by the doorway and didn't go further.

The room was crowded. Betty gave her a smile of
welcome across the room, but by now the children mill-
ing around Kylie formed an effective barrier between
Annie and the adults. Wrapping paper was being scattered everywhere. There was no room for Annie to pass.

Well, it didn't matter. She was content to stay where
she was, out of Tom's range.

Kylie opened Annie's gift first. Her eyes brightened
with pleasure when she saw the frieze.

'It's just perfect,' she crowed. 'I can put it in my
new bedroom, can't I, Mummy?' She turned to Annie
with the manners of a well-brought-up child. 'Thank
you, Dr Annie.' And then she turned to give Tom a
wide smile as well. 'And thank you too, Dr Tom. And
Hannah.'

Annie saw Tom's face still as her own heart sank. Annie had been right, then. He hadn't thought of this — that people would assume they'd share a gift.

Never mind. Annie stood and watched as Kylie opened gift after gift, and she thought of Hannah doing the same thing in six years. Would she herself be around to see it? Could she and Tom work out some relationship by then?

Then Kylie lifted another card, and sounded out the message on the card.

'Is this right, Mummy?' She frowned. 'I think it says it's from Dr Tom and Hannah. Didn't they already give me something?'

The room fell silent. Dear heaven. . .

'We're not very used to being married yet.' Annie's voice stammered into the uncomfortable stillness. 'Dr Tom and I bought a gift between us, but Hannah wanted us to give you her own gift. So one gift's from Hannah and one is from her mummy and daddy. We just got the messages on the cards wrong.'

'Oh.'

If it didn't quell the curiosity of the adults, at least Annie's explanation was satisfactory to Kylie. After all, two gifts were infinitely better than one. Kylie ripped off the wrapping — to reveal an identical frieze to the one Annie had given her.

Some moments are best forgotten.

For once in his life even Tom seemed stumped for words. He looked across at Annie and, as the various adults gave each other 'goodness, won't we be able to talk about this later' looks, Tom's face radiated pure mortification. As if he was suddenly seeing something he hadn't even known existed.

'But. . . Hannah didn't buy her present by herself, did she?' Kylie asked Annie, puzzled. 'Didn't she know what her mummy and daddy were buying? Didn't you tell her?'

'We'll change it for something else, Kylie,' Annie

said gently, her eyes on Tom. And some of the gentleness in her voice was for him. He hadn't known. Whatever family life he'd had in the past hadn't geared him for this. Hadn't geared him for her.

Blessedly, the door swung open just at that moment, and attention was diverted to Kylie's last guest.

'Daddy!' The identical gifts forgotten, Kylie hauled herself to her feet and reached her father without the use of crutches. 'Daddy, you came to my birthday!'

'Yeah, kitten, of course I came. Wouldn't miss it for quids.'

Rod Manning's voice was coarse and slurred with drink, and Annie winced. The man was dead drunk. It was obvious in the way he moved. He stood in the doorway and his body swayed. He tossed an unwrapped box down to the floor and then held onto the doorknob for support.

This was a Rod Manning Annie hardly recognized. He was unkempt and unshaven. His clothes looked as if they'd been slept in, and he couldn't have seen a bath for a week.

Kylie backed away uncertainly.

'Aren't you going to open my present?' Rod laughed and stared aggressively across at his wife, then back to Kylie. 'You open it now. I'll bet your mother hasn't spent as much on you as I have, sweetheart. I'll bet. . .'

Kylie gave him a scared glance and opened her parcel. It was a dress box and inside lay a frock — a fabulous frothy confection of tulle and lace. It looked over-the-top expensive, gaudy, and at least a couple of sizes two small.

'Thank you very much, Daddy,' Kylie whispered, her eyes scared. 'Grandma made me my dress for this birthday but this. . .this can be my next birthday dress. Or. . .' Her voice faltered. 'My Christmas dress.'

'You'll wear *my* dress for your birthday,' Rod growled. 'What do you mean, '*Grandma made me*. . .?' His voice was a cruel mimicry of Kylie's. 'My girl doesn't wear home-made dresses. Go and get changed.'

'But Grandma sewed me my dress while I was hospital.' There was a touch of defiance in Kylie's voice. She stood tall and faced her father square on. Rod Manning might be autocratic, but Kylie was her father's daughter. Rod wasn't having a bar of it.

'Kylie, you heard me. Change!'

'I won't.'

'You little. . .' Rod took a step forward and gave his daughter a ringing slap across the face.

'*No!*' Annie was the closest adult—the only one on Rod's side of the room. As Rod raised his hand again she dived straight at him. She caught his arm in mid-swing and held on like a terrier. 'No, Rod. . .'

'*Don't!*' Tom roared the command almost in unison with Annie's plea. He launched himself like lightning from the other side of the room, but he wasn't fast enough. He wasn't expecting what happened next.

No one was.

Annie was still clinging limpet-like to one of Rod's arms, but with his free hand Rod hauled a gun from the inside pocket of his jacket. And pointed it straight at Tom.

'Get back. Get back and leave my daughter to me.'

Tom stopped dead in mid-stride, wicked blue metal pointing straight at his heart.

'And you. . . Get away, bitch!' Rod pushed Annie away from him with a savage shove before he grabbed his daughter and hauled her close to him.

'She's wearing *my* dress and she's coming home with *me*,' he snarled. 'That's why I brought this.' He waved the gun. 'In case anyone here was stupid enough to object. You think I'd leave her in a dump like this? My kid? My kid doesn't wear home-made clothes and she doesn't live in any dumpy apartment.' He glared across the room at Betty, and his bloodshot eyes were crazy.

'And she doesn't live with you either, slut,' he snarled at his wife. 'Not now. Not ever. I've been to the lawyer's and they say I won't get custody of her. I can apply for access, they say. *Access!* Every bloody weekend and I have to stay off the booze to get her. You stupid bitch! Do you think I'll let you get away with that?'

He raised the gun higher over the heads of the children, pointed it straight at Betty — and his finger tightened on the trigger.

Whether or not he meant to shoot, Annie would never know. She couldn't wait to find out. He'd shoved her to the floor. Now she rose like one possessed and lunged over Kylie's head, hauling the gun sideways from the child and down — hauling with the determination of desperate terror.

'*Annie, no. . .*' Tom's roar came from across the room and he was moving again, but there were terrified children and gifts and furniture crowded between them. He couldn't reach her in time to help. Annie clung for dear life — and then the gun exploded.

One single explosion. Nothing more.

After the explosion — silence.

Annie fell silently, crumpling to the floor as her leg gave way under her.

'*Annie. . .!*'

The gun rose again, and this time it pointed straight at Kylie, still in Rod's grasp.

'Nobody move. No one!'

Tom froze. He had no choice.

Still gripping Kylie, Rod backed further from the group of horrified children, and stared down at what he'd done.

At Annie.

He looked only for a moment. Just long enough to see a circle of scarlet form and spread on the soft pastel skirt hugging Annie's thigh.

Then the gun moved away from Kylie and was levelled at Annie again — straight at her heart.

'*No!*'

There were still children between Tom and Rod. Between Tom and Annie. Tom couldn't reach her. His voice was hoarse with fear, but it wasn't fear for himself. It was fear for Annie. 'Manning, don't do it. No.'

'Get back, then.'

Rod grabbed his daughter tighter, and waved the gun around the room. 'Get back, all of you. In fact, you can all get outside. I don't want you here. Go. Now. Move! Leave me with my daughter.'

Tom took another step towards Annie.

'Go now! Or I'll shoot the bitch again! She stays here, too.' The gun swung back to Annie. She was huddled on the floor and the pool of crimson on her thigh was spreading down to soak the carpet. 'I mean it. It's good that I shot her. Good! She's the one that caused the trouble. Gave that sample to the cops. Made me lose my job. My family. It'll give me great pleasure to shoot her again—or let her bleed to death. *Just get!*'

'Manning, you don't mean this. Think of the trouble you're making for yourself if you make this any worse. Rod, don't. . .'

Tom's voice was an urgent plea. Around him, the birthday guests were reacting to terror in different ways. Most of the children were scrambling to reach adults at the far side of the room. One little girl stood stock-still and stared, white with shock, and a toddler picked up Kylie's birthday dress and tipped it out of the box onto his head.

And crowed with delight.

'Get them out! Now!' Rod was speaking directly to Tom—but his gun was on Annie.

'Mannning, she'll die. She's bleeding. . .' There was no mistaking Tom's fear. He gazed down at Annie with desperation and took another step towards her. 'Let me take Annie at least. . .'

'Move one step closer and she'll die a hell of a lot faster. And then the kids. See how many I can kill before someone stops me. I mean it. You clear this room right now — or she gets it. *Move!*'

There was nothing for Tom to do but obey. With one last, despairing glance at his wife, Tom turned to the door at the back of the room.

'All right,' he said heavily — dully. 'Everyone out. Move quietly and quickly.' He picked up Hannah's baby capsule.

Then he turned back.

'If you let her die, there won't be anywhere on God's earth you can hide,' he told Rod Manning, and then he took Betty's hand. The woman seemed stunned to immobility. 'Come on, Betty. We have to leave.'

'Kylie. . .' Betty's voice was a frantic moan. 'He'll kill Kylie.'

'No, he won't,' Tom said harshly, and gave her a push out of the door. 'Not if he has one brain left in his head. He won't do anything so stupid!'

The door swung shut. Inside the room there was silence.

From the other side of the door Annie could hear Betty's voice raised in frantic protest and Tom telling her to hush — to move the children quickly away from the building.

A child was sobbing.

Then there was nothing but Rod's heavy breathing.

Kylie hadn't said a word. She stood absolutely still in Rod's grasp, as if she were beyond protest.

There was blood oozing rapidly from Annie's leg. The bullet had sliced the inside of her left thigh. Annie looked down with detached interest and decided that, professionally, she should do something about it. She grabbed the first thing to hand — Rod's ridiculous party dress — wedged it between her thighs and clenched her legs together. Pressure should stop the bleeding. . . It didn't help much. The blood still came, but she couldn't think what else to do.

Somehow it didn't seem to matter what she did. The

whole room looked surrealistic. There were fairy cakes and sandwiches scattered over the floor, knocked there by one of the terrified children. A cake with pink icing lay by her hand, and there was a smatter of blood on its side.

'You've hurt Dr Annie. She's bleeding.' The voice was Kylie's — matter-of-fact and accusing.

'She deserved it.' Rod's slurred growl.

'No, she didn't, Daddy.'

'Shut up.'

'You shouldn't have shot her.'

'Hush, Kylie.' Annie made a huge effort to make her voice work, and somehow she got the words out. This was important. 'Leave Daddy be.'

'You shut your mouth.'

'What. . .what will you do now?' Annie asked. Her voice came from such a long way away. How much blood had she lost? Too much, she knew. She was feeling dizzy and sick.

'I'll wait, that's what I'll do.' Rod walked to the doors leading out of the room and shoved a bolt home on each. Then he turned to the window. The moment he let Kylie go the child dived to where Annie lay. She put her arms round Annie and huddled close. Annie tried to put an arm around her in return, but her arm seemed far too heavy.

How much blood was she losing? Dear heaven. . .

'Wait. . .wait for what?' she whispered.

'God knows. You to die?' Rod turned to watch her. 'I'd enjoy that.'

'Then you'd be up for murder.'

'Doesn't matter,' he said heavily. 'Lost my job. Without a licence, no job. Bank's foreclosing on the house. No bloody house. No wife. No kid.'

'You do have a child.' It was so hard to make herself speak.

'Look at her,' he sneered. 'What sort of a kid is that for a father to have? Wearing her bloody grandmother's dresses. Living with her mother. Doesn't even want to come near me.'

'Not when you frighten her,' Annie managed. 'And you don't have to frighten her.' She hesitated. 'Please. . . Let Kylie go outside,' she pleaded. 'Don't scare her any more.'

'The kid stays here. 'Till the end.'

Annie looked up into his face — and she knew what he intended. This man was suicidal. Drunk and suicidal. He pulled a bottle from a jacket pocket and took a long swallow of whisky — and then another — and Annie knew. He didn't have the courage to take his own life, but he wanted to be dead.

And he wanted Annie and Kylie to go with him.

After that the world started to drift. There were the sounds of sirens from a long way off.

Kylie was holding her hand and saying, 'Don't go to sleep. Please, Dr Annie, don't go to sleep. I don't want you to go to sleep.' It was so hard to keep her eyes open.

Annie tried desperately to hold Kylie close — to keep her safe — and promise that she wouldn't sleep. But she wasn't able to find the words she needed.

The pain in her thigh was fierce and throbbing.

Still there was silence. It went on and on. The room smelled of whisky and stale beer and, ridiculously, of the cocktail frankfurters congealing on the table.

Rod stood at the window, staring out at the backyard and willing anyone to come into range of his gun.

Kylie huddled closer to Annie, silently weeping.

Mustn't sleep. Mustn't. She had no choice. Annie's lids drifted lower — and suddenly jerked up.

There was a crash of breaking glass, a dull thud and then a vast and terrible smell. A smell that filled the room with fog, and burned and made Kylie choke. . .

But before the child could manage her first cough the silence turned to massive noise. Annie heard the splintering of wood and glass, crashing and shouts, and then a strong male body hurled itself from the stinking fog and covered both her and Kylie with his body.

There was a savage oath from above.

'Don't be a fool!'

A single shot rang out—and a scream.

Then Annie was being lifted and carried out through the fog—out through the burning mist. Somehow she and Kylie were being carried together and she wasn't sure whether one man was carrying her or two—but there was no way she was letting go of Kylie. No way at all.

Who was carrying her? Who? What was happening? Her head wasn't working. She was drifting towards unconciousness but there was one last thing she had to say. She must!

'You mustn't shoot her. I won't—'

'No one will shoot Kylie. Or you. You're safe, my love. You're safe.'

It was Tom. No matter how far away the world was, she'd know that voice anywhere. Her Tom.

She could let go now. Tom was here. She was safe, and he wouldn't let the world hurt Kylie.

And she knew nothing more for a very long time.

CHAPTER TWELVE

SHE shouldn't be in hospital.

Annie woke and stared up at the ceiling in concern. She was in the wrong place. In a ward. She had no business here. She should be standing over the bed, stethoscope in hand and ready to work. Not *in* the bed!

She lifted her head in bewilderment and pushed herself up, only to find strong hands holding her shoulders and pressing her back.

'And where do you think you're going?'

Tom!

'It's OK,' Tom said swiftly, seeing her confusion and flooding fear. 'It's fine, Annie. You're not to be upset. No one's hurt, except you.'

'Kylie. . .'

'Kylie's at home with her mum and her grandma and grandpa. The police have Rod in custody. He tried to turn the gun on himself, but failed.'

'But. . . Tom, I heard. . .I heard a shot. He didn't hurt you?'

'He fired once and missed. And once I stopped coughing I was fine. We used tear gas to get in. The police gave me a mask, but I couldn't see you fast enough so I hauled it off. Yeah, Rod shot at us — but he was blinded and panicking and he missed us by a country mile.'

'And. . .he's really OK?'

'He's really OK.' Tom lifted her hand and held it tightly between his. 'Stop worrying about everyone else, Annie. Think about you.'

'There's nothing. . .'

'Nothing wrong?' Tom closed his eyes, and there

were the shadows of haunting fear still on his face. 'Oh, God, Annie, if you knew how close. . .'

And then, as if he could bear it no longer, Tom gathered her into his arms. He held her, tubes and all. Plasma was being fed into her arm though an intravenous line. There was another line with what must be saline. . . She was strung up like a fish on a multitude of hooks and could go nowhere.

She didn't want to. Tom was holding her as if he'd never let her go, and that was just where she wanted to be.

'Annie. . .'

'Tom. . .what. . .?'

'No, hush and let me speak.' Tom's voice was a low growl, muffled by her hair. 'You've scared me half to death and you owe it to me to let me say what I must. I thought I'd lost the chance for ever.'

'You almost bled to death.' His arms tightened convulsively. 'Thank God the bullet didn't hit an artery. There's only soft tissue damage. The bullet's still in there but it can stay. We'll send you to Melbourne when your electrolytes are up a bit. Get a decent surgeon to remove the bullet and repair the damage. But, oh, Annie. . . You've still got a leg — and a life — but I've lost years from mine. Annie, love. . .'

There was raw agony in Tom's voice and Annie left herself drift, wonderingly, in his hold. There was nothing at all wrong with her when he held her like this. Nothing at all.

But Tom's voice was still filled with pain.

'God, Annie, when we had to go in. . . The police wanted to wait and try to talk him out. . .but I knew you were bleeding to death. We had to risk the tear gas.'

'Annie, I died a million deaths outside while they stuffed around with masks and cannisters and bullet-proof vests. All the time not knowing.' The agony in Tom's voice was turning to anger, but the anger wasn't directed at Annie. It was directed straight at himself.

'I've been such a fool. I thought. . .I thought if you died, you'd die not knowing. . .'

'Not knowing?' Annie's voice was a thread-like whisper, but it drifted out over the room. Filling it with hope.

Waiting. Waiting for a miracle. And the miracle came.

'Knowing that I love you. Knowing that I care for you so deeply. . .and knowing that I was too much of a coward to tell you.'

'Tom. . .'

'I was so damned scared of relationships,' Tom murmured, and his arms held her as if she were the most precious thing in the world. 'Of getting involved. And when I finally figured out just what you were. . .just what I felt for you. . .well, it scared me silly.'

He sighed and buried his face in her hair.

'So I thought I could sleep with you but hold our lives separate. That way. . .well, if you left —*when* you left — it wouldn't be so bad.' He gave a harsh laugh. 'I guess that's a legacy from my past. I loved my parents and they left. I loved my grandmother and she died. So I guess. . .subconsciously I was afraid to let myself love you. Afraid to love anyone. But I had no choice with Hannah. And today. . .from today I don't have a choice with you.'

'Tom, you don't have to. . .'

'Don't have to love you?' Tom's voice was almost a groan. 'You're kidding. Annie, you made the leap in love and trust. On our wedding night you offered me everything, and I shoved you away. I knew, you see. Even before you said you loved me, I knew. I could see it in your eyes. And, like a fool, I thought I could use that love — but not return it.'

He sighed and gently lowered her back on her pillows, then bent to stroke her hair.

He must have given her pethidine, Annie thought

drowsily. She was floating in a mist of love and light and wonder.

'I was a damned fool,' he said bitterly. 'I saw it at the birthday party with the gifts. . . Everyone's faces. . . Everyone seeing that we didn't have a proper marriage. I saw clearly then that the way I was treating you was wrong. But even then. . . While Kylie opened her presents I sat like a fool, trying to figure out whether I wanted to take it any further. Whether I wanted a real marriage, after all. And then some crazy lunatic with a gun comes blasting in and —' He stopped, his voice choking.

His hands moved to grip Annie's shoulders so that he could look clearly into her eyes. 'I've never been so terrified in my life,' he told her.

'Tom. . .'

He put his finger to her lips, silencing her.

'All my life I've held myself apart so that if I lost you. . .if I lost anyone. . .I could keep on being me. Independent Tom McIver.' He gave a bitter laugh.

'Only when Hannah arrived it shook my foundations. I could no longer exist being just me. I saw that. I couldn't bear Hannah being in the world and me not there. And today. . . Today I saw what it would be like. . .if I was in the world and my Annie wasn't.'

He held her hard, his hands gripping her with urgency and his eyes searching hers, while she looked wonderingly up at him.

And then he gave a rueful smile.

'Hell, sweetheart you're exhausted,' he told her. 'You've lost so much blood. You should be sleeping. But I couldn't let another moment go by without telling you. . .that I love you, Annie. I love you with my heart and my soul. I love you with everything I have. And if I lost you. . .if I lost you as I thought today I'd lost you. . .then a part of me I'm only just beginning to realize exists would wither and die. And anything's better than that. Annie, I never want to be apart from you again.'

'Tom, do you mean. . .?' Annie was weary and weak and confused, but she wasn't so confused she couldn't focus on what he was saying. Not so much on his words, but on what his eyes were telling her. Tom's eyes were sending a message all their own. A message of absolute commitment. A marriage vow all of their own.

'You mean you want to break down the wall between our apartments?' she whispered.

'Break down the wall?' Tom pulled her tenderly back into his arms, mindful of tubes and attachments. 'Hell, just hand me a sledgehammer. Annie, if there's so much as ten feet between us from now on it's too much. I'll never let you go again. If you'll have me, Annie. . . If you still want me. . .'

'Oh, Tom. . .' Annie's face nestled against Tom's chest. There was no pain. There was no terror or despair. There was only joy.

'I thought I was Sunday's bride,' she whispered into the place above his chest where his heart beat just for her. 'I thought I was lucky you married me before waiting for Monday's edition. But, Tom. . . Oh, Tom, Sundays last for ever.'

Jean Herrington stared out through the palm trees at the couple on the beach. She ought to go and clean out the third unit, she told herself. There was another honeymoon couple due in this afternoon.

But she didn't move. For the moment, Jean was content to stay where she was and watch one happy ending.

The Herringtons took only three couples at a time at their exclusive honeymoon resort. Emerald Palms was tucked into tropical rain forest on the coast of far north Queensland. Secluded gardens drifted down to the beach, and islands off the coast dotted the bay like jewels set in the glittering sea.

Emerald Palms was a honeymoon resort to dream of for ever.

Jean paid attention to detail, she did, and everything was just right. She should bustle on — but the group on the beach held her in thrall.

'I dunno, Bill,' she told her husband. 'I'm having trouble coping with who belongs where with this lot. Two honeymoon suites for one couple. . .'

'Yeah, but it's not just a couple.' Bill grinned. 'It's a honeymoon with a difference. A man and woman, a baby and a babysitter and two ruddy great dogs. . .' He shook his head and smiled benignly at his wife. 'I know you said we oughtn't take the dogs, but that fella could talk the Pope into turning Methodist!'

'*Bill*!' Jean gave a reluctant grin and conceded. 'I know what you mean, though. He is. . .persuasive. And, oh, Bill, they seem so happy.'

'Just perfect.' Bill came up behind his wife and gave her a squeeze around her ample waist. 'They're what we had in mind when we set this place up. I've never seen a pair so in love. Apart from us, of course.'

Jean wriggled happily in his grasp.

'You can tell the couples that'll last.' She sighed happily. 'And they will. They can't keep their eyes off each other. Or their hands.' Then she giggled at what her husband's hands were doing. 'Get away with you. We're too old to be engaging in hanky-panky at eleven in the morning.'

'We're not too old.' Bill looked out to where Tom was carrying his bride down to the surf. 'Do you reckon they'll ever be too old?'

'Maybe not.' Jean gave her husband a fond kiss and turned her eyes to the couple now knee-deep in the surf. 'I guess not.'

There was no doubt at all that they'd never be too old. Not in Tom's heart. Not in Annie's. Not in the minds of anyone who knew them.

'I hate the idea of this ending,' Annie whispered. She lay contentedly in the arms of her love and looked out over at the distant islands. 'We've only explored three islands and I can count at least five more. And we're going home tomorrow.'

'I have news for you,' her love informed her, kissing her tenderly on the lips. 'Ugh, you taste of salt.'

'Don't you want me, then?' Annie pouted, teasing, and Tom's eyes flared. There was no mistaking the message behind them.

He made a change of direction. He had been carrying her into the surf for a swim.

'*No!*' Annie protested as he turned to carry her up the beach to the honeymoon suite beyond the palms.

She shouldn't have teased him. What a thing to say! Red rag to a bull! It was far too close from here to the bedroom — and she'd wanted a swim.

Past tense.

Well, maybe a fast swim. And then. . .

'What news do you have?' she begged. 'Tell me, Tom, and stop thinking what you're thinking immediately.'

'Aren't you thinking what I'm thinking, too?'

She blushed. Annie's whole body started heating up, from the toes up. 'I might be,' she admitted. 'But tell me first. What news?'

'Just that the locum we employed so we could come away has agreed to take up a permanent position,' Tom told her, and his grip tightened on her near-naked body. 'So we can extend our honeymoon, and when we return we can keep the honeymoon going. When we're off duty, Annie, love, we're off duty together. We're a pair. Inseparable. Bonnie and Clyde. . . Darby and Joan. . .'

'Abbott and Costello?' Annie chuckled contendedly and wound her arms around the neck of her love. 'Ren and Stimpy? Oh, Tom. . . Oh, my Tom. . .'

'So now we have all the time in the world.' Tom sighed in utter contentment and nuzzled his face against her hair. Then he took a deep breath and, before she could utter any more protests, started striding swiftly up the beach with his bride held tightly in his arms.

'So. . .so why are you in such a hurry, then?' Annie said breathlessly, laughing. The heat in her body was escalating to white-hot. Her swim was forgotten. 'If there's all the time in the world.'

'Because I'm starting to think it's not long enough,' her love told her, and the passion in his voice was an aching need. 'Not long enough to even begin to share my love.'

'For ever won't be long enough for all the love in my heart.'

LIVE THE EMOTION

Modern Romance™
...seduction and
passion guaranteed

Tender Romance™
...love affairs that
last a lifetime

Medical Romance™
...medical drama
on the pulse

Historical Romance™
...rich, vivid and
passionate

Sensual Romance™
...sassy, sexy and
seductive

Blaze Romance™
...the temperature's
rising

27 new titles every month.

Live the emotion

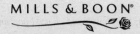

MB3

Next month don't miss –

SUMMER BRIDES

The perfect dress, a sexy bridegroom…but who will be the bride? These women each have a secret – they're head-over-heels in love! And now they're ready to risk all to walk up the aisle with the man of their dreams…

Available 4th July 2003

Available at most branches of WH Smith, Tesco, Martins, Borders, Eason, Sainsbury's and all good paperback bookshops.

0603/05

Live the emotion

... and get carried away with these three red-hot reads!

Miranda Lee
Caroline Anderson
Julia Byrne

MILLS & BOON

Don't miss *Book Eleven* of this BRAND-NEW 12 book collection 'Bachelor Auction'.

Who says money can't buy love?

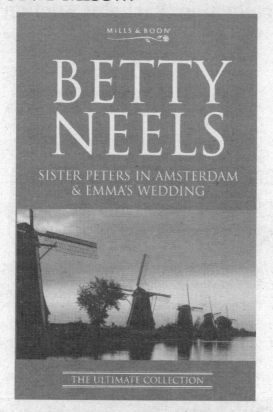

Modern Romance™
...seduction and passion guaranteed

Eight brand new titles each month

Take a break and find out more about
Modern Romance™ on our website
www.millsandboon.co.uk

Available at most branches of WH Smith,
Tesco, Martins, Borders, Eason, Sainsbury's,
and all good paperback bookshops.

GEN/01/RTL7